PENGUIN BOOKS

CHQ 20.12.14

— c

Kevin Brooks was born in Exeter, Devon, and he studied in Birmingham and London. He has worked in a crematorium, a zoo, a garage and a post office, before – happily – giving it all up to write books. Kevin is the award-winning author of nine novels and lives in North Yorkshire.

Praise for Kevin Brooks:

'Kevin Brooks just gets better and better, and given that he started off brilliant, that leaves one scratching around for superlatives'
– *Sunday Telegraph*

'He's an original. And he writes one hell of a story'
– Meg Rosoff, author of *How I Live Now*

D0321532

Books by Kevin Brooks

BEING
BLACK RABBIT SUMMER
CANDY
iBOY
KILLING GOD
KISSING THE RAIN
LUCAS
MARTYN PIG
NAKED
THE ROAD OF THE DEAD

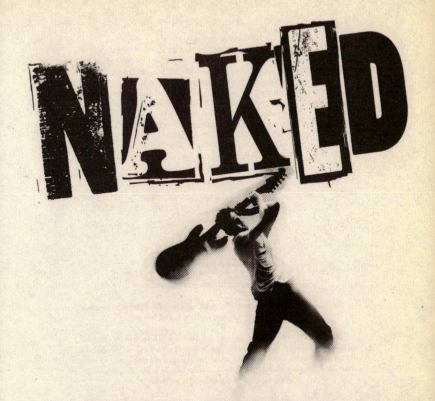

KEVIN BROOKS

PENGUIN BOOKS

PENGUIN BOOKS

Published by the Penguin Group
Penguin Books Ltd, 80 Strand, London WC2R ORL, England
Penguin Group (USA) Inc., 375 Hudson Street, New York, New York 10014, USA
Penguin Group (Canada), 90 Eglinton Avenue East, Suite 700, Toronto, Ontario, Canada M4P 2Y3
(a division of Pearson Penguin Canada Inc.)
Penguin Ireland, 25 St Stephen's Green, Dublin 2, Ireland (a division of Penguin Books Ltd)
Penguin Group (Australia), 250 Camberwell Road, Camberwell, Victoria 3124, Australia
(a division of Pearson Australia Group Pty Ltd)
Penguin Books India Pvt Ltd, 11 Community Centre, Panchsheel Park, New Delhi – 110 017, India
Penguin Group (NZ), 67 Apollo Drive, Rosedale, Auckland 0632, New Zealand
(a division of Pearson New Zealand Ltd)
Penguin Books (South Africa) (Pty) Ltd, 24 Sturdee Avenue, Rosebank,
Johannesburg 2196, South Africa

Penguin Books Ltd, Registered Offices: 80 Strand, London WC2R ORL, England

penguin.com

First published 2011
001 – 10 9 8 7 6 5 4 3 2 1

Text copyright © Kevin Brooks, 2011
All rights reserved

The moral right of the author has been asserted

Set in 10/14 pt Sabon by Palimpsest Book Production Ltd, Falkirk, Stirlingshire
Printed in Great Britain by Clays Ltd, St Ives plc

British Library Cataloguing in Publication Data
A CIP catalogue record for this book is available from the British Library

ISBN: 978-0-141-32611-5

www.greenpenguin.co.uk

Penguin Books is committed to a sustainable
future for our business, our readers and our
planet. This book is made from paper certified
by the Forest Stewardship Council.

For Phil, Pete, Sid, and Kenny

2

I didn't actually know Curtis Ray when I started at Mansfield Heath School in the autumn of 1970, but I knew who he was. *Every*one knew who Curtis was; he was that kind of kid. Although he was still only twelve at the time – a year older than me – he was already known for being *different*. He was Curtis Ray, the second-year kid with the long blond hair and the bolshy attitude, the hippy kid who wore surf beads and earrings and a black leather jacket, the kid who played electric guitar. He was the kind of boy you either loved or hated – and I'm pretty sure that even those who professed to hate him were secretly a little bit in love with him. And that applied to both the girls *and* the boys.

Of course, being a year older than me (and light years beyond my social circle at the time), Curtis wouldn't have known of my existence. I knew that *he* existed. I saw him in passing almost every day. But that's all he could ever be to me – a passing figure in the corridors at school, a reverently whispered name – '*look, there's Curtis Ray*' – a boy from another planet.

However much I dreamed about him – and I don't mind admitting that I *did* dream about him – I knew that they were only dreams. He *was* from another planet. He was cool, hip, rebelliously different. I was just different. He was so good-looking that even the girls who hated his long hair and his hippy music simply couldn't resist him. I, on the other hand, was generally considered to be 'not bad-looking . . . if you like that kind of thing'. And while Curtis seemed to know exactly who he was and what he wanted to be, my early teenage years were spent in a perpetual state of bewilderment. Not only did I have no confidence in myself, I also lacked faith in the sanity and purpose of everything around me. I just couldn't understand what the world was about, what it was all for, what it was supposed to mean . . .

All in all, I was a pretty *confused* kind of girl. And although Curtis's girlfriends over the years were both numerous and varied (in age, type, and character), the one thing they all had in common – apart from being beautiful and sexy – was a total *absence* of confusion. So there was simply no reason for me to believe that Curtis Ray could ever be anything more than a dream to me.

But on a blue summer's day in the first week of July 1975, my dream became a reality.

I'd been playing piano since the age of five, when my mum had taken me along to my first lesson. She'd always wanted to play the piano herself, so she claimed, and it was a constant source of regret to her that she hadn't had lessons when she was a child.

'It's not too late, Mum,' I used to tell her. 'I mean, it's not like you can only learn when you're a kid, you know.'

'It's my fingers,' she'd say. 'They're not supple enough any more.' Or, 'You know what my headaches are like, darling . . . I just wouldn't be able to concentrate.'

I think the real reason she didn't want to learn was that she knew it took a lot of hard work and dedication, and the only thing that Mum was dedicated to – apart from her various addictions – was avoiding hard work at all costs. Of course, she was perfectly happy to insist that *I* practised long and hard at the piano . . . and I did. But it wasn't hard work for me, because I enjoyed it. From that very first lesson when I was five years old, I just loved everything about it – the music, the magic, the wonderful world of sounds and songs . . . melodies, tones, structures, rhythms . . . it was all so enthralling. And I was good at it too. I wasn't a virtuoso or anything, but it all came very naturally to me, and by the time I was eight or nine I was already quite accomplished. For my tenth birthday I was given my very own piano – a really nice Bechstein upright, which I still play quite a lot now – and I carried on taking lessons and studying for my grades right up until I was almost seventeen. In fact, that's what I was doing on that hot summer's day in 1975 – I was in the music room at school, practising one of the pieces I was learning for my Grade 8 piano exam, which I was due to take in a few weeks' time.

Mansfield Heath School was a medium-sized public school in Hampstead, North London, where I lived. It was one of the first co-educational public schools in the country. The main school building, built in the seventeenth century, was one of those imposing old redbrick places with turrets and gargoyles and solid oak doors, and it was surrounded by lush green playing fields and ancient trees. The music room was in a small brick annexe building next to the chapel on the other side of the playing fields.

It was a Friday afternoon, that day, about two o'clock, and I had the room to myself. My music teacher – Mr Pope – let me practise whenever the room was free, and as I had a couple of free periods that afternoon and the room wasn't being used until three, I'd taken the opportunity to do some work on a particularly tricky passage of the piece that I was studying. So . . . there I was, alone in the music room, sitting at the piano, playing this passage over and over again, and I was concentrating so hard that I wasn't aware of the door opening and someone coming in. I just carried on playing. I'd just about got the hang of this problematic passage now, and I wanted to see how the work I'd done on it fitted in with the piece as a whole, so without pausing to rest I went back to the beginning and began playing the entire thing through.

It was a piece by Debussy, Arabesque No. 1. It's a wonderful piece of music, as light and dreamy as a perfect summer's day, and although I was still struggling slightly with some of the more technically difficult sections, that didn't stop me from losing myself in the beauty of the music whenever I played it. And when I got to the end, and the last quiet chord faded softly into the echoed silence . . . well, that was always a special thing for me. The sudden hush, the sense of the music floating in the air, the wonder of the melody still playing in my head . . .

I always took a quiet moment to savour it.

But that day, as I was sitting there enjoying the moment, the silence was broken by a soft round of applause from behind me. I turned round quickly, slightly startled, expecting to see Mr Pope, but instead of seeing the grey-bearded face of my music teacher, I saw the smiling face of Curtis Ray.

'That was *amazing*,' he said, still clapping quietly. 'Absolutely amazing . . .'

I stared at him. He was leaning languidly against the wall by the window on the other side of the room, his piercing blue eyes fixed on mine . . . and he was smiling at me. I couldn't believe it. He was Curtis Ray . . . he was here, with me. He was smiling at *me*.

'It's Debussy, isn't it?' he said.

'Sorry?'

'The music . . . the piece you just played, it's Debussy.'

'Oh, yeah . . .' I said, still quite dumbstruck. 'Yeah . . . the first arabesque.'

He nodded. 'It's really nice.'

I couldn't help glancing at the sheet music on the piano then, wondering if that's how he'd known it was Debussy – by reading it off the title page. But the title page wasn't showing. And by the time I turned back to him, I was already feeling embarrassed by my condescending assumption that he couldn't possibly have recognized the music by ear alone.

'Sorry,' I started to say. 'I didn't mean –'

'You're Lilibet Garcia, aren't you?' he said, pushing himself away from the wall and wandering casually towards me.

'Lili,' I told him.

'Don't you like being called Lilibet?'

'Would you?'

He smiled. 'I'm Curtis Ray.'

If the term *duh!* had been around then, I would have said it . . . or, at least, I would have thought it. But these were pre-*duh!* days, and I had to be content with thinking sarcastically to myself, 'No, really? Curtis Ray? I'd never have guessed . . .'

Actually, come to think of it, sarcasm was probably the last thing on my mind just then, and I probably didn't think anything *duh!*-like at all. I was too embarrassed, for one thing. Embarrassed by the tingling feelings in my heart, by my inability to stop staring at Curtis, by the sudden realization that while he was looking as cool as ever in his cool white T-shirt and jeans (because he was in the sixth form, and sixth-formers didn't have to wear school uniform), I was dressed in a totally uncool, and completely unflattering, pink school dress. And ankle socks, for God's sake. Embarrassing white ankle socks.

But the thing that embarrassed me most, the thing that made me feel really uncomfortable, was the simple fact that I *was* embarrassed. I *was* tingling and staring and squirming. I *was* behaving like a stupid little teenybopper. I *was* embarrassed by the clothes I was wearing. And that was all just *so* pathetic, and I hated myself for it.

But I just couldn't help it.

'You play really well,' Curtis said to me.

'Thanks,' I mumbled.

He was standing in front of me now. Not too close, but close enough for me to really see how stunningly good-looking he was. He'd always looked really good, even when he was going through that awkward thirteen/fourteen-year-old stage, but now – at seventeen – he'd grown up into a lean and hard-looking young man with a face that in some ways was almost *too* perfect to be true. It was the kind of face that seemed to have the ability to change, letting you see in it whatever you wanted to see in it. So if you looked at Curtis and believed that you were looking at the most beautiful boy in the world, that's what you saw. But you could also look at him sometimes and see a face of sadness, or heart-aching emptiness, or even cruelty . . .

But there was no sadness or cruelty in his face that day. Just a mind-blowing smile, a sheen of beauty, and those mesmerizing bright-blue eyes.

'Are you all right?' he asked me.

'Yeah, sorry . . .' I mumbled. 'I was just . . .'

I was just staring at him again, that's what I was doing. He'd taken a packet of cigarettes from his pocket now and was just about to light one.

'Are you sure that's a good idea?' I said. 'Mr Pope might be here any minute.'

Curtis laughed. 'Old Johnny won't mind,' he said, lighting the cigarette. 'He's always cadging fags off me. I've even shared a joint with him out here a couple of times.'

'Really?'

'Yeah . . . Johnny's a bit of an old hippy at heart.' He took a long drag on his cigarette and tapped ash to the floor. 'So, anyway,' he went on, 'do you play anything else?'

I looked at him, not sure what he meant.

'Apart from the piano,' he explained. 'Do you play any other instruments?'

'Oh, right,' I said. 'Well, not really . . . I mean, I can play the guitar a bit –'

'Yeah?'

I shook my head, realizing that I was talking to someone who – rumour had it – was an absolute genius on the guitar. 'I'm not any *good*,' I muttered. 'I just know a few chords, that's all . . .'

He smiled. 'What's your favourite?'

'Favourite what?'

'Chord. What's your favourite chord?'

'G major,' I said without thinking.

He nodded. 'Yeah, that's a good one. It's got a kind of *big*ness to it, hasn't it? An openness.'

I smiled, knowing exactly what he meant. 'What's *your* favourite?' I said.

He looked at me. 'Have a guess.'

I paused for a moment, giving it some thought, but I didn't really need to. The answer was instinctive. 'E major,' I said.

His smile told me I was right.

'Can you play bass?' he said.

'Double bass?'

'No, electric bass, you know . . .' He mimed playing a bass guitar. 'That kind of bass.'

'I don't know,' I said. 'I've never tried.'

'Do you fancy giving it a go?'

'What do you mean?'

'I'm looking for a bass player,' he said. 'For my band.'

'You're in a band?'

He nodded. 'We haven't played any gigs yet, but we've been practising on and off for about a year or so, and we're starting to get pretty good. The trouble is, Kenny – he's our bass player – well, he's suddenly decided that he doesn't want to play bass any more, he wants to play rhythm guitar.' Curtis took a long drag on his cigarette. 'Actually, to tell you the truth, Kenny's pretty shit on the bass anyway, so he's doing us a favour by packing it in. But now we need to find someone else . . .' He looked at me. 'What kind of music do you like? Apart from Debussy, obviously.'

It was a tricky question to answer. Or rather, it would have been a tricky question to answer if I'd tried to guess what kind of music Curtis liked and pretended that I liked it too, which I did actually consider for a moment or two. But although he wasn't really hippyish any more – his once-long hair was now hacked into something that looked like a lunatic bird's nest, and his scruffy old jeans were unfashionably, but very coolly, not flared – I naturally assumed that the kind of music he was into was the kind of music that I neither liked nor knew anything about, namely progressive rock – bands like Genesis and Yes and Pink Floyd. And if I'd told him that I liked Genesis, and he'd asked me which of their albums was my favourite, I wouldn't have been able to name one. And that really *would* have been embarrassing. So instead of trying to impress him, I simply told him the truth.

'Well, I've just got the new Cockney Rebel album,' I said. 'And I really like that.'

'Which one?' Curtis asked. '*The Best Years of Our Lives?*'

'No . . . the one before that.'

'*The Psychomodo?*'

'Yeah, that's it.'

He nodded knowingly. 'It's not as good as *The Human Menagerie.*'

I smiled. 'What *is?*'

He dropped his cigarette to the floor and stepped on it. 'Who else do you like?'

'I've been listening to the Sensational Alex Harvey Band quite a lot recently, and David Bowie . . . and I like some of the old Rolling Stones stuff –'

'What about the Stooges? Have you heard of them?'

I shook my head. 'I don't think so.'

'Iggy Pop and the Stooges . . . you've *got* to hear them. They're incredible. Really loud and *dirty*, you know?'

'Right,' I said, not quite sure what he meant. 'And that's the kind of stuff you like, is it?'

'I like all sorts,' he said. 'The Stooges, Velvet Underground, New York Dolls . . . the Faces, Dr Feelgood.' He looked at me. 'Have you seen the Feelgoods? They played the Rainbow in January. It was fan*tas*tic. They're an amazing band – really fast.'

I smiled. 'Fast?'

'Yeah.'

'So, basically, you like stuff that's loud and dirty and fast?'

'Yeah,' he grinned. 'That's pretty much it.'

'And is that what your band's like?'

'Why don't you come along and find out? We're rehearsing tomorrow. You can have a listen to what we do, and if you like it . . .' He paused, looking at me. 'Well, like I said, we need a new bass player, and I think you'd be just right.'

'Why?' I asked, genuinely perplexed. 'I mean, I could understand it if you were looking for someone to play keyboards –'

'God, no,' he said. 'We don't want any keyboards. We just need a bass player.'

'But I've never even played a bass –'

'Doesn't matter,' he shrugged. 'You'll soon get the hang of it. It's just like a guitar with a couple of strings missing.' He smiled. 'And, besides, it's not as if we're playing Debussy or anything.'

'Yeah, but I still don't get why you're asking *me* . . . I mean, there must be other people –'

'I don't *want* other people,' he said, his voice suddenly intense. 'I've tried other people, but that's all they are – other people. And that's not good enough. I need *special* people, people who *mean* what they do.' He stared intently at me. 'There's no point in doing *any*thing unless you really mean it, Lili. Do you know what I mean?'

'Yeah . . .' I said quietly, slightly taken aback by his passion. 'Yeah, I know what you mean.'

He stared silently at me for a moment longer, his eyes burning into mine, then all at once he relaxed again and his face broke into a carefree smile. 'Look,' he said, 'I know it's all a bit sudden, and it probably sounds kind of weird, but I just think you'd be perfect for the band, that's all. You love music, that's obvious. You can play. You're kind of kooky . . . *and* you look really good.' He grinned. 'I mean, what more could anyone want in a bass player?'

'Kooky?' I said, raising an eyebrow.

'Yeah . . .'

'You think I'm *kooky*?'

He smiled. 'It's a compliment.'

I knew what he meant, and I was perfectly happy to take it as a compliment. Kookiness was fine with me. I had no problem with kookiness at all. But Curtis had also said that I looked really good, and *that* was causing me all kinds of problems. Firstly, because no one had ever told me that I looked really good before, so it was hard to believe that he meant it. And if he *didn't* mean it . . . well, that would make him a pretty shitty person, wouldn't it? But if he *did* mean it, that would mean that Curtis Ray – *the* Curtis Ray – had told me that I looked really good. And that was something else altogether.

In fact, to tell you the truth, it made me feel so twistedly wonderful that I almost wished that he *didn't* mean it.

'So,' he said to me. 'What do you think?'

'About what?'

'The band . . . playing bass. Do you want to give it a go?'

I looked at him. 'Do you mean it?'

He nodded. 'Like I said, there's no point in doing anything unless you really mean it.'

'Yeah, all right,' I said. 'I'll give it a go.'

He smiled broadly. 'You won't regret it.'

As it turned out, he was both right and wrong about that . . . but I wasn't to know that then. And neither was he.

'This is where I live,' he said, writing his address on a scrap of paper and passing it to me. 'We're rehearsing in my dad's garage at the moment. It's not ideal . . . but until we find somewhere better, it's all we've got.'

I looked at the scrap of paper. Curtis's house was about a mile away from mine.

'Get there for about two o'clock,' he said. 'OK?'

'Tomorrow?'

'Yeah.'

I looked at him. 'What's the band called?'

'Naked.'

'Naked?'

'Yeah.' He smiled his smile. 'We're going to be *massive*.'

3

The next day, as I made my way through the streets of Hampstead towards Curtis's house, I was feeling so mixed up and nervous about everything that I came very close to chickening out. I just had so many doubts about everything – what would the rest of the band think of me? what if I made a complete fool of myself? what if Curtis realized that he'd made a mistake and I wasn't so 'perfect for the band' after all? And although I kept telling myself that how I looked and what I was wearing didn't matter, I couldn't help worrying that Curtis and the others just wouldn't think I was *cool* enough. I'd done my best – inexpertly slapping on a ton of black eye-liner and too much of my mother's red lipstick – but I'd never been too concerned about fashionable haircuts and clothes and make-up, and the simple truth was that I didn't actually know what was cool and what wasn't. I bought most of my clothes from jumble sales and charity shops, and – as far as I can remember – my hair at the time was a failed attempt at a Suzi Quatro-style layered cut, which might not have looked all that bad if I hadn't recently attacked it myself with a pair of blunt scissors . . . an exercise that resulted in me resembling a slightly deranged medieval waif. Actually, come to think of it, if you imagine a sixteen-year-old girl wearing too much eye-liner and mismatched secondhand clothes, with a haircut that wouldn't have looked out of place in a lunatic asylum . . . that's probably as good a description of me as you're going to get.

Anyway, as I said, I was feeling pretty nervous that day, worrying about all kinds of things, and the closer I got to Curtis's house the more tempting it was to just turn round and go back home. But as well as being racked with nerves, I was also – underneath it all – bursting with hope and excitement, and although the fear and anxiety were almost too much to bear, it was, in the end, the excitement that won the day. That's what kept me going – the buzz, the thrill, the kick of it all. Yes, I was scared. And, yes, I knew that I might make a fool of myself. But this thing I was doing, whatever it proved to be . . .

I *wanted* it.

I wanted to *do* it.

And I did.

Curtis's house was a reasonably large detached place in a reasonably nice part of Hampstead. It was nowhere near as big as my house, but then Curtis's father wasn't a film director like mine. Curtis's father was a doctor. As was his mother. And although I didn't know it at the time, they were both very straight-laced, very conservative, and they both found their son's choice of lifestyle *very* disappointing.

That afternoon though, when I got to Curtis's house, I had no idea of the conflict between him and his parents. I didn't know that they'd already banned him from using the garage as a rehearsal place, and that the only reason he'd arranged the rehearsal there today was that his father was away at a medical conference all weekend and his mother was spending the day with her parents in Maidstone. All I knew, as Curtis met me and took me into the garage and began introducing me to the others, was that my hands were shaking, my heart was trembling, and for a few terrible moments I was genuinely afraid that I was going to be sick. But, oddly enough, I also felt really good. Really *alive*. But scared to death and acutely self-conscious too. It was, I suppose, the kind of feeling you get when you're riding a rollercoaster – an exhilarating mixture of sickness, fear, and blood-twisting excitement.

'All right,' said Curtis, closing the garage door. 'Well . . . here we all are.' He smiled at me. 'Are you OK?'

I nodded. 'Yeah . . .'

'Good.' He ushered me over to the middle of the garage where the band's equipment was set up. 'This is Kenny,' he said, indicating a tallish boy with a bass guitar who was standing beside one of the speakers. 'And this,' Curtis said, turning to the other boy who was sitting at a drum kit, 'this is Stan.'

'Hi,' I muttered self-consciously, limply waving my hand. 'I'm Lili . . .'

While Stan glanced briefly at me and gave me a silent nod of acknowledgement, Kenny barely even looked at me. He just gazed vaguely in my direction for a fraction of a second, then turned his back and began tuning his bass. I recognized both him and Stan from school. They were in the same year as Curtis, and I'd seen them hanging around with him a few times. They'd never really struck me as being the coolest kids around, and I'd always assumed that they hung around with Curtis because they wanted to be seen with him, not because they were really *in* with him or anything, so I was slightly surprised to find out that they were in the band. They just didn't look like the kind of kids who played in a band.

Stan's real name was Phillip Smith, but – for reasons long forgotten – he'd always been known as Stan. He was a skinny kid, kind of gawky, with lank black hair and a long mournful face that never showed any emotion. He always gave the impression that he didn't really care about anything, which – when I first met him – I thought was just an act. But after a while, when I'd got to know him a bit better, I came to realize that it wasn't an act at all – he really *didn't* care about anything. He just lived his life, played his drums, did whatever he wanted to do . . . and, as far as he was concerned, that was it. That was all he needed.

Everything else – the rest of the world – simply didn't concern him.

And I always kind of admired Stan for that.

Not that he would have *cared* what I thought, of course . . . nor would I ever have told him. In fact, Stan had such little regard for what other people thought that he only ever spoke when it was absolutely necessary. In all the time I knew him, I don't think I ever heard him string more than a dozen words together. He was even quite reticent about counting the band in at the start of a song.

'Can't *you* do it?' he'd say to Curtis.

'All you've got to do is count to fucking four,' Curtis would tell him, shaking his head in exasperation. 'It's not *that* hard.'

'Yeah, I know . . .'

'Well, just fucking *do* it then.'

And he would. But then, for the next song, he'd just go 'One, two . . .' and start playing, or else he'd just bash his drumsticks together four times . . . and then Curtis would start arguing with him again.

But the arguments never really led to anything. And that was only partly because Stan just couldn't be bothered to argue. The main reason was that he was a hell of a good drummer, and Curtis was well aware that you can't have a good band without a good drummer, and he didn't want to risk losing Stan. So although he might argue with him every now and then, and he might sometimes get really pissed off with him, he'd never do anything to jeopardize Stan's place in the band.

When it came to Kenny though . . . well, that was different. As Curtis had already told me, he didn't rate Kenny Slater as a bass player, and I was soon to find out that he didn't actually rate Kenny at all. In fact, it turned out that Kenny was only in the band in the first place because he owned most of the equipment, all of which had been bought for him by his stinking rich parents, who – unlike Curtis's mum and dad – were more than happy to help their only son in any way they could. They were also the kind of parents who like to shower their offspring with expensive toys just to show everyone how fabulously wealthy they are . . . which, again, I didn't know at the time. But it wasn't too difficult to guess. Kenny's whole attitude was that of an over-indulged and unpleasant child whose brattish and sulky behaviour was only tolerated by other kids because he bought them sweets and let them play with his expensive toys.

I could have been mistaken, of course, but my overriding impression of Kenny that day was not only that he didn't like me, but that he didn't really like Curtis or Stan either, and – on top of all that – he didn't *really* want to be there. But there was no way that he was going to go home and leave the rest of them to play with *his* equipment.

'All right,' Curtis said to me, smiling as he slung a battered black guitar over his shoulder. 'Are you ready to hear the best band in the world?'

As I watched him walk over to the others and plug in his guitar, I couldn't help thinking how *perfect* he looked. This was his world, his environment . . . this was what he *was*. His guitar seemed almost part of him, and when he turned up the volume and effortlessly played through a series of blues riffs, I immediately knew that the rumours I'd heard were true – he really was a genius on the guitar. It wasn't that the riffs he was playing were particularly complicated or anything, it was simply the *way* he played them – with such natural ease and purity – and the raw beauty that he gave to the sound, and the way that the sound seemed to come not from the speakers, or even from the guitar, but from somewhere within Curtis himself . . .

It was truly stunning.

Satisfied with the sound of his guitar, he turned up the volume then and blasted out a chord, a big fat E major, and it was so incredibly loud that it literally shook the walls – and my stomach – it was all I could do to resist covering my ears with my hands.

I looked over at Curtis and saw him smiling at me, and I realized that he was reminding me that E major was his favourite chord.

I nodded at him, and smiled back.

He held my gaze for a moment, then turned to Stan. 'All right?'

Stan nodded.

Curtis looked at Kenny. 'OK?'

Kenny shrugged.

Curtis went over and stood in front of a microphone stand. 'This one's our signature tune,' he said into the mike, looking at me. 'It's called "Naked".'

He paused for a moment, closing his eyes, and then – bending over slightly, almost as if he was in pain – he opened up with a crash of chords that nearly knocked me off my feet. After a rapid four bars of guitar, the bass and drums came storming in, and I swear that the floor started shaking. It was a *huge* sound, and I knew then what Curtis had meant when he'd talked about music that was dirty and loud. And fast . . . God, they played *so* fast. It was breathtaking. Curtis was playing the guitar like a crazy man – hammering out the chords, bending and twisting all over the place, staggering backwards and reeling forwards – and when he lurched up to the microphone and started to sing, the sound that came out of his mouth was astonishing. It was so powerful, so loud, and raw, so basic and brutal . . . but at the same time, it was undeniably beautiful. Full of feeling, passionate and emotional . . .

It was a sound that came from his heart.

Apart from the chorus, when all three of them joined in on a guttural chant of 'Naked! Naked!', I couldn't really make out many of the words, but from what I *could* hear, I got the feeling that the song was something to do with decadence and poetry and monstrous souls.

I'd never heard anything like it before.

It didn't last very long – three minutes at the most – and as soon as they'd finished, Curtis shouted out, '"Monkeys"!' and they launched into another song. This one was a bit slower, a bit emptier, and not quite so manic as 'Naked', but it still had the same level of intensity and darkness, and it felt like the kind of song that gets better and better the more times you hear it.

The final song they played was something quite different. It was called 'Heaven Hill'. It started off quietly, with Curtis singing sorrowfully over a single haunting guitar line, and gradually it built up into a swirling echo of bitter-sweet harmonies over a mesmerizing heartbeat of throbbing bass and drums. Again, I'd never heard anything like it before, and if someone had asked me what kind of music it was, I wouldn't have known what to say.

It was, quite simply, unforgettable.

When the song ended, fading back to the original guitar line, Curtis turned to Stan and Kenny, nodded his head, then wiped a sheen of sweat from his face and looked at me.

'So,' he said, smiling. 'What do you think?'

'Fan*tas*tic,' I told him. 'Really . . . I loved it, especially the last one.'

'Yeah,' he agreed. 'It still needs a bit of work on the middle bit . . . but we've nearly got it now.' He removed his guitar, leaned it against the wall, and came over to me. 'So you really think we're all right then?'

'Yeah, really.'

He smiled again. 'Do you want to have a go on the bass now?'

I glanced over at Kenny, who was quietly picking out a few notes on his bass, and I wondered if he really *had* decided that he didn't want to play bass any more, or if it was more a case of Curtis not wanting him to. He looked fairly sulky about *some*thing, but sulkiness seemed to be his default setting, so it was hard to tell what he was really feeling. And although Curtis had said that he was 'pretty shit on the bass anyway', he'd sounded pretty good to me. But then what did *I* know about playing the bass?

And that was the problem – I *didn't* know anything about it. And yet there I was, being asked if I wanted to take over from Kenny, who as far as I could tell was a perfectly competent – and perhaps even better than average – bass player.

It wasn't a particularly comfortable situation to be in.

'Lili?' Curtis said.

'Yeah . . .' I muttered, looking back at him. 'Sorry, I was just . . .' I lowered my voice. 'Are you sure this is a good idea? I mean –'

'Yeah, of *course* it's a good idea,' he said breezily. 'Come on . . . just try it.' He put his hand on my arm and guided me over to where Kenny was standing. 'It's dead easy,' he said to me. 'Kenny's only been playing bass for a few months . . . haven't you, Ken?'

Kenny looked at him. 'What?'

'I was just telling Lili that it didn't take you very long to learn the bass.' Curtis grinned. 'And now you're shit-hot.'

Kenny just shrugged.

Curtis said to him, 'Give it here then.'

'What?'

'Your bass.' He sighed. 'Come on, Kenny . . . we haven't got all day.'

Kenny gave me a sideways glance, then – somewhat reluctantly – removed his bass and passed it over to Curtis. Curtis smiled tightly at him, waited for him to move away, then turned to me, holding up the bass. It was a Fender Mustang . . . not that I knew that then. All I knew then was that it looked *really* big.

'Right,' Curtis said to me, his smile back to normal again. 'I take it you're right-handed?'

'Yeah.'

'OK, let's try it on for size first.' He stepped up close to me and looped the guitar strap over my head, then gently lowered the Fender until the strap was taking all its weight. 'How's that?' he said.

'It weighs a *ton*,' I told him.

'You'll get used to it. Do you want me to adjust the strap? Or is it OK as it is?'

'I think it's all right.'

'OK,' he said, stepping back and looking me up and down. 'Yeah, it suits you. You look good.'

I didn't *feel* good. Not only was the bass as long as I was tall, it felt like it weighed the same as me too. Never mind trying to play the damn thing, it was difficult enough just standing there with it.

'Maybe it might be better if you sat down for now,' Curtis said, looking at me. 'Hold on, I'll get you a chair.' He went over to the back of the garage and came back with an old wooden straight-backed chair. 'There you go,' he said.

I felt slightly pathetic as I sat down and rested the bass on top of my thighs, but it *was* much more comfortable, and that easily outweighed my embarrassment.

'Better?' Curtis asked.

'Yeah, thanks.'

'All right . . . let's get started then.' He looked at me. 'Do you usually use a plectrum when you're playing the guitar? Or just your fingers?'

'Plectrum.'

'OK . . . well, with the bass you can either play fingerstyle, like Kenny, or use a plectrum. Fingerstyle players can sometimes get a bit snotty about using a plectrum, as if it's not the *right* way to play bass . . .' He glanced over at Kenny, half-grinning. Kenny ignored him. Curtis turned back to me. 'But, as far as I'm concerned, it doesn't really make any difference. I mean, as long as you get the right sound, who cares how you get it? Anyway, it's entirely up to you . . . but as you're already used to using a plectrum, you might as well use one to start with.' He passed me a plectrum. 'All right?'

'Yeah.'

'Right . . . well, all you really need to know is that it's tuned exactly the same as the first four strings of a guitar.' He reached over and touched the first string. 'So that's E, then A, D, and G. OK?'

'Yeah.'

'This is your volume,' he said, indicating one of two control knobs. 'And the other one adjusts the tone.' He looked at me. 'And that's pretty much it.'

'OK,' I said.

'So . . .' He smiled. 'Off you go then.'

I looked at him, guessing that he was waiting to see what I'd do. Would I hesitate? Would I ask him what he wanted me to do? Or would I just go for it?

I took a breath and went for it.

The only guitars I'd played before then were acoustic, and mainly classical acoustic, which have nylon strings and aren't particularly loud, so when I hit the open E string of that big Fender Mustang, and the *huge* throb of the bass note boomed from the speakers . . . well, it's hard to describe how *viscerally* thrilling it was. That deep, dark, *massive* sound, the *feel* of it . . . vibrating through the floor, into my flesh, my bones . . . it was just so unbelievably *good*.

I played some more, thumping the open E string – *doomp-doomp, doomp-doomp* – and then the A string – *domp-domp, domp-domp* – then back to E again. I reached down the neck of the bass, held down the E string on the third fret, and pumped out a big fat G. The string was incredibly thick and tight, much harder to hold down than the soft nylon strings of a classical acoustic guitar, and my finger started aching almost immediately. I played a few more notes, sliding up to A and then B, and then I had to let go of the neck and waggle my fingers in the air to ease the pain.

'All right?' Curtis said.

'Yeah . . . brilliant. It's just a bit hard to hold the strings down.'

'You'll get used to that too.'

He went over and picked up his guitar. 'Do you want to try playing along with us?'

'I don't know . . . I'm not sure I'm ready to –'

'You'll be all right,' he said. 'We'll just play a bit of 12-bar blues, you know . . . the basic three-chord stuff. E, A, and B . . . do you know what I mean?'

'Yeah, but I don't know –'

'Just keep to the single notes, you know – *dah-dah*, *dah-dah*, *dah-dah* – like you were doing just now. All right?'

I nodded. 'I'll do my best.'

'Good.' He turned to Kenny, who'd picked up a guitar and plugged it in and was standing by one of the speakers. 'Ready?'

Kenny nodded.

Curtis turned back to me. 'Just join in when you're ready, OK?'

I nodded.

Curtis turned up the volume on his guitar, ran through a couple of quick blues scales, made a slight adjustment to the tuning, and then – with a brief nod at Stan – he began to play.

He kept it quite slow, starting with a traditional descending blues intro, and then Kenny and Stan came in, driving the rhythm along as Curtis kept things going with some simple, but very effective, blues riffs. It was, as Curtis had promised, pretty basic stuff, and I knew in my mind how I *ought* to be playing along with it . . . at least, I knew what notes I ought to be playing and where and when I ought to be playing them. It was just a matter of actually *doing* it.

Don't think about it, I kept telling myself. *Just do it. Just get that rhythm into your head* – dah-dah, dah-dah, dah-dah, dah-dah – *and start thumping the open E string.*

I waited . . . while the key changed to B.

Dah-dah, dah-dah, dah-dah, dah-dah . . .

And then back to A.

Dah-dah, dah-dah, dah-dah, dah-dah . . .

And finally back to E again.

Dah-dah, dah-dah, dah-dah, dah-dah . . .

Dah-dah-daaaahh . . .

And then I joined in.

Although I was only playing single notes, it still took me a little while to work out how to play them with the solid thumping rhythm of a bass guitar, but after stopping and starting a few times to experiment with the positioning of my right hand, I finally figured out how to control the length and sustain of each note, which gave me a lot more control of the rhythm.

As we carried on playing that basic three-chord pattern over and over again, I gradually became more and more confident, and I soon felt competent enough to start adding a few extra notes here and there. I was still a long way from playing a bass *line* as such, but I wasn't just playing single notes any more. I wasn't feeling anxious or overly self-conscious any more either. In fact, after a while, I realized that I was actually really enjoying myself. Despite the almost stupid simplicity of the music, especially the part that I was playing, it was just as mesmeric – and easy to get lost in – as anything else I'd ever played, including Debussy. Perhaps even more so. It was addictive. I didn't want to stop. I just wanted us to keep going, to carry on playing that wonderfully idiotic music – *dah-dah, dah-dah, dah-dah, dah-dah* – over and over and over again . . .

But, in the end, my fingers began to hurt so much from holding down the bass strings that I simply *had* to stop. I physically couldn't play any more.

A few seconds after I stopped playing, the others stopped too.

'Sorry,' I said, waggling my throbbing fingers in the air.

'No problem,' Curtis said, smiling at me. 'It might be a good idea to keep your hand still for a minute.'

'What?'

'You're flicking blood all over the place.'

I stopped waggling my hand around and gazed at my fingers.

The bass strings had dug into my fingertips so much that my index finger was bleeding.

'Shit,' I whispered.

Curtis laughed.

I glared at him.

'Hey,' he said, still smiling. 'Welcome to the band.'

4

Everything changed for me after that weekend. I started spending a lot of time with Curtis, going round to his house a couple of evenings a week to practise the bass and learn Naked's songs . . . at least, that's all I *told* myself I was doing. And, at first, that *was* all I was doing.

We'd meet up after school, maybe go somewhere for a quick cup of coffee and something to eat, then we'd go back to his place and spend two or three hours in his bedroom together going through the songs. I'd sit on the bed with the bass, Curtis would sit next to me with his guitar, we'd plug in to a tiny little practice amp, and then we'd just go over the songs – again and again and again – until I knew them all off by heart. At the same time, Curtis was constantly giving me advice about how to play the bass, how to get the best out of it, how to get the right sound and – more importantly – the right *feeling* . . . and within a couple of weeks or so I'd not only become reasonably good at it, but I'd also gained a huge amount of confidence. So much so, in fact, that I even started to sing along with Curtis on some of the songs.

The songs were all written by him, both the music and the lyrics, and I soon found out that – unlike his carefree attitude to almost everything else – he took his song-writing *intensely* seriously. His songs were everything to him – they came from his heart, from his soul. And they were so personal, the lyrics so much a part of him, that although he was immensely proud of them, he was always quite adamant in his refusal to explain them.

'Songs are songs,' he told me once. 'They don't *need* explaining.'

'Yeah,' I'd said. 'But the words –'

'They're just words.'

Curtis was also very possessive and controlling about his music – very exact about how it should sound, very demanding about how it should be played – and he had no interest whatsoever in anyone else's opinions or suggestions. Kenny and Stan, I soon learned, didn't even bother trying to get him to listen to them any more – they just did whatever he told them to do. And it was at least a couple of months before Curtis would grudgingly acknowledge that my background in classical music and my years of study and training weren't totally irrelevant and worthless. Actually, he was probably right in the first place, because in terms of the kind of music we were playing, most of my classical training *was* totally irrelevant and worthless. But I did know quite a lot about music – how it works, how things fit together, how to make the most of rhythm and structure and melody – and Curtis eventually came to accept that some of my ideas were occasionally worth listening to.

But that was later . . .

In those first few months, I was perfectly content to keep my ideas to myself, listen to Curtis, and concentrate on learning the basics.

Another thing that changed was that as a result of playing the bass all the time, the skin on the fingertips of my left hand quickly hardened up, which stopped the bleeding and made it a lot less painful to play. On the downside, in terms of playing the piano, the roughening of my fingertips didn't help at all, and although I still managed to scrape through my Grade 8 exam, it was obvious that – to a certain extent – my piano-playing was suffering. Not that I really minded. Because, as time went by, although I still really enjoyed playing the piano, and I still really loved classical music, I gradually lost all interest in the *academic* side of playing. Music had become so much more to me now, and the idea of *studying* it just seemed so pointless, so artificial . . . so lifeless.

As well as spending a lot of time on my own with Curtis, we also spent as much time together with the rest of the band as we could – practising, rehearsing, working out new songs. It wasn't easy finding somewhere to rehearse. Curtis's parents had not only categorically banned him from using the garage, they'd even put a padlock on the door to stop him getting in when they were away. So we'd had to find somewhere else to play, and for a month or so we rehearsed a couple of times a week in a nightclub in Kilburn. The club was one of several in North London that Stan's father owned, and he was quite happy to let us use it whenever it was empty . . . until, that is, Curtis somehow managed to overload the club's PA system, blowing the speakers and causing about £5,000 worth of damage, which didn't go down too well with Stan's dad. After that, we practised in all kinds of places for a while – an abandoned factory, a lock-up garage, a dance studio, the basement of a squat in Seven Sisters . . .

Basically, as long as it had a roof and an electricity supply, it would do.

So . . . as the days passed by, and the summer holidays began, Naked took over my life. We practised hard, we learned new songs . . . and when I wasn't with the band, or practising the bass on my own, I was spending all my time with Curtis. I'd be lying if I said that there was nothing intimate about our relationship at that point, because I think we both knew what was going to happen from the moment we met in the music room, but there was no real physical intimacy between us during those first few weeks together. There was lots of smiling and joking, lots of playful flirting, and there were quite a few times when we'd sit side by side on Curtis's bed, playing our guitars, and Curtis would lean in close to me, take my hand, and gently guide my fingers over the fretboard, and my heart would start pounding, and I'd get all hot and flustered, wondering if he was going to kiss me, and how that would feel, and how I would feel if he wanted to do *more* than just kiss me . . .

I wondered about that quite a lot. Asking myself whether I really wanted to do it or not, imagining how it would be, how it would feel, what it would mean . . .

When the big moment finally came though, on a sultry Sunday afternoon in July, in Curtis's bedroom, when his parents were out . . . well, it wasn't really anything like I'd imagined. That's not to say it was terrible or anything, it was just . . . I don't know. It just wasn't how I'd imagined it was going to be. As I said, I'd kind of known all along it was going to happen eventually, and I was pretty sure that I wanted it to happen. I really liked Curtis. I admired him, I looked up to him . . . I was in awe of him, to tell you the truth. He was special. And I was, without doubt, physically attracted to him. So when he came back into the bedroom that afternoon, after excusing himself to go to the bathroom . . . when he closed the door and came over and sat down beside me on the bed, and he put his arm round my waist and gently kissed me on the lips . . . it *was* what I wanted. I still wasn't *entirely* sure if I wanted it to go any further, but I kind of knew that it would, and when it did . . . and we ended up in bed together, with Curtis murmuring breathlessly, 'Are you sure this is OK?' and me saying, 'Yes . . . yes, it's OK . . .'

And it *was* OK.

Sort of . . .

It was my first time, for a start, and I didn't really know how it was supposed to feel or what I was supposed to do. I didn't know if it was natural to feel slightly afraid of what was happening, and – to be perfectly honest – slightly turned off too. It was just the sheer physicality of it, I suppose. The reality of the sexual act, as opposed to the fantasy of falling in love. There was a big difference. And I think the reality of it was all just a bit too much for me. The naked reality of Curtis's body, his animal grunts and groans, his frighteningly desperate *need* . . . it had never been like that in my dreams.

I remember quite clearly lying in bed after that first time, watching Curtis as he pulled on his jeans and lit a cigarette . . . and I remember thinking to myself, *Is that it? Is that what it's all about?*

But, like I said, it was OK.

It was my decision as much as Curtis's, and I could have said no if I'd wanted to. It wasn't as if I was *forced* into it or anything. And Curtis, in his way, was quite gentle and kind. It was just . . .

I don't know.

It just changed things so much. It changed the way I saw Curtis. It made me realize that – in one way, at least – he *wasn't* any different to other boys. It changed me too, taking away the child in me and making me grow up too fast.

It changed *us*.

It changed everything.

And afterwards, there would always be a part of me that longed for the days before that Sunday afternoon, the days when I could go to bed at night and dream in innocence of the way Curtis had looked at me, or the way he'd smiled at me, or just the feel of his hand as he guided my fingers over the fretboard of the bass . . .

Before I met Curtis, I'd never been one for going out all that much. I wasn't a recluse or anything, and I'd been to my fair share of parties and clubs and gigs, but I wasn't the kind of person who went out on the town every night. With Curtis though . . . well, he *was* the kind of person who went out on the town every night, and now that I was *with* him, now that we were a couple, I started going out a lot too. Sometimes it'd just be me and Curtis, sometimes Kenny and Stan would come along, and sometimes Curtis would surprise me by bringing along people I'd never met before. He knew a *lot* of people, and even now I'm still not sure how he got to know them or where he met them. He just seemed to *know* them. They were all mostly arty kind of people – writers, musicians, poets, painters – and while some of them were OK, and none of them could be described as boring, a lot of them were far from pleasant. This didn't seem to bother Curtis. They could be loud, rude, disgusting, dirty . . . creepy, crazy, nasty, even dangerous – Curtis didn't care. As long as they were *different*, that's all that mattered to him. He *liked* abnormality. He found it entertaining. It was almost as if he saw life as a circus, and he was the ringmaster, surrounding himself with performing animals and clowns and freaks. And that made me wonder sometimes if that's how he saw me – as just another entertainment act in the circus of his life.

I have to admit, though, that we did have some really good times together. Curtis took me to see all kinds of bands in all kinds of places – bands I'd always wanted to see, bands I'd never heard of, bands who were great, bands who were awful. We saw Dr Feelgood, Eddie and the Hot Rods, Bazooka Joe, the Stranglers, the Count Bishops, the 101ers, Kilburn and the High Roads . . . and dozens more. Although I didn't know it at the time, a lot of these bands were, in a way, the forerunners of punk, and some of them included people who would eventually become really big names. The 101ers, for example, were Joe Strummer's band. Ian Dury was in Kilburn and the High Roads. Bazooka Joe featured Adam Ant.

And it was seeing these kinds of bands, and the people who went along to watch them, that first made me realize that something was starting to happen in the music world . . . at least in London, anyway. There was a change of mood in the air. There was a feeling that rock music had gone too far, that famous bands like the Rolling Stones and Led Zeppelin had become too pompous and out of touch. Simplicity was back in vogue. Rock 'n' roll was going back to the basics: short songs, no solos, everyday clothes, everyday people.

I liked it a lot.

What I didn't like quite so much was when Curtis started taking me to a clothes shop in Chelsea that everyone was talking about. The shop was called Sex, and over the years it came to be known as the birthplace of the Sex Pistols. When Curtis first took me there, in August 1975, it already had a growing reputation as *the* place to be. It was owned and run by Malcolm McLaren and Vivienne Westwood, and over the years its shop assistants included Glen Matlock and Sid Vicious, Chrissie Hynde (who later formed the Pretenders), and a punk girl called Jordan who was famous for wearing the shop's incredibly revealing and provocative clothes. A lot of the clothing was bondage gear – rubber stuff, hoods, T-shirts printed with pornographic images – the kind of clothing that was intended to shock. And that, to me, was what the whole place seemed to be all about – being shocking, being offensive, being outrageous. Which Curtis, of course, found fascinating. And that's one of the reasons he liked going there. Another reason – which he flatly denied – was that Jordan wasn't the only girl in the shop who wore revealing and provocative clothes. There were lots of them, all strutting around in their ripped fishnets and black PVC, most of them quite happy to try on the shop's clothes without bothering to go into the fitting room, just stripping off in the middle of the shop, the more people watching the better.

'It's nothing to *do* with sex,' I remember Curtis telling me once, after I'd caught him ogling a half-naked girl. 'It's about breaking taboos, you know . . . it's about *not* being hung up on traditional sexuality . . .'

'Yeah, right,' I'd told him. 'Of course it is.'

But although the girls – and the underlying sexual nature of the whole place – were undoubtedly part of the attraction for Curtis, his main reason for going there was simply that Sex was where it was happening. Not that Curtis – or anyone else – really knew what *it* was at the time, but his instinct told him that whatever it was, it was fresh and exciting, and it was different, and it was going to be big, and Curtis was determined to be part of it. So he spent as much time as he could just hanging around the shop, getting to know most of the regulars – the Sex Pistols, Johnny Rotten, Sid Vicious, Malcolm McLaren, Siouxsie Sioux, Steve Severin . . . the names and faces who would come to be known as pioneers of the nascent punk scene.

I didn't always go with him when he went down to Chelsea – sometimes he'd go with Kenny and Stan, sometimes he'd go on his own – and even when I did go with him, I didn't really get involved all that much. I'd talk to people if they talked to me, but mostly I just hung around in the background, keeping myself to myself . . . partly, I suppose, because I was still quite shy and a bit overwhelmed by everything, but I think the main reason was that I didn't actually *like* most of those people. They were interesting, and different, and there was no doubt that some of them were incredibly exciting . . . but, as far as I was concerned, most of them weren't very nice. Not that *nice* mattered to Curtis. All that mattered to him was the energy, the danger, the new ideas, new sounds, new clothes – the home-dyed spiky hair, the DIY fashions, the over-the-top make-up and attitude . . . all of it designed to shock.

Of course, nowadays it's perfectly acceptable to have spiky hair and dye it whatever colour you like, and it's quite commonplace for middle-aged parents to buy ready-ripped jeans from Asda, so it's hard to believe that these things were once considered outrageous.

But they were.

And Curtis took to them all with a passion.

On 6 November that year, we went to see the Sex Pistols play their first ever gig at St Martin's College. Curtis was really looking the part by then. His hair was hacked short and dyed bright green, he was regularly wearing eye-liner and lipstick, and he'd taken to wearing the same clothes pretty much all the time: dirty old straight-legged jeans, ripped at the knee; a threadbare T-shirt with the sleeves torn off, a pair of black motorcycle boots, and an ancient black leather jacket with *NAKED* daubed on the back in blood-red paint.

He was also, by that time, getting more and more into drugs.

It wasn't a new thing with Curtis. He'd always smoked a bit of dope now and then, ever since I'd met him, and while I didn't like it very much, I soon got used to it. I never really got *into* it myself – although I'd be lying if I said that I never touched drugs – but I couldn't help getting used to it, because in Curtis's world, which had become *my* world, it was simply something that every-one did. It wasn't a big deal. If you had some grass, you smoked it. If you had some speed, you snorted it. If you could get out of your head, you did. That's just the way it was.

That night in November though, the night of the Sex Pistols gig, when I met Curtis at the squat in Seven Sisters where we sometimes rehearsed, I knew straight away that he'd had some-thing more than just a joint or a line of speed. He was so strung-out, so bug-eyed and twitchy and sweaty and manic . . . it was frightening.

'What the hell have you taken, Curtis?' I asked him.

'What?' he grinned.

'What have you taken?'

'Nothing . . . I had a smoke, that's all. It's good stuff . . . you want some before we go?'

'No, thanks.'

'Come *on*, Lil,' he said, flinging his arm round my shoulder. 'Just a quick hit, get you in the mood –'

'I don't need to get in the *mood*,' I said coldly, shrugging his arm off. 'And don't call me *Lil*. You know I don't like it.'

'Yeah, all right,' he said defensively, stepping back. 'There's no need to get uptight –'

'I'm not *uptight*. I just –'

'Hey, you look fucking *great*,' he said, grinning crazily again. 'I mean . . . shit, *look* at you . . .' He stared at me, running his fingers through his hair. 'You know what you are, don't you?'

'What?' I sighed.

He smiled. 'You're the most beautiful girl in the world.'

'Yeah, right –'

'And you're mine.'

I looked at him, shaking my head, but I couldn't help smiling. 'Come on,' I said. 'Let's get out of here.'

Despite everything, the Pistols gig was amazing. Despite the state that Curtis was in, despite it being a cramped little venue with no stage and terrible acoustics, despite the sporadic outbursts of violence and venom, and the undeniable fact that – musically – the Pistols weren't actually all that good . . . despite all that, it was a night I'll never forget.

The headline act was Bazooka Joe, but I don't even remember what they were like. All I remember is standing with Curtis, Kenny and Stan, watching Johnny Rotten and the rest of the Pistols getting ready to play, the four of them slouching around like a gang of demented street urchins. Johnny was wearing baggy pinstripe trousers and his infamous 'I Hate Pink Floyd' T-shirt; Glen Matlock was wearing a pink blouse and paint-spattered jeans; and Paul Cook and Steve Jones . . . well, they just looked how they always looked – like a couple of happily-stoned criminals. I don't mind admitting that I wasn't expecting to like them very much, mainly because I simply didn't like them as people, but even before they'd played a note I could tell that something special was about to happen. I could feel it in the smoke-filled air, I could *sense* it . . . and so could everyone else. As they plugged in their instruments and got ready to play, Curtis leaned in close to me and whispered in my ear, 'Do you get it now?'

And I realized, quite suddenly, that I did.

As Steve Jones cranked up his amp and blasted out a buzz-saw chord, it dawned on me that the things I'd never liked about these people – their studied unpleasantness, their don't-care attitude, their desperate need to shock and offend – these were precisely the things that, as performers, made them so thrilling and unforgettable.

It wasn't the music, it was the attitude.

The energy.

The *chaos*.

As I said, in a strictly musical sense, the Sex Pistols weren't all that impressive that night. They weren't terrible or anything – I mean, they could all *play* – and although Johnny Rotten's voice was way out of tune at times, it was, without doubt, unlike anything else I'd ever heard . . . but overall, as a band, they were nowhere near as good as Naked. We were a much tighter band than them, our songs were far better, *and* more original, and although we hadn't actually played live yet, I was pretty sure that when we did, we wouldn't be as shambolic or ragged as the Pistols. They didn't even seem to know what they were doing most of the time.

'Look!' Curtis shouted in my ear during their second song. 'There's Malcolm!'

I looked where he was pointing and saw Malcolm McLaren down at the front, waving his hands around and shouting at the band, telling them where to stand and what to do. He had his usual entourage with him – Vivienne Westwood, Jordan . . . all the Sex regulars, most of them wearing clothes from the shop. When I looked back at Curtis, I saw him staring at one of the girls with Jordan. I didn't know what her name was, but I'd seen her before in Sex. She was a couple of years older than me – very pretty, very punky – and she always wore extremely revealing clothes. That night, as far as I can remember, she was wearing a black rubber miniskirt, a studded dog collar, a swastika armband, and not much else. As I watched Curtis leering at her, I saw her look back at him, all sultry and pouty at first, and then she smiled.

'Hey!' I said to Curtis, elbowing him hard in the ribs.

'Fuck!' he spluttered, spitting out the mouthful of lager he'd just taken. He wiped his mouth and glared at me. 'What the hell was that for?'

I didn't say anything, I just glared back at him for a moment, then went back to watching the band. He got the message though, and for the rest of the night he kept his wandering eyes to himself.

I'm not exactly sure what happened when the Pistols finished their fifth song, but there was some kind of bust up between the Pistols and a guy called Danny from Bazooka Joe – something to do with the PA, I seem to remember – and I don't know if it was Danny who cut the power, or someone else, or if the Pistols had borrowed some of Bazooka Joe's sound system and wrecked it or something . . . but whatever the reason, everything suddenly kicked off at the end of the fifth song. Johnny Rotten started yelling at Bazooka Joe, calling them a bunch of fucking cunts, then this Danny guy attacked Johnny, pinning him up against the wall . . . and then Malcolm McLaren and everyone else got involved, shouting and screaming, pushing and shoving . . . and, basically, that was it – a totally chaotic end to a totally chaotic gig.

While all this mayhem was going on, I remember turning to Curtis and seeing him just standing there, watching the after-gig chaos with as much – if not more – intensity than he'd shown when he was watching the actual gig. And I'm pretty sure that *that* was the moment when we both realized that although Naked were, in so many ways, a much better band than the Sex Pistols, that simply wasn't enough.

Yes, we had good songs. And they were *our* songs, not cover versions of old songs like the Pistols mostly played, and we could play them well. And, yes, that was all very important. But if we wanted to be something special, if we wanted to be a band that *mattered*, we had to have more.

It wasn't the music that mattered, it was the attitude.

The energy.

The chaos.

But as we headed home later that night, with Curtis jabbering away like a madman about everything we'd just seen and heard, telling me over and over again that *that* was the future, *that* was the way things were going, *that* was how Naked had to be . . . I was already beginning to have my doubts.

Did I really want Naked to be like that?

Did I really want Curtis to be like that?

Did I really want *myself* to be like that?

I wished I knew.

5

A lot of people have since claimed to have been at St Martin's College that night, and a lot of famous names have said that it was the Pistols first gig that inspired them to either form their own group or, if they were already in a band, to break it up and start a new one. And although I'm fairly sure that at least some of these claims aren't strictly true – mainly because, as far as I can recall, there simply weren't that many people there that night – there's no denying that it *was* a seminal event in the history of rock 'n' roll music. It made people realize that you don't have to be a genius to be in a band, you don't have to be a *vocalist* to sing, you don't have to be a godlike guitar-hero to play the guitar . . . all you have to do is learn a couple of chords, grab hold of a microphone, and start making some noise.

Simple as that.

It changed people's lives.

It certainly changed ours. Me, Curtis, Kenny, Stan . . . we were still the same band after that night, we were still called Naked and we still played the same songs, but now – as Curtis had put it – we'd seen the future of rock 'n' roll, and if we wanted to be part of it, we had to get moving.

Two days later, at our first rehearsal after the Pistols gig, Curtis sat us all down and laid out his plans.

'All right, listen,' he said. 'This band needs more bollocks, OK? We've got to crank it up . . . make it faster, louder, *nastier*. We've got to really fucking wind things up –'

'Why?' Kenny said.

Curtis glared at him. 'Why?'

'Yeah . . . why?'

'You were there the other night, weren't you?'

'Yeah, but I don't see what that's got to do with us.'

Curtis shook his head. 'That's the whole fucking *point*, Kenny. If we don't sort ourselves out, it *won't* have anything to do with us.'

'So what?' Kenny shrugged.

Curtis frowned at him. 'Don't you *want* us to make it?'

'Yeah , of course, but I don't see why we suddenly have to start copying the Sex Pistols. I mean, they can hardly even play –'

'Who said anything about *copying* them?' Curtis said. 'We're Naked, aren't we? We're the fucking *best*. But things are changing, you know . . . it's no good just being the best any more. It's not enough.'

'So what do you want us to do?' Kenny said. 'Play *badly*?'

Curtis shook his head again. 'Just play *harder*. Give it more energy, more speed . . . more *attitude*.' He looked at Stan. 'Do you know what I'm saying?'

Stan nodded.

Curtis turned to me. 'You need to hammer the shit out of that bass, all right?'

'Yeah . . .'

He smiled. 'I mean, really whack the fucker.'

'Hold on,' Kenny said. 'That's *my* bass, don't forget. I don't want it getting damaged –'

'Jesus *Christ*,' Curtis sighed.

'What?'

'You're *so* rock 'n' roll, Kenny. You really are.'

'Yeah, well . . . you wouldn't like it if someone broke *your* guitar, would you?'

'I'll tell you what,' Curtis said, giving him a patronizing look. 'If Lili *damages* your bass, I'll buy you a new one, OK?'

'Yeah, right . . . and where are you going to get the money from?'

'We'll have a record deal soon. We'll be rolling in cash.'

Kenny laughed. 'A record deal? We haven't even *played* anywhere yet . . . how the hell are we going to get a record deal when we can't even get a gig?'

Curtis stared at him. 'We'll get one soon enough.'

'How soon?'

'I'm working on it.'

'Yeah?'

'Yeah.'

The two of them just stared at each other for a while then, and I thought for a moment that either Kenny was going to storm out in a sulk, or Curtis was going to hit him or something. But eventually Kenny just kind of nodded and looked away, and Curtis lit a cigarette and said, 'Right, let's fucking do it.'

We plugged in, cranked it up, and launched into a 100 mph version of 'Naked'.

Curtis was as good as his word about getting a gig, and a couple of months later, on a cold Friday night in January, we piled all our gear into the back of a Transit van and headed off up the Seven Sisters Road towards a pub in Finsbury Park called the Conway Arms. The van belonged to – and was driven by – Stan's twenty-year-old brother, a Neanderthal-like guy known as Chief. He was as non-talkative, if not more so, than Stan, and he suffered from both a really bad BO problem and a tendency to fart quite a lot, neither of which made travelling in the unventilated confines of a Transit van all that pleasant. But as well as being the only person we knew who had a van, Chief helped us out in lots of other ways too – hefting equipment around, setting up lights, sorting out all the electrics . . . and, because of his sheer physical presence, he was a very useful person to have around when things got out of hand, which they often did.

There was another non-band member in the van that night too, a man in his mid-twenties called Jake Francis. Curtis had introduced us to Jake about a month before when we were rehearsing one night at the squat in Seven Sisters. None of us had ever met Jake before, and when Curtis brought him down to the basement and told us that he was going to be our manager . . . well, it didn't go down all that well, to say the least.

'He's going to be our *what*?' Kenny said indignantly.

'Our manager.'

'Since when?'

'Since I asked him,' Curtis said calmly.

Kenny shook his head. '*You* asked him to be *our* manager?'

'Yeah.'

'What about the rest of us . . . don't we get a say? I mean, fucking *hell*, Curtis . . . we've never even *talked* about having a manager, and now you just turn up, out of the blue, with someone we don't even know –'

'All right,' Curtis said. 'What do you want to know about him?'

'That's not the *point* –'

'He *knows* people, Kenny. He's got contacts . . . he used to manage bands in Manchester –'

'Yeah? Like who?'

Curtis looked at Jake.

Jake said to Kenny. 'Do you know the Black Angels?'

Kenny shook his head. 'Never heard of them.'

'How about Meat House?'

'Nope.'

'10cc?'

Kenny looked surprised. 'You managed 10cc?'

Jake grinned. 'No . . . but I'm a good enough liar to make you believe that I did. And that's exactly why you need me.'

Jake was kind of creepy-looking. Spider-thin, with short black curly hair, a bad complexion, and wire-framed granny glasses that made his eyes look really small. He always wore a greasy old dark green suit, dirty black plimsolls, and no socks . . . even in winter. He listened to reggae music all the time, at unbelievably loud volumes, and he *constantly* smoked dope, from first thing in the morning until last thing at night. Although, strangely, he never seemed to get stoned.

'So,' he said, turning to Stan. 'What do *you* think?'

'About what?'

'Do you want me to be your manager?'

Stan shrugged. 'I don't really care, to be honest . . .'

Jake looked at me. 'How about you?'

'I think we should talk about it first,' I said, glancing at Curtis.

'Yeah, of *course* you should talk about it,' Jake said. 'Take all the time you need, have a chat between yourselves, and if there's anything you want to know about me . . .' He grinned. 'Well, I'll do my best to tell you the truth.' He turned to Curtis. 'I'll be in the pub, OK?'

'Yeah . . .'

After Jake had left, we talked things over for quite a long time – asking Curtis lots of questions about Jake, most of which he couldn't answer, discussing whether or not we actually needed a manager at all – but, in the end, we couldn't come to an agreement. Kenny was still totally against Jake, Curtis was still for him, Stan still didn't care, and I couldn't make up my mind.

'Why don't we just leave it for now?' I suggested. 'We can think about it over the next few days and then, when we're all ready, we can get together and talk about it again.'

Apart from Curtis, everyone agreed that that was the best thing to do.

But it never happened.

Because the very next day, Curtis broke the news that Jake had got us a gig at the Conway Arms – which, although quite small, was a well-known venue with a good reputation for breaking new bands. And, according to Jake, if the first gig went well, there was a possibility of us being offered a residency, and that would mean playing the Conway *every* Friday night.

And even Kenny was impressed by that.

So, although we never officially asked Jake to manage us, and despite his undeniable creepiness, and the fact that none of us – Curtis included – actually liked the man, he somehow just sort of *became* our manager.

So, anyway, there we all were that night, the six of us crammed into Chief's stinking Transit van – Curtis and Jake in the front with Chief; me, Kenny, and Stan stuffed in the back with all the equipment – making our way along the Seven Sisters Road towards the Conway Arms. Jake, as ever, had a big fat joint going, and Curtis and Chief were both chain-smoking cigarettes, and the smoke was so thick inside the van that I could barely breathe.

'How about opening a window?' I said, coughing.

'It's too cold,' Jake replied.

'I'm suffocating back here.'

'We'll be there in a minute.'

'I could be dead in a minute.'

Curtis looked over his shoulder at me and smiled. 'Excited?'

'I would be if I could breathe.'

He didn't say anything else, he just carried on looking at me, and as I gazed back at him through the smoke, I suddenly realized how blissfully happy he was. This was what he'd been waiting for – this coming moment, this day, this night. This was his dream. To get up on stage and play his songs . . . this was all he'd ever wanted.

'Yeah,' I told him, smiling. 'Yeah, I'm excited.'

We stared at each other in silence for a while, sharing an intimate moment, and then Curtis took a drag on his cigarette and turned to Kenny, who was squatting down awkwardly between two stacks of speakers.

'You all right there, Ken?' Curtis grinned.

'Yeah, fucking great.'

'Ready to rock?'

Kenny actually smiled. 'Yeah, I'm ready.'

Curtis looked at Stan. 'You ready?'

Stan grinned. 'Fucking A.'

'Let's do it then,' Curtis said. 'Let's go out there and give the world something to remember.'

I'm not sure if we were *that* memorable that night, but anyone who was there will tell you that it was probably one of the best debut gigs that London has ever seen. And I know that I'll never forget it. The whole experience . . . it was all just so raw, so pure, so wrought with primitive emotion. Even the simple process of walking into the Conway Arms at eight o'clock in the evening, when it was already quite busy, and announcing ourselves as 'the band', and then being taken upstairs to the bar where we'd be playing, and being shown into the 'dressing room', which was actually just a converted toilet . . . even all that gave me a weird kind of thrill. A nervous thrill, perhaps. But a thrill nevertheless. And then we had to unload all the gear and set it up on the stage, which meant traipsing up and down the stairs for an hour or so, lugging our equipment out of the van and carrying it through the downstairs bar, which was gradually becoming more and more crowded, which meant that we all had to put up with quite a lot of staring – which wasn't too bad – and a few friendly comments – 'what kind of stuff do you play?' – and quite a few *not* so friendly comments – 'who the fucking hell do you think you are?' And, of course, because most of the crowd were men, most of whom had been drinking, and I was a sixteen-year-old girl – and, what's more, I'd been persuaded by Curtis to 'dress up a bit', so I'd 'borrowed' a lacy white cocktail dress from my mother's vast wardrobe, and I was wearing it with blue-and-white striped tights, bright red DMs, and half a ton of make-up – so, obviously, I was the subject of a fair bit of attention myself.

Some of it was OK – young men doing their best not to stare, others just smiling shyly – but a lot of it consisted of out-and-out leering, which was really unsettling, together with the kind of remarks that you'd expect from a pub full of men. Comments such as 'Show us your tits, love,' or 'Listen, darling, if you're looking for a father-figure . . .'

Arf arf arf.

I did my best to stay cool about it, but I felt really angry inside.

So by the time we'd got all the gear set up, done a quick soundcheck, and gone back to the dressing room to wait for the crowd to amble upstairs, I'd already been through enough different emotions to last me a week. I'd been thrilled, I'd been nervous, I'd been angry . . .

And now?

Sitting there in that cold windowless room, with Curtis tuning his guitar, a smoking cigarette lodged in his mouth . . . and Stan winding strips of tape round a drumstick . . . and Jake all twitchy and hyper, pacing up and down, puffing away on a joint . . . and Kenny just standing in the corner, staring nervously at the floor, his face deathly pale . . .

How did I feel now?

I could hear the room filling up outside – voices, laughter, chinking glasses . . . a hum of expectation. I could feel the butterflies in my stomach, the fear of what I was about to do, the rush of excitement, the edginess of not knowing what was going to happen . . .

Would I be OK?

Would I remember the songs?

Would I mess everything up?

I heard Jake saying, 'Here,' and when I looked up I saw him passing something to Curtis, a small rectangle of folded paper. Curtis opened it up, carefully tipped out a line of white powder onto the back of his hand, then lifted his hand to his nose and snorted up the powder through one nostril.

'What's that?' I said.

'Nothing . . .' Curtis sniffed, wiping his nose. 'Just some speed . . . you want some?'

'No, thanks.'

Curtis nodded, looking around. 'Anyone else?'

Stan shook his head, Kenny said nothing.

Curtis passed the speed back to Jake.

I looked at Curtis, feeling slightly disappointed. I'd sort of hoped that the gig itself – the excitement of it, the buzz – might have been enough for him, and that, just for once, he could have gone without any artificial stimulation . . .

But I didn't say anything.

I didn't want him to think I was *uptight*, did I?

There was a quick knock on the door then, and as it swung open, the noise from outside rolled in, like a breaking wave of chattering voices. The man who ran the pub popped his head round the door and said, 'You ready?'

Jake and Curtis both said, 'Yeah.'

The man nodded. 'Good luck.' And walked off, leaving the door open.

I could see the people outside now. There were about fifty, maybe sixty of them. Some of them were from the bar downstairs, but there were quite a few who I guessed had arrived at the last minute – younger people, cooler people, the kind of people who go to see bands. And, hanging around at the back, I could just make out a raggedy bunch of over- and underdressed figures who I recognized from Sex: Malcolm McLaren, Jordan, Sid Vicious, Siouxsie Sioux . . .

The girl with the swastika armband was there too, the one Curtis had ogled at the Sex Pistols gig. I'd found out since that she called herself Charlie Brown. Whether that was her real name or not, I had no idea – and, to be perfectly honest, I couldn't have cared less either way.

I just didn't want her to be there.

47

'Come on, Lili,' Curtis said to me. 'This is it – we're on.'

As I got to my feet and followed him and the rest of the band out of the dressing room and across the room towards the stage, it suddenly felt as if all the emotions I'd already been through that night were now swirling around inside my belly in a sickening cocktail of dizzied confusion. And as I climbed onto the stage and plugged in my bass, I was convinced that I was going to throw up.

'Ladies and gentlemen,' a voice announced over the PA system. 'Please put your hands together for . . . Naked!'

6

The houselights went down, and just for a moment everything hummed in a darkened silence. Then a spotlight came on, picking out Curtis at the front of the stage, and as he leapt into the air like a maniac and began thrashing out the first four bars of 'Naked', I just knew that everything was going to be all right. The sound was electrifying, stunning, the crash of chords ripping through the air like a thunderous shot of adrenalin, and when I started playing – coming in at *precisely* the same time as Kenny and Stan – and the stage erupted in a blaze of lights, it all felt so good that I thought for a moment my heart was going to explode. The sound was almost too good to believe. We were so loud, so fast, so tight . . . we were so *there* . . . it was incredible. The machine-gun beat of Stan's drums, the punching rhythm of Kenny's guitar, the booming thump of my bass . . . and, above it all, the screaming craziness of Curtis's guitar and the mesmerizing sight of him twisting and reeling and staggering around the stage . . .

He looked so out of it, so lost and manic, that I thought for a second he wasn't going to get to the microphone in time to start singing the first verse, but I needn't have worried. At the very last moment, he spun round, lunged across the stage to the mike, and launched into the first verse with perfect timing. He sang as if his life depended on it – spitting out the words with venom and passion, his eyes squeezed shut, his neck straining – and although I'd heard him singing so many times before, I was still taken aback by the sheer brutal beauty of his voice. The words screamed out of his mouth as if they'd been torn – ripped and bleeding – from his heart:

> *IDLE BLACK EYES*
> *AND DRUG-YELLOWED SKIN*
> *THE DREAM FLOWERS DIE*
> *ON HER COLD NAKED SIN . . .*

His passion was infectious, and when we all joined in on the chanted chorus –

> *I'M NAKED!*
> *YOU'RE NAKED!*
> *WE'RE NAKED!*
> *. . . NAKED!*

– we sounded like a bunch of mad demons.

It was awesome.

The song only lasted about three minutes, and as soon as we'd finished it – with a final crashing chord and a deliberate screech of feedback from Curtis's guitar – we went straight into the next number, a song called 'Crack Up'. It was another very short and very fast song, similar in style to 'Naked', but with a slightly jerkier rhythm. It was probably my least favourite of all our songs, but the audience seemed to like it, and by the time we'd played the final chorus and begun the introduction to 'Heaven Hill', there were plenty of people dancing down at the front.

As far as I was concerned, 'Heaven Hill' was easily the best song that Curtis had ever written. It was so haunting and memorable that every time we played it my skin would shiver and I'd get a weird kind of fluttery feeling in my heart. It was a slightly unusual song in that it didn't follow the typical verse/chorus/verse/chorus structure, consisting instead of three separate

– but interlinked – parts that gradually built up into a final swirling chorus that brought everything together in a wonderful burst of multilayered melodies. Curtis had helped me to develop the bass line, showing me a simple chord technique that gave the bass a much deeper and more melodic sound, which I absolutely loved. I also loved playing 'Heaven Hill' because Curtis and I sang together on it – him taking the lead, me singing harmony – and at some point during the song Curtis would always glance across at me with a look on his face that said, *Isn't this great?*, and I'd always smile back at him in silent agreement . . .

It was our special little moment.

And that night, as we began singing the final chorus together –

HEAVEN HILL, REMEMBER
HEAVEN HILL, REMEMBER
HEAVEN HILL . . .

– and Curtis looked over at me with a smile that said, *Isn't this just THE best thing in the world?* and I smiled back like a lovestruck fool, it was even more special than ever.

That, for me, was the high point of the night.

Unfortunately, it was followed soon afterwards by a couple of not-so-high points, the first of which occurred during the very next song, a two-minute slab of blood-curdling noise called 'Stupid'. In keeping with its title, the lyric of the song boasted only one word, the eponymous 'stupid', which Curtis screamed out at the top of his voice, over and over again. Towards the end of the song, as the music got louder and faster and crazier, he lurched right up to the edge of the stage, fixed his eyes on a girl at the front, and began howling the by-now almost unintelligible word at her – *STUPIDSTUPIDSTUPIDSTUPID . . .*

The girl didn't seem to mind all that much – in fact, I think she was quite flattered by the attention – but the man who was with her, a greasy-haired biker drinking beer from a bottle, he didn't like it at all. I saw him glaring at Curtis for a moment, waiting to see if he'd stop, and when he didn't – when Curtis carried on leaning towards the girl and yelling like a lunatic into her face – the biker took a swig from his bottle, pulled the girl out of the way, and swung the bottle at Curtis's face. Curtis, though, had seen it coming and had already moved back from the edge of the stage, so the beer bottle missed him by miles. This only made the biker even angrier, and as Curtis carried on playing – with a mocking grin on his face – the biker drew back his arm and hurled the bottle with all his strength. Curtis leapt to one side, trying to get out of the way, but he wasn't quite quick enough and the bottle caught him a glancing blow on the side of his head. He staggered slightly, shaking his head, but he didn't stop playing. Even as a trickle of blood began oozing down the side of his face, he kept chopping away at his guitar, hammering out the chords, seemingly oblivious to any pain. Jake, meanwhile, who'd been looking on from the right-hand side of the stage, was now striding towards the biker, shouting obscenities at him, clearly intent on sorting him out. Which, although quite admirable, was patently never going to happen, as the biker was roughly twice the size of Jake and at least fifty times tougher. So I wasn't surprised when the biker turned towards Jake, looked him up and down, and floored him almost dismissively with a single punch to the head. But then, as if out of nowhere, I saw a giant-sized fist rise up from the crowd behind the biker, and I caught a quick glimpse of Chief's Stone Age face, and I watched in awe as he brought his fist down, hammering it into the top of the biker's head, and the biker collapsed to the floor in a heap.

Just as he hit the floorboards, we finished the song, and for a moment or two there was a stunned and menacing silence. Then Chief stepped out from the crowd, gave the thumbs-up to Curtis, and started helping Jake to his feet. At the same time, another biker appeared and began dragging his still-unconscious friend away, and Curtis chose that moment to step up to the mike and stare out at the crowd, his face a mess of blood and sweat-streaked mascara.

'That was "Stupid",' he said, grinning momentarily at the bikers. 'And this . . .' he continued, looking back at the crowd, '. . . this is "Inside You".'

I started playing first, thumping out the big heavy bass line to the song, and then Stan brought the rest of the band in with four razor-sharp beats on the snare drum. Although it was a really good song – dark and menacing, with a disjointedly hypnotic rhythm – I'd never been too keen on the lyrics.

> *I WANT YOUR HEART*
> *I WANT YOUR BLOOD*
> *I WANT YOUR SKIN*
> *I WANT YOUR FLESH . . .*

When I told Curtis once that I didn't like the words, he'd actually got quite indignant with me.

'Why?' he'd said. 'What's the matter with them?'

'Well, you know . . . they're just a bit . . .'

'A bit *what*?'

'Nasty.'

'*Nasty*?' he sneered. 'What do you mean, *nasty*?'

'Come on, Curtis,' I sighed. 'You know what I mean . . . it's like you're talking about a girl as if she's just a piece of meat or something.' I shook my head. 'It makes you sound like a serial killer.'

He laughed.

I glared at him. 'It's not *funny*.'

His laughter stopped quite abruptly, which was kind of disconcerting, and he stared at me. 'You just don't *get* it, do you?'

'Get what?'

'Look,' he sighed. 'Just because *I* write the words and *I* sing them, that doesn't necessarily mean that they're coming from me.

I mean, Jesus Christ, Lili . . . you *can* write from other people's points of view, you know.'

'Yeah, but –'

'And, besides, the song isn't about *physically* wanting someone anyway. It's about wanting someone so much, *loving* someone so much, that you actually want to *be* them.' He looked hard at me. 'Do you understand? You don't just want to be *with* them, or be part of their life. You want to be *inside* them.'

Although, at the time, his explanation had seemed perfectly reasonable, I was still far from convinced, and every time we played 'Inside You' I still felt slightly uncomfortable. And that night, as we finished the first verse of the song, and Curtis started singing the chorus –

> *I WANNA BE*
> *I WANNA BE*
> *I WANNA BE*
> *INSIDE YOU*

– I suddenly realized that he was staring intently at someone at the front of the crowd as he sang, and when I followed his gaze to see who he was looking at, I saw the sickeningly pretty figure of Charlie Brown. She wasn't dancing or anything, she was just standing there, all on her own, as cool as you like, her smouldering black eyes fixed on Curtis as he sang to her. And that's what he was doing, without a doubt – he was singing *to* her.

> *I WANNA BE*
> *INSIDE YOU* . . .

It didn't last very long, this intimate little serenade, and by the end of the song Charlie Brown had turned round and coolly slinked off, glancing coquettishly over her shoulder at Curtis as she went. I did my best to be mature about the whole thing, trying to convince myself that it didn't really mean anything, that it was all just part of the show . . . that Curtis was, after all, the front man in a rock 'n' roll band, so he was *supposed* to do this kind of thing . . . I mean, I couldn't expect him to behave like my boyfriend when we were on stage, could I?

The trouble was, no matter how hard I tried to be mature about it, I simply couldn't do it. I *wasn't* mature. I was sixteen years old. Curtis was my first proper boyfriend. He was the first boy I'd ever slept with . . . we were *lovers*, for God's sake. I wasn't entirely sure what that meant, if anything, in terms of our commitment to each other, or our future together, but that wasn't the point. The point was, he was *my* boyfriend, and seeing him singing to that girl, singing those words to her, right in front of me . . .

It tore me up.

And for the next couple of songs, I found it really hard to concentrate. I didn't make any major mistakes, but I did hit a couple of bum notes, and I very nearly messed up the ending of one song. I don't think anyone in the audience noticed, but Curtis definitely did, and when he came over to me before the start of the next song – tuning his guitar on the way – I was fully expecting him to have a go at me, or at least just point out my mistakes, and I was building myself up to say something back to him, something cutting and harsh, or maybe I'd just totally blank him, or give him a withering look . . . but none of that happened. Instead, he just came up to me with a heart-melting smile, briefly took hold of my hand, and then leaned in so close that I could feel the warmth of his lips as he whispered in my ear, 'I love you.' And before I had a chance to say anything back, he kissed my neck, let go of my hand, and loped back to the front of the stage to introduce the next song.

I knew that they were just words, of course – *I love you* – and I knew that they *shouldn't* make any difference to how I felt, that they *shouldn't* make up for anything, that they *shouldn't* make me feel any better . . . and I knew how pathetic it was that they *did* make me feel better. I *knew* that it was shallow and stupid of me, and I knew that I ought to be ashamed of myself. And I was.

But that didn't change anything.

I still felt really good.

Deluded or not . . .

I felt *wanted* again.

And that was enough for me.

'This next song's for Lili,' I heard Curtis announce. 'It's called "The Only Thing".'

We played ten songs that night, and when we finally left the stage, the audience carried on clapping and cheering and stamping their feet for a good five minutes or so. It was a wonderful feeling – sitting in the dressing room, sweaty and drained, exhausted and ecstatic, listening to the crowd crying out for more – and I think we were all very tempted to go back out and play another song or two, but Jake was adamant that we shouldn't.

'Always leave them wanting more,' he said, lighting up a joint. 'If they want to hear you again, they'll come and see you again.'

So we all just stayed where we were for a while, talking and drinking, laughing about this and that, teasing Jake about his 'fight' with the biker and his already blackening eye . . . and gradually everything began to calm down a little. The owner of the bar came in and congratulated us on the gig, then Jake went off with him to sort out 'some business', which I assumed meant getting our payment for the gig, and maybe negotiating terms for a residency.

Curtis came over to me then, gave me a big sweaty hug, and asked me if I was all right.

'Yeah,' I told him. 'I'm fine.'

'God, that was *good*, wasn't it?'

'Yeah . . .'

'I mean, that was *it*, wasn't it? That was fucking *it*.'

I guessed he'd taken some more speed at some point, because his eyes were darting all over the place and he kept licking his lips all the time. The cut on his head where the bottle had hit him had opened up again, and a thin trickle of blood was oozing down his face.

'Listen, Curtis,' I started to say. 'Maybe you should –'

'Do you want a beer or something?' he said, glancing over his shoulder at the open dressing-room door. 'I'm just going to try and find Malcolm before he goes, see what he thought of us.' He looked back at me. 'All right?'

No, I thought to myself, suddenly consumed by jealousy again, *it's not all right. Because you're probably* not *going to see if you can find Malcolm, are you? You're probably going to see if you can find Charlie Brown . . .*

Curtis smiled at me. 'I'll bring you a beer when I come back, OK?'

'Yeah . . .'

He kissed me – a quick peck on the forehead – and left.

I sat there for a moment or two, just looking down at the floor, feeling kind of sorry for myself . . . and then I remembered that I wasn't alone. I raised my eyes and glanced over at Kenny and Stan. They were sitting quietly in the corner together – Stan with a bottle of beer in his hand, Kenny wiping the sweat from his guitar strings with a cloth.

Stan smiled at me. 'All right?'

I nodded.

Kenny stopped cleaning his guitar and looked over at me. He didn't say anything for a second or two, he just sat there gazing quietly at me. And when he looked back down at his guitar and started wiping the strings again, I thought that was it.

But I was wrong.

'He doesn't mean it,' he said softly, without looking up.

'Sorry?'

7

My mother's maiden name was Mari Ellen James, and she was born and brought up in a small farming village just outside Bangor in north Wales. Her mother was an alcoholic, her father a man who revelled in violence. My mother left school at fifteen, became pregnant at sixteen, and lost the baby a week before she was due to get married. The marriage was inevitably postponed, and while my mother was recovering from the miscarriage, her prospective husband – a farmer's son from a neighbouring village – slipped out of his parents' house one night, walked to Holyhead, and caught the first ferry to Dublin.

My mother never saw him again.

A year or so later, while working as a waitress in a tea room in Bangor, she was approached by a customer – a smartly dressed man with an English accent – who claimed to own a modelling agency in London. He asked my mother how old she was, gave her a business card, and told her that if she was interested in becoming a model she should get one of her parents to give him a call at the end of the week when he'd be back in his office in London.

My mother, of course, didn't dare say a word to her parents about this smartly dressed man from London. Instead, on the following Friday morning, she left home for work at the usual time, caught her usual bus into Bangor, but rather than getting off at her usual stop near the tea rooms, she stayed on the bus all the way to the railway station where she bought herself a ticket to London.

By two o'clock that afternoon, she was standing outside a shabby-looking office building in Regent Street, gazing up at a row of hand-written company names listed on the wall by the door.

'World Class Models' was the second name from the top.

She reached up and pressed the buzzer.

'I know it all *sounds* rather seedy,' I remember my mother telling me. 'And there were lots of times when it *was* . . . but modelling is a seedy business, Lili. It always has been, and it always will be. And, of course, I was very young, and all on my own, a long way from home, so I was quite vulnerable . . . but, on the whole, it wasn't as bad as it could have been.'

She never went into any more detail about the seedier side of her modelling life – at least, not with me – preferring instead to reflect on the good times. How she stuck at it, how she learned the business, how she worked really hard and gradually built up a name for herself, until eventually – at the age of nineteen – she was offered a contract by one of the top three modelling agencies in the country.

'And within a year,' she told me proudly, 'I was travelling all over the world and earning more money than I'd ever *dreamed* of. I bought a car, a flat in London . . . I had money in the bank. I had everything I'd ever wanted, Lil. *Every*thing . . .'

But she didn't.

Her mother, by then, had drunk herself to death, and her father was serving a ten-year sentence for manslaughter.

She didn't have a husband.

She didn't have a child.

She was still all alone.

But in 1958, on her twentieth birthday, she met a man called Rafael Garcia.

Thirty years earlier, at the age of fifteen, Rafael had left his home in Mexico and illegally crossed the border into the USA. Within a few months, he'd not only made his way to Los Angeles, he'd also managed to find himself work as a gopher in the movie industry. It wasn't much of a job – making tea, running errands, that kind of thing – and the movie company he worked for was basically a Mafia-controlled money-laundering operation. But in the same way that my mother made the best of a bad job, so did my father. He stuck at it too. He learned the business, he worked really hard and gradually climbed the ladder, until eventually – at the age of thirty-seven – he directed his first feature film.

By the time Rafael met my mother, he was forty-five years old and had already directed or co-directed over a dozen films. Most, if not all, of them were dreadful – B-movies, cheap horror movies, run-of-the-mill Westerns – but while Rafael might not have had much creative talent, he knew how to make films that raked in the money, and that's why he eventually became one of the most sought-after directors in Hollywood. His films didn't cost very much, they didn't take long to make, and they never pretended to be anything more than mindless entertainment. When you went to see a Rafael Garcia film, you knew exactly what you were going to get: excitement, thrills, a fair bit of violence, and lots of sexy girls. His films weren't explicitly sexual or anything – especially not by today's standards – but they were fairly raunchy for their time, and that was the main reason for their commercial success.

When Rafael met my mother, at a VIP party celebrating the premiere of his latest movie, he was already in a relationship with the star of the film, a relatively unknown young actress called Barbara Shelley. He'd previously been involved with another young starlet called Deborah Layne, who'd appeared in one of his earlier films, and there were rumours that Rafael had been with her on the night she'd committed suicide some years earlier, but that he'd left her apartment before the ambulance had arrived . . . rumours that he strongly denied. But there wasn't any doubt that he had a history of dating much younger women, especially the young actresses who appeared in his films, and when he met my mother – who, at the time, was on a modelling assigment for a cosmetics company, and was generally regarded as one of the most beautiful women in the world – he fell for her immediately.

After the VIP party, in the early hours of the morning, she went back to his luxury apartment with him, and for the next couple of weeks they were barely out of each other's sight. Within the month, they were not only engaged to be married, but Rafael had also promised her a starring role in his next film.

The next few months were the happiest days of my mother's life.

Living with Rafael in Los Angeles, soaking up the sunshine and the celebrity lifestyle, taking acting lessons, making plans for her wedding . . . she absolutely adored every moment. The marriage took place in October that year, by which time she was already pregnant with me, and when they left the wedding reception for their honeymoon, and were driven off to the airport in a shiny white limousine, my mother still didn't know where they were going.

'It's a secret,' Rafael kept telling her. 'You'll find out when we get there.'

My mother didn't really care where they were going, as long as it was somewhere exotic, somewhere hot, somewhere romantic, and – knowing Rafael – she was sure that she wouldn't be disappointed. But ten hours later, when the private jet finally landed, she realized – with a sinking heart – that they were actually back in London.

She thought at first that it was just a stop-over, and that they'd soon be flying off to their *real* destination, but when they got off the plane and got into another limousine, and the limo drove off, leaving the airport behind . . .

'Where are we going now, Rafa?' my mother asked, trying to keep the disappointment from her voice.

'I have a present for you,' he said, smiling. 'A wedding present.' He glanced at his watch. 'We'll be there very soon.'

When they arrived in Hampstead, and the limousine stopped outside a huge old gothic house, and my mother slowly realized that the house was her wedding present . . . she simply couldn't believe it. It was so big, so dark, so monstrous, so ugly . . .

'What do you think?' Rafael said to her, smiling. 'Isn't it splendid?'

She just stood there, unable to speak, gazing up at the black-ened stone walls.

'I knew you'd like it,' Rafael went on. 'As soon as I saw it . . . I just *knew* you'd fall in love with it.'

My mother looked at him. 'You *bought* this?'

'Of course.'

'But what about the house in Los Angeles?'

He shrugged. 'We live there, we live here . . . LA for work, here for your home. For our child.' He looked at my mother. 'America is no place to bring up a child.'

'But what about the movie –?'

'We shoot the movie here, in London.'

'Really? I didn't know that. I thought –'

'We start in two weeks.' He smiled at my mother and patted her belly. 'Before you get too big.'

'But what about –?'

'Hey,' he said, putting his finger to her lips. 'No more questions, OK? No more work talk. We're on honeymoon, remember?' He took her by the hand and started leading her up to the house.

'You're going to be very happy here, Mari,' he assured her. 'I can feel it in my bones.'

Rafael stayed in Hampstead while the film was being made, but as soon as shooting had finished he flew back to Los Angeles to begin editing the movie, leaving my mother all alone in a house she hated. The film – a third-rate gangster movie called *The London Mob* – was no better or worse than any of his other films. My mother's performance though – playing the part of a gangster's moll called Rita – was awful. She *looked* really good, and her Cockney accent wasn't *quite* as laughable as some of the other actors' attempts, but the undeniable truth was that she simply couldn't act.

And she knew it too. She knew that her performance was embarrassingly bad, and she knew that when the film was released the critics would tear her apart, and she knew that her acting career was over before it had even begun.

And if that wasn't enough, she also knew that Rafael didn't love her any more . . . if, indeed, he ever had. Three months after leaving for Los Angeles to edit the film, he'd come back to see her just the once – and that was only a two-day visit to get her to sign some legal contracts. She pleaded with him to stay, even going so far as to get down on her knees at one point and beg him not to leave.

'I *need* you here, Rafa,' she sobbed. 'It's so *lonely* in this house –'

'I'm sorry, Mari, but I have to work.'

'But I'm going to have our *baby*. What if something goes wrong –?'

'Nothing's going to go wrong.'

'It did before.'

'You'll be fine, trust me. I'll make sure you have all the best people –'

'I don't want fucking *people*!' she screamed at him. 'I want *you*! You're supposed to be *with* me, for God's sake. You're my fucking *husband*.'

He didn't stay. He flew back to Los Angeles the following day, and – as far as I know – he never went back to Hampstead again. By the time I was born, in June 1959, Rafael had filed for divorce, and was publicly dating another young actress who would later become his second wife. When the divorce was finally settled, my mother was awarded an initial lump sum of $3,000,000, with further payments of $500,000 per year for the remainder of her life. She also kept the house in Hampstead.

And gradually lost her mind.

Of course, I didn't realize that there was anything wrong with my mother until I was about nine or ten. I simply accepted, as all children do, that my life – my home, my mother – was normal. I didn't *know* anything else. I didn't know that mothers aren't supposed to lock themselves in their bedroom for weeks on end, leaving you in the hands of a series of uncaring nannies. I didn't know that most mothers aren't wildly unpredictable – one minute loving you to death, the next minute screaming at you with hatred burning deep in their eyes.

I didn't know that my mother was a broken woman.

To me, she was just my mother.

It wasn't until I began making friends at school, and they'd talk to me about things, about their families, and they'd invite me round to their houses for tea or a birthday party . . . it wasn't until then that I realized that my life wasn't quite so normal after all. Most of my friends had fathers, for a start. And even if their parents were divorced, they still got to see their fathers now and then. I'd never even laid eyes on mine. And, as far as I knew, most of my friends' mothers weren't constantly struggling with some form of addiction, or obsession, and their day-to-day lives weren't ravaged by depression and mania.

The older I got, the more aware I became of my mother's suffering. It wasn't always obvious, and there were long periods when everything seemed perfectly normal. Weeks would go by, even months sometimes, when she wouldn't sleep all day, or get drunk all the time, or be out of her head on prescription drugs. She wouldn't slop around the house in dirty old clothes, she wouldn't wash her hands every five minutes, she wouldn't go out every night and come home with a different man. She would, for a while, do normal things. She'd cook, go shopping, read books, watch TV. She'd talk to me, tell me stories. She'd tell me about her life. But then, often quite suddenly, something would just snap, and the mania or depression – or whatever it was – would take over again, and she'd develop a new addiction, or a new obsession, and all I could do was hope that it wasn't going to be too bad.

One final thing about my mother, and it's a question that you've probably been asking yourself. If she hated the house in Hampstead so much, why did she stay there? Why not just sell it and move somewhere else?

I asked her once. She was in the grip of a cleaning obsession at the time – maniacally scrubbing the walls, washing the windows, polishing the furniture . . . going at it like crazy, not bothering to eat or sleep or even stop for a moment's rest – and I'd just made her some soup and was trying to persuade her to drink it, when all of sudden she burst into tears and slumped down to the floor.

'This fucking house,' she moaned. 'I fucking *hate* it.'

'So why don't we move, Mum?' I said. 'With the money you get for this place we could get somewhere really nice, a little flat in the middle of London or something.'

She shook her head. 'I can't leave here.'

'Why not? I mean, if you hate it so much . . .?'

She looked at me, her eyes slightly unfocused. 'I have to be here for Rafa,' she said distantly. 'He'll be back soon . . . I have to be here for him.'

And that, for now, is all you need to know about my mother.

Curtis didn't want to go home after the gig at the Conway Arms that night, and we had to drive back to the squat in Seven Sisters anyway to drop off Jake and unload some of the gear, so Curtis suggested that we stay the night there. Someone had just moved out, apparently, and their room was still empty. We'd stayed the night at the squat a couple of times before, and although I didn't really like it there, I didn't really want to go home either. My mother was going through one of her sexually promiscuous phases at the time, and she was also hooked on some new slimming pills that she'd got from her doctor which kept her awake for days on end, so I knew that if I went home she'd probably be with some moron she'd dragged back from the pub, and if she hadn't managed to find anyone – which was highly unlikely – she'd want to sit up all night talking to me. And I wasn't really in the mood for either of those things. So I told Curtis I'd stay the night, and while he got on with unpacking the van, I went over to a phone box across the road and called my mother.

I knew that it was little more than a gesture, and that in her state of mind she probably wouldn't have noticed – or cared – if I'd come home or not anyway. And, besides, she'd told me before that I didn't need her permission to stay out all night.

'You're sixteen now,' she'd told me. 'Almost seventeen . . . you're not a child any more.'

Which, at the time, I'd kind of appreciated. But recently I'd begun to realize that there was a part of me that secretly yearned for her to be a bit less liberated, a bit more protective . . . a bit more caring, I suppose.

'Hey, Mum,' I said when she answered the phone. 'It's only me –'

'Just a minute,' she muttered. 'Hold on . . .' I heard her cover the mouthpiece and speak to someone. I heard laughter, a cough, the chink of glasses. Music was playing in the background – 'Tumbling Dice' by the Rolling Stones. 'Lili . . .?' Mum said. 'Is that you?'

'Yeah, Mum . . . listen, is it OK if I stay over with some friends tonight?'

'Course,' she mumbled. 'Course you can, love . . .'

Her words were slurred. She sounded drunk.

'I'll be back in the morning,' I told her.

'Mmmm . . .'

'Are you all right, Mum?'

'All right . . .? What . . . yeah, I'm all right. I'm *fine* . . . how did it go?'

'Sorry?'

'The gig – how did it go?'

'Yeah, it was great. Really good.'

'Good . . . good . . .' She covered the mouthpiece again, whispered loudly at someone, then came back to me. 'So, how did it go tonight? The gig . . . was it good?'

'Yeah . . . look, Mum, I have to go now, OK?'

'Right . . .'

'I'll see you tomorrow.'

'Yeah . . . see you later, darling. Have a good time.'

I put the phone down.

It was dark outside, the High Road quiet in the night. Lights blazed from the windows of the squat across the street, and when I opened the door and stepped out of the phone box, I could hear the deep thudding bass of reggae music blaring out of the house.

I paused for a moment, gazing up at the infinite black sky . . .

Wondering so many things.

Then a car sped past, and an empty beer can came flying out of the window, clattering to the pavement at my feet. The driver honked his horn, laughter cackled from the open windows, and as the car disappeared down the High Road, I crossed the road and went back to the squat.

8

The squat was a four-storey Victorian townhouse in a dead-end street that ran parallel to the High Road. I didn't really know anything about it – who actually owned it, how long it had been used as a squat – all I knew was that it was a big sprawling house with dozens of rooms, and that all kinds of people were continuously moving in and moving out, which meant that you never really knew who was actually living there at any given time. The house itself was in fairly good condition. It had electricity, gas, running water. It wasn't overly dirty. Everything worked. All in all, it was just a slightly shabby, slightly rundown, slightly messy old house.

But it wasn't the house that I didn't like – it was the people who lived there.

Some of them were OK, I suppose, but most of them were a bit like Jake – that is, they spent a lot of time taking drugs, and they were kind of creepy. A lot of them were in bands, so there was always music playing somewhere in the house, and it was inevitably played *really* loudly no matter what time of day or night it was.

Which was why I didn't get any sleep that night.

The room Curtis and I were sleeping in – or were *supposed* to be sleeping in – was on the top floor of the house. There was no furniture or anything, no curtains, no bed, nowhere to sit. It was basically just an empty room with some cushions and a couple of blankets thrown on the floor. I didn't feel all that comfortable about sleeping in blankets that had recently been slept in by someone else, but by then I was simply too tired to care. It was late, around two o'clock, and I was exhausted. I just wanted to sleep. But Curtis was still hyper, and he couldn't keep his hands off me . . .

At three o'clock in the morning, we were both still wide awake. Curtis was sitting cross-legged on the floor, smoking a cigarette and scribbling furiously in a notebook, and I was lying face down on the blankets with a cushion clamped over my head, trying to keep out the booming thud of the reggae music that was still blaring out from somewhere downstairs.

'Curtis?' I said.

He didn't answer.

I removed the cushion from my head. 'Curtis?'

'What?'

'I can't get to sleep.'

'Why not?'

'Why do you think?' I turned over and sat up. 'Are they going to be playing music *all* night?'

'Probably.'

'Why do they have to play it so *loud*?'

Curtis smiled. 'It's reggae . . . it's *supposed* to be loud.'

'Couldn't you just go down and ask them to turn it down a bit?'

He laughed. 'Yeah, right . . . that'd be a really *cool* thing to do, wouldn't it?' He put on a simpering voice. 'Would you mind *awfully* turning it down a bit?' He laughed again, and went back to writing in his notebook.

I sighed. 'What are you doing?'

'Lyrics to a new song,' he said.

'What's it called?'

'Don't know yet.'

I sighed again, resigned now to not getting any sleep, and I just sat there for a while, not saying anything, just watching

71

Curtis, looking around the room, gazing out through the curtain-less window at the empty starless night . . .

'Did you speak to Jake?' I asked Curtis.

'Uh?'

'Did you speak to Jake?'

'About what?'

'The Conway Arms . . . he said something about a residency –'

'Oh, yeah, didn't I tell you? We've got it. Every Friday night, ten o'clock. We can either take a straight fifty quid or a cut of the door money. Jake's still trying to work out which is best. We've arranged to meet Arthur on Monday morning to sort out all the details.'

'Who's Arthur?'

'The guy who owns the Conway.'

'Right.' I looked at him. 'You know we're back at school on Monday, don't you?'

'I'm not going.'

'What?'

'I'm not going back.'

'What do you mean?'

He stopped writing and looked up at me. 'I'm not going back to school, Lili. This is what I want to do – the band, the music, you know . . . this is my *life*. It's all I want.'

'Yeah, but what about your A levels –?'

'Fuck 'em,' he said, laughing. 'I don't need A levels, do I? Not for this . . .' He tapped his notebook. 'If I'm going to write songs I need a *life*, not a fucking A-level certificate.'

'Yeah, but –'

'Naked are going to *make* it, Lili,' he said, his voice suddenly intense. 'Believe me, we're going to be big.' He shook his head. 'I haven't got *time* for school any more.'

'Have you told your parents?'

'Not yet.'

'They're not going to like it.'

72

He sniffed. 'Yeah, well . . .'

He was staring down at his notebook now, not writing anything, just staring down at the page. And I could tell that he was thinking about his parents, about what they'd say when he told them he was leaving school . . . I could see the confused mixture of resentment and fear in his eyes. He never liked talking about his parents, and I think, in a way, he despised them simply for what they were – conservative, middle-class, comfortably wealthy. It was almost as if he resented the fact that he hadn't been born poor, so he didn't really have anything to rage against. He knew, deep down, that his rebelliousness had no cause, and he blamed his parents for that. Yet, at the same time as despising them, he couldn't get away from the simple fact that they were his parents. His mother, his father. They'd brought him into this world, nurtured him, cared for him, looked after him. He was their son. And I don't think he ever worked out how to deal with that.

I looked at him.

He was still staring blindly at his notebook.

'Curtis?' I said.

No answer.

'Curtis?'

He looked up. 'Yeah . . .?'

'It'll be all right,' I said quietly. 'I'm sure . . . it'll be OK.'

He grinned. 'Fucking right.'

9

I didn't hear from Curtis again until the following Wednesday. I was due to take my mock A levels that year, and because of all the stuff with the band and everything I hadn't done any revision, and I was quite a long way behind in my course work too, so I'd been making an effort to stay at home and try to catch up a bit. I'd called Curtis on the Monday to find out what had happened at the meeting with Arthur, but when his mother answered the phone she told me that Curtis wasn't there.

'Do you know where he is?' I asked her.

'No,' she said bluntly.

'Oh, OK . . . well, when he comes home, could you tell him that Lili called, please?'

She didn't really say anything, she just made an odd little sniffing noise, a contemptuous kind of snort, and put the phone down.

I tried ringing him again the next night, but this time nobody answered. I let it ring for quite a long time, then eventually I hung up and called Kenny. But all he could tell me was that Curtis hadn't been at school for the last two days.

'What about Stan?' I asked him.

'What about him?'

'Do you know if he's heard from Curtis at all?'

'No idea.'

'He hasn't said anything to you?'

'About what?'

I sighed. 'About *Curtis*.'

'No, he hasn't said anything. What's this all about anyway?'

'Nothing . . . I'm just trying to get in touch with Curtis, that's all.'

'Yeah, well . . . you know what he's like.'

'Yeah . . .'

It was around six o'clock on Wednesday evening when Curtis finally called me. He was ringing from a phone box. I heard the pips going, then Curtis muttering and swearing as he tried to put the coins in . . .

'Fuck . . . shit, hold on –'

Beep, beep, beep . . .

'Curtis? Is that you?'

'Lili?'

'Yeah –'

'Can you hear me?'

'Yeah, where are you?'

'The phone box opposite the squat . . . God, it *stinks* in here –'

'What's going on, Curtis? Where've you been? I've been trying –'

'They threw me out, didn't they?'

'*What?*'

'My fucking parents, they threw me out of the house.'

'Why?'

'Fuck knows . . .'

He sounded really wired, like he was totally wrecked on something.

'What happened?' I said softly, trying to calm him down. 'Just tell me what happened.'

It took a while to get the full story out of him, mainly because he kept changing it all the time, but in the end I managed to piece it all together. Basically what happened was that he'd stayed at the squat until Sunday evening, and then around eight o'clock he'd finally gone back home. He was planning on telling his parents about his decision to leave school that night, but as soon as he got back, as soon as he walked through the front door, his father came storming up to him, grabbed him by the shoulders, and dragged him into the kitchen. Sitting at the table, crying her eyes out, was his mother. And on the table in front of her was a small lump of cannabis resin wrapped in clingfilm.

'I must have left it in one of my pockets,' Curtis told me. 'Mum probably found it when she was doing the washing.'

'What did your dad *say*?' I asked him.

Curtis laughed. 'He asked me what it was, and what the *bloody hell* I was doing with it.'

'And what did you tell him?'

'The truth. I told him that it was just a bit of dope, and that there was no need to make a big deal about it.'

'I bet that went down well.'

He laughed again. 'Yeah . . . he just started yelling at me then, screaming at me like a crazy man. I thought his head was going to explode. And the more he shouted, the more Mum cried . . . which made him shout even more. It was ri*dic*ulous. After a while, I just turned round and started to walk out. But then Dad grabbed me again and started spitting out all this stuff about *no more stupid music, no more pop groups, from now on you do what I say* . . . I didn't even bother saying anything, you know? I just stood there and stared at him. Then he said something about coming straight home from school on Monday, and I told him that I wasn't going to school on Monday, that I wasn't going to school at *all* any more, and then it all kind of kicked off again. In the end . . . well, he came up with that old "my house, my rules" thing, so I just told him that he could keep his fucking house, and I walked out.'

'So he didn't actually throw you out then?'

'Shit, Lili, whose side are you *on*? I mean, *Jesus* . . .'

'I didn't mean –'

'Anyway, it doesn't matter . . .'

'What doesn't matter?'

'Any of it . . . all of it. I don't know . . .'

There was a silence on the line for a while. I could hear Curtis breathing, short sharp breaths. I heard him sniff a couple of times. I imagined him in the phone box, chewing his lip, his eyes darting around, watching the traffic outside.

'What are you going to do?' I asked quietly.

'It's no problem,' he said casually, trying to sound upbeat. 'I've moved into the squat, that room we were in the other night. I'll get it cleaned up, get some furniture in, a chair, a proper bed . . .'

'What will you do for money?'

'Sign on, like everyone else.'

'What about all your stuff?'

'What stuff?'

'From home . . . all your records, your clothes –'

'I don't need them. I've got my guitar here, that's all I need.'

'Oh, Curtis . . .' I sighed.

'Don't *pity* me, Lili,' he said coldly.

'I'm not –'

'This is what I *want*, all right? This is how it's *supposed* to be.'

Over the next month or so, things began to settle down a bit, and I managed to establish some kind of routine in my life. During the week, I'd get up every morning and go to school, where I'd try to forget about everything else – my mother, Curtis, the band – and just concentrate on schoolwork. After school, on Mondays, Wednesdays, and Thursdays, I'd go straight home. Tuesdays, I'd travel by underground to the squat for a band rehearsal, and after that I'd usually stay the night with Curtis. Fridays, I'd rush home after school, quickly get changed, then head off to the squat to help load up the van and get everything sorted out for that night's gig at the Conway Arms. After the gig, I'd stay the night with Curtis again, and then – more often than not – we'd spend the rest of the weekend together, rehearsing again on the Sunday, after which I'd finally get the tube back to Hampstead.

The Friday night gigs at the Conway were getting better and better all the time. Curtis was writing better songs, we were getting better at playing them – both individually and as a band – and the audiences were getting bigger every week. We were starting to build up a following, and after about the second or third gig I was amazed to see people in the audience singing along to our songs. Not everyone liked us, of course, and there was always some kind of trouble whenever we played. Fights would break out in the audience, bottles and glasses would get thrown, idiots would try to get up on stage to attack Curtis. There was always a threat of violence at a Naked gig. And if the threat didn't materialize of its own accord, Curtis was always more than happy to stir things up. He *liked* causing trouble. He enjoyed the thrill of it, the adrenalin rush, the natural high . . .

Not that he needed much of a *natural* high.

Since moving into the squat, his use of drugs had steadily increased, and by the end of January, I began to realize that he was under the influence of *some*thing virtually all of the time. I guessed that this was only partly due to the increased availability of drugs at the squat, and that Curtis himself had much deeper reasons for wanting to be out of his head so much, but whenever I tried talking to him about it, he'd either shrug it off – *I'm just having a good time, that's all* – or he'd lose his temper – *who the fuck are* you *to tell me what to do?* – or he'd simply ignore me, play deaf, and change the subject.

So, in the end, I simply stopped trying.

His drug-taking still bothered me, and I wished he wouldn't do it *all* the time, but it hadn't yet reached the stage where it got in the way of everything else. I mean, at that point in his life, Curtis was still a long way from being totally out of control . . . in fact, if anything, I'd say that it was around then that he was at his creative peak. His new songs were fantastic, his singing and guitar playing were out of this world . . . he even *looked* more amazing than ever. And when he was on stage, doing his thing, his presence was so electrifying, so captivating, that even *I* found it hard to take my eyes off him.

When he wasn't on stage, and when he wasn't hanging around the squat getting stoned, Curtis spent most of his time with Jake, trying to find other gigs for us, or trying to persuade record company people to come and see us at the Conway. But they didn't have much luck. Although the Sex Pistols had played a few gigs in London – and there were rumours of other punk bands starting up – it would still be a good few months before the punk scene really got going, and even longer before the record companies began to show any interest. At the same time, most of the regular venues around London were still only booking either big name bands or 'pub rock' bands like Eddie and the Hot Rods, who basically played fast rhythm and blues. And Naked, of course, didn't fit into either category. Jake tried lying about us, pretending that we were just another pub rock band, but on the couple of occasions that this actually got us a booking, the gigs weren't all that good. *We* were as good as ever, but we weren't right for the audience, and they weren't right for us.

Mind you, it was actually one of these gigs that got us our first *NME* review. It was only a couple of lines, and it only really mentioned us because we were supporting a band called Roogalator, who just happened to be the *NME*'s pet band at the time, but still . . .

It was a review.

And it called us a 'shit-hot new band from North London'.

So we weren't complaining.

Talking of complaining, though . . .

At around that time, towards the end of January 1976, the people who lived next door to the squat started making complaints about the noise. Apparently, it wasn't so much the general noisiness of the squat that bothered them – the all-night music, the constant to-ing and fro-ing, the occasional drug-fuelled revelry – it was, quite specifically, the sound of us rehearsing in the basement that caused all the problems. Which wasn't really all that surprising. For a good few months now we'd been rehearsing twice a week, and we always played as loudly as possible, for at least a couple of hours, so I didn't really blame the neighbours for eventually getting fed up with it.

But Curtis did.

When Jake told him that we'd have to find somewhere else to practise, he went completely ballistic.

'I don't have to listen to *them*, for fuck's sake. *Jesus!* Who do they think they *are*? Fuck them! What are they going to do about it anyway?'

'They'll probably call the police,' Jake explained calmly, passing Curtis a joint. 'And if the police come round here . . .'

He didn't have to explain any further.

Curtis took the joint, looked at it for a moment, then shook his head. 'Fuck.'

'It's all right,' Jake told him. 'I've been looking for a better rehearsal place for you anyway. And I've found this place just up the road that's absolutely perfect . . .'

The rehearsal building that Jake had found for us wasn't quite as *absolutely perfect* as he'd made out, but it *was* a lot better than the basement. And it *was* just up the road too – about five minutes' walk from the squat, at the south end of West Green Road. It was a big old brick-built warehouse, with high ceilings and thick walls and a solid stone floor, and it was set back from the street behind a fenced-off area of wasteground. There were no residential properties close by, and the nearest buildings were a row of takeaway food places on the other side of West Green Road. So, basically, we could play as loudly as we liked without any problems.

When Curtis asked Jake if we had – or needed – permission to use the building, and if so, what it was going to cost us, Jake just touched his finger to his nose and said, 'Don't worry about it, it's all sorted.'

And it was here, in the warehouse, that the final bust-up between Curtis and Kenny took place . . . the bust-up that would eventually lead to everything else that happened that summer.

10

The showdown between Curtis and Kenny was always going to happen at some point, and the only real surprise when it finally came about was that it hadn't happened before. They were polar opposites in almost every way – in their attitude, their outlook, their behaviour – and although it had always been fairly obvious that they didn't particularly like each other, their relationship now had deteriorated to such an extent that they barely even talked to each other any more.

The friction between them had been simmering for so long that I think we all knew it could erupt at any point, and we also knew that it wouldn't necessarily take anything major to spark it off.

And we were right.

It was a Sunday afternoon and we were rehearsing at the warehouse. It was only the second time we'd practised there, and I, for one, really liked it. It had windows, for a start – unlike the basement – so it didn't feel like we were stuck in a dungeon, and unlike in the cramped confines of the basement, there was plenty of room to move around, which *should* have meant that there was less likelihood of us bumping into one another, or causing an accident, or breaking something . . .

But, ironically, it was precisely this freedom of movement that led to the accident that eventually led to the meltdown between Curtis and Kenny.

And it was all my fault.

As far as I can remember, I was actually in a pretty good mood at the time. I don't recall why, exactly – although it might well have been simply because we weren't at the squat – but, whatever the reason, I'm fairly sure that in the moments before everything kicked off, I was feeling uncharacteristically light-hearted. Earlier on, Curtis had suggested that it might be a good idea if I tried moving around a bit more when I was on stage.

'What do you mean?' I'd said.

'Well, most of the time you just stand there –'

'What's wrong with that?'

'Nothing . . . it's just . . . well, apart from me, we probably come across as being a bit kind of *static* on stage, you know? Kenny doesn't move, Stan *can't* move . . .'

'You want me to *move*?'

He smiled at me. 'It'd give us a lot more energy if you did.'

'I'm not *dancing* –'

'You don't have to dance. Just, you know . . . move around a bit.'

'What, like you?'

'However you want, it doesn't matter. Whatever feels natural.'

'I don't know . . .' I said hesitantly. 'I'm not sure I can play and move at the same time.'

Curtis shrugged. 'Just try it, OK? See how it feels.'

And that's what I was doing when it happened. We were in between songs, and Curtis was talking to Stan, trying to work out a tricky little drum section, and I think Kenny was just standing around, not doing anything as usual . . . and I was off on my own, doing what Curtis had asked me to do. I'd turned down the volume on my bass, and I was practising playing and moving at the same time, and – to my surprise – not only could I do it, but I was actually enjoying it too. Skipping around, jumping up and down, moving to the rhythms inside my head . . . it was fun. In fact, I was enjoying it so much that I got a bit carried away. I was trying to see if I could play the bass and spin round in circles at the same time, and at first I couldn't work out how to do it without getting my legs tangled up in the guitar lead. But then I realized that if I spun round in one direction for a while, then stopped and spun round the other way, the guitar lead would unravel itself from my legs and I'd be free to keep on twirling. Unfortunately, I forgot all about the dizzying effect of whizzing round in circles, and as I whirled across the room like an idiot, still playing the bass, my legs went all wobbly, my head started spinning, and I totally lost control of where I was going. I didn't even see the wall, I was just kind of tottering around, trying to stay on my feet, and the next thing I knew I was crashing backwards into the warehouse wall and slumping down to the floor. I didn't hurt myself or anything, and I probably would have just laughed it off if it wasn't for the fact that as I hit the ground I heard something snap, and almost at once I realized that as I'd fallen I'd slammed the bass into the hard stone floor.

'Fucking *hell*!' I heard Kenny shout. 'What the *fuck* are you doing with my bass?'

I sat up, still quite dizzy, and looked at the bass. I couldn't see any damage at first, and I thought maybe I'd imagined the snapping sound, but then I heard Kenny's angry voice again – 'You've broken a fucking machine head!' – and I realized that he was right. The E-string machine head – the metal peg for tuning the string – had snapped off when the bass had hit the floor.

'Shit,' I said. 'I'm sorry, Kenny –'

'I *knew* this would happen,' he spat, striding towards me. 'I fucking *knew* it.'

'I'll get it fixed,' I told him. 'I'll pay for it –'

'Too fucking right you will.' He stopped in front of me, staring down at the broken bass, angrily shaking his head. 'Jesus *Christ* . . .'

'Look, I'm sorry, OK? It was an accident –'

'An *accident*?' he hissed, glaring at me. 'You were spinning round all over the place, you stupid fucking –'

'Hey, Kenny,' I heard Curtis say. 'That's enough.'

We both looked round at the sound of his voice. He was standing a few feet away from Kenny, fixing him with a steady gaze.

Kenny turned towards him. 'She broke my fucking bass –'

'*She*?'

Kenny hesitated. 'Look, I know she's your girlfriend and everything –'

'Her name's Lili, Ken. Not *she*, OK?'

'Yeah, well . . . maybe it's about time that *Lili* started using her own fucking bass instead of borrowing mine all the time, *OK*?'

'No,' Curtis said calmly, 'it's not OK. We're supposed to be a band. We do things together, we own things together, we break things together . . . and we don't fucking blame each other when something goes wrong. We're all in this together –'

'Really?' Kenny sneered.

'Yeah, really.'

'So how come you auditioned for another band a couple of weeks ago?'

There was a deadly silence for a few moments then, with everyone staring at Curtis, waiting to see what he'd say.

Eventually, after staring really hard at Kenny for a few seconds, he said, 'I don't know what you're talking about.'

'No?'

'I haven't auditioned for anyone.'

'That's not what I heard.'

'Really?' Curtis smiled. 'Go on then, tell me who I've been auditioning for.'

'London SS.'

Curtis laughed.

Kenny shook his head. 'You can't deny it, Curtis. You were seen –'

'So fucking what?' Curtis said. 'I *know* them, all right? I hang around with some of them sometimes. And, yeah, I might well have been around when they were auditioning . . . but you know what London SS are like, for Christ's sake. They're *always* auditioning. That's all they ever do. I mean, they've never played anywhere, they've only got about two songs, and they've never had the same line up for more than a week . . . do you really think I'd want to *audition* for a band like that?'

Kenny said nothing for a while, he just stared back at Curtis, and it was clear to me from the look in his eyes that he knew that this was the moment . . . the moment when he either stood up to Curtis, or backed down again. And he knew that if he backed down this time, having gone so far as to accuse Curtis of being disloyal to the band . . . well, he just couldn't back down after that.

'You know what, Curtis?' he said slowly. 'I think you're full of shit.'

Curtis smiled. 'Yeah?'

'Yeah.'

Curtis carried on smiling at him for a while, not saying anything, then – with a slight shrug of his shoulders – he turned to me and held out his hand. I was still sitting on the floor with the broken bass resting in my lap. 'Are you all right?' Curtis asked me.

'Yeah . . .'

He reached down, took my hand, and helped me to my feet. 'Here, let me take that,' he said, reaching for the bass. I lifted the strap from my shoulders and let him take the bass off me. Holding it by the neck, he smiled calmly at me. 'You might want to move back a bit.'

'Sorry?'

He nodded his head. 'Just stand over there.'

Puzzled, I moved back a few steps and stood by the wall and watched as Curtis turned back to Kenny. Still smiling, still hold-

86

ing the bass by its neck, he glanced briefly at the broken machine head.

'It was an accident, Kenny,' he said softly. 'Lili didn't mean it.'

'I know –'

'If she'd meant it, she would have done this.'

He stepped back and raised the bass above his head, holding it by the neck in both hands, and then he spread his legs and swung the bass like an axe, crashing it down into the floor. The body of the bass cracked in half, and a pick-up went flying across the room. But Curtis hadn't finished yet. As Kenny stepped back, his face pale with shock, Curtis raised the bass over his head again, and this time he just started pummelling it into the ground, over and over again – *bam, bam, bam, bam* – until all that was left of it was a mess of broken wood on the floor, bits of plastic and metal all over the place, and the remains of the snapped-off neck in his hand.

Curtis was still smiling.

'Here,' he said to Kenny, tossing him the broken neck.

'What the fuck –?'

He shut up suddenly as Curtis stepped towards him, thinking – as I was – that Curtis was going to hit him. But he didn't. Instead, he bent down and gathered up as much of the broken bass as he could, cradling the bits in his arms, and then he straightened up, looked at Kenny for a moment, and started lobbing the broken bits at him. Kenny caught the first one or two, but after that his hands were full, so all he could do was try to get out of the way.

'There you go, Kenny,' Curtis said, throwing another bit at him, a bit harder this time. 'Here's your bass back. Thanks for letting us borrow it.' A lump of wood hit Kenny's shoulder. 'Whoops,' Curtis said. 'Mind your head.' As he flung another piece at Kenny's head, Kenny turned, ducking his head, and started heading for the door.

'You're fucking insane, Curtis,' he muttered. 'You're out of your fucking head.'

'Send me the repair bill, Kenny, OK?' Curtis called out, laughing now as he chucked a big splinter of wood at his back. 'And feel free to come and see us any time . . . any time at all.'

Kenny had reached the door now. He paused for a moment, looking back over his shoulder, and he was just about to say something when Curtis stepped forward, swung his arm, and whipped a chunk of metal across the room at him. Kenny legged it through the door, slamming it shut behind him just in time. The chunk of metal crashed into the door, leaving a fist-sized dent where Kenny's head would have been.

No one spoke for a while.

Curtis looked at me, breathing hard, but still smiling. I looked back at him, too stunned to say anything. And after a few moments, we both looked at Stan. He was just sitting there, as blank as ever, idly whirling a drumstick in his fingers.

'Well . . .' I said eventually.

Curtis lit a cigarette. 'Well what?'

I shrugged. 'I suppose I'm going to *have* to buy myself a bass now.'

Getting a new bass wasn't a problem. All I had to do was ask my mother for some money, take a trip to Charing Cross Road with Curtis, and let him do the rest. He knew all the music shops in the area, and once I'd told him that I simply wanted to buy another Fender Mustang, exactly the same as Kenny's, and that I didn't care how much it cost, he just led me along to a specialist guitar shop and we picked out a brand-new Fender.

'Do you want to try it out first?' he asked me.

The shop was full of people trying out guitars and basses, all of them looking very serious as they showed off their rock 'n' roll skills. Most of them, for some reason, seemed to be playing Led Zeppelin's 'Stairway to Heaven'.

'No,' I told Curtis. 'I don't want to try it out. Let's just pay for it and get out of here.'

My mother had given me more than enough money, so I bought myself a nice hard guitar case and some extra strings too. As I handed over the cash, and the shop assistant started putting the bass into the case, I looked at Curtis and saw him shaking his head.

'What?' I said to him.

He smiled. 'Nothing . . . I was just thinking, that's all. Maybe you could ask your mum to buy me a new guitar.'

I knew that it was meant as a joke, or at least that he didn't really mean anything by it, but just hearing him say the words 'your mum' suddenly made me realize how rarely he ever mentioned her. Apart from things like, 'Do you have to ring your mum?', he never asked me anything about her, never talked about her, never showed the slightest interest at all. And while that had never really bothered me before – at least not consciously – it just seemed to hit me at that moment, and for a few fleeting seconds I kind of hated him for it.

'What?' he said, frowning at me. 'What did I say?'

'Nothing,' I said, letting it go. 'It's all right . . . I just . . .'

'What?'

'Nothing.' I smiled coldly at him. 'Come on, let's go.'

We talked over with Jake whether we should try to carry on as a three-piece or start looking for a new rhythm guitar player.

'I mean, we can *do* it as a three-piece,' Curtis said. 'It's not a problem. There's nothing we *can't* play without a second guitar, it just means that the sound's going to be slightly different on some songs.'

'In what way?' Jake said.

Curtis shrugged. 'A bit emptier in parts, maybe. Not so *full*.'

We played through a couple of songs to show him what Curtis meant, and Curtis was right – it *wasn't* a problem, we *could* play them as a three-piece, and to most people they probably wouldn't have sounded any different. But *we* could tell the difference. We knew that we'd developed the songs to be played with a second guitar, and that they sounded better with a second guitar. So, for us, there was really no argument.

'I know a few people who *might* be all right,' Curtis said. 'But it's not just a case of how *good* they are. I mean, Kenny was a pretty good guitarist, but he was never right for Naked, was he? So I don't know . . . I'm not sure the people I know would fit in.'

'We can advertise,' Jake suggested. 'Put an ad in the *NME*.'

'Yeah . . . if we put it in this Thursday's, we could hold auditions at the warehouse next weekend.'

'You'll still have to play *this* Friday with just the three of you.'

'Yeah, well, if that's what we have to do . . .'

The advert appeared in the *Musicians Wanted* section of the *NME* on Thursday 5 February 1976.

> **Rhythm guitarist wanted for gigging band. Pistols, Dolls, Stooges. No hippies, no Kennies. no limits.**

'No *Kennies*?' I said to Curtis when I saw it.

He just smiled.

I said, 'Is that how you spell "Kennies"?'

He shrugged. 'Who cares?'

Friday's gig at the Conway Arms went ahead as usual, and apart from playing a slightly shorter set – missing out a couple of songs that we hadn't had time to rework for just the one guitar – everything else was fine. It was kind of strange playing without Kenny, and we all had to work a little bit harder to make up for his missing guitar, but we soon got used to it. And by the end of the set, I think we all realized that we somehow felt a lot closer as a band without Kenny. We hadn't changed our minds about needing another guitar player, but with Kenny gone . . . well, it just seemed to change the *dynamics* of the band. With the four of us, there'd always been a sense that the band was split down the middle, with me and Curtis on the one hand, and Kenny and Stan on the other. But now, with only the three of us, that split was gone. We were all on the same side now, we were all working together.

We didn't actually talk to each other about this, and I was only really guessing that Curtis and Stan felt the same way as me. For all I knew, I could have been totally wrong. I did try asking Curtis how he felt after the gig, but, as usual, he was too busy with his post-gig socializing to spend much time with me. He had people to talk to, autographs to sign, drinks to drink, drugs to take . . . and that night he also had potential rhythm guitarists to see. At least, that's what he told me. And I did see him talking to a couple of vaguely familiar faces who, according to Stan, had both 'played guitar in some shitty little band from Paddington'. But later on, when I went downstairs to use the toilet, I also saw Curtis talking to Charlie Brown.

They were in a little booth together at the back of the bar, and although they weren't alone – one of Charlie's friends was there too – they were definitely sitting too close to each other for my liking. And the way they were talking to each other – eye to eye, intimate and intense – they might as well have been alone. As I stood there staring at them from across the bar, Curtis suddenly looked up and saw me. For a very brief moment, he had the look of someone who's been caught out – a quick flash of surprise, embarrassment, panic – but almost immediately his face broke into a welcoming smile and he casually waved me over. I held his gaze for just a second, keeping my face as blank as I could, then I looked away and headed off into the toilets.

Neither of us mentioned this little episode until a few hours later when we were lying in bed in Curtis's room back at the squat. It was around two o'clock in the morning, and for once the house was relatively quiet. Someone was playing an acoustic guitar somewhere, picking out some nice lazy blues riffs, but they were at least a couple of floors away, and it was quite a relaxing sound anyway.

I still didn't really like staying at the squat, but it wasn't quite so bad now that Curtis had made an effort to make his room a bit more comfortable. He'd furnished it mostly from skips – there was a manky old armchair, a reasonably clean settee, an old kitchen table and a couple of hard-backed chairs – and the room always felt slightly damp, and smelled slightly musty. But, all in all, it wasn't too bad. The bed wasn't actually a *bed*, just a secondhand mattress on top of a wooden pallet. But, again, it wasn't as bad as it sounds. At least it was *our* secondhand mattress.

Curtis, as usual, was too wired to sleep that night, and as I lay there, turning things over in my mind, he was sitting up in bed beside me, smoking a joint and reading a book about Paul Verlaine. I knew in my heart that there was really no point in saying anything to him about Charlie Brown, because whatever I said, and however I put it, I knew that he'd have an answer. So I kept telling myself to just forget it, just stop thinking about it, keep your mouth shut, and go to sleep. But I knew that was never going to happen.

'Curtis?' I said quietly.

'Yeah . . .?'

'Did you have any luck tonight?'

His breathing stopped for a moment. 'Sorry?'

'You said you were seeing some guitar players. I was just wondering how you got on.'

'Oh, right . . .' he said, breathing out. 'Yeah, I spoke to a couple of people I know . . .' He puffed on the joint. 'I don't think they're right for us, but I told them to come along to the audition anyway. Jake's booked the warehouse for next Friday and Saturday. Oh, and there's no gig on the Friday, by the way. The Conway's closed for a couple of days for some renovation work or something.'

'Right . . .' I said. 'Is Charlie going to be auditioning?'

'What?'

'Charlie Brown . . . the swastika girl. You were talking to her in the bar tonight –'

'Yeah –'

'So I just *assumed*, you know, that she was one of the guitarists you told me you were going to see.'

93

There was a moment's silence then, and although I was facing away from him, I could sense that Curtis had put down his book and was looking down at me.

'She's just someone I know, Lili,' he said softly. 'That's all.'

'Right . . .'

He put his hand on my shoulder. 'Come on, Lili . . . hey . . .' He leaned over me. 'What's the matter?'

'Nothing . . .'

'Look at me.'

I said nothing.

'Lili, come *on* . . .' He gave me a gentle tug. 'Just look at me a minute, OK?'

I sighed, rolled over, and sat up.

Curtis smiled at me. 'Look, I was only talking to Charlie because she knows Siouxsie Sioux and some of the others from Bromley, and some of them know people who're getting bands together, so I just thought that Charlie might have a few ideas about guitarists –'

'I'm not *stupid*, you know.'

He took hold of my shoulders and looked me straight in the eyes. 'I'm not *lying* to you, Lili. I mean, do you *really* think I fancy Charlie or something?'

'It had crossed my mind.'

He shook his head. 'She means nothing to me – honestly. Absolutely *nothing*.' He cupped my chin in his hand and spoke softly. 'You're the only one for me, Lili . . . you *know* that. There's no *reason* for me to want anyone else. I mean, how many times have I told you that you're the most beautiful girl in the world?'

'Once.'

He smiled his most irresistible smile. 'Isn't that enough?'

I really wanted to talk to him then. I just wanted to *talk*. I wanted to tell him how I felt about things, how I felt about myself, about my mum, about him, about us, and I wanted him to *listen* to me . . . but as he took me in his arms and kissed me, and we lay down on the bed together, I knew that the time for talking was over.

You should have listened to yourself before, a voice in my head said as Curtis climbed on top of me. *You should have just kept your mouth shut and gone to sleep when you had the chance.*

12

Curtis and Jake took care of all the arrangements for the auditions – sorting through the replies to the advert, deciding who to see and who not to see, working out how long it would all take, and so on – and all I had to do was be at the warehouse, with my bass, at two o'clock in the afternoon. I had no idea what to expect – how it was going to work, how many people would be there – and when I got to the warehouse for the first day of auditions on the Friday, I was really surprised to see a good dozen or so people already waiting outside. They were a real mixture – young and old, cool and not so cool, short-haired, long-haired, tough-looking, weird-looking. The only thing they had in common, apart from being male, was that they all had guitars.

When I went into the warehouse, the others were already there. Curtis and Jake were setting up an amp and a mike in the middle of the room, and Stan was sitting at his drums as usual, tapping out a rhythm on the rim of the snare. Chief was there too, squatting on the floor at the back of the room, reading a Batman comic.

'Have you seen how many people there are outside?' I said to no one in particular.

'There should be thirteen of them,' Jake said. 'And tomorrow we've got another twelve.'

'Why don't you let them wait in here?' I suggested. 'It's really cold outside.'

'Pressure,' Jake said, looking far too pleased with himself. 'It's all part of the audition process. We keep them on edge so we'll find out how they cope with the pressure.'

'They're guitar players,' I said. 'Not astronauts.'

Stan laughed.

Jake gave me one of his creepy – and condescending – little grins, then turned to Curtis. 'Tell her, Curt,' he sighed.

'Tell her what?'

'What we said, about making them wait –'

'No, Lili's right,' Curtis said, smiling at me. 'Go and let them in, Jake. There's no point keeping them out there.'

'Yeah, but –'

'Just do it, OK?'

It turned out to be a long and fairly tedious day. One by one, Jake asked the guitarists to step up to the mike and plug in their guitars, and then after he'd asked them a few simple questions – what's your name? where are you from? what kind of experience have you got? – Curtis took over. His audition technique was pretty straightforward.

'All right?' he'd say.

And the shy ones would just mumble something back – 'Yeah, thanks,' or just 'Yeah . . .' – while the more confident characters might try to start a conversation – 'Hey, yeah . . . how you doing? This is really great, by the way . . . I mean, I've seen Naked *so* many times . . .' – in which case, Curtis would just let them ramble on until it finally dawned on them that they were talking far too much.

Then Curtis would simply say, 'OK, play something.'

I thought that this was kind of cruel at first – and I suppose, in a way, it was – but as the day went on, I began to realize that it was actually a really efficient way of finding out what we needed to know, because each guitarist dealt with it in his own individual way.

Some of them just looked confused.

Others said, 'What do you want me to play?'

The ones we liked the best – the ones who understood that we were looking for a *rhythm* guitarist – they just kind of nodded, looked down at their guitars, and started playing chords, some of them just strumming, others really hammering away, and others giving us a mixture of both.

The ones we liked the worst were the ones who immediately began showing off, playing really *difficult* stuff, guitar-hero stuff, or those who just played stuff they'd copied note for note from other bands . . . there was even one guy called Damon who started playing the riff to 'Smoke on the Water', for God's sake. As soon as Curtis realized what he was playing – which took him about two seconds – he just stood up and said, 'Yeah, thanks, Damon. We'll be in touch.'

Out of the thirteen candidates, there were only two who Curtis thought were worth a second listen. They were both about eighteen or nineteen, and they were both pretty good, and so Curtis sat them down and quickly taught them how to play 'Naked' – which, out of all our songs, was easily the simplest to learn – and once they'd got the hang of it, we asked each of them to play through the whole song with us a couple of times.

'Don't worry if you mess it up or get lost or anything,' Curtis told them. 'We'll just carry on playing, and you come back in when you're ready. OK?'

By the time we'd gone through 'Naked' with each of them – twice with one and three times with the other – and then thanked them for coming and taken their details and told them we'd be in touch, it was getting on for nine o'clock and I was pretty tired. Curtis and Jake had been snorting speed for most of the day, so they were both full of energy, but me and Stan had kept our noses clean, and neither of us could stop yawning. Chief had barely moved all day. He was still sitting on the floor at the back of the room, still staring silently at his Batman comic.

'So . . . what do you think?' Curtis said.

The general opinion seemed to be that the two guys we'd picked out were definitely the only two worth considering, and that although they were both potentially good enough musically, the first one lived in Colchester, which was about seventy miles away, and he'd made it quite clear that he had no intention of moving to London.

'So what would he do if we *did* ask him to join the band?' I asked.

'He said he'd *commute*,' Jake sneered.

We all agreed that having a commuter in the band was simply out of the question. And we also all agreed that the other guitarist, while probably the better of the two, was just a really unpleasant person. Kind of snotty, far too full of himself, and no sense of humour whatsoever.

'He's also *really* ugly,' Curtis said.

'That's not fair –' I started to say.

'It's true, though, isn't it?' Curtis said, grinning. 'I mean, the guy looks like a fucking *gargoyle*.'

'Well, yeah,' I agreed. 'But –'

'But *nothing*, Lili,' he said quite seriously. 'We're going to be famous, don't forget. We're going to be photographed all over the world. Kids are going to put posters of us on their walls.' He grinned again. 'I don't want Naked to be remembered as "that band with the gargoyle on guitar".'

'It'd be good for you though, wouldn't it?' I said.

'How's that?'

I smiled at him. 'Well, it'd make you seem better-looking . . .'

'Better-looking than a gargoyle, you mean?'

'Yeah.'

We sat around for a while longer, just talking and messing about, then Curtis and Jake decided they wanted a drink, so they went off to the pub, and Stan and Chief said that they were going home. I was too tired to go to the pub, and I didn't want to go back to the squat on my own, so I asked Chief if he could give me a lift back to Hampstead.

And that was pretty much it for the day.

When I woke up the next morning, I had no idea that within a few hours I'd be meeting the person who'd change my life for ever. Of course, there was no reason that I *should* have had any idea. I mean, that's not how it works, is it? Premonitions, déjà vu . . .? None of that kind of stuff is real. So, no, when I woke up that Saturday morning, there was nothing to suggest that today was *the* day – nothing in the air, nothing in my mind, nothing in my heart. It was just another cold February day. Dull and windy, not much to look forward to, just another long day of auditions.

My mother was still in bed when I left the house and headed off to the underground station. I'd made her a cup of coffee and asked her if she wanted anything to eat before I'd left, but she'd barely even opened her eyes.

'I'll probably be back on Sunday night,' I'd told her.

'Uh huh,' she'd muttered.

The walk to the underground station was the same as ever, as was the tube journey to Seven Sisters, and when I got to the warehouse the only thing that seemed to have changed was that the waiting guitarists weren't hanging around outside in the cold. They were hanging around *inside* in the cold. Apart from that, everything else was almost exactly the same as the day before. Curtis and Jake were setting up the amp and the mike, Stan was sitting at his drums . . . even Chief was in the same place as before, squatting on the floor at the back of the room. This time, though, instead of a Batman comic, he was reading a copy of *Sounds*.

Everyone seemed a bit jaded, as if there was no real hope of the day being a success. Jake was in a really bad mood, for some reason, constantly scratching at his hair and cursing under his breath all the time. And Curtis looked badly hungover. His eyes were bloodshot, his skin deathly pale, and when he came over and kissed me hello, his breath almost knocked me out.

'Christ,' I said, recoiling. 'How much did you have to drink last night?'

'It was Jake's fault,' he mumbled. 'He took me to this party . . .'

'Have you had any sleep?'

'I'll be all right,' he said, glancing over his shoulder at Jake.

'Listen, Curtis,' I said. 'Why don't you –?'

'Yeah, look . . . we'd better get started, all right? You ready?'

'Yeah,' I sighed. 'I'm ready.'

The auditions proceeded in exactly the same way as the day before, and by the end of the first stage we'd once again whittled down the candidates to just two – a tall gangly guy with a spider's web tattooed on his face, and a slightly unsettling young man with staring eyes and trembling hands. I didn't think either of them were suitable for us. In fact, to be honest, I found them both a little bit scary. But Jake and Curtis thought it was worth seeing what they were like when they played with us, so Curtis went through the same process as before – showing them how to play 'Naked' – and then the first one, the gangly guy, joined us for a couple of runs through the song. He messed it up pretty badly the first time, completely forgetting where the chorus came in, and on the second run-through his nerves got the better of him and he did even worse.

Then it was the trembly-handed guy's turn. He was pretty good on the first take, keeping it nice and simple, concentrating on getting the rhythm just right, and when we got to the end of the song, Curtis looked reasonably pleased. He went over and had a few words with Trembly, giving him some advice about how to play the chorus slightly differently, and then we started again.

And it was while we were playing the song through for the second time that something caught my eye on the other side of the warehouse – a movement, a change in the light – and when

I looked over to see what it was . . . that's when I saw William Bonney for the very first time.

He'd just come in through the door – which accounted for the brief change in the light – and now he was just standing there, with his hands in his pockets, watching us play. There was an air of cautious curiosity about him, like that of a wary animal investigating something new. He was obviously intrigued by us, but I also got the feeling that, while he wasn't scared, he was perfectly prepared to run at the first sign of danger. He was fairly slight, and not that tall, and my first impression was that he was just a young boy, maybe thirteen or fourteen years old. But after watching him for a while, I realized that I was wrong. He was young . . . but he wasn't *that* young. The odd thing was, the more I studied him, the *less* sure I became of his age. One second I'd think he was about sixteen or seventeen, the next second he'd turn his head slightly . . . and all of a sudden he'd somehow gain a couple of years. And then, just a moment later, I'd begin to think that I was right in the first place and that he really was only fourteen years old.

It was really weird.

The way he was dressed was kind of confusing too. His clothes were slightly tattered – but clean – and it looked to me as if he'd obviously had them for quite a while. They had a sort of dated – yet somehow timeless – feel to them. Narrow-legged trousers with an old leather belt, plain brown shoes, a well-worn black suit jacket, and a washed-out white cotton shirt with frayed cuffs. It was a look that reminded me vaguely of some vagabond street kids I'd seen in a 1950s black-and-white movie.

I must have been watching him for about twenty seconds or so when I suddenly realized that he'd stopped watching *us* play and was instead looking directly at me. My instinctive reaction was to look away, but I just couldn't seem to take my eyes off him. It wasn't that he was stunningly good-looking or anything – at least, not in a conventional sense, like Curtis – but there was just something about him . . . something indefinable, something very special. He had dark brown hair that was neither long nor short, a pale complexion, a slightly crooked smile, and his eyes . . . God, his eyes. They were the most incredible pure, bright, hazel-brown . . . so clear and radiant, so full of life . . .

'*Lili!*'

I looked over at Curtis and suddenly realized that he'd stopped playing . . . *every*one had stopped playing. Except me. The song had finished, but I was still playing. And everyone was looking at me.

'What the fuck are you *doing*?' Curtis said.

I stopped playing. 'Sorry,' I said, feeling myself blush. 'I was . . . uh . . .'

'You were what?'

I shrugged. 'I don't know . . . I just –'

'Who's that?' Curtis said, noticing William for the first time. He turned towards him. 'Who the fuck are you?'

'Me?' William said, looking back at him.

'Yeah, are you here for the audition?'

'The what?'

'The *audition*.'

William smiled. 'What audition is that?'

Curtis sighed. 'What are you doing here, exactly?'

'Nothing.' William shrugged. 'I was just passing by and heard the music, that's all.' He glanced at me and smiled again, then looked back at Curtis. 'It's a good song, I like it.'

His voice was soft, much deeper than I'd expected, and he spoke with a strong Northern Irish accent. 'Do you want me to go?' he asked Curtis.

Curtis frowned at him. 'What? No . . . just . . . I don't know. Just hold on a minute.' He turned to Trembly. 'Right, OK, thanks . . . yeah, that was good. We've got your phone number, we'll get back to you in a couple of days, OK?'

As Trembly nodded and started putting his guitar away, I saw

William ambling across the warehouse towards us. He nodded at Jake, who was standing off to one side, smoking a joint. Jake nodded back and offered him the joint.

William looked at it for a moment, then shook his head. 'You wouldn't have a normal cigarette on you, would you?'

Jake took a packet of cigarettes from his pocket and gave one to William.

'Thanks,' William said, lighting the cigarette from Jake's joint. He took a puff on it and looked at me. 'Hey,' he said, smiling. 'How are you doing?'

Annoyingly, I felt myself blush again. 'Yeah . . .' I muttered. 'Yeah, I'm fine, thanks.'

'Well, that's good.'

I held his gaze for a moment, trying to think of something to say, but all I could do was stare like an idiot into those wondrously bright hazel eyes . . .

'So you like the song?' I heard Curtis say, and I saw William look over as Curtis walked up to him, smoking a cigarette.

'I do, yeah.'

Curtis nodded, looking him up and down. 'Well, that's good.'

If William noticed the slight touch of sarcasm, he didn't show it. He just smiled at Curtis and said, 'This is your band then, is it?'

Curtis nodded. 'We're called Naked.'

The warehouse door creaked open then, and I looked over and saw Trembly walking out.

'Thanks again!' Curtis called out after him.

He turned in the doorway, nodded, then went out and closed the door.

Curtis turned back to William. 'What do you think of him?'

'What do *I* think?'

Curtis grinned. 'Yeah, we're looking for a new rhythm guitar player, and he was the last to audition. Do you think he was any good?'

I didn't really know what Curtis was up to, but he was definitely playing some kind of game with William, and I didn't like it at all. William, though . . . well, he either didn't realize that Curtis was mocking him, or he simply didn't care.

'Do you really want to know what I think?' he said to Curtis.

'Yeah, of *course*.'

William took a drag on his cigarette. 'He doesn't pay enough attention to the drums.'

Curtis just looked at him, clearly a little bit shocked.

'I mean,' William went on, 'you've got a really good drummer there, good drums, excellent bass . . .' He smiled briefly at me when he said this, then turned back to Curtis. '. . . and *you* obviously know what you're doing. So there's the two of you working together with your drummer, but then the guy who just left, he's not even *listening* to him, he's just concentrating on the rhythm that *he's* playing . . . do you know what I mean?'

'Yeah . . .' Curtis said, nodding in agreement. 'Yeah, I know *exactly* what you mean.' His tone of voice was quite genuine now, no hint of mockery at all. 'So . . .' he continued, 'do you play anything yourself then?'

William shrugged. 'This and that . . .'

'Guitar?'

'A bit.'

'You any good?'

'I can hold a tune.'

Curtis grinned. 'Hold a tune?'

'Just about, yeah . . .'

'Are you good enough to play with us?'

William looked at him. 'That's not really for me to say, is it?'

'Are you interested?'

'I could be . . .'

'All right then.'

Curtis went over and picked up his guitar. 'What's your name, anyway?' he said, bringing it back.

'William Bonney.'

Curtis stopped. 'William *Bonney*?'

'Yeah.'

Curtis stared at him. 'That's *really* your name?'

'Yeah, why?'

'Billy the Kid,' Curtis said, laughing. 'You know, the outlaw . . . Billy the Kid? That was *his* real name – William Bonney.' He carried on walking over to William, still chuckling. 'I can't believe it, you've got the same name as Billy the fucking Kid.'

'Really? I didn't know that.'

'Yeah . . . so where do you come from, Billy?'

William aimed a thumb over his shoulder. 'Just up the road there.'

'No, I mean where are you from *originally*. Which part of Ireland?'

'Belfast.'

'Belfast?'

'Yeah.'

'Right . . . well, OK . . .' Curtis passed his guitar to William. 'All right, Billy the Kid. Let's see what you've got.'

13

Even before he'd played a single note, it was obvious that William knew what he was doing with a guitar. The way he took if from Curtis and casually slung the strap over his shoulder, the way he held it, even the way he adjusted the strap – shortening it slightly to bring the guitar higher up his body – it all looked perfectly natural to him. And he didn't wait for Curtis to tell him what to play either, he didn't wait for anything. He just started playing.

And when he did . . .

It was breathtaking.

For the first five seconds or so, as his fingers skipped over the fretboard and the most wondrous guitar music filled the air, all I could do was hold my breath and stare in amazement at him. He played without a plectrum, picking and strumming the strings with a combination of both thumb and fingers that I'd never seen before. And the sound it produced – a simultaneous mixture of bass notes, chords, and melodies – was unlike any other guitar sound I'd ever heard. It was almost as if there were two guitars playing at once.

He didn't play anything obviously recognizable at first – in fact, I'm fairly sure that almost everything he played was improvised at the time – but the stuff he started off playing definitely had an Irish feel to it. At the same time though, it was equally definitely *not* a traditional Irish sound. It's really hard to describe, but he somehow managed to produce a sound that combined the melody and rhythm of traditional Irish music with a much harder, much *spikier*, blues style.

It really was amazing.

I glanced over at Curtis to see what he thought, and from the stunned look on his face, I guessed that he was, if anything, even more enthralled than I was.

For the next few minutes, William carried on improvising. The Irish feel to what he was playing gradually faded out, and the blues took over for a while. Then, quite seamlessly, the blues gave way to a series of really impressive little jazz riffs, which in turn he developed into an incredibly weird, and oddly syncopated – but surprisingly catchy – heavy-rock beat.

And then, if that wasn't enough, he stopped playing for a fraction of a second, leaving a long wailing note hanging in the air while he quickly adjusted both the tone and the volume controls, and then he launched into the opening chords of 'Naked'.

Not only did he play them perfectly – at the perfect tempo and with the perfect feel – he played them in *exactly* the same way as Curtis. Same guitar sound, same rhythm, same emphasis . . . he even had the *volume* just right. And I don't know whether it was this uncanny replication of Curtis's intro that caused Stan and me to start playing, or if it was simply our instinctive reaction to hearing those oh-so-familiar chords . . . but, whatever it was, we both came crashing in as usual, and it all felt so totally natural that I didn't even *think* about Curtis until just before the vocals were about to come in. My immediate thought was that he wasn't going to be liking this, that he'd think William was trying to take over from him or something, and that he'd either be angry about it, or resentful, or jealous, or maybe just sulky . . . but when I looked over to see what Curtis was doing, I was pleasantly surprised to see him standing at the microphone, getting ready to sing, and I was even more surprised to see that he was really getting into the music – his eyes closed, nodding his head to the beat, doing all his usual weird little movements. William was also moving to the music now, hopping and skipping in a strangely endearing little jig – his feet twitching and jerking, his head and shoulders bobbing up and down. It was a really *enjoyable* thing to see. And when Curtis started to sing, everything just felt – and sounded – fantastic. The song sounded great, William's guitar sounded great, Curtis sounded great . . . we all just sounded really, *really* good.

And what was even more incredible was that after hearing us play 'Naked' just *once*, William played the whole song through without a single mistake. He got absolutely *everything* right – verse, chorus, middle-eight, key change . . . he even remembered that we ended the song, somewhat unexpectedly, on the *sixth* repetition of the final chant (rather than the more traditional fourth or eighth repetition), an odd little quirk that had taken *me* ages to get used to. But not only had William got the ending dead right after hearing it played just once, the one time he *had* heard it was the time I'd messed it up, so he'd actually got it dead right after hearing it played *badly* just once.

Which really *was* impressive.

We all knew how special he was . . . I could tell straight away. As the echo of the final chord howled round the warehouse, and we all just stood there for a few moments, soaking up the electric silence, I could feel something different in the air. It was as if we'd suddenly just found something that we'd been looking for for a long time . . . which, of course, in a way, was exactly what *had* just happened. But there was much more to it than that. Because we all *knew* that what we'd just found, what we'd accidentally stumbled upon, was the rarest of shining jewels. And we all knew that if we could keep hold of that jewel, if we could get William to play with us, we wouldn't just be better than before, we'd be a hundred times better than before . . .

And the prospect of that was *hugely* exciting.

So much so, in fact, that as I gazed round at the others, they all had the same goofy look of stunned excitement on their faces. Jake, Curtis, Chief . . . even Stan was grinning like a fool.

'Well . . .' Jake said eventually, breaking the silence. 'That was . . . uhh . . .'

'Yeah . . .' said Curtis, nodding his head. 'Yeah, it was . . . abso*lutely* . . .'

'What did you say your name was again?' Jake asked William, offering him a cigarette.

'William Bonney,' he said, taking the cigarette.

'Billy the fucking Kid,' Curtis muttered.

Jake turned to Curtis. 'So, what do you think?'

Curtis stared thoughtfully at William for a few moments, slowly nodding his head, then he turned and looked at me. 'What do you think, Lili?'

'Yeah,' I said casually, smiling at William. 'I think he can hold a tune.'

William smiled back and gave me a little bow of appreciation.

I turned to Curtis. 'What do *you* think?'

'Yeah,' he said, stepping up to William and lighting his cigarette for him. 'I think we've just found our man.'

For half an hour or so after that, we all sat around and talked things over. Curtis and Jake did most of the talking, of course – telling William all about Naked, about our residency at the Conway Arms, the other gigs we'd played, why we were looking for another guitar player, what we hoped to achieve, and so on. William didn't say very much at this point, he just listened. And when Curtis and Jake began asking him questions, he kept his answers fairly simple.

'So, I mean . . . what do you think about joining us?'

'Do you get paid for these gigs you do?'

'Yeah . . . we get a cut of the door money at the Conway, and for the others it's usually a straight fee. I mean, it's not a fortune at the moment, but –'

'How do you split the money?'

'After expenses, Chief gets ten per cent, and the rest is split equally. Jake gets an equal share.'

William nodded. 'Sounds fair enough.'

'So, is that a *yes*?'

William glanced at Stan, then at me. 'If you all think I've got what it takes, yeah . . . I'll give it a go.' He looked at Jake. 'Do I have to sign anything?'

Jake shook his head. 'We just need to check a few things first though.'

'Like what?'

'You live locally, yeah?'

William nodded. 'West Green Road. It's not far from here –'

'Yeah, I know where it is. What about school? Where do you go to school?'

William laughed quietly. 'I don't go to school.'

'Do you work?'

He shook his head.

'Sign on?'

'No.'

'So what do you do for money?'

'This and that . . .'

'This and that?'

'Yeah.'

Jake glanced at Curtis. Curtis just shrugged. Jake turned back to William. 'So you won't have any problems getting to rehearsals or gigs then?'

'No problems, no.'

Jake turned to Curtis again. 'Is there anything else?'

'Yeah,' Curtis said, looking at William. 'I take it you've got a guitar?'

'Well . . . not exactly,' William said.

'And what exactly does *not exactly* mean?' Curtis asked.

'I can get one.'

'Sorry?'

'I can get one, it's not a problem. I just don't have one at the moment, that's all.'

'Right . . .' said Curtis, doubtfully. 'And when can you *get one* by?'

'When do I need it?'

'We rehearse every Tuesday and Sunday.' He grinned. 'So, basically, you'll need a guitar by tomorrow night.'

'OK,' William said.

Curtis stared at him. '*OK?*'

'Yeah.'

'Where the *fuck* are you going to get a guitar from by tomorrow night?'

William smiled sheepishly. 'Well, it's kind of complicated . . . I know someone who knows someone who can usually get hold of things . . . you know?'

'Right . . .'

'What kind of guitar do you think I should get?'

'What *kind*?'

'Yeah, you know, what *make* . . .? I mean, should I get the same as yours?' He peered over at Curtis's guitar. 'What make is that . . .?'

'It's a Danelectro.'

'Is that a good one?'

Curtis shrugged. 'It's all right. I mean, it's the best I could afford.'

'Should I get one of those then?'

Curtis grinned, shaking his head in disbelief. 'Well, if you've got a *choice*, I'd suggest getting a Gibson Les Paul or a Vintage Telecaster, something like that.'

Curtis was only messing about – the guitars he mentioned would have cost thousands – but William seemed to be taking him seriously.

'OK,' he said. 'Well, I'll see what I can do.'

'Yeah, right,' Curtis laughed. 'And while you're at it, if there's one going spare . . .'

The smile William gave him was impossible to read, and just for a moment I saw a flash of something in Curtis's eyes that I'd never seen in him before, and because it was so unfamiliar it took me a while to work out what it was. But then I got it: it was a look of uncertainty. Which might not *sound* all that strange, but if there was one thing that Curtis had never suffered from, it was uncertainty.

'Anyway . . .' he said after a while, having lit another cigarette to compose himself. 'I think that's probably all for now. Unless anyone else has got anything . . .?' He looked at Stan. Stan shook his head. Curtis looked at me. 'Lili? Is there anything you want to ask Billy?'

'No,' I said. 'I don't think so . . .'

'OK, well . . . what's the time?'

Jake glanced at his watch. 'Just gone seven.'

'What time does this Pistols thing start?' Curtis asked him.

'I don't know,' Jake shrugged. 'Ten, eleven . . . maybe later.'

Curtis turned to William. 'Are you up for a good night out?'

'I suppose so, yeah . . .'

'It's all free,' Curtis said, grinning. 'Free drink, free to get in . . . *and* you'll get to see the Sex Pistols.'

'The who?'

'No,' Curtis said, 'not The Who, the Sex Pistols –'

'Hold on a minute,' I said to Curtis. 'What are you talking about?'

'It was a *joke*, Lili –'

'Yeah, I know that. I meant what's this Pistols thing you're talking about?'

'The Valentine's Ball,' he said, slightly impatiently. 'You know . . . the thing at Andrew Logan's place tonight?'

'Who's Andrew Logan?'

'The *artist*,' Curtis said, shaking his head. 'Come *on*, Lili, I've already *told* you about this –'

'No, you haven't.'

'Yeah, I have.'

'When?'

'I don't fucking know . . . the other day, whenever it was.'

'Curtis,' I said slowly, trying to stay calm. 'You haven't told me anything about a Valentine's Ball, OK? You've never mentioned anyone called Andrew Logan, and I don't know anything about a Pistols gig tonight.'

'Yeah, well,' he muttered. 'I definitely *told* you –'

'No, you *didn't*.'

He shook his head again. 'I think you'll find I did.'

I very nearly told him to fuck off then, but for some reason I found myself feeling embarrassed about losing my temper and swearing at him in front of William . . . which didn't make any sense at *all* to me. But – understandable or not – my desire not to embarrass myself seemed more important to me than the anger I felt towards Curtis, so instead of telling him to fuck off, I just took a few deep breaths, waited until I'd calmed down a bit, and then smiled politely at him.

'All right,' I said quietly. 'Let's just forget about whether you told me or not, OK? Just *pretend* that you didn't.'

'Right,' Curtis said, smiling. 'But I *did* . . .'

'OK,' I said, gritting my teeth. 'Well, just humour me then. Tell me again.'

The Valentine's Ball was an invitation-only party at Andrew Logan's studio in Butler's Wharf, just south of the Thames. Logan was a well-known artist – sculptor, painter, aesthete, performance artist – and he was a key social figure in the London art/fashion scene at the time, a scene which included Malcolm McLaren and Vivienne Westwood. Logan's parties were infamous, and he had links with all kinds of people – film-makers, actors, writers, musicians – so McLaren had persuaded him to let the Pistols play at his Valentine's Ball in the hope that it would boost their profile.

Curtis had got to know McLaren quite well by this time, and Jake – though, in some ways, a rival – had also become part of the same burgeoning punk 'social circle'. So, in short, it turned out that McLaren had given Jake and Curtis four invites to the Valentine's Ball, and that, apparently, was where we were going.

'All right?' Curtis asked me after he'd explained all this.
   'Yeah, thanks.'
   'So . . . do you remember me telling you about it now?'
   I just sighed.
   He grinned. 'It's OK, Lili, you don't have to be –'
   'Curtis?' I said, not caring any more.
   'What?'
   'Fuck off.'

14

It wasn't until after he'd asked William to come with us to the Valentine's Ball that Curtis remembered that there were now actually six of us – me, Curtis, Jake, William, Chief, and Stan – and we only had enough tickets for four. Luckily for Curtis, though, as well as not saying anything to me about the party, he'd also forgotten to tell Stan and Chief about it, and they'd already made other plans, so they weren't really bothered. In fact, after listening to Curtis go on and on about Andrew Logan's arty friends and his wonderfully *theatrical* parties, I think they were both quite relieved that they *didn't* have to go. And, to be quite honest, when they dropped us off at the squat and drove off to wherever they were going, I kind of wished I was going with them. Whatever they were doing for the rest of the night, it had to be better than traipsing halfway across London for a party in an art studio with the Sex Pistols and Malcolm McLaren and God knows who else.

'Cheer up, Lili,' Curtis said breezily as we climbed the stairs to his room. 'It's going to be great. Everyone's going to be there – the music press, reporters, photographers . . . Jake reckons there might even be a film crew.' He stopped, put his hands on my shoulders, and leaned in close to me, smiling radiantly. 'This could be it, Lili,' he said, his eyes alight with excitement. 'I mean, you never know . . . this *could* be our night.'

I didn't really understand *how* this could be 'our night', but his intense and almost childlike enthusiasm was so irresistible that, as I followed Jake and William into his room, I began to think that maybe I was wrong . . . maybe tonight wasn't going to be as bad as I thought.

As it turned out, I *was* wrong. It wasn't as bad as I thought – it was a whole lot worse.

Everything started out OK. We all just sat around in Curtis's room for a while, and then Curtis went and borrowed another guitar from someone in the squat, and while he sat down with William and began teaching him some of our songs, I just sat there and listened to them play. They sounded really good together, and it was kind of nice just sitting there, not doing anything, just quietly enjoying their presence. Curtis seemed really happy, and he clearly liked playing his songs to William, and William's ability to learn them was absolutely amazing. Just like before, pretty much all he had to do was hear the song once, and that was it.

After a few songs, Jake went out and got a big bottle of cheap red wine from somewhere, and then Curtis and William stopped playing and we all just sat around drinking and talking for a while. Jake put a record on, and for once it was something that I actually liked. It was The Velvet Underground's third album – the one with 'Pale Blue Eyes' and 'Candy Says' – which I'd always really loved. Inevitably, as the record played, Jake skinned up a joint and began passing it around. I had a couple of quick puffs before passing it to William, and although he seemed quite at ease taking it from me – giving me a small nod of thanks and a heart-flipping smile – he didn't actually smoke any of it. He just passed it on to Jake and went back to smoking a cigarette.

Again, without quite knowing why, I found myself feeling oddly embarrassed. I also realized that the red wine and the dope had gone straight to my head and I was beginning to feel a little bit stoned already. And I knew I had a long night ahead of me, so for the next hour or so I didn't smoke any more and I just sipped at my glass of wine.

Curtis and Jake, on the other hand, just got on with it – smoking joint after joint, guzzling the wine . . . and at one point I saw them both popping some kind of pill, which I guessed was probably speed. William, I noticed, while drinking his fair share of wine, didn't seem remotely interested in either the dope or the pills, despite the frequent offers from Curtis and Jake. He didn't make a big deal about it, he just smiled politely, quietly shook his head, and that was that.

Which I thought was pretty cool.

So, anyway, that's how it went for the next couple of hours – music, drinking, smoking, talking. I virtually clammed up completely and just listened to the music and the conversation. It was good for a while. Curtis picked up his guitar and began quietly playing along to The Velvet Underground, picking out some beautiful little melodies, and at the same time he talked almost non-stop to William – asking him all kinds of questions about his life, what kind of music he liked, where he was from . . . but the funny thing was that although I was really concentrating on both Curtis's questions and William's answers, and although William *seemed* perfectly at ease with the questions, and he *seemed* to be answering them quite openly, it suddenly struck me after about an hour or so that he hadn't actually said anything of any significance about himself at all. Of course, I did wonder briefly if perhaps it was just the drink and the drugs playing tricks with my mind, but I quickly dismissed that idea. It was over an hour ago since I'd had those two quick puffs on the joint, and in that hour I'd barely touched my glass of wine . . . so, no, I wasn't mistaken. I had no idea how he'd done it, but William had been talking about himself, answering questions about himself, without so much as mentioning a single personal fact. And as far as I could tell, he'd done it in such a way that neither Jake nor Curtis were aware of what he'd done.

Which, again, I thought was kind of cool.

What wasn't so cool was when Curtis sloped off out of the room and was gone for a good ten minutes or so, and when he came back I knew straight away that he'd taken something else. His eyes were huge, his face was pale, he was sweating like crazy, and he couldn't stop grinning like a lunatic. I didn't know what he'd taken, but there'd been a lot of LSD going round the squat over the last few months, so it wouldn't have surprised me in the least if Curtis was taking the odd tab of acid now and then.

'All *right*!' he said, far too loudly. 'We'd better get a move on if we're going to this fucking Ball. You ready, Jake? Billy?'

William and Jake stood up.

Curtis turned his bug-eyed gaze on me. 'You going to get changed, Lil?'

I stared back at him. 'Are you?'

'No . . .'

I said nothing, just shrugged and got to my feet.

'I just thought –' Curtis started to say.

'What?'

'Well, you know . . . I just thought you might want to doll yourself up a bit, that's all.'

'Doll myself up a bit?'

'Yeah . . . I mean, it is a Valentine's Ball . . .'

I looked down at myself, pretending to study my clothes. I was wearing a short black skirt, ancient plimsolls, and a raggy old mohair jumper. I looked up at Curtis. 'This isn't good enough for you?'

'Yeah, of course . . . you look great. You always look great, Lili –'

'What would you *like* me to wear?' I said sarcastically. 'A swastika and a black leather bra?'

'No, no . . . I didn't mean . . . I just meant –'

'Yeah,' I sighed. 'I know what you meant.'

'Hey, come on,' he pleaded. 'Don't be like that . . . please?' He gave me his most endearing smile. 'You look fan*tas*tic, Lili. Really –'

'Yeah, all right,' I muttered. 'Let's just get going, shall we?'

And before he had a chance to say anything else, I crossed the room, opened the door, and started heading down the stairs. Curtis came scampering after me, followed closely by Jake and William, and although Curtis had enough sense to leave me alone for the moment, he just couldn't leave it.

'Doesn't she look great, Jake?' I heard him say. 'I mean, *doesn't* she?'

'Uh huh . . .'

'Just *look* at her.'

'Yeah.'

'Billy?'

'What?'

'What do you think?'

'About what?'

'Lili . . . how do *you* think she looks?'

'Oh, right, yeah . . . I think she looks fine.'

That was it, I couldn't take any more. I stopped suddenly and turned round, glaring angrily at Curtis. 'All *right*!' I snapped. 'That's *enough*! Jesus Christ . . . just fucking leave it now, OK?'

Smiling broadly at me, he held up his hands. 'OK, OK . . . I'm sorry . . .'

'Not another *word*, all right?'

Still smiling, he held his lips together and mimed turning a key.

'Shit,' I muttered, turning round and continuing down the stairs.

*

The next time he spoke, we were standing on the platform at Seven Sisters underground, waiting for the tube. I heard him muttering something to Jake, and then I saw him glance at William, and then I heard him say, in a stupid mock-Irish accent, 'Oh, roight, yeah . . . I tink she looks foin.' And as he laughed, too loudly again, and gave William a playful shove on the shoulder, I really felt like killing him. It was just such a pathetic thing to do, making fun not only of William's accent but also – and, in a way, this was even worse – mocking the words that Curtis himself had forced William to say about me just a few minutes earlier. He'd even got the accent completely wrong. Not that it really mattered, but Curtis's stereotypical thick Irish brogue was absolutely nothing like William's distinct Belfast accent.

I really hated Curtis then.

But I didn't say anything to him.

I thought if I did, it'd just make things worse. And William seemed to be dealing with it perfectly well anyway. He was giving Curtis that steady-eyed look again, the smile that had bothered Curtis so much before, and this time it wasn't quite so unreadable to me: it was the lazy kind of look that a lion gives a zebra when it's not hungry.

Things got even worse on the tube journey. It was a long trip, all the way down to London Bridge underground, and at some point I think Curtis must have taken another pill or another tab of acid or something, because as the journey progressed he gradually became more and more out of control – singing and laughing, acting really weirdly, being incredibly rude to complete strangers . . . it was excruciating. So much so that even Jake began to look a little bit flustered.

As Curtis got to his feet again and started bellowing out the words to 'Naked' while lurching all over the place with the movement of the tube, William, who was sitting next to me, leaned over and spoke in my ear.

'I think it might be a good idea if you got him to sit down.'

'Yeah, I know,' I said, whispering loudly above the roar of the train. 'I'm *really* sorry about this . . . he's not usually *quite* so bad. I mean, I know how embarrassing it is –'

'It's not that,' William said. 'Some F Troop boys just got on the next carriage at the last stop and they've been eyeing up your man for a few minutes now. If he doesn't sit down and shut up, there's going to be trouble.'

I looked through the connecting door into the next carriage and saw half a dozen or so tattooed skinheads. They were all watching Curtis with naked hatred in their eyes. It was a look I'd get used to over the coming months – the look of the skinhead or teddy boy or biker who wanted to beat up a punk – but this was the first time I'd ever witnessed it. And I didn't like it at all. I glanced over at Jake to see if he was going to do anything, but he was just sitting there with a weird kind of half-stoned, half-scared-to-death look on his face.

'Curtis!' I said, starting to get up. 'Curtis, that's enough –'

'Leave him,' William said, putting his hand on my shoulder and gently easing me back into the seat. 'It's too late now. They're going to get him whether he stops singing or not.'

I looked back at the skinheads again. They'd all moved towards the connecting door now and were clearly intent on getting to Curtis. He was aware of them now, and there was no doubt that he *knew* they were after him, but that didn't deter him from singing and shouting. In fact, he'd started to sing *at* them now, taunting them, leaning forward and yelling at the top of his voice – '*NAKED! NAKED! NAKED! NAKED!*' – and I knew that William was right, it was pointless trying to stop him.

'What's F Troop?' I asked William, just for the sake of something to say.

'Football hooligans, Millwall boys. Don't stare at them.'

I looked away. 'Are they coming through the door?'

'They're trying it . . .'

I heard the door rattling . . . then a fist slamming hard on the glass. I heard Curtis laughing . . . then yelling again.

'*NAKED! NAKED! NAKED! NAKED!*'

'The connecting door's locked,' William said.

'What will they do now?'

'Wait for the next stop.'

'*NAKED! NAKED!*'

More fists slammed against the glass. Shouts rang out – 'You wanker! You're fucking dead! You're all fucking dead!'

'*NAKED! NAKED!*'

And now I could feel the train slowing down . . . we were pulling into a station. And I was petrified. I felt sick. Any second now, the doors were going to open, the skinheads were going to jump out, run along the platform, jump into our carriage . . .

I looked down at my hands.

They were shaking.

'Wait for me at London Bridge,' I heard William say.

I looked at him. He'd got to his feet and was watching the skinheads as they gathered round the doors of their carriage, waiting for the train to stop.

'What?' I said.

William smiled. 'Just wait for me at London Bridge, OK?'

'What are you *doing*?'

But the train had pulled to a stop now, and William had moved away from me and was standing at the doors, waiting for them to open. Curtis was still bawling away like a lunatic . . .

'*I'M NAKED! YOU'RE NAKED! WE'RE ALL FUCKING NAKED!*'

. . . and I was too frightened, too confused, too totally mixed up to do anything. All I could do was sit there and watch as the doors slid open with a weary hiss, and William – incredibly –

stepped out onto the platform and moved calmly towards the skinheads, who were piling out of their carriage and racing towards ours. I thought he'd had it then. I was fully expecting the skinheads to simply launch into him, punch him to the ground, kick the shit out of him, then carry on into our carriage. But as William approached them, smiling pleasantly and holding up his hands, I saw the two leading skinheads hesitate for a moment, looking slightly confused. And that was all William needed. He went up and said something to the first one – a huge young man with horns tattooed either side of his forehead – and although I couldn't hear anything above the echoed roar of the tube station, I could see the effect that William's words had on the skinhead. He froze for a moment, and then almost immediately his eyes filled with rage and he spat in William's face. William didn't react at all. He just stood there, watching as the first skinhead turned to the others and yelled at them, pointing at William, telling them, I guessed, what William had just told him. Their reaction was the same as his – a sudden surge of rage – and as they all started moving menacingly towards William, that's when he made his move. In a blur of speed, he grabbed the big skinhead by the shoulders, jumped in the air, and hammered his forehead into the skinhead's face. And then, before the others had a chance to grab him, he leapt to one side, kicked the second skinhead in the groin, and sped off along the platform.

The train doors were closing now, but the skinheads weren't bothered. They'd forgotten all about Curtis. The big one was staggering around holding his face, his nose broken, blood streaming everywhere. The second one had collapsed to his knees and was moaning and cursing in agony. And the rest of them were now stampeding along the platform after William. As the train began pulling away, I got to my feet and went over to the doors, desperate to see if William was getting away. The train picked up speed, rattling and roaring towards the tunnel, and as it passed the chasing pack of skinheads I could see them shouting and yelling at each other as they ran, pointing up ahead . . . and then, a second or two later, just as the train entered the tunnel, I caught a very quick glimpse of William running at top speed down a dark little corridor marked NO EXIT, STAFF ONLY . . .

And then he was gone.

15

There were plenty of times back then when I wondered why I stayed with Curtis. Why did I put up with him? Why did I tolerate his increasingly uncaring and chaotic behaviour? Why didn't I just face up to the truth – that he was spiralling out of control, that he was hurting me more and more, and that for a lot of the time I was finding it really hard to actually *like* him any more, let alone love him . . .?

Why *was* I still with him?

Looking back on it now, I think there were probably a thousand different mixed-up reasons, but I'm sure a big part of it was that I'd never really been shown much affection before – growing up with no father, and not much of a mother – and now that I'd been given at least some kind of love, I just couldn't bear to let it go. I needed it. And no matter how *wrong* it was to stay with Curtis, no matter how painful things had become, the idea of *not* being with him any more, of being on my own again, was even more painful.

And I think, deep down, that I probably equated being on my own with being like my mother, and the thought of ending up like her was absolutely terrifying.

It's hardly an ideal reason for staying with someone, I know. But back then I don't think I was even aware of it. All I knew at the time was that there was something inside me – something much stronger than rationality and common sense – that wouldn't let me leave Curtis, whether *I* wanted to or not.

*

That night, as the tube train disappeared into the dark roar of the tunnel, I stood by the train doors for a while, staring forlornly at the blackened reflections in the glass, trying to calm the fear and anger beating in my heart. Curtis wasn't singing or shouting any more, and I couldn't see him anywhere in the reflected glass, so I guessed that he'd either sat down or moved along the carriage or something . . . not that I cared where he was. I really didn't. For the second time that night, the only thing I felt for Curtis was hatred.

It was Jake who finally came over and spoke to me. 'Come on, Lili,' he said. 'It's all right now –'

'Yeah?' I snapped back at him. 'You think so?'

'Curt didn't know what he was doing –'

'He *never* knows what he's fucking doing, does he?'

'Yeah, I know,' Jake sighed. 'I know . . .' He gently touched my arm. 'Come on, why don't we sit down?'

I glanced behind him and saw Curtis slumped in a seat. He wasn't asleep – his eyes were open – but he didn't seem particularly conscious either. He was just sitting there, perfectly still, staring at nothing, as if he was in a trance. There was an empty seat next to him, but I didn't want to be anywhere near him just now, so I turned away from the doors and started heading for another empty seat further along the carriage. I had to pass Curtis on the way, and I had no intention whatsoever of even looking his way as I passed, but just as I drew level with him I heard his voice.

'Hey, Lili . . . how's it going?'

And he sounded so infuriatingly casual, as if everything was perfectly all right, that my rage boiled over and I stopped in front of him, glaring angrily into his face.

'*What* did you say?' I hissed at him.

He just stared at me for a moment, then he blinked a couple of times and shook his head, and then – with a puzzled grin – he said, 'What's going on? Are we there yet? What time is it?'

I didn't bother answering, I just shook my head in despair.

'What?' he said, gazing around the carriage. 'Where is everyone?' He looked back at me, grinning crookedly. 'Where's Billy the Kid, Lil?'

'Saving your life, you cretin.'

And, with that, I walked off and left him to it.

The rest of the journey passed off without incident. I sat on my own, not speaking to anyone, just seething quietly to myself. Jake went over and sat next to Curtis. And Curtis, after jabbering incoherently to Jake for a while, suddenly slumped back into his trance-like state and stayed there, silent and motionless, until we got to London Bridge.

Jake had to help him off the train and up the escalators when we got there, and I'm sure he would have liked some help from me, but he didn't get it. I went on ahead of them, stopping only when I got to the ticket hall. *Wait for me at London Bridge*, William had said, and that's what I was going to do. I was going to wait. Whatever Jake and Curtis wanted to do, I was going to wait . . . it was the least I could do.

It was *all* I could do.

I found a spot with a good all-round view of the ticket hall, leaned against a wall, and set about waiting.

A few minutes later, I saw Jake and Curtis coming towards me. Curtis was still looking pretty spaced out, weaving around and staggering from side to side, but at least he was walking unaided now. And despite the bugged-out glassiness of his eyes, he seemed to be regaining some kind of awareness of what was going on. In fact, as he came up to me, smiling and running his fingers through his hair, there was even a slight hint of remorse on his face.

'You all right, Lili?' he asked quietly.

'Yeah, great,' I said coldly. 'Never been better.'

He smiled nervously, looking around. 'Where's Billy?'

I just shook my head, utterly speechless. I didn't know if he was pretending to have forgotten what had happened, or if he genuinely couldn't remember. But it didn't matter. Either way, it was pathetic. And he could stand there giving me his poor-little-boy smile as much as he liked, he wasn't getting my forgiveness this time.

I shook my head again, sighed, and looked away.

'Jake?' I heard him say. 'What the fuck's going on?'

And Jake started telling him. He actually stood there and told him what had happened, telling it as if Curtis hadn't been there – the singing and the shouting, the skinheads, the train stopping, William getting off . . .

'He got off the train?' Curtis said.

'Yeah . . .'

'Why?'

'Jesus Christ . . .' I muttered.

'What?' Curtis snapped, turning to me. 'What the *fuck's* the matter with you now?'

'What's the matter with *me*?'

'Yeah.'

I sighed. 'You just don't get it, do you?'

'Get what?'

'*Every*thing . . . *any*thing . . . I mean, you're just so –'

'Where's the toilets in this place?' he said, totally ignoring me and looking around the ticket hall. 'I'm absolutely *dying* for a piss.' He grinned at me. 'Sorry, Lil, but I *really* need to go. Do you know where they are?'

When I didn't answer him, he turned to Jake. 'Any idea?'

Jake shook his head.

Curtis lit a cigarette and looked around the hall again. 'Yeah, well . . . I'd better go and find them.' He turned back to Jake. 'You wait here, OK?'

Jake nodded, and Curtis wandered off without so much as a glance at me.

I really wanted to leave then. I just wanted to get back on the tube, get back to Hampstead, get into my bed and sink down into the solitary darkness. Forget about everything. Just go to sleep and dream of nothing.

'He can't help it,' I heard Jake say.

I looked wearily at him.

'Curtis . . .' he muttered. 'I mean, I know he can be really difficult sometimes –'

'Jake?' I said.

'What?'

'Just shut up, OK?'

Fifteen minutes later, when Curtis still hadn't returned, I began to wonder what had happened to him. I didn't *want* to be concerned, and it kind of annoyed me that I was, but there wasn't much I could do about it. It was getting pretty late by then, and the ticket hall wasn't that busy, but there was still a regular stream of people coming in and out of the station. A lot of them had clearly been drinking, and although me and Jake were both dressed relatively conservatively – I mean, we didn't look *too* outrageous or anything – we were still obviously quite different to everyone else, and that was enough to draw their attention. It was mostly just dirty looks and muttered curses, the odd shouted insult or two, and at one point someone lobbed a half-empty beer can in Jake's general direction . . . but that was as far as it went.

Saturday-night drunks.

Saturday-night violence.

Find someone who's not the same as you, and laughingly beat the shit out of them.

I didn't want be there any more.

I didn't want to be part of this . . . whatever it was. I just wanted to go home and forget about everything . . . just go to sleep and sink down into the solitary darkness –

'Thanks for waiting.'

The sudden voice startled me for a moment, and the fear must have shown in my face, because when I looked up and found myself gazing into William Bonney's clear hazel eyes, the first thing he said was, 'Sorry, I didn't mean to scare you.' Considering everything that had happened, William seemed remarkably calm and composed. As I jabbered away at him, asking him a dozen disjointed questions, he just stood there smiling at me, waiting for me to finish, then he asked Jake for a cigarette, took his time lighting it, took a long drag, and blew out a stream of smoke with an audible sigh of satisfaction.

'So . . .' he said slowly. 'You got here all right then?'

'Yeah, yeah,' I said, trying to hide my impatience. 'But what about *you*? Did you get away from them all right?'

'The skinheads?'

'Yes, the skinheads.'

He just shrugged. 'They weren't up to much.'

'What do you mean?'

He smiled. 'I've run away from a lot worse than them before.'

'But why did they go after you in the first place? I mean, what did you say to them to make them so angry?'

He grinned again. 'I told them I was IRA.'

'You what?'

'IRA,' he repeated. 'I told them I was in the IRA.' He laughed quietly. 'If there's one thing a skinhead hates more than anything else, it's a Provo. They can't *stand* them.'

I didn't know what to say for a moment. I just couldn't believe what he'd done, the risk he'd taken, the danger he'd put himself in, and all for the sake of three people he'd known for less than a day . . . one of whom had caused all the trouble in the first place.

'Where is he, anyway?' William said. 'Where's Curtis?'

I was just about to say 'Who cares?' when I heard a carefree shout from across the ticket hall:

'Hey! There he is! *There's* my Billy boy!'

And we all turned to see Curtis swaggering across the hall towards us, grinning crazily and waving his hands.

'*Billy!*' he cried, coming up to William and giving him an overzealous hug. 'My *hero* . . . you saved my *life*, man!'

He wasn't serious, of course – he *couldn't* be serious – he was just trying to make a big joke out of it, as he always did when he didn't know how to deal with something. But that wasn't what annoyed me the most. No, what annoyed me the most was how he'd suddenly seemed to have regained his memory about what had happened on the tube train.

'I owe you one, Billy,' he was saying now. 'Really . . . I mean, Jesus . . . you're an honest-to-God fucking *hero*. Here, have a cigarette . . .'

'Thanks,' William said, taking a cigarette from Curtis's packet even though he was already smoking one. 'I'll save it for Ron,' he said, smiling and tucking the cigarette behind his ear.

'Ron who?' Curtis said.

'Later Ron.'

Curtis frowned for a moment, then all of sudden he got the joke and began laughing and cackling as if it was the funniest thing he'd ever heard. 'Later *Ron* . . . yeah, good one, I like it . . . later on . . .'

William just stood there, smiling quietly, like a patient parent putting up with an overexcited child. And that was another thing I was really annoyed about – Curtis's sudden overexcitement. Which, of course, was the result of whatever he'd taken during his unnecessarily long 'trip to the toilet'. And whatever it was – and my guess was speed – I was pretty sure that he'd taken a *lot* of it. His eyes were as big as saucers, his face was drained white, and he was twitching so much it looked like his skin was alive.

'Yeah, yeah, anyway,' he said to no one in particular. 'Yeah . . .

so are we going to this fucking party or what? Jake? Do you know where it is?'

'I thought *you* knew.'

'Yeah . . . yeah, I know where it is.' He gazed quickly around the ticket hall, pointed to one exit, then changed his mind and pointed to another. 'It's this way, come on . . .'

I looked at William. 'Do you want to go? I mean, it's probably nearly over by now –'

'Course he wants to go,' Curtis said, grabbing William by the arm. 'You want to go, don't you, Billy?'

William looked down at Curtis's hand on his arm.

Curtis took the hint, grinned sheepishly, and let go.

William turned to me. 'Well, I really don't mind what we do, to be honest. But seeing as we're already here, and it's taken most of the night to get here . . .' He shrugged his shoulders and smiled. 'But, like I said, I really don't mind.'

I looked back at him for a few seconds, deliberately ignoring Curtis, and I was fairly sure that if I told William the truth – that I didn't want to go to the party, that I just wanted to go home – he'd probably offer to get the tube back with me, and for a moment or two I actually found myself imagining it . . . sitting on the tube with William, feeling safe and comfortable, the two of us just talking about things, or not talking about anything if we felt like it . . . and then, when the tube finally got to Hampstead, he'd shyly offer to walk me back home, and I'd just *know* that there'd be no strings attached, that he wouldn't be trying anything on, and I might even find myself wishing that he would . . .

And then a shout rang out from across the ticket hall – 'Fucking *weirdos*!' – and Curtis yelled back – 'Fuck off!' – and as I looked at him, and he looked back at me, grinning with idiot pride, I realized, with a silent sigh of resignation, that I wasn't going home without him.

I couldn't, could I?

For a thousand different mixed-up reasons . . .
I just couldn't.

'Come on, then,' I said wearily. 'Let's get it over with.'

16

I don't know how we ever found the studio where the Valentine's Ball was taking place, because Curtis was the only one who knew where it was – at least, he kept *telling* us he knew where it was – and all he kept doing was running around the maze of South London side streets, shouting at everyone he came across – 'Hey, d'you know Andrew Logan? Do you know where Butler's Wharf is?' And when that didn't work – mainly because most people thought he was a lunatic – he just put his hands to his mouth, raised his head to the cold night sky, and started screaming at the top of his voice:

'*HEY, MALCOLM! JOHNNY! WHERE THE FUCK ARE YOU?*'

Unsurprisingly, this didn't get us very far either.

Eventually, though, after stumbling around the streets for what seemed like a lifetime, we somehow managed to get close enough to the studio to hear the distant boom of the music blaring out. Even from a distance, you could tell it was incredibly loud. And very raucous. And unmistakably angry.

'That's the Pistols,' Curtis said.

All we had to do then was follow the sound of the music.

It was utter mayhem when we finally got there. The Sex Pistols were still playing, and Johnny Rotten was *completely* off his head – crawling around on the beer-soaked floor, bug-eyed and rotten-toothed, howling and sneering like a madman – and the

rest of the band were pretty much out of it too. The studio itself was all decked out with weird sculptures and mannequins,
shop fittings and film scenery, and the place was absolutely jam-
packed with a seething crowd of very loud, very drunk, and
very stoned people. I recognized quite a few of them. The usual
McLaren/Sex Pistols crowd was there, and a bunch of others
who I found out later were (or had been, or would be) members
of the Clash and/or the Banshees and/or the soon-to-be-defunct
London SS. But there were all kinds of other people there too
– journalists, film-makers, photographers, artists, oddballs . . .
most of them drinking and posing and doing their best to out-
shock one another.

It was a nightmare.

A circus from hell.

Curtis, of course, couldn't get enough of it. As soon as
we got there he started zipping around all over the place
like a crazed tornado – talking to anyone and everyone, waving
his hands around, laughing and shouting, chain-smoking
cigarettes and guzzling wine from a bottle – and for the first
half-hour or so he insisted on dragging me and William around
with him.

'This is Billy,' he told everyone he came across. 'Billy the Kid,
our new guitar player. He's a fucking *genius*. He's going to make
us big. You watch . . . he's a fucking *star*. Hey, Malcolm! Come
over here . . . *Malcolm*! This is Billy, Billy the Kid . . .'

And on and on and on . . .

Throughout all this, William didn't do or say very much at all,
he just kept smiling, nodding his head, shaking hands, occasionally glancing at me . . . and, as usual, I wasn't saying or doing
anything either. I was just going along with it all – trying not to
look too bored, trying not to hate everything too much, trying
not to keep looking round to see if Charlie Brown was there . . .

It was hard work.

And when Johnny Rotten started making a commotion on

stage – shouting and swearing, throwing the mike stand around, smashing up the band's equipment – and everyone in the room was suddenly drawn to his manic behaviour, William and I were both thankful for the opportunity to slope off to the back of the studio and get away from everyone else for a while. As we sat down on the floor and leaned back against the wall, I could hear Malcolm McLaren's excited voice urging Jordan to take off her clothes. All the music press were there, and I guessed he thought that a naked punk girl would do wonders for the Pistols' profile.

'Go on, Jords!' I heard him yell. 'Get 'em off!'

'No . . .'

'Go *on*!'

And then I saw her jumping up on stage – a diminutive figure dressed all in black, with a big blonde beehive haircut and heavily made-up eyes – and Johnny Rotten started tearing her clothes off, and all the photographers and film-makers started rushing to the front to get pictures . . .

'Do you know her?' I heard William say.

I looked at him. He had a cigarette in one hand, a can of lager in the other, and he was watching the spectacle on stage with a look of bemused curiosity on his face.

'She's called Jordan,' I told him. 'She works at Malcolm McLaren's shop.' I glanced over at the stage and saw that Jordan wasn't alone now. Some of her friends, including Charlie Brown, were showing themselves off for the photographers too – taking their tops off, flashing themselves about, striking outrageous poses. The music press were loving it, as were most of the men – leering, gesturing, shouting, urging the girls on. Curtis was there too, standing with Jake next to Malcolm McLaren, a half-bottle of vodka dangling from his hand. But, unlike the others, Curtis wasn't shouting or gesturing – he was just watching, silently, his whacked-out eyes fixed intently on Charlie Brown's now-naked torso.

'Why are some of them wearing swastikas?' William asked me, taking a sip of lager.

'It's just a punk thing,' I told him. 'They like to shock people, to cause offence . . .'

'Why?'

I looked at him. 'I don't know, really. It's just . . .' I shrugged. 'It's just what they do.'

'Is that why Curtis acts like an idiot sometimes? To cause offence?'

I smiled. 'Curtis *is* an idiot sometimes . . . most times, actually.' I looked over at the stage again. Curtis was still just standing there, ogling Charlie Brown, and I could tell that he was incredibly drunk now. The top half of his body was wavering, moving loosely in aimless circles, and his head was lolling all over the place. I watched him take a long shuddering slug from the vodka bottle, then I turned back to William.

'Why did you do it?' I asked him.

'Do what?'

'Why did you go out of your way to save Curtis from getting beaten up?'

William shrugged. 'Why not?'

'You could have got hurt.'

He smiled. 'But I didn't.'

I looked at him. 'What's a Provo?'

'Sorry?'

'Earlier on . . . you said that skinheads hate Provos –'

'Oh, right . . . yeah.' He shrugged again. 'Provo is just a slang term really . . . the Provos, you know? The Provisional IRA.'

I nodded, pausing for a moment to glance over at Curtis, and then I looked back at William. 'You're not *really* in the IRA, are you?'

'Why?' he asked, smiling. 'What would you do if I was?'

'I don't know . . .' I shrugged. 'Not much, I suppose.'

'You wouldn't turn me in?'

For a moment or two, I really wasn't sure if he was pulling my leg or not. He was still smiling, and I was *almost* convinced that he *was* only joking, but there was just something about him – a distant glint of hidden darkness – that made me wonder . . . what if? What if he really *was* in the IRA? There'd been a series of shootings and bomb attacks in London over the last few months – Oxford Street, the Hilton Hotel, Green Park underground – and in December there'd been an armed siege at a flat in Marylebone involving four IRA men on the run from the police . . . so there was no doubt that the IRA had a presence in London at the time. Not that that *meant* anything, of course. All it meant was that it wasn't *impossible* that William was in the IRA. Extremely unlikely, yes. But not impossible. And if he really *was* a Republican terrorist – a killer, a murderer, a bomber . . .? How would that make me feel? Would I be scared of him? Would he disgust me? Would I try to understand him? Or, as he'd just suggested, would I simply turn him in?

'It's all right,' he said lightly, touching my arm. 'I'm only messing about.'

'I know you are.'

'Really?'

'Yeah . . .' I smiled at him. 'I mean, you're far too short to be a terrorist, for a start.'

'I'm not short.'

'You're not *tall*.'

'All right,' he said, grinning. 'But how do you know that the IRA don't have a specialist "midget brigade"?'

'I think I would have heard of such a thing, if it existed.'

'Not if it was a *secret* midget brigade.'

'A secret midget brigade?'

'Yeah . . .'

'Right,' I said, nodding. 'And why, exactly, would the IRA *need* a secret midget brigade?'

'I can't tell you that.'

'Why not?'

'It's a secret.'

We carried on talking for a while, mainly about Naked – how long we'd been together, how I'd joined, how many gigs we'd played . . . that kind of thing – and after about twenty minutes or so, I realized that, once again, William wasn't telling me anything about himself. He was just sitting there, smoking and drinking, perfectly content to listen to me as I prattled away, answering his questions.

But just as I realized this, and just as I was about to start asking *him* a few questions, he touched my knee and pointed across the room at Curtis. He was still near the front of the stage, but he was sitting on the floor now – cross-legged, his head slumped down on his chest, his eyes almost closed, the half-bottle of vodka in his hand empty. He was on his own, just sitting there, totally wrecked, while the party carried on all around him.

'God . . .' I sighed, shaking my head.

'It looks like he could do with a bit of help,' William said.

'He could do with *some*thing,' I muttered.

'Maybe we should get him home?'

'Yeah, I suppose . . .' I started looking around the room. 'Have you seen Jake anywhere?'

'He left about ten minutes ago.'

'He left?'

William nodded. 'He was with a girl.'

'Which girl?'

'The short blonde one with the dog collar round her neck.'

I nodded, half-remembering the girl. I didn't know who she was, but I'd seen Jake talking to her earlier on.

I looked back at Curtis. He hadn't moved.

'What time is it?' I asked William.

He shrugged. 'One thirty, two o'clock . . . something like that.'

'Really?'

'Yeah.'

'Shit,' I said. 'The underground won't be running now . . . how the hell are we going to get back?'

'Night bus?'

'Where from?' I looked at him. 'I don't even know where *we* are, let alone where the bus goes from.'

William nodded. 'We'll have to get a taxi then.'

'I haven't got enough money for a taxi. It'll cost a fortune at this time of night.'

'What about Curtis?'

I laughed. 'Curtis has *never* got any money. How about you?'

William didn't say anything, he just looked at me for a moment, then turned away and began gazing around the room as if he was searching for someone in particular. I didn't have a clue what he was doing, and I was just about to ask him, when his eyes suddenly fixed on someone on the other side of the room.

'I'll be back in a minute,' he said, getting to his feet.

'Where are you going?' I asked him.

'Nowhere,' he smiled. 'Just the toilet.'

I watched him as he walked away from me, crossing to the other side of the room, and I watched – increasingly perplexed – as he turned to the left and headed towards a group of people standing by the wall. There were about five or six of them, gathered in a semi-circle, talking animatedly about something. I didn't know who most of them were, but the one doing most of the talking was Malcolm McLaren.

As William approached the group, his gait began to change. He started staggering a bit, walking unsteadily, as if he was drunk. And then, just before he got to McLaren, I saw him look over his shoulder without stopping, as if someone had called out his name, and when he turned back he was so close to McLaren that he couldn't help stumbling into him. It looked *exactly* like a drunken accident – William wrapping his arms round McLaren to steady himself, McLaren spilling his drink and looking annoyed, William letting go of him and stepping back, wiping the spilled drink from his clothes, then holding up his hands in profuse apology . . .

McLaren shook his head, exasperated.

William carried on apologizing.

McLaren held *his* hands up – 'OK, OK . . .'

Smiling drunkenly, William said something to him. McLaren just frowned. William mimed a gunfighter drawing his pistols, then pointed over at Curtis, and I guessed he was reminding McLaren that he was Billy the Kid, the new guitarist in Curtis's band – 'Remember? Curtis introduced us earlier on . . .?'

McLaren nodded vaguely, pretending to remember – 'Oh, yeah, right . . .' and then, as William gave him a clumsy pat on the shoulder before lurching off towards the toilets, McLaren turned back to the others with a disdainful shake of his head – 'Fucking idiot . . .'

And that, for the moment, was that.

I still didn't have a clue what William was up to.

While I waited for him to come back, I looked over at Curtis again. He was still sitting down, but he'd slumped right over now – his head face down on the floor, his arms hanging loosely at his sides – and I guessed he'd probably passed out. It was really tempting to just leave him there. *Why not?* I asked myself. *Just leave him to it, let him stew in his own stupidity, go home without him . . .*

I wished I could.

After a minute or two, I saw William coming back from the toilets. He was walking normally again now – perfectly sober and steady – and there was a look of quiet satisfaction on his face. He had to pass Malcolm McLaren and the others to get back to me, and as he approached them I saw him glance ahead at a group of people coming towards him from the opposite direction. He momentarily slowed down, as if he was going to stop to let the other people past, but as they neared the spot where McLaren was standing, William speeded up again, reaching McLaren just as the others were passing him. There wasn't a lot of room, and as William pushed his way through a gap on McLaren's side, someone must have given him a shove, because he suddenly lurched to one side and bumped into McLaren again.

The encounter was a lot briefer this time.

A quick coming together, a steadying hand, a hurried apology – 'Sorry! Me again! Sorry!' – a smile, a step back, another quick smile . . . and William was gone before McLaren had a chance to say anything.

As he crossed the room back to me, I realized that – unlike almost everyone else in the room – he didn't seem to care what anyone else thought of him. He didn't look at people to see if they were watching him, he didn't try to be cool, he didn't *try* to be anything . . . he just walked across the room, true to himself, content with himself, his smiling eyes fixed on me.

'All right?' he said, stopping in front of me.

'Yeah . . .'

'Are you ready?'

'Ready for what?'

'Sleeping Beauty over there,' he said, glancing at Curtis. 'We should get him back home before he turns into a pumpkin.'

'Yeah, but I've already told you, we don't have enough money for a taxi.'

'Yeah, we do,' William said, reaching into his pocket. Making sure that no one else could see what he was doing, he pulled out a thick handful of £10 and £20 notes. 'That should be enough, shouldn't it?' he asked me.

I stared at the money for a moment – guessing the total to be at least £100 – and then I slowly looked up at William. He smiled at me. And, at last, I got it: it was Malcolm McLaren's money. William had stolen his wallet when he'd first 'drunkenly' stumbled into him. He'd taken the wallet into the toilet, removed all the cash, then replaced the wallet in McLaren's pocket when he'd bumped into him again on the way back.

'You're a wicked person, William Bonney,' I said, smiling.

He smiled back at me. 'You don't know the half of it.'

It was quite a struggle getting Curtis to his feet and out of the studio, but between the two of us we just about managed it in the end. It was a cold night outside, the streets veiled with a misty rain, but luckily we didn't have to wait long for a taxi. Unfortunately, though, as the cab slowed down and pulled in to the kerb, the driver took one look at Curtis, shook his head, and drove off without stopping.

'Great,' I muttered, wiping rain from my face.

'It's all right,' William said, peering up the street. 'There's another one coming.' He glanced over at Curtis, who was half-slumped, half-leaning against a wall, then he turned to me. 'Can you see if you can make him look a bit less wrecked?'

I went over to Curtis, grabbed him by the shoulders, and straightened him up. His eyes half-opened and he started to moan.

'Shut up, Curtis,' I told him. 'Just keep quiet and stand up straight, OK?'

'*Unnhh . . .?*'

I took hold of his face in both hands, leaned in close, and whispered harshly at him, '*Please . . . shut . . . UP!*'

He stared at me for a moment – his eyes all bloodshot and bleary – then he sighed heavily and dropped his head. I breathed out, almost gagging on the alcohol stink of his breath, and looked back at William. The taxi was just pulling up beside him now. It stopped, William approached it, and the driver wound down his window.

'Where to, mate?'

'Seven Sisters, please.'

The driver looked over at Curtis and me. 'Are they with you?' he asked William.

144

'Yeah . . .'

'No way,' the driver said shaking his head. 'I'm not having him puke up in the back of my cab. Sorry, mate.'

As he turned away and started to wind up the window, William stepped forward and put his hand on the glass. 'How much do you want?' he said to the driver.

'Get your fucking hand off –'

'Fifty quid?'

The driver looked at him.

William said, 'And if he throws up, I'll give you another ten. How's that?'

The driver thought about it for a moment, then said, 'Sixty up front, and you're on.'

'OK.'

'But if he makes any trouble –'

'He won't.'

We didn't speak for a while as the black cab rumbled along through the rainy South London streets, we just sat together in the back of the taxi – Curtis on my right, William on my left – the three of us lost in our own inner worlds. Curtis was slumped against the window, snoring and drooling and occasionally muttering unintelligibly to himself; William was gazing quietly out of the window, watching the streets pass by; and I was just staring blindly at the raindrops on the glass, trying not to think about anything at all. I wanted to forget everything, to empty my mind, to leave all the chaos and crap behind . . .

But it wasn't easy.

Because the thing about things that have just happened – especially the things that you wish *hadn't* happened . . . well, that's just the thing: you can't make them unhappen. You *can't* just leave them behind, because once they've happened, they're part of you, part of your past, and their memories become part of your present, and their consequences become part of your future.

Things that happen *become* you.

And you can never leave yourself behind.

I turned to William. 'You got it wrong.'

He looked at me. 'Sorry?'

'About Sleeping Beauty and the pumpkin . . . you got it all wrong.'

'Did I?'

I nodded. 'It was Cinderella who went to the ball, not Sleeping Beauty. And neither of them turned into a pumpkin. That was Cinderella's coach. If she didn't get home before midnight, her coach would turn back into a pumpkin.'

'Right . . .' William said.

I smiled at him. 'I just thought you'd like to know, that's all.'

'Yeah, well . . . thanks. Thanks for pointing out my mistake.'

'No problem.'

He smiled at me.

I said, 'Do you mind if I ask you a question?'

'Is it about fairy tales?'

'No, it's not about fairy tales.'

'In that case, no . . . I don't mind.'

'You stole Malcolm McLaren's wallet, didn't you?'

He shook his head. 'I didn't steal his wallet, I just borrowed it so I could steal his money. I gave his *wallet* back to him.'

'Right,' I said, 'OK . . . but you still picked his pocket, didn't you?'

'I did, yeah.'

'Why? I mean, you could have just asked him to *lend* us some money.'

William shook his head again. 'That would have been begging.'

'No –'

'I don't beg for anything.'

'You'd rather steal?'

'Yep.'

I didn't say anything for a while, I just looked at him, wondering if he was going to say anything else. I'm not sure what I was expecting – an explanation, perhaps . . . some kind of justification – but I knew in my heart that I was wasting my time. He did what he did; he didn't need to *justify* it to anyone.

'Can I ask you something else?' I said.

'Sure,' he said, smiling again. 'Ask away.'

'How come you know how to pick pockets?'

'Ah, well . . . now that's a long story.'

'We've got a long way to go,' I said, glancing out of the cab window.

'Maybe some other time.'

I gave him a look – slightly disappointed, but not really surprised – and said, 'All right then, let me ask you something else. How long have you lived in London?'

'Two years.'

'And you moved here from Belfast, right?'

'That's right.'

'Why?'

'Why what? Why did I move here? Or why did I leave Belfast?'

'Both.'

He grinned. 'I thought you were only going to ask me one question.'

'I never said that.'

'No, but that's what you implied.'

'I didn't *imply* anything. All I said was that I wanted to ask you something else –'

'Exactly . . . some*thing* else. Singular.'

'Stop changing the subject.'

'I'm not changing the –'

'Why did you leave Belfast?'

Something changed in him then, something in his eyes. It didn't last long, but I definitely saw a momentary flicker of darkness, a darkness borne of pain and sorrow . . . and worse. And his eyes held a warning too – *don't go there*. But whether it was meant for me, or whether it was just an instinctive reminder to himself to stay away from the darkness, I just couldn't tell.

'I'm sorry,' I started to say. 'I'm being too nosy –'

'No, it's all right,' he said, bringing the lightness back to his face. 'It's just . . . it's nothing. It was just . . . family reasons, you know . . . that's why I left Belfast.' He shrugged. 'Just family stuff.'

I nodded, as if I understood. Which I didn't, of course. But I didn't want to push him any further. Not yet, anyway.

'So,' I said breezily. 'Is it very different here?'

'Different than Belfast, you mean?'

'Yeah.'

He grinned. 'A *little* bit, yeah.'

'In what way?'

'Well, London's a lot bigger, for a start. And there's a lot more people here. I mean, in Belfast, if I go into town, I'm almost *guaranteed* to meet at least half a dozen people I know. But here, you never see the same person twice. Which is actually kind of nice, once you get used to it. And another thing I like about London is that you don't get stopped and searched every time you go into a shop or a pub or something.'

'Is that what happens in Belfast?'

'Yeah, all the time. You can't go anywhere without getting pushed up against a wall by a squaddy. Especially if you're . . .'

I looked at him. 'If you're what?'

He gazed out of the window and sighed. 'It's different here . . . I mean, it's a completely different world. In Belfast . . . well, you can't know what it's like unless you know what it's like.'

'I don't understand.'

He nodded his head at the passing streets. 'If we were in Belfast, every one of these streets would be either Catholic or Protestant. They might even be Catholic on one side and Protestant on the other. And whichever you are, Catholic or Protestant, you're born into hating the other side.' He looked at me. 'If this was Belfast, and the driver there was a Protestant, he wouldn't have stopped to pick me up. And if he was a Catholic, and this was a Protestant area . . . well, we wouldn't actually be here, because a Catholic cabbie would *never* drive through a Protestant area. But if he did, and I was sitting in the back, we'd both be absolutely shitting ourselves.' William paused for a moment, his eyes lowered, seemingly lost in thought. Then, after letting out another long sigh, he looked back up at me again and said, 'That's it really. That's how it is.'

When we finally got back to Seven Sisters, William helped me get Curtis out of the taxi and we walked him up to the front door of the squat. He was still only semi-conscious, walking like a zombie, and I was pretty sure that he had no idea where he was.

'Do you want me to help you get him inside?' William asked.

'No, I'll be all right now, thanks.'

'Sure?'

'Yeah,' I said, smiling at him. 'You've done more than enough for us as it is. You should just get on home now.'

As I said this, the taxi driver put his cab into gear and started pulling away from the kerb.

'*Hey!*' I called out after him. '*HEY! Just a minute* –'

'It's OK,' William said calmly. 'Let him go.'

'Yeah, but you paid him –'

'Really, it's all right. I don't mind walking from here. It's not far.'

'But it's raining.'

He smiled. 'I like the rain. It reminds me of home.'

'Are you sure? I mean, there's probably a spare room in here somewhere –'

'Thanks, but I'd better get back.'

'OK . . .'

'Billy?' Curtis suddenly spluttered. 'Is that Billy?'

We both looked at him. He was leaning against the porch wall, and he was trying to turn his head to focus on William . . . but he wasn't really succeeding. It was as if his head was simply far too heavy for him to control. So, after a few moments, he gave up, letting his head loll back against the wall.

'Billy?' he mumbled. 'Right, uhh, yeah . . . t'morrow . . . OK? Yeah . . . seven, yeah? R'earsal . . . seven . . . shit . . .'

He groaned, heaved, clutched his stomach, then doubled over and threw up.

17

By seven thirty the next night, when William still hadn't turned up at the warehouse for the rehearsal, I was fairly sure that I was never going to see him again. He'd obviously changed his mind about joining the band, and after everything that had happened the night before, I didn't really blame him. I mean, why would anyone in their right mind want to throw in their lot with a walking disaster like Curtis? It just wasn't worth all the hassle, was it?

I looked across at him now – sitting on a wooden crate, picking away at his guitar, his face deathly white, his eyes ringed with heavy black circles.

He'd been unusually quiet all day.

After finally waking up around midday, he'd spent most of the afternoon either throwing up or just lying in bed, moaning and groaning, and I'm sure that was part of the reason for his uncharacteristic silence. But it was also his way of saying sorry. Sorry I fucked up. Sorry for embarrassing you. Sorry for putting you through hell again. Of course, it would have meant a lot more to me if he'd actually *said* he was sorry, and I would have appreciated it if – while he was at it – he'd thanked me for looking after him too.

But that wasn't Curtis's way.

And, unlike William, I didn't seem able to just take it or leave it. I just had to take it. Which made me think that, unlike William, I wasn't quite right in my mind.

'What time is it now?' I heard Curtis call out.

'Twenty to eight,' Jake replied.

Curtis looked over at me. 'He's not coming, is he?'

I wasn't *strictly* not speaking to Curtis, but I was avoiding it whenever possible. Like now. So I didn't answer him, I just shrugged.

He glanced over at Stan. 'What do you think? Shall we just get started without him?'

Stan shrugged too.

Curtis lit a cigarette and turned to Jake. 'Do you want to go up to the phone box and try ringing him?'

'He's not on the phone,' Jake said.

'What?'

'That's what he told me. He hasn't got a phone.'

'Shit . . .' Curtis muttered.

And that's when the warehouse door opened and William walked in. He was dressed exactly the same as the day before – same jacket, same shirt, same trousers – and he was carrying two guitar cases, one in each hand. As he shut the door and came over to us, the pall of lethargy that had been hanging over the whole room suddenly seemed to evaporate. It was as if a light had been turned on.

'Sorry I'm late,' he said. 'I got held up.' He smiled at me. 'You all right?'

'Yeah . . . yeah,' I said. 'I'm fine, thanks.'

He turned to Curtis. 'How are you feeling today?'

'Yeah, great,' Curtis said grumpily, staring at the guitar cases. 'What have you got there?'

'Well,' William said, putting the guitar cases on the floor. 'I couldn't get a Gibson Les Paul, like you suggested, but I managed to get these.' He opened up the two cases, revealing two Fender Telecasters. One of them looked brand new, its Sunburst finish still glossy and sleek, but the other one was clearly pretty old, its pale butterscotch body covered in dents and scratches. 'Will they do?' William asked Curtis.

Curtis was virtually drooling at the sight of the guitars. 'Are these *yours*?' he said, not quite believing his eyes.

'They're *ours*,' William told him.

'Ours?'

'Yeah . . .' He looked at Curtis. 'You said you could do with another guitar, didn't you?'

'Well, yeah, but –'

'You can have whichever one you want,' William said. 'I mean, I don't mind having the crappy old one . . .'

Curtis stared open-mouthed at him. 'You *are* joking, aren't you?'

'No, you can have the new one –'

'That's a '68 Telecaster,' Curtis said, almost reverentially, indicating the older guitar. 'It might even be a '66. That's like . . . I mean, that's like the *god* of guitars.'

'Really?'

Curtis shook his head in utter disbelief. 'Where did you *get* them from?'

'It's probably best if you don't ask,' William said.

'Are they stolen?'

'Well, like I said . . .'

'Don't ask.'

'Right.'

Curtis turned back to the guitars, his face a picture of pure delight. He looked like a child on Christmas morning.

'So . . .' William said, sharing a smile with me. 'Are we going to practise or what?'

By the end of that week, William had learned all the songs and we were more than ready to start playing as a four-piece band again. And when we did start playing – at the Conway Arms on Friday night – we all knew, straight away, that something special had happened. We'd always been a great band, with great songs and tons of energy, and Curtis had always been a stunningly good, and naturally mesmeric, frontman. But now that William had joined us, we'd suddenly become so much more than just a great band. We were a *special* band now. The kind of band that really *means* something. William's presence had taken us to a different level.

It's hard to describe exactly what it was that William gave us. There was his guitar playing, of course, which somehow managed to make every song sound a hundred times better. And his singing, his understated harmonies, which added tones to Curtis's vocals that simply hadn't existed before. And then there was his stage presence – his weird little dancing movements, his jerky legs and twitching feet – and the way he somehow induced us all to interact with one another on stage, creating a sense of energy and emotion that mirrored the music and gave it more passion.

But above and beyond all these things – as crucial and pivotal as they were – it was William's relationship with Curtis that changed us the most. Again, it's a difficult process to explain, and it was a relationship that was to change so much over the coming months that it's almost pointless trying to describe it, but in those early days – before it all began to go wrong – there was an incredibly strong creative dynamism between the two of them.

It was clear from the start that Curtis respected William as a musician. And although his attitude towards him as a *person* wasn't quite so clear – at least, not at first – it was obvious to me that, while he'd never admit it, Curtis was slightly in awe of him. He'd do virtually anything to disguise it – mocking William all the time, teasing him, laughing at him – but there was always an underlying feeling that if ever William told him to stop, or told him to shut up, or just looked at him in a certain way, Curtis wouldn't hesitate to do what he was told.

But William never did tell him to shut up.

He was always content to just smile quietly to himself and totally ignore him.

And when William began making suggestions about how to improve some of our songs, which he did after a couple of weeks, Curtis not only listened to him – albeit grudgingly at first – but in the end he actually *agreed* with him. Which, for Curtis, was almost unheard of. But there was no doubt that William's input *did* make the songs better.

One of the first things he questioned was why we played everything so fast.

'We're a punk band, that's why,' Curtis told him. 'We play loud and fast.'

'Yeah, but why?'

'Why not?' Curtis grinned.

'I just think –'

'It's all about *energy*, OK?' Curtis snapped. 'It's about power and speed, simplicity. Three-minute songs, no solos, no fucking about –'

'Just like everyone else, you mean?'

'What?'

'All the other punk bands. You want to sound just like them?'

'No, of course not –'

'I thought punk was supposed to be about doing your own thing?'

'Well, yeah . . .'

'So why copy everyone else?'

'It's not *copying*, it's just . . .'

'Listen, Curtis,' William said quietly. 'You write really good songs, OK? I mean, they're *really* good songs. But you don't need to play them all at a hundred miles an hour. They've got enough energy already. And they'll sound even better, and even more powerful, if you play them just a little bit slower.' He looked at Curtis. 'The energy doesn't come from how fast you play, it comes from the song itself. The power comes from the *way* you play, not the speed. Look, I'll show you what I mean.'

And he showed us, playing the chords to 'Stupid' at a slower speed and with a slightly different rhythm, and he was right – it did sound better. More powerful, more emotional, more energetic, more everything. And it was the same with most of the other songs too. A slight change in tempo here, a different rhythm there . . . and, all at once, it was as if we had a brand-new set of songs.

Better songs.

A better sound.

A better band.

Curtis got it all straight away, naturally finding the new rhythms and the new ways of playing each song, and once he'd shown me what he was doing, I quickly caught on as well. But Stan had a few problems at first. It wasn't that he *couldn't* change the way he played, or that he didn't have the ability, he simply needed someone to tell him what to do.

'Like *this*,' Curtis kept telling him. '*Duh-dah-dah, duh-dah-dah . . . chshh, chshh* . . . just play it like that.'

And Stan kept saying, 'What does that *mean*? *Duh-dah-dah, duh-dah-dah . . . chshh, chshh . . .*? That doesn't mean *anything* to me.'

But then William stepped in. 'Here,' he said, unstrapping his guitar and moving over to Stan. 'Let me show you.' And he just sat down at the drums and showed Stan exactly what to play and how to play it. Just like that. It was incredible. And he was good, too. A really good drummer. Not *quite* as good as Stan, but not far off.

It was something we'd all get used to over the months to come – this ability of William's not just to play almost any musical instrument, but to play them all really well – and eventually we'd get round to incorporating all kinds of different instruments into the band – violin, banjo, accordion, harmonica – all of them played by William. And that was another thing that made us special and gave us the edge over other bands – we weren't just another guitar/bass/drums outfit any more. We were different. We had more depth, more variety . . . more everything.

It wasn't *all* down to William though.

As I said, in the early days, there was an incredible creative dynamism between him and Curtis, and while William may have been the one who suggested new ideas and new ways of playing the songs, it was still Curtis who wrote them, and he never just accepted William's ideas, he built on them, he developed them, and he also worked them into even better songs, which William in turn would further improve with yet more ideas.

Of course, it wasn't always a tension-free process, especially towards the end. But even at the beginning there were times when Curtis would suddenly revert to his old untouchable, uncriticizable self.

I remember one occasion, about a few months after William had joined us, when we'd just finished playing 'Naked' at a rehearsal, and Curtis was having a quiet word with Stan about something, and out of the blue William suddenly said to him, 'Is it "Idle black eyes" or "Idol black eyes"?'

'What?' Curtis said, turning to him.

'In the first line of the song, you know – "Idle black eyes and drug-yellowed skin" . . .?'

'What about it?'

'Is it "idle" as in "lazy", or "idol" as in "God"?'

'I-D-L-E,' Curtis said, spelling it out. 'As in lazy. Why?'

'No reason, really,' William shrugged. 'It's just . . .'

'Just what?'

'It reminds me a bit of a line from a Rimbaud poem, that's all.'

'Yeah?'

William nodded. 'From "The Illuminations", a piece called "Childhood". There's a line that goes something like, "That idol, black eyes and yellow mane . . ."' He smiled at Curtis. 'Do you know the poem I mean?'

'What are you trying to say?'

'Nothing. I was just –'

'Are you accusing me of *stealing* my lyrics from Rimbaud?'

William held up his hands. 'No, no . . . not at all. I just remember the line for some reason, that's all. And I wondered if you were alluding to it or anything, you know?'

'*Alluding* to it?' Curtis sneered.

'Yeah.'

Curtis just stared at him for a while then, his eyes hard and cold, and I got the feeling that he wanted to take it further, that he *wanted* to really let rip at William, but something was holding him back. And that something, I guessed, was the fact that William was probably right. Curtis was always reading Rimbaud, he loved his stuff, and although I was pretty sure that he wouldn't blatantly steal from him, I wouldn't be at all surprised if – as William had suggested – he occasionally *alluded* to Rimbaud's work in his lyrics.

Eventually the coldness left Curtis's eyes and he decided it was best to just laugh the whole thing off.

'What the fuck do you know about Rimbaud anyway?' he said, grinning at William.

'Not much,' William replied, putting on a mock Irish brogue. 'I mean, what would an ignorant bogtrotter like me know about nineteenth-century French poetry?'

'Exactly,' Curtis said.

And that was the end of it.

Although, in hindsight, it was only the beginning.

People soon began to take notice of the new-look Naked. Although we'd already built up a good-sized following, and our Friday-night gigs at the Conway had always attracted a fairly big crowd, it wasn't until William joined us that we really began to take off as a band. And it all happened relatively quickly. Within a month or so of our first gig with William, the crowds at the Conway had almost doubled in size, and the atmosphere at the gigs was becoming more and more crazy by the week. More people, more fans, more madness, more singing and dancing . . . every time we played it got hotter and bigger and louder and better . . .

We were on the way up.

We were Naked.

We were *hot*.

As well as playing the Conway, we began getting other gigs too. They were still mostly pub venues – places like the Red Cow, the Nashville, the Pied Bull – but the pub circuit was where it was happening at the time. The crowds were good, the gigs were always advertised in the music press, and most importantly – at least from Jake's and Curtis's point of view – there was always a pretty good chance of being seen by journalists and record-company people.

The record companies were just beginning to show some interest in bands like the Sex Pistols and Naked around then, but it was little more than just interest. The punk scene was still in its early days, and while it was creating a lot of buzz around London, it was yet to really take off anywhere else. And even in London, it was still pretty much a word-of-mouth phenomenon. There were constant rumours about various other punk bands getting together, but in the spring and early summer of 1976, the only real punk bands who were regularly gigging were Naked and the Sex Pistols. The Clash and the Damned wouldn't make their debuts until July that year, and both Subway Sect and Siouxsie and the Banshees didn't play live until September. So although the record companies were aware of punk, they were still a long way from buying into it.

But that didn't stop Curtis and Jake from pursuing them. To Curtis and Jake, a record contract was the be-all and end-all. Without a record contract, a band was nothing. But *with* a record contract . . . well, that was it. That was the dream. To make records. To sell records. To become stars. As far as Curtis and

Jake were concerned, that's what it was all about. Getting a record contract.

As for the rest of us . . .

Well, Stan – as usual – was happy enough with whatever came along. If we got a contract, fine. If we didn't, so what? Stardom didn't mean much to him. He just liked playing the drums, and it didn't really make any difference to him if he was playing at the warehouse or playing in front of a hundred thousand people.

William, too, seemed perfectly content with how things were. It was obvious that he loved playing, that he loved the music, but the rest of it – the social side, the business side, the whole sex and drugs and rock 'n' roll thing – well, that didn't appeal to him at all. He didn't have anything against it, and it never bothered him what anyone else did, but – for the most part – I think he just found the rock 'n' roll world a bit ridiculous. The only time he ever showed any interest in record contracts was when the subject of money came up, which at the time, in view of his otherwise unmaterialistic outlook, I found quite odd. But there was a lot about William that I didn't know then, a lot that I didn't understand . . .

There was a lot that I didn't know about myself too.

Did I want to be famous? Did I want to be a rock 'n' roll star? Did I want to make records and play big venues and have my photograph taken all the time?

I didn't know.

Did I want to stay at school and go to university? Did I want a career? Did I want to fall in love and get married and buy a nice house and have a family?

I didn't know.

Did I want to stay with Curtis for the rest of my life?

I really didn't know the answers to any of these questions, and most of the time I didn't even bother thinking about them. I just lived every day as it came. Being with Curtis, hanging around with the band, playing gigs all over the place . . .

It was all OK.

And from February onwards, after William joined the band, I started enjoying it all a lot more. There was still a lot going on that I *didn't* enjoy, in particular the growing sense of violence at most of the gigs, which Curtis continued to both encourage and thrive on, and I still didn't like most of the people involved in the music business – the other bands, the hangers-on, the wheelers and dealers, the groupies, the predators, the drug addicts and crazies – but I was learning all the time how best to avoid them. It was actually a lot easier to avoid them now that William was around, because he didn't like them either. And while he'd quite often just disappear on his own after a gig or a rehearsal, sloping off quietly without saying a word, we'd also sometimes sneak away together for a bit of peace and quiet. Stan and Chief might join us occasionally, but mostly it'd be just William and me. And mostly we wouldn't really talk about anything. William might smoke a cigarette – if he'd managed to cadge one off somebody – and we might share a bottle of beer or two, and maybe talk about what had happened that night – the gig, the songs, the people we'd seen . . .

But it never went much further than that.

Which was fine with me.

Or so I kept telling myself . . .

The truth was, I wanted to know more about William. I wanted to know who he was, and where he came from, and why . . . I wanted to know what he thought about things, and how he felt about things. I wanted to know where he lived, who he lived with, what he did when he wasn't with the band . . .

I wanted to know all about him.

Purely out of curiosity, of course. There was nothing more to it than that.

Or so I kept telling myself . . .

But I never pushed him. If he didn't want to talk about himself, that was his right. He didn't owe me anything. He didn't *have* to open himself up to me. He didn't have to share with me the secrets of his heart . . .

But on a warm night in May, much to my surprise, that's exactly what he did.

18

As far as I was aware, the party at the squat that night wasn't actually in celebration of anything, it was just a party. A Saturday night free-for-all, just for the hell of it. There were no invitations, no guest lists, no limits. The door was left open all night, and anyone who turned up was welcome, as long as they brought something to drink or smoke or snort or whatever. And even if they didn't bring anything, no one really cared. It was that kind of party.

I wasn't looking forward to it at all.

I'd seriously considered not going, but I was practically living at the squat by then, and not going would have meant either going back home to Hampstead for the night, which wasn't particularly appealing, or going somewhere else for the night, which wasn't really an option, because I didn't have anywhere else to go. And besides, even if *I* didn't go to the party (not that I'd actually have to *go* anywhere), Curtis was still going to be there – he wouldn't have missed it for the world – and I knew that if I wasn't there with him I'd probably spend the whole night worrying about him, wondering what he was getting up to, who he was with, how much he was drinking/smoking/snorting/whatever . . .

And I knew that he *would* get wrecked.

Although he'd cut back on his drug use to a certain extent since that night at the Valentine's Ball, it was still very rare for him not to be under the influence of *some*thing – a small joint in the morning, a couple of beers in the afternoon, a line of speed most evenings. The only thing that had changed, really, was that he'd learned not to take too many drugs all at once. Or, at least, not when I was around anyway.

So I didn't doubt that he *would* get stoned out of his head at the party, whether I was there or not. But if I *wasn't* there, there was a pretty good chance that he'd not only get stoned out of his head but he'd take the opportunity to drink and smoke and snort himself into oblivion. And I simply wasn't going to let that happen.

The party didn't really get going until after the pubs had closed, which back then was at 11 p.m. on Saturdays. I'd spent most of the night with Curtis and Jake in a pub called the Seven Sisters, which was just around the corner from the squat in Broad Lane. There were a bunch of other people there too, most of them from the squat, but Stan and Chief turned up at some point during the night, and they brought some friends with them, and then a bit later on a motley group of punks slouched in, most of whom I recognized vaguely as friends and acquaintances of Curtis and Jake – musicians, poets, artists, designers . . .

I didn't *mean* to drink very much in the pub, but we were in there for a good few hours, and it was loud and noisy and hot and sweaty, and I was finding it really hard to deal with all the talking and posing, everyone acting like idiots, and the more I drank, the easier it was to ignore everything . . .

So by the time the pub closed and we all started walking back to the squat, I was already quite drunk. Curtis wasn't in too bad a state. He hadn't had much to drink, but he'd been speeding all day, and he'd been keeping himself topped up with numerous snorts of sulphate in the pub toilets, so he was zipping around all over the place like a hyperactive lunatic, but he was still pretty much in control of himself. Once he started on the drink though – which he always did when he'd been speeding all day – well, that's when the problems would start.

But, for now, he was OK.

In fact, despite his almost exhausting over-exuberance, I was actually having a pretty good time with him.

'You want a ride, Lili?' he said to me as we headed back to the squat.

I raised my eyebrows at him.

He laughed. 'No, I meant a piggy-back. Here . . .' He turned his back to me and bent over. 'Jump on.'

I hopped up onto his back and put my arms round his neck, and he grabbed hold of my legs and started running.

'Not so fast!' I cried out.

'Hold on tight!'

As he hurtled down the road towards the squat, jiggling me up and down on his back, I closed my eyes and screamed like an excited kid on a rollercoaster. The screams almost turned to real screams as we reached the squat, and I suddenly realized that Curtis was going too fast to stop, and as he tried to turn the corner into the squat he lost his balance and we both toppled over into a hedge and ended up flat on our backs in the front yard. It was a fairly heavy fall, but after a few moments' silence – which reminded me, there and then, of the silence you hear just after a child has fallen over, just *before* they start to cry – we both realized that we weren't hurt, that nothing was broken, and we both sat up, brushed ourselves down, and began to laugh.

'Fuck!' gasped Curtis.

'Yeah . . .'

'That was your fault.'

'*My* fault? I *told* you not to go so fast –'

'*You* had the reins.'

'*What* reins?'

He grinned at me. 'The piggy reins.'

It wasn't *that* funny – in fact, it wasn't really funny at all – but for some reason we both found it hilarious, and for the next minute or so we just sat there on the ground together, laughing ourselves stupid. People were streaming past us now, heading up the path into the squat, and music was blaring out of the house – 'Beat on the Brat' by the Ramones – and the night was warm, the still air carrying the music far into the night, and for the first time in ages I briefly felt like a young girl again . . .

It was a good moment.

'Come on,' said Curtis, getting to his feet and offering me his hand. 'Let's party.'

It was hot inside the house. There were hundreds of people milling around, the air was thick with the sweet smell of marijuana, and the front room downstairs was a seething mass of sweaty dancers. There'd been a mini heatwave that week – a portent of the summer to come – and although the temperature now was beginning to cool, it was still, for May, a ludicrously hot night.

I spent a while with Curtis, just mooching around, drinking wine, saying hello to people, watching people dance. The first Ramones album had recently been released, and that night it was being played almost continuously. The songs were ridiculously short – two or three minutes at most – incredibly fast, and wonderfully simple. But it wasn't the easiest music to dance to. Pogo-ing had yet to take off, and most people were still trying to work out *how* to dance to punk music. A dozen or so hardcore punks were just throwing themselves around the floor, not bothering to move to the music at all, just leaping up and down and crashing into each other, but – for the most part – the people who wanted to dance had to wait for something more danceable to come on. Which, more often than not then, was reggae.

So, as the last snarling 'Oh yeah . . .' of the Ramones' 'Judy is a Punk' faded out, and the first big bass beats of Big Youth's 'Screaming Target' boomed round the room, the dance floor suddenly filled up again.

'You dancing?' I yelled in Curtis's ear.

He smiled at me. 'You asking?'

Considering his love of the limelight, and the ease with which he presented himself on stage, Curtis was a surprisingly self-conscious dancer. He also wasn't all that good at it . . . and maybe that was why he found it so awkward. He just wasn't used to *not* being good at something. But we did sometimes dance together, and that night was one of those times. It didn't bother me that he wasn't a great dancer – I wasn't that hot myself – and, besides, with reggae music you can't really go wrong. As long as you've got at least some sense of rhythm, all you have to do is move. Move anything – your head, your hips, your feet . . . it doesn't matter. Just close your eyes, feel the music, and move with it.

And that's what we did.

Just the two of us, alone together in a sea of people, swaying and rolling, not thinking, not talking, just floating along, moving to the music, just dancing . . .

And, after a while, even Curtis began to enjoy himself.

We carried on dancing together for the next few songs – two more reggae tracks from the Big Youth album followed by the Stones' 'Hey Negrita' – and then whoever was in charge of the music at that point, which was basically anyone who *wanted* to be in charge, put the Ramones album back on again, and although me and Curtis both loved it, neither of us really fancied trying to dance to it.

'I need a wee, anyway,' I said to Curtis.

'Right,' he said, looking around the room. 'Have you seen Jake anywhere? I need to see him about something.'

'Try the kitchen,' I said. 'And Curtis?'

'Yeah?'

'Don't go mad, OK?'

'What do you mean?'

'You know what I mean. Just . . . you know . . . don't overdo it, that's all. For my sake.'

He smiled at me. 'OK.'

'Thanks,' I said, giving him a kiss.

'You're welcome,' he said, kissing me back.

I watched him walk off towards the kitchen, knowing full well that he was after more drugs, then I went upstairs and joined the long queue for the toilet.

Twenty minutes later, when I came back down and went into the kitchen, Curtis was nowhere to be seen. I wiped a sheen of sweat from my face, took a cold can of beer from the fridge, and went outside to get some fresh air.

There was no back garden as such, just a small brick-walled yard of cracked concrete with a tangled border of overgrown weeds and nettles. In a pathetic attempt to build a bonfire, the rotted trunk of a long-dead apple tree had been uprooted from the corner of the yard, doused in petrol, and set alight, and now it lay smouldering – and stinking of petrol – in the middle of the yard. A sad-looking punk with purple hair was standing alone in front of the blackened tree, staring at nothing and idly tapping a length of charred wood against his leg, and two dead-eyed hippies were sitting cross-legged on the ground by the far wall, mumbling incoherently to each other as they shared a bottle of wine. Apart from that, the yard seemed empty. I moved away from the smouldering tree to get away from the petrol fumes, and then I just stood there for a while, with my back to the house, breathing in the clear night air and soaking up the relative peace and quiet. A pale white moon hung high in the sky, its outline shimmering with an eerie blue light. There was something about this light, something about the sheer *blue*ness of it, that reminded me – unsettlingly – of my mother's eyes . . .

I sighed, looking down and trying to shake the image from my mind. I didn't *want* to think about my mother – it was all too confusing, too complicated – but I couldn't help wondering what she was doing right now. Was she at home? Was she alone? Was she out somewhere? Was she with someone?

I sighed again and decided to go back inside.

Just as I turned to leave, though, I heard a voice calling out softly from behind me – 'Hey, Lili' – and when I looked round, I saw William. He was sitting on an upturned milk crate against the wall of a little alleyway that led round the side of the house. There was a half-empty bottle of wine at his feet, and he had a half-smoked joint in his hand.

'William!' I said, unable to keep an audible exclamation mark from my voice. 'What are you doing?'

'Not much, he replied, smiling. 'Just sitting around, you know . . .'

'I wasn't sure you were here,' I said. 'At the party, I mean . . .'

'Yeah, I'm here.'

I smiled, feeling a bit foolish, not knowing what to say.

'Don't let me stop you,' William said. 'I mean, if you were going back in –'

'No . . . no, that's all right. I was just . . .'

'Looking at the moon?'

I laughed. 'Yeah, something like that.'

He gazed up. 'It's a nice one tonight.'

'Yeah, it is.'

He looked back at me. 'Do you want to sit down?'

'Yeah, OK,' I said, walking over to him.

He pulled up another milk crate, and I sat down next to him. He took a plastic lighter from his pocket, relit the joint, and took a drag on it.

'I thought you didn't smoke,' I said, watching him. 'Dope, I mean . . . I thought you didn't use drugs.'

He shrugged. 'I asked someone for a cigarette earlier on and they gave me this.' He looked quizzically at the joint. 'It's better than nothing, I suppose . . .'

'Do you ever buy your own cigarettes?' I asked.

He smiled. 'Are you saying I'm stingy?'

'No . . .' I looked at him. 'Well, yeah, actually. Yeah, I am.'

He laughed.

I took a small sip from the can of beer I'd taken from the fridge.

'Do you want some of this?' William said, offering me the joint.

I shook my head, swallowing the beer. 'I'm already a bit stoned from just being in there,' I told him, indicating the house. 'That's partly why I came out here, to clear my head.'

'Yeah, I know what you mean.'

I took another sip of beer. 'Did you come on your own?'

'What – out here?'

I looked at him. 'How come you always answer a question with another question?'

'Do I?'

'You've just done it again.'

'Have I?'

I gave him a stern look.

'All right,' he said, smiling. 'What was the question again?'

'I just asked if you came to the party on your own, that's all.'

'Yeah, I did.'

'You didn't bring any friends with you or anything?'

'No, I didn't bring any friends.'

I smiled. 'Have you *got* any friends?'

'One or two.'

'How about a girlfriend?'

'No.'

'Really?'

'Yeah, really.'

'I find that hard to believe.'

He just shrugged.

'Is there someone back home?' I said. 'Is that it? You've got a girlfriend in Belfast and you're saving yourself –'

'You ask a lot of questions, don't you?' he said.

'I'm just curious, that's all.'

'Why?'

'Because . . . I don't know. It's just . . . well, I don't know anything *about* you.'

He looked at me. 'I don't know anything about *you*.'

'Aren't *you* curious?'

He didn't say anything for a while then, he just looked at me, his eyes almost golden in the moonlight, and I had absolutely no idea what he was thinking. His face was a mask, his heart and soul impenetrable. After what seemed like a minute or two, but was probably only a couple of seconds, I saw his eyes dart to the right, drawn by something in the backyard, and then he smiled at me and said, 'Just a second,' and I watched him as he got to his feet and went over to the sad-eyed punk by the smouldering tree. The punk was smoking a cigarette, and I realized that William had just seen him light it, and now he was asking him if he could have one. The punk gave him two. William thanked him, put one behind his ear, lit the other one, and came back over to me.

'All right,' he said, sitting down. 'What do you want to know?'

'Sorry?'

'You said that you didn't know anything about me . . .'

'Yeah . . .'

'So what do you want to know?'

'Well . . . anything, really,' I muttered, taken aback by his sudden candour. 'You know . . . whatever you want to tell me about . . . your family, your home, why you came over here . . .'

'OK,' he said. 'I'll tell you as much as I can . . . but on two conditions.'

'Which are?

'Firstly, that you don't repeat *any*thing I'm about to tell you to anyone else.' He gave me a deadly serious look. 'Not a single word, OK?'

'Yeah, of course.'

'This is strictly between you and me. Do you understand?'

'Yes, I understand. What's the second condition?'

'You have to tell me everything about your family too.'

'No problem,' I said, holding my hand out for him to shake. 'You've got yourself a deal.'

He looked at me, a trace of sadness in his eyes, and for a moment I thought he was going to change his mind. And I wondered briefly if I was doing the right thing – was I forcing him to do this? was I making him do something he didn't want to do? – and I began to think that maybe it would be best if he *did* change his mind. But then he took my hand, gave it a quick shake, and before I had a chance to say anything else, he began telling me his story.

William was born and brought up in the Falls Road district of west Belfast, a staunchly Republican area. His father, Joseph, was a labourer. His mother, Catherine, worked part-time in a local library. William's brother, Joseph – known to the family as Little Joe – was three years younger than him.

'We were a fairly normal family really,' William told me. 'My parents worked hard, we went to mass every Sunday, and most summers we'd go and stay at my grandparents' farm near Antrim. I mean, we never had much money or anything, but neither did anyone else, you know? There was always enough to eat, we never really missed out on anything . . .' He shrugged. 'It was kind of hard at times . . . but you just get on with it, don't you?' He paused for a moment, staring thoughtfully at the ground, and then he went on. 'And I suppose that's what we were doing when it happened – just getting on with it, trying to live our lives . . .'

It was January 1970, and the conflict in Northern Ireland was getting worse all the time. British troops patrolled the streets of Belfast, gunfire rang out almost every night, and there was constant rioting between Republicans and Loyalists. William's family, like most other families in the neighbourhood, did their best to carry on as usual and not get directly involved, but it simply wasn't possible. They were Catholic, they lived in a close-knit Republican area . . . they were, by default, targets

...oyalist violence. And it worked the other way round too. ...rdinary Protestant families, living in Loyalist neighbourhoods, were the targets of Republican hatred. So every night the battle lines would be drawn – makeshift barriers of corrugated iron and burned-out cars – and streets would be blocked off, and then the rioting would begin. Kids throwing stones and bottles, petrol bombs flying through the air, guns going off, the mobs swelling, the ferocity growing . . . and then, sometimes, the security forces would arrive – British soldiers or the RUC, the Royal Ulster Constabulary – and sometimes they'd try to take control and calm things down, and sometimes they succeeded, and the rioting would gradually die down, the combatants melting away into the darkened streets, and everything would be quiet again . . . until the following night.

But, according to William, there were other times when the security forces had no intention of calming things down.

'I'd seen them do it before,' William told me. 'The fucking police . . . I'd seen them standing by, doing nothing, while a mob of Loyalists broke through a barrier and ransacked a whole fucking *street*. I mean, they were beating the shit out of people, dragging them out of their own houses . . . whole families, little kids and everything . . . and the police just stood there and let it happen.'

'Why?' I asked. 'Why would the police do that?'

He looked at me. 'Because that's how it is . . . that's how it's always been. You're either this or that – Protestant or Catholic, Rangers or Celtic, punk or skinhead, black or white, orange or green . . . it doesn't matter what any of it means, what any of it *stands* for, all that matters is which side you're on.'

'And you're saying that the police in Belfast are on the side of the Loyalists?'

'All I'm saying is what I know, what I've seen . . . what I saw that night.'

*

His home was a small terraced house in a narrow street on the north side of the Falls Road. The rioting that night had been particularly violent, and there'd been a series of running battles in the surrounding streets between local residents and rampaging Loyalists.

'There was a handful of Provos with us that night,' William said. 'And some of them were rumoured to have machine-guns. They were mostly local men, but the ones with the guns were a couple of big names who'd come down from the north to help us out . . . which, as it happened, only ended up making things worse . . .' William sighed. 'Anyway, we had a pretty good barrier up at the end of our street, and it seemed to be doing its job, and although there were plenty of RUC around, they weren't really getting involved in anything, they were just kind of hanging around in the background – close enough to keep an eye on things, but not close enough to get petrol-bombed. So it looked for a while as if nothing much was going to happen, it was just going to end up in the usual stalemate. But then, around midnight, a couple of UVF guys turned up in a JCB – you know, one of those big road-digger things – and they just drove it straight through the barrier, and then all hell broke loose.'

William was sitting perfectly still now. His eyes were fixed blindly on the brick wall of the alley, and his face was pale and empty. His voice, when he spoke, was the bewildered voice of the ten-year-old child he'd been that night.

'They just broke in . . . just kicked the door down and stormed into our house and started smashing everything up. I was upstairs in my room with Joe . . . we could hear it all going on – the stomping boots, the shouting and crashing, my dad yelling at them to stop . . . and Joe's crying, and I'm trying to comfort him, and then we hear Mum's sobbing voice downstairs – '*Leave him alone!*' – and suddenly Joe goes running out of the room, calling out for Mum, and I run off after him,

175

shouting at him to come back, but he's halfway down the stairs now . . . and as I go racing down after him I see all these men in our house – big men, in hats and black coats – and some of them have got hammers and clubs, wooden clubs, pick-axe handles, and they're smashing everything up – furniture, ornaments, windows, lights . . .'

William paused for a moment, swallowing hard, and then he went on. 'They were in the front room, the two RUC men. They had heavy coats on, but I could see their uniforms underneath. One of them had a pick-axe handle and the other one had a pistol. When I went into the front room, Joe had run up to Mum and she was holding him tight, and they were both crying their eyes out and watching in horror as the cop with the pistol laid into Dad. Dad was being held from behind by two Loyalists, and the RUC guy was screaming questions into his face – '*WHERE ARE THEY? COME ON, YOU FENIAN BASTARD! WHERE THE FUCK ARE THEY?*' Dad's face was all smashed up and there was blood streaming from his nose, and when the cop began yelling at him again, Dad sniffed hard, drew his head back, and spat blood in his face. The cop went crazy then, cracking the pistol repeatedly into Dad's head, and that's when Mum went for him. She let out this piercing scream and grabbed a heavy candlestick from the mantelpiece and lunged at the cop who was hitting Dad, swinging the candlestick at his head . . . but the other cop, the one with the pick-axe handle, he was ready for her. He just shoved her at first, just kind of grabbed her and flung her back against the wall, but that didn't stop her. I mean, she was strong, my mum . . . she was a fighter. She just . . . she just kind of stood there for a moment, shaking the dizziness from her head, and then she went for them both again, wailing like a banshee and swinging the candlestick over her head . . . and then this cop . . . the bastard who'd shoved her . . .' William swallowed again, wiping a tear from his eye. 'He just *hit* her . . . just like that. The fucking *bastard* . . . he just swung the pick-axe handle like it was a baseball bat and hammered it into her head . . . and I heard it . . . I fucking *heard* it . . . this terrible awful *cracking* sound . . . and Mum . . . she just . . . she just dropped, you know? Like a sack . . . she just dropped to the floor, her head all cracked open . . . and there was just nothing there any more. No life . . . just like that . . .'

William paused for a while then, just sitting there silently, breathing, thinking . . . lost in his memories. And I didn't know what to do. I didn't know what to say. What *could* I say? There was nothing that would *mean* anything. So I didn't say anything. I just sat there, sharing the silence.

Eventually, after a minute or two, William straightened up, took the cigarette from behind his ear, and lit it. 'They killed her, Lili,' he said quietly. 'Just like that . . .' He clicked his fingers. 'They killed her . . . *and* they got away with it.'

'They got *away* with it?' I said.

He nodded. 'They said she just fell down the stairs . . . I mean, there was barely even an investigation. The police claimed to have information that we were harbouring known terrorists, and that during the search of our house my mother attacked an RUC officer, and as he tried to defend himself she stumbled and fell down the stairs . . . and that was it.'

'But there were witnesses –'

'No, there weren't. According to the police, the only people present when it happened were the two RUC officers and us. And neither of the officers were armed. They even claimed to have found a loaded pistol in the house.' William looked at me. 'They kept my dad in custody for two days, beat the shit out of him, and promised him that if he didn't keep his mouth shut about what really happened, he'd be thrown in jail, locked up for years, and me and Joe would be taken into care.'

'Christ . . .' I whispered. 'So what did he do?'

'He kept his mouth shut,' William said simply. 'What else could he do? He came back home, cleaned up the house . . . he spent hours and hours with me and Joe, talking to us, taking care of us . . . and a week later we all went to Mum's funeral.' William took a drag on his cigarette. 'That night, after the funeral, Dad joined the Provisional IRA.'

Over the next few years, William went on to tell me, his father's life became more and more bound up with the IRA. At first, he was only involved on a volunteer level – attending meetings, collecting and passing on information, running errands, hiding guns – but as time went on, and his capabilities became recognized, he gradually rose up through the ranks, and by 1974 he'd become an active member, at an operational level, of one of the three battalions that made up the Belfast Brigade. The IRA had become his whole life.

'What exactly does "at an operational level" mean?' I asked William.

'Organizing and taking part in operations.'

'Right, I see. And by "operations" you mean . . .?'

'Everything,' William said. 'Bombings, shootings . . . you name it.'

'Killing people?'

William looked at me. 'It's a war, Lili . . . them against us. You either lie down and let them stomp all over you, or you stand up and fight back.' He shrugged. 'It's a war . . . people get killed in wars.'

'And you think that makes it OK?'

'It's not a question of being OK or not. It's just how it is. If you're in the army, and your country's at war, it's your job to kill people.'

'Yeah, but the IRA's not a *real* army –'

'Yes, it is. It's the Irish Republican Army. The only reason the

Provisionals split from the old IRA in 1969 was that the old IRA weren't doing their job any more, they weren't defending their people. And that's what an army *does*.'

I was really quite confused about everything now. I didn't know much about the history of the conflict in Northern Ireland. I didn't know when it had started, or why . . . I didn't even really understand what it was all about. All I knew was that almost every night there'd be TV news reports of another bombing, another shooting, another horrific terrorist attack . . . and now I was faced with the fact that William's father was personally involved in such terrible atrocities. And that was really disturbing. But at the same time, I could *kind* of understand his motivation. I could, to a certain extent, sympathize with his hatred of the security forces, and his desire to avenge his wife's murder . . .

And yet . . .

I knew in my heart that it was *wrong*. It's wrong to kill people, no matter what. It's just wrong.

I looked at William. 'What's he doing now?' I asked. 'Your father . . . I mean, is he still –?'

'He's dead.'

Joseph Bonney met Nancy Dougan in November 1974. A Belfast girl, born and bred, she was a nurse at the Royal Victoria Hospital, and when Joseph was rushed to the emergency ward one night with sudden appendicitis, Nancy's was the first face he saw when he woke up after the operation.

For Joseph, it was love at first sight.

But Nancy had other ideas.

She came from the Falls Road area too, she'd lived there all her life, so she knew who was who, and what was what . . . and she'd heard all about Joseph Bonney. She knew what he was, and what he did, and she didn't like it at all. In her job, she saw the bloody consequences of paramilitary actions every day. She saw the torn-off limbs, the shattered knee caps, the burned faces . . .

she saw it all. And she didn't want anything to do with a man who caused such suffering and pain.

So she looked after Joseph, she nursed him, she was even reasonably cordial to him, because that was her job. But that was as far as it went. She didn't respond to his cautious smiles, his gentle jokes, his gracious manner. She wasn't won over by his quiet ways, his kindness, his thoughtfulness. She didn't let his crushing sadness cloud her perception of what he was . . . not at first, anyway. But gradually, as he slowly recuperated from his operation – and an infection that had complicated his recovery – Nancy found herself becoming inextricably drawn to him. She didn't *want* to like him, and she tried her best not to, but she just couldn't help it. And by the time Joseph had fully recovered, and was ready to be discharged, he and Nancy had spent countless hours talking to each other, often in the dead of night, and they both knew in their hearts that despite all the seemingly insurmountable difficulties, they were *meant* to be together.

It was as simple as that.

They just *had* to be together.

So, after Joseph had been discharged, they set about making it possible.

The first hurdle to overcome was Joseph's membership of the IRA.

'I can't be with you if you stay with them, Joe,' Nancy told him bluntly. 'I can't be with a man who wilfully hurts and maims people . . . I can't live with a killer. I just can't. And whatever your reasons are, whatever justification you think you have, right or wrong . . . whoever or whatever you're fighting for or against, it doesn't make any difference. I'd feel exactly the same if you were in the UVF or the UDA . . . they're all fundamentally the same. They all try to solve problems with violence. And I'm not saying that's intrinsically wrong, because I don't think you can say that about anything, but it's not right for *me*. I mean, I know that violence is never going to stop, and there's nothing anyone can do to change that, but *I* have a choice, Joe. I can decide what's right and wrong in *my* life. Do you understand what I'm saying?'

Joseph nodded.

Nancy looked at him. 'I can't have you in my life if you carry on doing what you're doing. It's as simple as that. You can either have me . . . or you can stay as you are. It's up to you.'

Joseph didn't say anything, he just smiled – a smile from his heart – then he took her in his arms and kissed her.

The next obstacle to overcome was the IRA itself, or – more specifically – the IRA's unwritten membership policy of 'once in, never out', which basically meant that once you were a member of the IRA, you were *always* a member of the IRA. No matter how much you'd achieved or sacrificed for the cause, retirement simply wasn't an option. So Joseph knew that he couldn't just arrange a meeting with his brigade commander and tell him that he wanted out, because not only would his request be refused, but it would also mark him out as a potential security risk, and Joseph was well aware of how the IRA dealt with threats to their security.

So the only choice he had, as far as he could see, was to lie about his state of health. And that's what he did. His recent appendectomy, he claimed, was still causing him serious problems. The infection had flared up again, it had spread to his small intestine, he was in so much pain sometimes that he could barely walk . . . there was simply no *way* that he could return to active service yet. If nothing else, he'd be a liability – a risk to his colleagues and to the operation itself.

'And did that work?' I asked William. 'Did they buy it?'

'Most of them did . . . for a while, anyway. There was no reason not to. The trouble was, there was a guy in Dad's battalion who'd had it in for him for ages, a really nasty piece of work called Franky Hughes. There'd been a lot of talk going round that Franky was a grass, and Franky had got it into his head – mistakenly, as it turned out – that my dad was behind all these rumours. So he was always looking for a way to get back at him. And when Dad came out of hospital and began making his excuses, Franky decided to check him out, just to make sure that he really was as ill as he claimed. And, of course, he not only realized that he wasn't, but he also found out that Dad was seeing Nancy.'

'Why did that matter?' I said. 'I mean, I can see how it was bad for this Franky guy to find out that your dad was lying, but what did it matter if he was seeing Nancy? What did that have to do with anything?'

'Nancy's a Protestant,' William said.

'Oh, right . . . I see.' Although, to be honest, I didn't. Not really. 'So is that why she made your dad renounce the IRA? Because she was a Protestant and he –'

'He didn't renounce the *IRA*,' William corrected me. 'He never stopped believing in the cause. He simply renounced *his* use of violence, that's all. And Nancy didn't *make* him do it either, she gave him the choice. And it was nothing to do with her religion, it was just her.'

'OK . . .' I said. 'I'm sorry. I didn't mean –'

'Yeah, I know you didn't,' he said, half-smiling at me. 'Sorry. It's all right, it's just . . . it's me.' He shook his head. 'I can't help it. Whenever I start thinking about Franky *fucking* Hughes . . .'

'What did he do?' I asked.

William sighed. 'He bided his time, he waited . . . watching Dad, following him around, gathering evidence . . .'

'Evidence of what?'

'Well, *some* of it was genuine. Evidence that Dad wasn't ill – photographs that showed he was perfectly healthy, pictures of him out and about with Nancy, smiling and laughing . . . but the rest of it, the stuff that *really* did for him, that was all false. Franky made it all up.'

'What kind of stuff do you mean?'

'Well, it turned out that Franky actually *was* a grass. He'd been passing on information to an MI5 agent for years, so he knew better than anyone what kind of evidence was needed to prove that someone was an informer, and all he had to do was provide it. I'm not exactly sure how he did it – although I wouldn't be surprised if he got some help from MI5 – but a couple of months later he went to the brigade commander and presented him with enough evidence to prove beyond doubt that Dad was working for the British intelligence services and that Nancy was his go-between. There were forged documents, falsified records, doctored photographs, transcripts of non-existent telephone conversations . . .' William sighed again. 'Dad never stood a chance.'

'What happened?' I asked quietly.

'They killed him . . . they killed them both, Franky and Dad.' William's voice was cold and empty. 'Their bodies were found in a patch of wasteground about a mile from our street. Their hands were tied behind their backs, their eyes were taped shut, and they'd both been shot in the back of the head.'

'God, William . . .' I whispered.

'He only went out to get some fish and chips,' William went on, slowly shaking his head. 'Me and Joe had just got back from school, and Dad hadn't had time to make us anything to eat, so he just popped out to the chip shop instead . . . and he never came back. I thought at first . . . I don't know. I thought maybe he'd stopped off for a drink or something, but when he still wasn't back by seven, I rang Nancy to see if she knew where he was, but she hadn't seen him all day. When I told her that he'd been gone for hours, she knew straight away that something was wrong. She came rushing over to our place and we spent the next few hours ringing round, trying to find out if anyone had seen him, and then about ten o'clock the police turned up. We all knew then . . . as soon as we saw them, we knew what had happened.' William shook his head again. 'They told us to go upstairs,' he continued, his voice edged with bitterness now. 'The police . . . they didn't want me and Joe to hear them breaking the news to Nancy, so they told us to go upstairs and wait in the bedroom. But we didn't. We went upstairs and then sneaked back down and listened at the door. The police knew that it was an IRA execution from the way the bodies were found, and once they'd told Nancy what had happened, they immediately started asking her all these questions about Dad . . . I mean, they didn't even wait for her to stop crying, the bastards. And I really lost it then. I went running into the front room, shouting and screaming at them, telling them to fuck off and leave us alone . . . and then Little Joe ran in and started laying into them too . . .' William smiled sadly. 'He actually bit one of them on the leg . . . just ran up to the bastard and *bit* him. They didn't stay long after that.'

He paused for a moment, taking a drink from the bottle of wine, and then he sighed heavily again and carried on.

'We didn't stay very long, either. As soon as the police had gone, Nancy sat down with me and Joe and we all just cried our hearts out for a while, and then eventually, when the tears had begun to dry up, Nancy did what she had to do.'

Although Joseph hadn't known that Franky Hughes was setting him up, he'd been well aware that the IRA would eventually find out that not only had he been lying about his health, but also that he was in a relationship with a Protestant woman, and while that probably wasn't enough in itself to put his life in danger, the risk was always there.

'And if they ever suspect me of betraying them,' he'd told Nancy, 'they're probably going to assume that you had something to do with it. And you know what that means, don't you?'

Nancy nodded. She knew exactly what it meant.

'It'll probably never come to it,' Joseph went on, 'but if

anything *does* ever happen to me, I want you to promise me something.'

Nancy just nodded again.

'I want you to promise me that you'll leave Belfast as soon as you can, OK? Don't bother packing or saying goodbye to anyone, don't wait for *anything*, just get out of the country as soon as you can. All right?'

'But –'

'No buts, just do it. Do you promise?'

'Yes . . . yes, I promise.'

'And I want you to take William and Joe with you.'

'Why?' Nancy said. 'The IRA's not going to go after *them*, are they?'

'It's not that.'

'What then?'

'It's William,' he said. 'If they kill me, and he stays here, there's a chance that he'll go after them. And if he does that, he'll end up with a bullet in the back of his head. And then Little Joe's going to grow up knowing that his father *and* his brother were killed by the IRA . . . do you see what I'm saying? I don't want my sons ending up like me.'

'They won't,' Nancy said.

'You promise? You'll take them with you?'

She nodded. 'I've got a friend who lives –'

'Don't tell me,' Joseph interrupted. 'Don't tell anyone. If the time ever comes, and you have to go, just go.'

'Right . . .' She smiled. 'But the time isn't going to come . . . is it, Joe?'

'No,' he assured her. 'Everything's going to be all right.' He returned her smile. 'In fact, I wouldn't be at all surprised if we both lived for ever.'

The morning after William's father was killed, Nancy and the two boys took the first available ferry to Liverpool. From

Liverpool, they travelled by train to London, and by late afternoon they were sitting in the kitchen of a council flat in a tower block on the Cranleigh Farm estate in West Green Road. The flat belonged to an old friend of Nancy's from nursing college, a woman called Rhoda Devlin. Rhoda had grown up with Nancy, they'd played together in the streets when they were kids, so she knew all about the Troubles. She understood how the paramilitaries worked. And once Nancy had explained what had happened and why she'd had to leave, Rhoda had no hesitation about letting her and the boys stay at the flat. In fact, as it turned out, she'd been thinking about leaving the flat to move in with her boyfriend, but it had taken her so long to get the council flat in the first place that the idea of giving it up now really irked her.

'But if *you* wanted to stay here,' she told Nancy. 'You and the boys . . . well, I could move in with Derren *and* keep the flat in my name. Which might come in useful if things don't work out at Derren's . . . which knowing *my* luck with men, they probably won't. So, anyway, what do you think?'

'Would I have to pretend to be you?' Nancy asked.

'Only as far as the council's concerned. And as long as the rent gets paid, they don't really care who you are.'

So that was pretty much that. Rhoda moved out a week later, and William and Little Joe began a brand-new life with Nancy. New life, new home, new town, new country, new 'mother'.

'Not that she ever asked us to consider her as our mother,' William said. 'She was just . . . I don't know. Just Nancy, I suppose. She was all we had left . . . she still is.' He looked at me. 'She's everything to us – mother, father, sister . . .'

'She must be a remarkable woman,' I said.

'Yeah, she is.'

'How does she manage?' I asked. 'Money-wise, I mean. Is she still nursing?'

William shook his head. 'It's still a bit difficult . . . she can't really get a proper job until she gets some new ID, because if she uses her real name and real ID . . . well, we just have to be really careful, you know?'

'Do you really think the IRA will be looking for her?'

'I *know* they are.'

'How do you know?'

He shrugged. 'Contacts, people back home, people who hear things . . . it's a small world back there.'

'But a big one here.'

He smiled. 'Yeah . . .'

'Isn't there any way you can put things right with the IRA?' I asked. 'I mean, if they knew the truth, if they knew that Franky Hughes had set up your father and Nancy –'

He shook his head. 'It wouldn't make any difference now. They don't acknowledge mistakes – it's a sign of weakness. The truth doesn't matter, the truth's irrelevant. All that matters to them is their honour and reputation.'

'Their *honour*?'

He just shrugged.

For a moment then, I almost lost my temper. I just couldn't understand how he could possibly accept such a ridiculously twisted sense of morality. Of course, I knew that he didn't *agree* with it, and that his acceptance of it was really no more than a resigned acknowledgement of the way things were . . .

But still . . .

I think I just wanted him to show some hatred for the IRA.

Which just goes to show how incredibly naive I was at the time.

'So if Nancy can't get any work,' I said to him, 'how do you manage to –?'

'She can get *work*, she just can't do anything *officially* until she gets some fake ID. But fake ID costs a lot of money, which is

187

hard to come by because Nancy can't get a real job until she *gets* the fake ID . . . so all she can do at the moment is cash-in-hand stuff, which doesn't really pay very much. But we manage, you know? And I do as much as I can to help out . . .'

'So you *have* got a job?'

'No,' he said, grinning. 'I just steal stuff.'

'Right . . .'

He looked at me. 'Sometimes you just have to do whatever it takes.'

I didn't say anything, I just looked at him. And as I gazed deeply into those haunted eyes, I thought about everything he'd been through – his mother's death, his father's life with the IRA, his father's murder *by* the IRA – and I tried to imagine how it must have been for him, how it must have made him feel . . . but it was beyond me. I didn't even know how it made *me* feel. I felt *some*thing though – there was no doubting that – and, whatever it was, it moved me so much that I wanted to take hold of William and never let go.

But this was the real world – Saturday night, Sunday morning, the backyard of a house in Seven Sisters, the brutal beauty of the Ramones blaring out from the wide-open windows – and I knew that in this *real* real world, I couldn't put my arms round William and hold him for ever . . .

But I *could* put my arms round him for now.

And when I did – not holding him *too* tight, and not feeling the need to say anything – it felt *so* right, so absolutely perfect, that I wished we were in another world, a world that *wasn't* real, a world where we *could* hold each other for ever. And we *were* holding each other now . . . it wasn't just me with my arms round William, we were embracing each other.

And although that's all it was – a simple embrace, with nothing else to it – it was, for me, an incredibly intimate moment, and for the first time in my life I knew how it felt to be at *one* with somebody. I felt complete, content . . . I didn't need anything else at all. Just this.

I felt totally *liberated*, as well. There were no expectations, no rules, nothing to be embarrassed about. It felt perfectly all right to be silent, but at the same time, if I wanted to say something, *anything*, I knew that I could. I didn't have to *think* about what to do. So when I felt a question forming in my mind, I didn't stop to consider if I ought to ask it or not, I just opened my mouth and let the words come out.

'Do you mind if I ask you something else?' I murmured.

'Is it about fairy tales?'

I smiled, remembering the night of the Valentine's Ball. 'No,' I said, just as I'd said that night. 'No, it's not about fairy tales.'

'In that case, no . . . I don't mind.'

'Is William Bonney your real name?'

He didn't say anything for a while, he just carried on holding me, and then after a few moments he gently let go – without moving away from me – and looked into my eyes. His eyes, I noticed, were traced with tears. But his smile was a good one – a smile from the heart.

Just as he was about to answer my question – or, at least, just as he was about to say *some*thing – a horrible screeching sound came from inside the house, and the music suddenly stopped, and we both heard the unmistakable sound of fighting – raised voices, bodies crashing around, shouting and swearing. It was coming from the room downstairs where people had been dancing.

'What the hell –?' I started to say.

'Listen,' William said.

I kept quiet for a moment, and then I heard it. An all too familiar drunken voice, angry and stupid and out of control:

'Come on then, you *fucker*! Come *on*!'

I looked at William.

'Curtis?' he said.

I sighed. 'Who else?'

20

The fight at the party that night sounded a lot worse than it actually was. In fact, Curtis and the other guy – a punk called Andy – were both so stoned that it wasn't really a fight at all, just a lot of pushing and shoving, a lot of shouting and swearing, and a fair amount of falling over and rolling around on the floor. When I asked Curtis later what the fight was about, he told me that it was nothing, just 'one of those things, you know . . .' And when I pressed him further, he claimed that Andy had been bad-mouthing Naked.

'He said we were *fakes*, for Christ's sake . . . public-school fakes. I mean, what the fuck is *that* supposed to mean?'

I don't know if Andy really did say that – although I wouldn't be surprised if he had – but I doubt if that was the true cause of the fight, because some weeks later I found out that Andy was going out with Charlie Brown – who wasn't there that night – and I think it's more likely that they came to blows after Curtis had said something to Andy about Charlie, or Andy had said something to Curtis . . .

Whatever the reason, it was all pretty pathetic.

But then, in all honesty, a lot of things seemed kind of pathetic after hearing about William's troubled life that night. In comparison to what he'd been through – and was *still* going through – so much of everything else suddenly seemed so trivial and insignificant. Me and Curtis, the band, school, music . . . I saw it all in a new perspective now. None of it was a matter of life and death. None of it mattered *that* much. Even my mother's continuing problems weren't quite so distressing in light of what had happened to William's parents. I mean, at least my mother – and father – were both still alive. Of course, I'm not saying that I suddenly realized how wonderful my life was or anything . . . I just realized that it could easily have been a whole lot worse.

21

The weather cooled a little towards the end of May, but the days
began to warm up again in June, and by the end of the month
the whole country was bathed in scorching blue skies and swel-
tering heat. In what was to become the hottest summer since
records began, temperatures soared to 80° F for days on end, often reaching well over 90° F. Throughout June and July, and into
the early weeks of August, the heat bore down relentlessly. There
was no respite – no rain, no cooling breezes – and even at night
the temperatures barely dipped. Some nights were so hot that
people took to sleeping on rooftops. And as the summer went
on, the never-ending heat and the continuing lack of rain began
to take its toll – pavements cracked, roads melted, rivers ran dry,
and water supplies had to be rationed. There were devastating
forest fires, plagues of ladybirds, widespread crop failures, all
kinds of economic and industrial problems . . . none of which,
to be perfectly honest, had any effect on me whatsoever. And
it was the same for everyone else I knew too. Our world was
our world – our streets, our houses, our days, our nights – and
anything beyond that, which pretty much meant everything else
on the planet, simply didn't concern us. We weren't interested
in politics, we didn't keep up with foreign affairs, we couldn't
have cared less about nuclear weapons or the war in Vietnam
or anything else that the rest of the world – at least, the rest of
the *adult* world – deemed important. And while it was true that
William had far more experience of life – and death – than the

rest of us put together, even his relationship with the rest of the world was relatively insular.

Of course, I realize now how narrow-minded and self-obsessed that probably sounds, but it's just the way it was back then. We didn't watch TV, we didn't read newspapers . . . we just lived our lives.

That summer, for us, was just *our* summer: we enjoyed the heat, we cursed the heat, we sweated, we burned . . . we did what we did. We spent our days just hanging around in the sun or rehearsing at the warehouse, and in the evenings we'd either hang around some more, or go to the pub, or – more often than not – drive across London to play another gig.

Our gigs were coming thick and fast now. Two, sometimes three, a week . . . the venues were getting better all the time, the crowds getting bigger, the buzz getting louder. The punk scene in London was really starting to take off, with more and more bands emerging all the time. At the beginning of July, the Ramones played two nights at the Roundhouse, and on the night we went to see them, everyone who was anyone was there, including just about every music journalist in London. The same month saw the debuts of the Clash, the Damned, and the Buzzcocks. The music press was still divided over how good these new bands really were – some of the papers hated them, others quickly fell in love with them – but, either way, punk music was beginning to get a lot of media attention. The Ramones' gigs in particular were *huge* events. And as a result of all this publicity, the record companies were gradually starting to show some real interest in punk . . . some of which was coming our way.

It wasn't much yet – mainly just rumours and vaguely promising possibilities. Jake was forever telling us that he'd spoken to so-and-so from Polydor or A&M or whoever, and that they were 'seriously' interested in us, or that they were coming to see us at our next gig, and a deal was 'definitely on the table' . . .

But, so far, nothing had come of it.

We were getting fairly regular coverage in the music papers too – reviews, reports, interviews – and the overall feeling among most of the journalists was that while we were undoubtedly a punk band, at the forefront of the burgeoning scene, we weren't quite the same as all the other bands. Yes, we were loud, and sometimes really fast. And, yes, we embraced and embodied the punk sensibilities. But we didn't *just* do the 1-2-3-4, bam-bam-bam stuff. And while that occasionally led to accusations that Naked weren't a punk band at all – which I always thought was a pretty pointless thing to say – it mostly worked to our advantage.

'If you want to get noticed,' Jake said once, 'it's no good being exactly the same as everyone else, you have to be different. You have to stand out from the crowd.'

We'd also been together a lot longer than most of the other bands – the Pistols excepted, of course – and, musically, that gave us an edge too. We knew what we were doing. We were tight. We were *good*.

What more could a record company want?

We had great songs.

A unique sound.

We had Curtis, who was born to be a rock 'n' roll star.

And we had William.

Although Naked had always been Curtis's band – he was the songwriter, frontman, singer, lead guitarist – and although it was still always his name, his voice, his picture that dominated all our press coverage, it was also becoming apparent now that there was a growing interest in William. Reviews and articles about us began to focus not only on Curtis, but on William too . . . or Billy the Kid, as they insisted on calling him right from the start. There was praise for his guitar-playing, his singing, his looks . . . even his dancing got rave reviews. Billy the Kid, it was generally agreed, was an exceptionally cool individual.

William never bothered reading any of the music papers. He had no interest whatsoever in other people's opinions, either of the band or of himself, and when it came to doing interviews, his view was exactly the same. He had no interest in them at all. He'd happily sit in with the rest of us during interviews, and he was never rude or dismissive to any journalists, but he never actually talked to them. Never said a word, never offered an opinion, never answered any questions. In all the time I knew him, the only words I ever heard him say to an interviewer were, 'You haven't got a spare cigarette, have you?'

Jake was forever trying to persuade William to say *some*thing, but he always flatly refused.

'It's just music,' he'd say. 'What's there to say about it?'

Which was kind of strange, because I remembered when Curtis had said something very similar to me shortly after we'd met. 'Songs are songs,' he'd said. 'They don't *need* explaining.' And yet now here he was, just a year or so later, regularly and volubly – and very publicly – discussing his music at the drop of a hat. Not that I held it against him or anything, it just struck me at the time how quickly things can change . . . for better or worse.

Things change.

William never changed though. He just carried on saying nothing and keeping his thoughts to himself, and I think he just kind of assumed that in the end the media would eventually get used to it and leave him alone, but that didn't happen. Instead, his refusal to play the game only *increased* the amount of interest in him. It added to his 'coolness'. It gave him a sense of mystery and intrigue. And there's nothing the media likes more than a mystery.

Of course, I was the only one who knew that William's desire to keep a low profile wasn't *just* a matter of personal choice, it was potentially a matter of life and death. In fact, it was around this time that he confided in me that he'd been seriously considering quitting the band because of the possible risk that any media exposure might pose to Nancy and Little Joe.

'I know it's not really *much* of a risk,' he told me. 'I mean, it's pretty unlikely that the IRA are going to find out about me by reading the *NME*, you know? And even if one of them *did* happen to come across a photo of the band, they wouldn't recognize me.'

'Yeah, well,' I said, 'you *are* very good at making sure you're looking the other way whenever anyone takes a picture of us.'

He grinned. 'You've noticed, have you?'

I nodded. 'I don't think I've ever seen a photograph of the band that clearly shows your face.'

'Well, that's good . . . I mean, I look a lot different now to how I looked when I was in Belfast. I'm taller, my hair's longer, I'm two years older . . . so I doubt if anyone would recognize me anyway, but still . . .'

'You can't be too careful.'

'Exactly.'

'But the IRA aren't even after *you*, are they? They're looking for Nancy –'

'Yeah, but they know that I'm with her. So if they find me, they find her.'

'And you're still convinced that they really *are* looking for her?'

'Well . . .' he said cautiously, 'that's the thing. I know that they'd like to find her, that they'd *like* to take her out of the picture, but – from what I've heard – it's not particularly high on their list of priorities right now. I mean, if they happen to find out where she is, if someone brings her to their attention, then fine – they'll deal with her. But, according to my contacts, they're not *actively* looking for her any more.'

'Well, that's good, isn't it?'

'I wouldn't say it's *good* –'

'Yeah, but if they're not going out of their way to look for her, you don't have to leave the band, do you?'

'That's exactly what Nancy said.'

I looked at him. 'You've talked to her about it?'

'Yeah.'

'So what does she think?'

'She thinks I should stick with it. The way she sees it, the risk of exposure is so slight that it's hardly worth bothering about, and as long as I don't get my picture on the front page of the *Sun*, there's no need to worry.' He lit a cigarette. 'She thinks it's good for me anyway . . . you know, being in the band. It keeps me occupied, keeps my mind off other things . . . and it brings in a bit of money too, which always helps.' He gave me a slightly embarrassed look. 'And it's kind of a family thing, as well . . . the music. My grandparents always played, my dad was a pretty mean fiddler . . . so, you know, in a way, I'm just kind of following the family tradition.' He smiled. 'That's what Nancy thinks, anyway. She says my mum and dad would have been proud of me.'

I smiled warmly at him.

He said, 'So, yeah, I'll just have to see how it goes, I suppose. I mean, if things start getting any bigger for us . . . well, I might have to reconsider. But, for now, I think I'll probably carry on with the band.'

'Good,' I said, nodding my head a little too vigorously in a dismal attempt to hide the true depth of my relief. 'That's . . . well, it's really good . . .' I smiled at him again. 'And, besides, it's not as if anyone's going to come across your *real* name in the papers, is it?'

He looked at me. 'You mean the whole "Billy the Kid" thing?'

'No,' I said, holding his gaze. 'You know very well that's not what I mean.'

'Do I?'

I shook my head. 'You're doing it again.'

'Doing what again?'

'Answering questions with another question.'

He smiled. 'Well, you know me . . . Mr Mysterious.'

'Is that it?'

'What?'

'Mr Mysterious – is *that* your real name?'

'Damn,' he said, laughing. 'Found out at last.'

The attention that William was starting to attract wasn't easy for Curtis to deal with. He still admired and respected William, and – although he'd never admit it – he still looked upon him with something approaching reverence, but when it became clear that other people were beginning to admire and revere him too . . . well, for Curtis, that was different. That wasn't the way it was supposed to be. *He* was the star, the leader, the genius, and while it was fine for *him* to rave about William, he resented the admiration of others towards him.

He was jealous, basically.

He didn't like it.

Again, he'd never actually admit it, and he always tried to keep his true feelings to himself, but it was obvious – at least, to me – that William's growing popularity was really tearing him up. What made it even worse for him, I think, was that he was perfectly aware of how essential William was to the band, and that without him – without everything he gave us – we probably wouldn't be attracting half as much attention from the press and the record companies.

So, in one sense, William was helping Curtis to achieve his dream . . . but at the same time he was stealing his thunder. Which, naturally, Curtis found pretty confusing. But although I understood and accepted his confusion, that didn't make it any easier to cope with. I mean, Curtis was difficult enough at the best of times – but a permanently confused and conflicted Curtis . . .?

No, it wasn't easy.

He was very good at keeping his feelings to himself when he needed to, and the only times he publicly showed any animosity towards William were on a couple of occasions when William was late for rehearsal, and when he did finally turn up he gave no explanation. He just said, 'Sorry, I got held up.' And even then, Curtis didn't let rip at him or anything, he just kind of scowled at him all night. Another time though, when William missed a rehearsal altogether, Curtis really did go mad at him.

It was towards the end of July, as far as I can remember. It had been another stiflingly hot day, the temperature way up in the 80s, and even at seven o'clock in the evening the warehouse felt like an oven. Because we were gigging a couple of times a week now, we didn't really need to practise quite so regularly any more, but Curtis had recently written some new songs that he was keen to get into the set, so we'd booked the warehouse for two consecutive nights to give ourselves time to learn them.

By seven thirty, there was still no sign of William.

We sat there, waiting . . . sweating . . .

Eight o'clock came and went.

Eight thirty . . .

'We'll give him until nine,' Curtis said. 'And if he's not here by then . . .'

He wasn't.

'*Fuck* it,' Curtis spat. 'Who the *fuck* does he think he is?'

The next night, William turned up at the warehouse at seven o'clock on the dot. He didn't say anything when he came through the door, he just walked in, crossed over to where all the equipment was set up, and put down his guitar case. He seemed a bit distracted, as if he was pre-occupied with something, and I don't think he was even aware of Curtis, let alone that he was standing there glaring angrily at him. Which, of course, made Curtis even angrier.

'Fucking *typ*ical,' he sneered.

William looked at him. 'Sorry?'

'You just stroll in without a fucking word –'

'*What?*'

'Where were you?'

'When?'

'When do you fucking think?'

'Oh, yeah, last night,' William said casually. 'Yeah, sorry about that. Something came up –'

'Yeah, I bet it fucking did,' Curtis said, shaking his head. 'It's always the same with you, isn't it? "Something came up . . . I got held up . . ."' He was mocking William's accent now. '". . . oh, yeah, *sorry* about that . . ."' He stared at William. 'I mean, what is it with you, eh? You think you're *better* than the rest of us, is that it? We have to be here on time, but you can just pick and choose when you want to turn up, and if you can't be bothered to show up at all . . . well, it doesn't really matter, does it? We'll all forgive you anyway because you're so fucking wonderful.'

William said nothing, just stared back at him.

'You know what your trouble is, don't you?' Curtis went on. 'You're starting to let all that crap in the papers go to your head . . . you're actually starting to *believe* it. You're Billy the fucking Wonder Kid, you can do whatever the fuck you want –'

'All right,' William said calmly. 'That's enough.'

'No, you fucking listen to me –'

'You've made your point, Curtis,' William went on, his voice slightly harder now. 'But don't push it, OK?'

'Or else what?'

William sighed. 'Look, I'm sorry about last night, OK? I'm sorry I couldn't be here, and I'm sorry it pissed you off so much. But I had to do something –'

'Yeah? And what was that then? What exactly was this *vitally* important thing you had to do?'

'That's my business.'

Curtis shook his head. 'We sat here for two fucking hours waiting for you – the least you owe us is an explanation.'

'I don't owe you anything.'

'No?'

William just stared at him for a few moments then, and I could tell from the tired-out look in his eyes that he'd had enough of this now. I don't think he was particularly annoyed with Curtis, and he certainly wasn't angry with him, he'd simply had enough. And as I stood there, watching and waiting, I was fully expecting William to just turn round and walk out. I knew that's what he was going to do . . . I just *knew*. And I could already feel the emptiness in my heart.

But I was wrong.

He didn't walk out.

Instead, he looked down at the ground for a moment, let out a quiet sigh, then looked up at Curtis again and said, 'Do you want me to go?'

'What?' Curtis said.

'If you want me to go, just say it. You won't see me again.'

Curtis looked puzzled. 'What do you mean?'

William sighed again and picked up his guitar case. 'What do you want me to do?'

'Stay,' I heard myself say.

Curtis looked at me, his eyes momentarily shocked, then angry, then confused . . . and just for an instant I saw a flash of bitterness too, and something cold and calculating . . . but it was all so mixed up, so chaotic and fleeting, that before I could make any sense of it, Curtis had looked away from me and was smiling, quite genuinely it seemed, at William.

'Hey, come *on*, Billy,' he said breezily. 'Lighten up, for Christ's sake. I was only . . . you know . . . like you said, I was just a bit pissed off, that's all. I mean, it's no big *deal* or anything . . . all right?'

William looked at him for a second or two, making him wait, then – with no expression at all – he just nodded.

'OK,' Curtis said, trying his best to sound upbeat, but not quite managing it. 'Let's get on with it then. I want to see if we can get these new songs sorted out before Friday . . .'

*

After the night at the party, when William had told me all about his life, we hadn't had much chance to talk to each other again. Not on our own, anyway. William didn't socialize with the rest of us very often. He'd sometimes hang around after a gig or a rehearsal and share a couple of drinks with us, but most of the time, once the gig or the rehearsal was over, he'd just pack up his guitar and go. And even when he did hang around with us, I was always with Curtis, so we were very rarely actually on our own together. Even so, the closeness we'd shared that night at the party was never far from my mind, or my heart, and I didn't have to be alone with William to know that he felt the same. The closeness between us, our innocent intimacy, was always just *there* . . . in a shared glance, a fleeting smile, a knowing silence.

It felt good.

But wrong.

Like a purity tainted with sin.

That night, during a break in the rehearsal, I waited for Curtis to go to the toilet and then I went over and spoke to William.

'Are you OK?' I asked him.

'Yeah . . .'

'Sorry about Curtis, you know . . .'

'No problem,' he said, smiling at me. 'Thanks for speaking up for me.'

I shrugged. 'Curtis would never have let you go anyway.'

'You reckon?'

I smiled. 'You're his hero.'

'Yeah, right,' he said, laughing. 'Billy the fucking Wonder Kid . . .'

I glanced across the warehouse, checking to see if Curtis was coming back yet. He wasn't. I turned back to William and lowered my voice. 'Is everything all right? You know, with Nancy and everything . . .?'

'Everything's fine.'

'What about last night . . .? I mean, was that anything to do with –?'

'No.' He looked at me. 'No . . . it was just . . .'

'Something you had to do?'

'Yeah.'

The heat that night was so thick and muggy that it was almost impossible to sleep. After the rehearsal, William had left straight away, and I'd gone to the pub with Curtis, Stan, and Chief. We'd stayed until closing time, then me and Curtis had gone back to the squat and just sat around in his room for a while – listening to music, reading . . . not really talking very much. It was too hot for talking. It was too hot for *any*thing. The window was wide open and we had a little fan going – Curtis had found the fan in a skip a while ago – but the air was so heavy that nothing really made any difference. Curtis was drinking Special Brew and smoking joint after joint, and when he went over to his desk and started scribbling away in his notebook, I decided that I might as well try to get some sleep. I stripped off and lay down on top of the bed, closed my eyes, and tried to think cooling thoughts. I pictured myself sitting beside a mountain stream, dipping my bare feet in the ice-cold water. It was springtime, I imagined, a fresh afternoon in April. The air was crisp and scented with grass, the world was quiet, and a refreshing breeze was drifting down from the mountains, cooling the back of my neck . . .

None of it worked, of course.

I just lay there, covered in sweat, only too aware that far from sitting barefoot beside a mountain stream, I was in fact lying on a clammy bed in the suffocating air of a shabby little room in North London.

I don't know what time it was when I eventually fell asleep, and I don't know what it was that woke me again either. All I knew, as I groggily opened my eyes and sat up in bed, was that

Curtis was sitting in a chair by the window, leaning towards me, his arms resting on his knees, staring intently into my eyes. He was bare-chested, his skin glistening with sweat, and his face in the darkness looked so cruel, so *alien*, that for a moment or two I didn't recognize him. I didn't doubt that it *was* Curtis, I just doubted that I'd ever really known him. He was like a stranger wearing Curtis's skin.

'Curtis . . .?' I mumbled sleepily, rubbing my eyes and glancing at the clock. 'What's going on? It's four o'clock in the morning –'

'What do you think of him?' he said quietly, still staring at me.

'What?'

'Billy . . . William . . . what do you think of him?'

I rubbed my eyes again. 'I don't understand . . . what do you mean?'

He leaned towards me and spoke very slowly. 'What . . . do . . . you . . . think . . . of . . . him?'

'I don't know . . .' I muttered, beginning to feel a little bit scared now. 'He's all right, yeah . . . you know . . . he's OK . . .'

Curtis smiled coldly. 'He's OK?'

'What's this all about, Curtis? Why are you –?'

'You think he's *OK*, do you?'

'Yes,' I sighed. 'Is that a problem?'

'A problem?' he said quickly, leaning back in the chair. 'Why should it be?'

I realized then, as his body slumped to one side, and he tried, but failed, to sit up straight, that he was so stoned out of his head on something that he'd virtually *anaesthetized* himself. All he could do was sit there, slumped sideways in the chair, like a puppet without any strings.

'What do you think of me?' he said.

'I think you need to go to bed. You're totally wrecked –'

'Do you love me?'

'Yes, I love you,' I lied. 'What have you taken tonight?'

'It's a *reasoned* derangement, you know . . .'

'Listen, Curtis –'

'Of all the senses . . . it's a *reasoned* derangement . . . all shapes of love, suffering, and madness . . .' He sighed heavily. 'God, I'm tired.'

'Come on, Curtis,' I said, getting to my feet and going over to him. 'You really need to go to bed now. Here, give me your hand . . . Curtis?'

When he didn't answer, I leaned down and looked at him. His eyes were closed.

He'd passed out in the chair.

22

It'd been rumoured for a while that Malcolm McLaren was trying to arrange a big event in August to showcase the Sex Pistols, and when he finally announced that they'd be playing at the Screen on the Green cinema in Islington on 29 August, supported by the Buzzcocks, the Clash, and Naked, Curtis and Jake were absolutely convinced that this was the chance we'd been waiting for.

'It's going to be *massive*,' Jake said excitedly. '*Every*one's going to be there – journalists, photographers, all the record companies . . . it's just going to be *huge*.'

'Yeah,' Curtis agreed. 'I still think Malcolm should have put us higher up the bill though. I mean, we shouldn't have to play *first*, for Christ's sake. It should be the Buzzcocks first, then the Clash, *then* us, and then the Pistols.'

'Yeah, I know,' Jake said. 'But you know what Malcolm's like . . . he's always doing deals behind the scenes, all kinds of sneaky shit. By the time he agreed to include us in the line-up it was either bottom of the bill or nothing.'

'Yeah, well,' Curtis muttered. 'We'll just have to blow the rest of them off the stage, won't we?'

'Exactly.'

A couple of days later, the significance of the Screen on the Green gig became even greater when Jake told us that he'd just come back from another meeting with Polydor records – who'd been showing a lot of interest in us for a while – and that they were now very close to offering us a contract.

'How close is "very close"?' Curtis asked him.

'Well, they're still being a bit cautious, so it's hard to say for definite, but I kind of got the impression that they're going to make a final decision after the gig in Islington. Most of them are going to be there, and I think they just want to see us one more time before they make up their minds.'

'No pressure then,' Curtis said.

Jake grinned. 'Like you said, all you've got to do is blow everyone else off the stage . . . do that, and we're made.'

The concert was advertised as a 'Midnight Special', with films being shown in the cinema until midnight, and then live music from midnight until dawn. So, even as the first group to play, we still weren't due on stage until just gone twelve. Curtis, though, was adamant that we should get there a lot earlier.

'Everything's got to be dead right,' he explained. 'The sound-check, lights, equipment . . . we can't afford to get anything wrong. There's too much at stake. So I think we should aim to get there for seven o'clock at the latest.'

'That's *five hours* before we're due to start,' I pointed out.

'So?'

'Well, it's a long time to hang around.'

'It's better than being late and fucking things up.'

I was fairly sure that the *real* reason he wanted to get there so early was to make sure that nothing happened without him. All the big names were going to be there – the Pistols, the Clash, the Buzzcocks . . . Rotten, Strummer, Devoto – and there was no way that Curtis was going to let anyone forget that he was a big name too. And if that meant getting to the gig five hours early . . . well, so be it.

The plan, then, was for Chief and Stan to pick us all up from the squat on Sunday evening around six thirty.

'So if you aim to get here about an hour earlier,' Curtis said to William, 'we can get all the gear ready –'

208

'It's easier for me if I meet you there,' William said.

'Where?'

'At the Screen on the Green.'

Curtis looked at him. 'Why?'

'It's my little brother's birthday on Sunday. We're going to the zoo in the afternoon and then he's having a birthday party in the evening. It won't finish until around sevenish –'

'A *birthday* party?' Curtis said, shaking his head in disbelief. 'You're going to be late for the gig because you're going to a fucking *birthday* party?'

'Did I say I was going to be late for the gig?'

'Well, no –'

'And it's not *a* birthday party, it's my *brother's* birthday party. And I promised him I'd be there.'

'Oh, well,' Curtis said sarcastically, 'that's all right then.'

'Yeah,' William said, staring at him. 'I know it is.'

It was obvious that Curtis wasn't happy about William making his own way to the gig, but I think he realized that there wasn't much he could do about it. He couldn't *force* him to change his plans. And if Curtis changed *his* plans – if he offered to wait at the squat for William, having already committed himself to leaving at six thirty – that, to Curtis, would be a sign of weakness. And there was no way he was going to let William think he was weak.

'Don't worry,' William said to him. 'I'll be there by seven thirty, OK?'

'Seven thirty?'

'Eight o'clock at the very latest.'

Things didn't get any better for Curtis when, on the Saturday night before the gig, I came back to the squat, after ringing home from the phone box across the road, and told him that I had to get back to Hampstead as soon as possible because my mother was having some kind of breakdown.

'What do you mean?' he said. 'What kind of "breakdown"?'

'I'm not really sure,' I said, quickly gathering all my stuff together. 'It was a friend of hers on the phone – Laura. She's staying for the weekend and they were supposed to be going out somewhere tonight, but apparently Mum started acting really weird . . . like she was convinced that someone was after her –'

'*After* her?'

'That's what Laura said. Mum thought that someone was coming to get her.'

'Who?'

'She didn't say . . . she just started panicking, really losing control, and then she locked herself in the bathroom and she wouldn't come out. Laura said Mum was terrified . . . crying and screaming –'

'She's probably just stoned.'

I looked at him. 'What?'

He shrugged. 'It can do that to you sometimes, cannabis. It can make you feel really paranoid.'

'Yeah, well . . . whatever it is, I have to go –'

'Are you coming back tonight?'

'I don't *know*, Curtis,' I said impatiently, heading for the door. 'Probably not, OK?'

'What about tomorrow?'

'Ring me,' I said, hurrying out. 'I'll let you know.'

By the time I got home, Laura had called Mum's doctor and he'd come over and given her something to 'calm her down'. Dr Samaros – or Doc Sam, as he liked to be called – was a 'private' physician, with a very select clientele, and Mum had been using him for years. I'd never really liked or trusted him that much, partly because he always looked so unhealthy – permanently off-colour would be a good way of describing him – and, the way I saw it, if he couldn't look after himself properly, how could he look after anyone else? But the main reason I disliked and mistrusted Dr Samaros was that all he ever seemed to do was give Mum drugs. It didn't matter what she claimed to be suffering from, his answer was always the same – take these pills. God *knows* what he gave her over the years – uppers and downers, slimming pills, painkillers . . . packets of pills, bottles of pills, whole boxes of pills – he dished them out like sweets. And Mum, being Mum, never asked any questions. She was more than happy to take whatever he gave her.

Her medicine cabinet was the size of a small wardrobe.

That night, when I got there, Dr Samaros was just on his way out.

'She's sleeping now,' he told me, putting on his coat. 'I've given her a mild anti-psychotic and something to calm her down, and she should be quiet now for the rest of the night.'

'An anti-psychotic?' I said, somewhat alarmed.

He smiled. 'It's all right, Lili, it's only a precaution. Your mother's probably just a little overstressed, that's all . . . you know how she gets.'

'Yeah, but –'

'A good night's sleep and she'll be fine, don't you worry.'

'I *am* worried.'

He smiled again and ruffled my hair, as if I was six years old. 'I'll call round again in the morning, OK?'

And, with that, he was gone.

I gave Laura a quick hug, and thanked her for calling the doctor, then I went up to Mum's bedroom to see how she was doing. The lights were off in her room, and she was curled up in bed, her knees tucked up to her chest and her hands clamped over her head.

'Mum?' I said quietly, sitting down next to her. 'Mum . . .?'

She was fast asleep.

I put my hand on her shoulder and whispered to her again, but there was no response whatsoever. No movement, no sound . . . nothing. She wasn't just fast asleep, she was as good as unconscious. On her bedside table was an open bottle of pills. I picked it up and tried to read the label, but the writing was illegible. I sighed, put the lid back on, dropped the bottle in my pocket, and went downstairs.

Laura told me a little bit more about what had happened. They'd been getting ready to go out, she said, helping each other choose what to wear, and everything had seemed fine.

'We were just enjoying ourselves,' she told me. 'You know, having a bit of a laugh, looking forward to going out, and then suddenly your mum just kind of flipped. She went to the bathroom, and I carried on getting dressed, and when she came back she just started ranting and raving . . .' Laura shook her head. 'It was if she'd suddenly become a different person.'

'What was she ranting and raving about?'

'She kept saying that there was someone downstairs, a man . . . she could hear him walking around. She said she knew who he was, he'd been after her for weeks, but she couldn't tell me his name. And when I asked her *why* this man was after her, she said he was going to kill her.'

'Did *you* hear anything?'

'No,' Laura said, shaking her head. 'There was no one there. I went down and checked. When I went back upstairs, your mum had locked herself in the bathroom. She was absolutely *petrified*.'

'Had she been taking anything? You know, drugs, pills . . .?'

'We had a couple of glasses of wine . . .'

'Nothing else?'

'Not that I'm aware of . . .'

She looked away then, and I was pretty sure she was lying. I knew how it was when she got together with Mum for a night out – a couple of lines of coke to get themselves in the mood, a bottle of wine, a few joints . . .

And maybe Curtis was right, maybe Mum *had* just had a bad

reaction to the dope or the cocaine or whatever . . . maybe that's all it was. She wasn't losing her mind, she'd just had a bad reaction . . .

I wished it was true.

But I knew that it wasn't.

'Has she ever done this before?' Laura asked me.

'No . . .' I said cautiously. 'I mean, she hasn't done *this* . . . but . . . well, you know . . .'

Laura nodded. 'She's been through a lot.'

'Yeah . . .'

We spent the next few hours just sitting around talking . . . mostly about Mum. Laura told me lots of stories about the 'old days', laughing and joking about all the crazy things that Mum and her used to get up to when they were models, before Mum was married. I'd heard most of the stories before, but I didn't really mind hearing them again. It was nice to imagine Mum being happy. Later on, Laura asked me how I was doing – school? boyfriend? the band? – and I managed to avoid telling her anything about school or Curtis by concentrating on Naked instead. The who, the what, the where . . . the music, the punk scene, the gigs . . .

'Have you played anywhere I'd know?' she asked.

I named a few places, but she hadn't heard of any of them.

'How about the Screen on the Green?' I said. 'Have you heard of that?'

She nodded. 'It's a cinema, isn't it? In Islington.'

'Yeah, we're playing there tomorrow night with the Sex Pistols and a few other bands . . .' I started to tell her, but then I remembered Mum. 'Well, we're *supposed* to be playing there tomorrow night . . . I mean, if Mum's not any better –'

'I'm sure she'll be fine tomorrow,' Laura said. 'And I'll be here anyway – I'm staying till Monday at least. So you don't have to worry . . .' She smiled. 'I'll babysit for you.'

*

I checked on Mum again before I went to bed, but she was still completely dead to the world. I covered her up and tucked her in, fetched her a glass of water in case she woke up during the night, and then I went to bed.

The next morning, when I took her a cup of coffee, Mum was already awake and out of bed. She wasn't dressed or anything, she was just sitting in a wicker chair by the window, still in her nightdress, reading a book and smoking a cigarette.

'Hello, love,' she said, surprised to see me. 'What are *you* doing here?'

'I came round last night,' I told her, putting her coffee on the windowsill. 'How are you feeling, Mum?'

'Fine,' she said. 'I'm fine . . . is anything wrong? You haven't had a fight with Curtis, have you?'

'No . . . why?'

She smiled. 'Well, you don't usually come home on a Saturday night . . .'

'I was worried about you.'

She frowned. 'Why?'

'Well, last night . . . you know . . .'

She shook her head, perplexed. 'What *about* last night?'

'Laura told me what happened, Mum.'

'I'm sorry, love, but I really don't know what you're talking about.'

'You were frightened . . .'

'Frightened of what?'

'You thought there was someone in the house –'

'Who?'

'I don't know . . . a man. You told Laura that he was after you, that he was trying to hurt you –'

Mum laughed. 'No one's *after* me . . . why would Laura think that?'

'Is it Dad?'

'Your *father*?'

'Yeah . . . I mean, did you think it was him in the house last night?'

She shook her head in dismay. 'Why on *earth* would I think that?'

'I don't know –'

'Did Laura tell you that Rafa was here?'

'No, she was just worried about you –'

'Why?'

'You were terrified of something.'

'Don't be silly,' she said, laughing again.

'You locked yourself in the bathroom, Mum.'

'No, I didn't –'

'You were crying –'

'That's ri*dic*ulous.'

'Do you remember Doc Sam being here?'

'When?'

'Last night. He gave you some pills –'

'That was last week.'

'Do you remember going to bed?'

She looked at me, blinking rapidly, trying to remember . . . but she couldn't. Or perhaps she just didn't want to.

'Is Laura still here?' she asked suddenly.

'Yeah –'

'What time is it?'

'About ten . . .'

'Is Laura still here?'

Dr Samaros came round a little bit later, and as always he in-sisted on seeing Mum privately, in her bedroom . . . just the two of them. I tried arguing with him, telling him that I should be with her, that she was *my* mother, but he just did what he always did – gave me a patronizing smile and told me that he was only following my mother's instructions.

215

'If you'd like to ask her . . .' he said.

I shook my head, knowing full well what her answer would be, and left them to it.

Half an hour later, when Doc Sam finally came out of Mum's bedroom, all he had to say was, 'She's fine.'

'But she doesn't remember anything about last night,' I pointed out.

'Well, that's not unexpected really . . . it's nothing to worry about. In fact, it's probably best if she *doesn't* remember.'

'Yeah, but –'

'I'm sorry, Lili,' he said, glancing at his watch. 'I really have to go.' He gave me that condescending smile again. 'If she starts playing up again, just call me, OK?'

Nothing much happened for the rest of the morning. Mum seemed to be doing OK. A bit detached perhaps, not altogether *there* . . . but that wasn't unusual. Without actually discussing it, Laura and I decided to avoid any mention of the night before. We just kind of pretended that nothing had happened. We ate lunch together, drank coffee, sat around talking . . .

And then Curtis rang.

I took the call on the phone in the hallway.

'How is she?' he asked.

'Not too bad at the moment,' I said, keeping my voice down. 'She's just a bit . . . I don't know. It's hard to explain –'

'Are you coming back this afternoon?'

'I don't know, Curtis . . . I think I'd better stay for a while, just in case –'

'But you just said she was fine –'

'No . . . I said she wasn't too bad –'

'Same thing.'

'No, it's not –'

'Well, anyway . . .'

'Lili?'

I turned at the sound of Mum's voice. She was standing at the end of the hallway, staring angrily at me. Her body was rigid, her face tense.

'Who are you talking to?' she snapped.

'It's just Curtis –'

'Don't *lie* to me.'

'I'm not –'

'Lili?' I heard Curtis say. 'What's going on?'

'Just a second,' I said into the phone.

'It's *him*, isn't it?' Mum hissed.

'Mum –'

'I know what you're doing!'

'Mum, please –'

'Give me that!' she yelled, grabbing for the phone.

As I instinctively yanked it out of her reach, she suddenly flinched, turning her head away from me as if I was going to hit her.

'No . . .' she muttered. 'Please . . .'

'It's all right, Mum,' I said, reaching out to comfort her. 'I'm not –'

'Don't *touch* me!'

I pulled my hand back.

She stared at me for a few seconds then, her lips moving, but no sound coming out . . . and I knew – I *knew* – that just for a moment she didn't know who I was.

'It's OK, Mum,' I said softly. 'It's me . . . Lili . . . everything's OK –'

'Lili?' Curtis said over the phone.

Mum stared at the handset, her head cocked to one side.

'What's she doing?' Curtis said.

Mum's eyes widened and she clamped her hand over her mouth, suddenly terrified.

'It's *Curtis*, Mum,' I said. 'It's only Curtis –'

'Don't tell him anything,' she pleaded, her voice a broken whisper. 'Please . . .? Don't tell him I'm here . . .'

'Are you there?' I heard Curtis say.

Mum just turned and ran then, clattering hysterically up the stairs, almost falling over in her haste to get away.

'Mum!' I called out after her. '*Mum!*'

I heard the bathroom door crashing open, then slamming shut . . . and then all I could hear was the sound of muffled sobbing. I couldn't move for a while. I just stood there, staring hopelessly up the stairs, my heart beating hard and my eyes filling with tears . . .

'Lili . . .?' I heard Curtis say. 'Are you still there? Lili?'

I slowly put the phone to my ear. 'Yeah, I'm still here.'

'What the fuck's going on –?'

'Not now, Curtis,' I said emptily. 'I'll tell you later.'

'How *much* later?' he said angrily. 'When are you –?'

'Just ring me later.'

'Yeah, but –'

I hung up.

It was two or three hours before Mum stopped crying and came out of the bathroom. While she was in there, I must have called Dr Samaros at least a dozen times, but he was either out somewhere or just not answering his phone. Mum looked exhausted when she finally came out of the bathroom – her eyes red and puffy, her skin deathly pale, her movements slow and heavy.

'Are you OK, Mum?' I asked her.

'Tired,' she muttered. 'Just tired . . .'

Laura helped me get her into bed, and then . . . well, then I just sat with her for a few hours. She slept restlessly – tossing and turning, twitching, shivering . . . muttering to herself now and then . . . whispered words of madness.

I just sat there.

Laura was still trying to get through to Dr Samaros on the phone downstairs, and every time she picked up the phone and put it down again, the phone on Mum's bedside table made a soft tinging noise.

Ting . . .

The curtains were still drawn, and the dimmed afternoon light seemed old and heavy. The air was hot and humid, and through a small gap in the curtains I could see dark clouds hanging low in the sky. Every now and then, faint rolls of thunder murmured in the distance.

I just sat there.

Ting . . .

It was around five o'clock when Laura brought me up a cup of coffee.

'I got through to him at last,' she told me. 'The doctor . . . he said he'll be here in about an hour.'

'Thanks,' I said, taking the coffee from her.

Laura looked at Mum. 'How is she?'

I shrugged. 'It's hard to tell . . . she's just sleeping . . .'

'Are *you* all right?'

'Yeah . . . you know . . .'

'What time's your concert tonight?'

'Well, we're supposed to be there at seven, but –'

'You don't *have* to stay, Lili,' she said kindly. 'I can sit with your mum –'

'No, it's all right, thanks. I'll stay –'

The telephone rang.

I picked it up. 'Hello?'

'Lili? It's Curtis. What's going on?'

'The doctor's coming round in an hour,' I told him.

'An *hour*? It's gone five already.'

'Yeah, I know –'

'So what time will you get here?'

'Look, Curtis, I don't know if I can make it tonight –'

'*What?*'

'Mum's really ill –'

'You can't *do* this, Lili,' he said angrily. 'You *can't* fuck this up . . . not tonight.'

'I'm sorry, Curtis, but I can't just leave her –'

'Yeah, well, you're just going to have to, aren't you?'

'No –'

'Or bring her with you.'

'What?'

'If you can't leave her, bring her with you.'

'Don't be *stupid*.'

'Fuck's *sake*, Lili,' he screamed. 'What's the *matter* with you? This is *important*. Don't you get it? This . . . is . . . *fucking* . . . *important*!'

'So is this,' I said quietly, and put the phone down.

I looked quietly at Mum . . . her troubled face, her worn-out beauty . . .

I looked at Laura. She smiled sympathetically.

The phone rang again.

I picked it up. 'Yeah?'

'Listen, Lili,' Curtis said quickly. 'I'm sorry, OK? I'm *really* sorry . . . I didn't mean to yell at you, I was just –'

'I'll get there if I can,' I told him.

'Yeah?'

'If I'm not at the squat by seven, and I probably won't be, go on without me.'

'Well, OK, but –'

'Just shut up and *listen* to me, Curtis, OK?'

'Yeah, yeah, of course.'

'*If* I think it's all right to leave Mum,' I said wearily, 'I'll make my own way over to Islington as soon as I can. But I'm not making any promises, all right?'

'Yeah . . .'

'If I'm not there by eleven, you can assume that I'm not coming and you'll just have to manage without me.'

'We can't –'

'William can play bass . . . or you can.'

'Yeah, but –'

'That's *it*, Curtis,' I said firmly. 'I'm not arguing with you. Have you got that?'

'Yeah . . .'

'I'll see you if I see you.'

By eight o'clock, Dr Samaros had been and gone, and Mum was sleeping deeply.

'I've given her something that'll keep her out for at least twelve hours,' Doc Sam had told me. 'She might be a little woozy when she wakes up, but with a bit of luck, a good long rest will clear her mind and she won't have any more of these episodes.'

'With a bit of luck?' I said.

'Call me tomorrow,' he said, ignoring my sarcasm. 'Let me know how she's doing.'

After he'd left, I sat with Mum again for a while . . . not really knowing what to do, or how to feel . . . just sitting there, listening to the rumble of distant thunder . . . too tired to do anything, too wired to sleep . . .

Laura came in at some point and quietly gave me a hug.

'You might as well go, Lili,' she said softly.

'Sorry?'

'Your concert . . . I mean, if you feel like it, you might as well go. There's no point in staying here, is there? Your mum's going to be asleep all night, there's nothing you can do for her. All you're going to do if you stay is sit here all night worrying.' She smiled at me. 'It'll be all right . . . I'll sleep in here, just in case she wakes up. And I can always ring you at the cinema if necessary . . . the Screen on the Green, wasn't it?'

'Yeah . . .'

She grinned. 'And I'm sure Curtis will be happy to see you.'

I allowed myself a little smile. 'You wouldn't say that if you knew him.'

'Really?'

I nodded. 'He's not really a "happy" kind of person.'

'He's more of a dark, brooding type, is he?'

'Yeah, you could say that.'

If it had been just another gig that night, I think I probably would have stayed at home, but it wasn't just another gig. It was a gig that could change our lives for ever. And while the prospect of getting signed by a record company didn't mean all that much to me, it meant the world to Curtis. It was the gateway to his everything. And however I felt about him just then, whatever he meant to me, I couldn't just let him down, could I? I couldn't ruin his dream.

And so, with a mixed-up heart – and a pocketful of cash I'd taken from Mum's purse – I told Laura I'd call her later, kissed Mum goodbye, and went out to look for a taxi.

23

It was just gone nine o'clock when I arrived at the Screen on the Green. The streetlights were on, the air was still hot, and the night sky was heavy with rolling black clouds. After wandering around the cinema for a while, trying to work out where I was supposed to go, I finally found Curtis in a smoke-filled room backstage. It wasn't a very big room, and there were so many people and bits of equipment in there – guitars, amps, speakers, drums – that I could hardly get through the door. I didn't have a clue who most of the people were. Some of them, I guessed, were roadies, others were probably just friends of the bands, or people who *wanted* to be friends of the bands. Steve Jones and Paul Cook from the Pistols were there, sharing a bottle of vodka with a couple of scantily dressed punk girls. And I could just make out Jake, over in the corner, rolling a joint and laughing about something with a middle-aged man in a suit who I'd never seen before. It took me a while to spot Curtis, but eventually I saw him – sitting on the floor at the back of the room, talking animatedly to Mick Jones and Paul Simonon from the Clash.

Rather than wade through all the bodies, I just called out to him from the doorway. And when he looked up at the sound of his name, I could tell from his eyes – which were popping out of his head – that he'd taken a lot of speed.

'Lili!' he cried out, quickly getting to his feet. 'Thank *God* you're here.'

As he hurried across the room towards me, his amphetamine

eyes darting all over the place, it suddenly struck me that within the space of half an hour or so I'd gone from one extreme to the other. From Mum, at home, sedated out of her head . . . to Curtis, here, *speeding* out of his head.

What, I wondered, was *that* all about?

Before I had time to think about it, Curtis came stumbling up to me, grabbed me by the arm, and said, 'I need to talk to you,' and the next thing I knew he was bundling me out into the corridor.

'All right,' I told him. 'Take it easy. There's no need to –'

'Do you know where he lives?'

'Who?'

'Billy . . . do you know where he lives?'

'Why?'

'He's not fucking *here*, is he? That's why. It's gone nine o'clock and the little bastard's still not here.' Curtis shook his head. 'I *knew* I couldn't trust him . . . I just fucking *knew* it.'

'I'm sure it's all right,' I said. 'He's probably just –'

'No,' Curtis said angrily. 'It's not *all right*. He said he'd be here by eight at the latest.'

'And he hasn't phoned or anything?'

'I would have *told* you if he had, wouldn't I?'

'All right,' I said, trying to keep calm. 'I'm only trying to –'

'West Green Road, isn't it? That's where he lives – somewhere on West Green Road.'

'Cranleigh Farm,' I said.

Curtis looked at me.

'It's an estate on West Green Road,' I told him.

'That's where Billy lives?'

I nodded. 'I mean, I don't know which flat or anything –'

'How do you know he lives there?'

'He told me.'

'When?'

'I don't know,' I said, not quite sure why I was lying, or why

I felt guilty. 'He just mentioned it once, that's all . . . I can't remember *when* . . .' I looked at Curtis. 'Does it matter?'

He just shrugged and lit a cigarette.

'Anyway,' I said, 'I'm sure he'll be here soon. I mean, it's still only half past nine. As long as he gets here before midnight –'

'And what if he doesn't?'

'We'll just have to play without him, won't we. We've done it before . . . played as a three-piece. We can do it again.'

'Yeah,' Curtis said. 'But it wouldn't be the same, would it? I mean, without Billy . . .' He hesitated, puffing hard on his cigarette, uncomfortable about saying what he wanted to say. 'Well, we need him, don't we?'

'You don't have to be embarrassed about it,' I said.

'About what?'

'How you feel.'

'How I feel about *what*?'

'About William . . . I mean, just because he really pisses you off –'

'All I care about right now is this gig, OK? Everything else is irrelevant.'

'Is that why you haven't asked me about my mum?'

'What?'

'My mum . . . she's really ill, remember?'

'Yeah, I know –'

'You could have at least *pretended* to care.'

'I *do* care –'

'No, you don't. You haven't even asked me how *I* am.'

'Yeah, I know, but . . .' He blew out his cheeks. 'It's just that I've hardly had time to think –'

'You've had enough time to shovel a load of speed up your nose.'

'Yeah, well . . . I'm having to organize everything on my own, aren't I?'

'Poor you.'

He didn't like that, and for a moment I thought he was going to lose his temper with me, but he just about managed to control himself.

'You want to try thinking about someone other than yourself now and then,' I said. 'I mean, you're not the only one with problems, you know.'

He lowered his eyes, trying to show me how utterly ashamed of himself he was.

It was pathetic.

And for a moment, I really felt like slapping him.

But then, quite suddenly, I realized that I just didn't care any more. He was Curtis; he was how he was. And that's all there was to it. I could take him as he was . . . or I could leave him.

'All right,' I sighed. 'What do you want to do about William?'

The way Curtis saw it, there was no point in all of us staying there and just hoping that William would turn up, so one of us might as well drive out to West Green Road and see if we could find him.

'I know it's a long shot,' Curtis said, 'and it'll probably be a complete waste of time . . . but, like I said, we don't *all* have to hang around here, do we?'

'I suppose not . . .'

'And if you get going with Chief right now –'

'Me?'

'Yeah . . .'

'Why me?'

'Because . . .'

'Because what?'

'Because if *I* go, and I find him, and it turns out that he just couldn't be bothered to get here on time, or he forgot all about it or something . . . well, you know what I'm like. I'll probably start yelling at him, and then he'll get really pissed off . . .' Curtis looked at me. 'But he likes you, Lili. He'll listen to you.'

I was slightly taken aback for a moment. I just wasn't *used* to Curtis being like this . . . whatever *this* was. It was almost as if he was behaving like a normal person – being reasonable, being aware of his own faults, being honest. Of course, it was perfectly possible that he was just being whatever he thought I wanted him to be, in order to get what he wanted . . .

'So what do you think?' he asked me, glancing at his watch. 'If you leave now, you should get to West Green Road by ten. It shouldn't be too hard to find this Cranleigh Farm place, then all you have to do is ask around and see if anyone knows where Billy lives –'

'And what if they don't?'

'We won't be any worse off than we are now, will we? I mean, as long as you start heading back by eleven-ish, you'll be back here no later than eleven thirty, and if he's still not shown up by then . . . well, in that case, we *will* have to play without him.' Curtis looked at me. 'I think it's worth *trying* to find him though, isn't it?'

It'd been a long tiring day, and my head felt really frazzled, and the last thing I wanted to do just then was go driving round London in a crappy old Transit van . . . but I could see that Curtis had a point. I probably *wasn't* going to find William, but it made sense to at least make the effort. And, besides, the only alternative was to hang around here for the next couple of hours with Curtis and Jake in a room full of roadies and wannabes and Sex Pistols and half-naked punk girls and creepy old men in suits . . .

'OK,' I told Curtis. 'I'll give it a go.'

While Curtis went off to find Chief, I called home from a pay-phone in the corridor. Mum was still sleeping, Laura told me, everything was fine . . . there was nothing to worry about. To be honest, I was getting a bit sick of people telling me that there was nothing to worry about, but I knew that Laura meant well – and that I was in a particularly irritable mood anyway – so I just thanked her, told her that I'd ring again in an hour or so, and said goodbye.

When I hung up the phone and turned round, I almost bumped into Chief. He was standing so close to me that I had to step back to look up into his face.

'Hey,' he said.

'Hey, Chief,' I replied, looking around for Curtis. 'Where's Curtis?'

Chief just shrugged. 'The van's round the back.'

'OK . . .'

He looked at me for a moment, nodded, then walked off.

I followed him – along the corridor, through the double doors, along some more corridors – until, eventually, we came to an unlocked fire door that led us out to the back of the building. The night air was still quite warm, but it was just beginning to rain now, and as we hurried across to the Transit van, a roar of thunder ripped through the sky and almost immediately the rain started crashing down. I wasn't wearing a coat – just a T-shirt and jeans – and by the time we got to the van, I was already soaked to the skin. Chief seemed to be taking ages to unlock the doors, and when I looked over to see what was keeping him, I saw him standing at the side of the van staring down at the ground.

'Come on, Chief,' I shouted over the rain. 'Open the doors . . . I'm getting soaked here.'

He looked up slowly at me, shaking his head.

'What is it?' I said. 'What's the matter?'

'Flat.'

'What?'

'Flat tyre.'

A flash of lightning lit up the night for a moment, followed seconds later by another huge crack of thunder. It was a lot louder this time, a lot closer.

'Have you got a spare?' I shouted.

He shook his head. 'Flat.'

'A *spare* tyre,' I yelled. 'Have you got a spare tyre?'

'It's flat.'

'The spare's flat?'

He nodded.

'Shit.'

Chief didn't seem bothered at all, he was just standing there in the pouring rain, not saying anything, not doing anything . . . apparently not feeling anything. He was just kind of *being* there, just accepting the moment for what it was – which was pretty much what he did all the time – and it suddenly struck me that it wasn't such a bad way to live your life. No complications, no catastrophes, no calamitous ups and downs . . .

I shook my head.

'Hey, Chief!' I yelled. 'Open the doors, will you? We might as well get out of the rain for a minute.'

'Eh?'

I mimed turning a key. 'Unlock the doors!'

'They're open.'

'What?'

'They're already open.'

The sound of the rain hammering down on the roof of the van was, for some reason, oddly comforting. It somehow made me feel safe, secure, almost cosy. And I wouldn't have minded just sitting there for a while – watching the rain streaming down the windscreen, looking out for the lightning, listening to the thunder . . .

But I had things to do.

I turned to Chief, who was sitting beside me in the driver's seat, calmly smoking a cigarette. 'I'm going to have to get a taxi,' I told him. 'Can you let Curtis know?'

He nodded.

I reached into my pocket and pulled out the money I'd taken

from Mum's purse, making sure I had enough for a taxi. I'd actually got a lot more than I thought, well over £100, which was more than enough.

'Just tell him that I took a taxi to Cranleigh Farm,' I said to Chief. 'And that I'll get a taxi back, OK?'

Chief nodded again.

I said, 'I'll be back by eleven thirty at the latest.'

'Right . . . eleven thirty.'

'OK,' I said, peering through the windscreen. 'Well, it doesn't look as if this rain is going to stop any time soon, so I might as well get going now.'

'Hold on,' Chief said, reaching over the back of the seat. 'Here . . . take this.' He passed me a coat, a big black donkey jacket, the kind of thing that workmen wear. 'It's not pretty,' he said, 'but it'll keep you dry.'

'Thanks, Chief,' I said, smiling at him.

'And this . . .' he added, passing me a dusty old biker's cap.

I stuck the cap on my head, still smiling at him. 'How do I look?'

'Beautiful,' he said, and for the first time in my life I saw him smile.

I leaned across and kissed him on the cheek. 'See you later, Chief.'

He grinned. 'Not if I see you first.'

I smiled at him again, then opened the van door, put on the donkey jacket, and scurried off into the rain.

24

Cranleigh Farm wasn't the worst council estate in North London, and it probably wasn't the biggest either, but for someone like me – a public-school girl from a wealthy family, with a big house in Hampstead – it was like stepping into a whole different world. And as I stood in the middle of the concrete square where the taxi driver had dropped me off, and I gazed all around me at the high-rise blocks and the ruined playgrounds, the rusted iron railings and the graffitied walls . . . I couldn't help wondering what the hell I was doing here.

This wasn't *my* world . . .

This wasn't where I belonged . . .

This was *scary*.

The thunderstorm had faded away now, but the rain was still coming down pretty heavily, so it wasn't surprising that there weren't that many people around. An old black guy was walking his dog across the square, and there was a group of kids hanging around the entrance to one of the tower blocks, but apart from that, the estate seemed deserted. I knew that it *wasn't* deserted though. I could hear music playing somewhere – the Bee Gees – and from somewhere else, the sound of Alice Cooper. I could hear a car revving up, and voices in the distance . . . someone laughing, someone shouting. And I could *feel* people watching me too. People in the tower blocks, watching me from their windows . . . wondering who I was, and what I was doing here . . .

I felt really uneasy.

I didn't *want* to feel uneasy. I wanted to feel how I thought I *should* feel – not scared, not out of my depth, not like a prim little rich girl haughtily sniffing the dirt . . .

But I was what I was.

And, like it or not, there wasn't much I could do about it.

I looked at my watch. It was 10.05. I pulled up my coat collar, tucked my hair into my hat, and started heading over to the kids by the tower block.

There were four of them – three boys and a girl, all of them about seventeen or eighteen – and they'd been watching me on and off since I'd got out of the taxi. One of the boys was a tough-looking black kid wearing a black leather coat and platform shoes, the other two were slightly younger-looking white boys. They both had longish hair, parted in the middle, and they both wore round-collared shirts and flared denim jeans. The girl had feathercut hair and was dressed in a tank top, miniskirt, and long brown boots.

I had no idea if they were friendly or not, but I was glad that I'd forgotten to get changed before I left the house, so I wasn't wearing the kind of clothes that I usually wore for a gig. If I'd been wearing anything even remotely punky . . . well, back then, in a place like this, it really wouldn't have been a good idea. As it was though, in my T-shirt and jeans, and Chief's donkey jacket and cap, I was reasonably sure that I didn't look *too* weird. And even if I did look a *bit* weird – which, come to think of it, I probably did – it wasn't in an obviously identifiable way. As long as no one could look at me and think *she's a punk*, I'd probably be OK.

That's what I was hoping anyway.

'Excuse me,' I said, walking up to the four kids. 'I'm looking for a boy –'

'Aren't we all?' the girl said, grinning.

I smiled.

She stopped grinning.

The black kid said, 'You got any cigarettes?'

'Uh . . . no, sorry –'

'Got the time?'

I looked at my watch. 'It's nearly ten past –'

'Nice . . .'

'Sorry?'

'The watch . . . very nice.' He looked at one of the other boys. 'Looks like yours, Dave, doesn't it?'

'Yeah.'

The black kid looked back at me. 'Dave lost his watch . . . someone nicked it. Looks just like yours.' He moved towards me, smiling. 'Where do you get it?'

'It's mine,' I said, stepping back. 'Look, I don't want any –'

'What?' he said, suddenly stopping. 'You think I'm going to *rob* you?'

'I don't –'

'Now why would you think that?' he said, grinning.

I didn't know what to say then. I was frightened, confused . . . not sure if I ought to be frightened or not . . .

'What do you want?' the black kid said, not grinning any more.

'I'm looking for someone –'

'Who?'

'William Bonney. He lives somewhere on this estate –'

'Bonney?'

'Yeah . . .' I said, realizing that they were all staring at me now, and that their demeanour had suddenly changed. It was as if, at the mere mention of William's name, they'd all become smaller, less confident . . . less scary.

'Do you know him?' I asked.

The black kid shook his head. 'No . . .'

As I looked over at the others, I saw one of the boys glance briefly at the block of flats to his right.

'Is that where William lives?' I said to him.

'Eh?'

'Do you know which flat he's in?'

The boy shook his head. 'I don't know anyone called Bonney.'

It was obvious that he was lying.

But not so obvious why.

And when I asked the other boy and the girl if they knew anything about William, they were both equally evasive – mumbling and shaking their heads, avoiding eye contact. I turned back to the black kid. He'd lit a cigarette now and was moving away from me.

'I'm a friend of William's' I told him. 'You don't have to worry –'

'You're not listening,' he said. 'We don't know him, OK?'

'Yeah, but –'

'You're starting to piss me off, girl,' he said, staring hard at me. 'And that's not something you want to do, do you understand?'

'Well, yeah –'

'Good. Now why don't you just turn round and fuck off back to wherever you came from, all right?'

We stared at each other for a while then, and I realized – somewhat to my surprise – that I wasn't quite so frightened of him now. I still didn't feel confident enough to push him any further about William, but I certainly didn't feel threatened any more.

'See you then,' he said, still staring at me.

I held his gaze for a few more moments, then nodded, turned round, and calmly walked away.

I didn't look back until I was halfway across the square, heading for the exit to West Green Road. All four of them were still just standing there, watching me, so I turned back and carried on walking. The rain had almost stopped now, but the air was still heavy and thick, and I was pretty sure the storm wasn't over yet.

I went out through the gates of the estate, turned right, and walked along the pavement for a while. When I stopped in the shelter of a big old plane tree and looked back at the estate again, I saw the four kids heading across the square towards the tower block that one of the boys had glanced at earlier.

I stepped back behind the tree, making sure that I had a clear view of the kids and the tower block, and then I just watched and waited.

I watched them going into the block.

I waited.

I kept my eyes on the tower-block windows, scanning them for any sudden movement – a face at the window, a light coming on, a light going off . . .

I knew that it was probably a waste of time. I was only guessing from the boy's reaction that this was where William lived, and even if my further assumption was right – that the kids not only knew him, but that they knew him well enough to keep their mouths shut about where he lived, *and* that he'd want to know immediately if anyone started asking questions about him – well, even if that *was* what they were doing right now – letting him know about me – the chances of me spotting him when, and if, he looked out of the window were still fairly slim. He might be in one of the flats with no lights on, he might live on the other side of the block, he might not be home at all . . .

But I carried on watching anyway.

And after a minute or two I *did* see something.

It wasn't William's face, it was the face of a woman. I only saw it for a moment – a brief twitch of a curtain, a face looking out, scanning the streets . . . it could have been anyone. But then, just before the curtain closed again, I saw someone else at the window, someone standing behind the woman, talking to her and pointing down at the square . . .

The girl in the tank top.

The curtain closed, but I kept my eyes on the window, fixing its position in my mind: seventh floor, last window on the left . . . *my* left. I muttered this over and over again to myself – *seventh floor, last on your left . . . seventh floor, last on your left* – until I was absolutely sure that I wouldn't forget it, and then I just waited.

It didn't take long.

After a few minutes, the four kids came out of the tower block and began wandering back across the square. When they got to the other tower block, the one they'd come from, the two boys and the girl went inside and the black kid carried on without them. I watched him as he wandered off across the estate, heading – I guessed – for whichever block he lived in, and I didn't stop watching until he was out of sight. I waited a couple of minutes, just to make sure that he wasn't coming back, then I stepped out from behind the plane tree and went looking for the woman whose face I'd seen at the window.

There was no one around as I entered the tower block and got into the lift. I hit the button for the seventh floor, waited for the doors to close, and shook the worst of the rain from my coat. As the lift groaned and rattled its way up, I found myself looking around at everything – the graffitied walls, the rows of buttons, the printed instructions on what to do in case of an emergency – and it wasn't until the lift had almost reached the seventh floor that I realized what I was actually doing. I wasn't just looking around at everything, I was trying to sense William's presence. I was trying to imagine him travelling up and down in this lift every day, trying to imagine his face, his eyes, his thoughts, his feelings . . .

The lift tinged.

And stopped.

Seventh floor.

The doors opened, and I stepped out into the corridor. It was empty. A desolate silence hung in the air, and as I turned right and headed down the hallway, the sound of my footsteps on the hard linoleum floor seemed to resound with the weariness of age-old echoes.

I stopped outside the door at the end of the corridor, double-checking in my mind that I was in the right place. The window had been the last on my *left* when I was facing the tower block, so now that I was actually in here, facing the other way, it was the last on the *right*.

Was that right?

I was pretty sure it was.

I lifted my hand to knock on the door, then hesitated . . .

What if I was wrong? What if this wasn't the right flat? Or what if it *was* the right flat but I was wrong about everything else? What if the girl in the tank top I'd seen at the window wasn't *the* girl in the tank top? What if she was just *a* girl in a tank top? Or what if she *was* the Tank Top girl, but she was just visiting the woman who lived here . . . and the woman who lived here wasn't Nancy at all, she was just a woman, and she'd just happened to be looking out of the window earlier on to see of it was still raining or something? Or what if . . .?

'Shut *up*,' I muttered to myself. 'For Christ's sake . . . just shut up and get on with it.'

I took a deep breath, let it out slowly, and knocked on the door.

'Who is it?'

It was a woman's voice, a Northern Irish accent.

I leaned in close to the door and said, 'My name's Lili, I'm a friend of William's. We play in the band together –'

'What's your surname?'

'Pardon?'

'Your second name, what is it?'

'Garcia.'

'What's your band called?'

'Naked.'

'And what instrument do you play?'

'Bass guitar. Is William –?'

'Name one of your songs.'

'Sorry?'

'Give me the name of one of your songs.'

'Well . . . there's one called "Heaven Hill". And another one –'

'All right, just a second.'

I heard lots of bolts being unlocked then – bolts, chains, locks – and eventually the door swung open and I was face to face with the woman I'd seen at the window. There was little doubt in my mind now that she *was* Nancy – who else would have asked me all those questions? – and the smile on her face as she opened the door was enough to banish any remaining doubts from my mind. It was a good smile – kind and friendly and true – but it was a troubled smile too. Tired, sad . . . the smile of a weary soul.

'Hello, Lili,' she said. 'It's so nice to meet you at last. William's told me all about you. I'm Nancy.'

I nodded, suddenly unsure what to say.

Nancy smiled again. 'Would you like to come in?'

'Uh . . . no,' I muttered. 'No, thanks . . . I'm just . . . I was just –'

'You're *soaking* wet,' she said, looking at me. 'Why don't you just come in for a minute and get dried off?'

She stepped back, opening the door to let me in.

I hesitated for a moment, not really sure *why* I was hesitating, and then – with a slightly embarrassed smile – I went inside.

*

Before I had a chance to ask her about William – who obviously wasn't there – Nancy showed me into the bathroom, gave me a towel, and went off to fetch me some dry
clothes. I tried telling her not to bother, that I was fine, but
she insisted.

'Here,' she said, coming back with a T-shirt and a pair of jeans.
'I think they should fit you OK. We're just about the same size.'

'Thanks . . .'

She smiled. 'I'll go and make us a cup of tea, OK?'

'Yeah.'

The clothes were a fraction too big for me, but it *was* nice to
get into something dry at last. And despite their slight bagginess,
and the fact that they belonged to a woman at least twice as old
as me, the T-shirt and jeans were actually not bad at all. Faded
blue denims, with narrow legs and patched-up knees, and a
short-sleeved black T-shirt with a question mark printed on the
front.

Nancy, I decided, was a pretty cool person.

She was younger than I'd imagined – in her mid- to late-thirties
– and the way she looked and dressed was also quite different to
the picture of her I'd built up in my mind. For some reason, I'd
come to think of her as being fair-haired and pale-skinned, with
a slim figure and a rather stern face. Whereas, in fact, she had
shoulder-length dark red hair, a fairly full figure, and a classically
beautiful face. And in place of the traditional nurse's uniform
that I'd – quite stupidly – always imagined her wearing, she was
dressed almost hippyishly in a pair of denim dungarees over a
lacy white vest.

I thought for a moment about *my* mum . . .

And then I had to remind myself that Nancy *wasn't* William's
mum . . .

And also . . .

I looked at my watch.

It was 10.45, a *lot* later than I'd thought.

I quickly towel-dried my hair, hung my wet clothes on a drier by the door, and went out to find Nancy.

'I'm sorry, Lili,' she told me. 'I really don't know where William is.'

We were in the sitting room now, sipping from mugs of steaming hot, and very strong, tea. I'd quickly explained the situation to Nancy – about the gig and William and everything – but so far she hadn't been able to help. William hadn't said anything to her about the gig, she told me, and she hadn't seen him since he'd left the flat around six o'clock. It was tempting then to ask her about Joe's birthday party, but I'd already had a pretty good look around the sitting room, and I hadn't seen any evidence of either a party or a birthday. No birthday cards, no cakes, no balloons, no presents. So, unless Little Joe's birthday party had been the most unparty-like party imaginable, I had to assume that William had been lying.

'Did he say where he was going?' I asked Nancy.

She shook her head. 'He rarely does.'

'What about when he'd be back? Did he give you any idea . . .?'

'No . . .' She looked at me. 'Actually, come to think of it, I don't *think* he had his guitar with him when he left.'

'No, he wouldn't have,' I told her. 'He left it at Curtis's place on Saturday.'

'Oh, right . . .' She took another sip of tea. 'Joe might know something . . . I'll give him a shout.'

'Don't wake him if he's asleep,' I said.

'Asleep?' She laughed. 'That boy *never* sleeps.' She turned towards a door at the far end of the room. 'Joe!' she called out. 'Can you come here a minute, please?'

The door opened almost immediately and Little Joe stepped into the room. Apart from the fact that he was a few inches shorter than William – and a couple of years younger, obviously

– he looked almost exactly the same as his brother. Same face, same hair, same eyes . . . even his posture was virtually a carbon copy of William's.

'This is Lili,' Nancy told him. 'She's looking for William. Do you know where he is?'

Joe looked at me, then looked back at Nancy and shook his head.

'When did you last see him?' Nancy asked.

'Just before he went out.'

'Did he tell you where he was going?'

'No, he just went out.'

'OK . . .' She smiled at him. 'Lili plays in William's band.'

He looked at me. 'You're in Naked?'

'Yeah.'

'I'm thinking of forming a band.'

'Really?'

He nodded. 'I'm going to be the singer.'

I smiled. 'Good choice.'

'Yeah, I know.' He looked at Nancy. 'Is William in trouble?'

'No, love, he's not in trouble . . . we just want to find out where he is, that's all.'

Joe just nodded.

Nancy smiled at him again. 'I'll see you in a minute, OK?'

After another quick nod, and a brief glance at me, Joe went back through the door and closed it quietly behind him.

'Wow,' I said quietly. 'He's the spitting *image* of William.'

'I know,' Nancy said, smiling. 'And he's getting more and more like him every day.'

'How old is he?'

'He was thirteen in June.'

So I was right about the birthday party. William *had* lied.

I glanced at my watch. It was 11.05.

'Are you all right for time?' Nancy asked.

'Well, I'd better get going really, if you don't mind.'

'Of course not.' She got to her feet. 'If William does come back tonight, what do you want me to do?'

'You couldn't just punch him in the head for me, could you?'

She laughed. 'No problem.'

'Actually,' I said, standing up, 'you know what's going to happen, don't you?'

Nancy nodded. 'He's going to be at the cinema when you get back.'

'Exactly.'

'He'll be sitting there, calm as you like, smoking a cigarette and drinking beer, wondering what all the fuss is about.'

'Yep.'

'And then you'll come in, soaking wet again and really fed up –'

'And *I'll* punch him in the head.'

'Ex*act*ly,' she said, and we both burst out laughing.

On the way out of the flat, I thanked Nancy for the T-shirt and jeans and told her that I'd get them washed as soon as possible and give them to William to bring back to her.

'Why don't you just bring them back yourself,' she suggested. 'There's no rush to get them back, and it'd be lovely to see you again. And you can pick up your clothes while you're here.'

'Yeah, OK,' I said. 'I'd like that.'

'Good.' She smiled at me. 'Well, I hope everything turns out all right tonight.'

'I'm sure it will.'

She unlocked all the bolts and chains on the front door, went to open it, then paused. After a moment's silence, she turned to me and looked me in the eye.

'William has a good heart,' she said quietly. 'He doesn't always do the right thing, and there's no excuses for that, and sometimes he gives the impression that he doesn't care enough about other people's feelings. But deep down, in his heart, he's the most selfless and *truly* caring person I've ever known.' She smiled sadly. 'That probably doesn't make any sense at all, does it?'

'Yes, it does,' I said. 'It makes perfect sense.'

25

It didn't dawn on me until I was leaving the tower block and heading back across the square to West Green Road that Nancy hadn't given me any explanation for all the questions she'd asked before letting me in. I didn't *need* an explanation, of course, I knew that she was just checking to make sure that I was who I said I was, and I knew why she was doing it. But *she* didn't know that. Or maybe she did? Maybe William had told her that he'd confided in me . . . and maybe that was why she hadn't said anything about the four kids either, or asked me how I'd worked out exactly where she lived . . .?

Or maybe, I thought, she just didn't *want* to talk about those kinds of things?

Not that it really mattered.

She was nice, that was the main thing.

And I liked her.

The rain was really starting to pour down again now, and there was a stormy stillness to the air that felt as if it was going to break any minute. I hurried out onto West Green Road, hoping that I wouldn't have to wait long for a taxi. And I didn't. Just as the night sky seemed to lower itself to the ground, darkening the rainswept street, and the first faint roll of thunder crackled through the air, I saw the welcoming yellow light of a black cab coming down the road.

I put my hand out, stepped back as the taxi pulled up, and got in the back.

It was 11.20 now, and as the taxi rumbled along Green Lanes I wondered if I should ask the driver to stop at a phone box so I could ring Curtis and let him know where I was and what was happening. I'd thought about calling him from Nancy's flat, but then I'd remembered that she didn't have a phone. I looked out through the rainswept windscreen and saw the blurred red glow of a phone box up ahead, and I was just about to ask the driver to pull up beside it . . . but then I changed my mind. Islington wasn't that far away now. The roads were free of traffic. I'd be back in less than fifteen minutes. And what good would ringing Curtis do anyway? If William was there, he was there. If he wasn't, he wasn't.

I sat back and gazed out at the passing world.

Despite the thunderstorm – and the fact that it was gone eleven o'clock on a Sunday night – the streets were still fairly busy. It was well past closing time, but a lot of the pubs hadn't finished for the night yet, and even in some of those that did look closed there were figures moving around in dimly lit back rooms. There were people sheltering from the rain in shop doorways, people hanging around in kebab shops and mini-cab offices . . . there were people smoking joints and drinking from cans of Red Stripe . . .

And there was William.

My first thought when I saw him was that it had to be someone else, someone who looked just like him. My mind was playing tricks on me, that's all it was. It was dark, it was raining . . . I couldn't see clearly through the rain-dazzled glare of the street-lights . . .

But even as I wound down the window to get a better look, I knew that it *was* him.

He was with three other men, and they'd all just come out of a shabby little pub called the Black Horse on the corner of a side street and were heading off down the street, away from Green Lanes. I didn't know what it was that stopped me from calling out through the window to William, but there was just something about him . . . something about the men he was with, something that didn't feel right. He seemed so *different* somehow, so unlike the William I knew. Harder, older . . .

He looked heartless.

And I got the feeling that if I *did* call out to him, he'd either ignore me, pretend that he didn't know who I was . . . or just tell me to fuck off.

'Can you stop here, please?' I said quickly to the driver.

'Sorry, love?'

'Stop here. I want to get out.'

'Right here?'

'Yes!' I snapped, looking back through the rear window.

He pulled up at the side of the road, about thirty yards past the pub. I gave him a £5 note, told him to keep the change, and ran off up the street towards the pub.

By the time I got there, William and the three men were halfway down the side street, about forty yards away from me. I waited on the corner, keeping out of sight, and watched them. Two of the men were in their mid-twenties, the other one was older, around fortyish. The older man was unshaven, wearing a heavy black overcoat, workman's boots, and a flat cap. One of the younger men was pale and thin, with long brown ratty hair, the other one had bushy black hair and a beard. Ratty was wearing a faded denim jacket. Bushy was dressed in a parka. They all looked like the kind of men who were used to walking the streets at night.

I looked at my watch.

It was almost 11.30.

If I jumped in a taxi right now, I could still get to Islington by midnight. If I ran after William and dragged him into a taxi, we could *both* still get there on time.

I looked down the street again.

William and the others were turning off into another little side street now, and I noticed that all three men glanced quickly over their shoulders as they went. I hesitated for a moment, not knowing what to do, and then I looked back along Green Lanes to see if there were any taxis in sight. *If there's one coming,* I promised myself, *I'll take it. But if there's not . . .*

A black cab was approaching, its yellow light on.

It drew level with me, slowing down as the driver caught my eye . . .

And then, as I looked away, it drove straight past.

I shook my head, wondering what the hell I was doing, and then I started to run.

The road they'd turned into was a grubby little backstreet that ran alongside a railway track. Most of the streetlights were out, and the rain was still lashing down, and for a moment or two I thought I'd lost them. I stood on the corner, breathing heavily, trying to see where they'd gone . . . but all I could see in the thundery darkness was a row of dilapidated houses, a couple of parked cars, and a patch of wasteground at the end of the street.

'Shit,' I muttered.

I took my hat off and ran my fingers through my hair.

I carried on looking.

Nothing moved.

I looked at my watch. 11.35.

'Shit.'

Lightning flashed, ripping across the sky, and I thought I saw a movement at the end of the street, to the left of the wasteground. A vague shadow, shifting across the ground. I kept watching, waiting for the next bolt of lightning . . . and then I heard a low creak, the sound of a heavy wooden door opening, and just for a moment a pale light flickered in the spot where I'd seen the shadow.

Thunder rumbled.

The pale light went out.

A door slammed shut.

I put my hat on and headed up the street.

The railway track was on a raised verge behind the houses on my left, and when I got to the end of the street I saw that the track carried on over an arched brick bridge that followed the perimeter of the wasteground. Some of the arches under the bridge were empty, but most of them were clearly in use as workplaces. They had big wooden double doors at the front, heavy machinery outside, signs that said CRASH REPAIRS, MOTS, SCRAP WANTED. They were all locked up, all silent and dark . . .

All except one.

It was the second workshop along. A battered metal sign on the wall said *WARWICK MOTORS*. There was no window at the front, and the double doors were closed, so I couldn't see inside, but there was definitely somebody in there. A pale light was showing through a gap at the foot of the doors, and in the light I could see faint shadows of movement. I moved a little closer, hoping to hear something, but with the roar of the rain all around me, and the thunder still rumbling away, it was impossible.

I looked at my watch.

11.40.

I looked up, startled by a sudden screeching sound, and saw a freight train rattling along the track above me. As it approached the arches, the beam of its headlights lit up the darkness either side of the bridge, briefly revealing that one of the arches – the one nearest to me – was actually a tunnel that led through to the other side of the bridge.

I waited for the train to pass, then looked at my watch again.

11.41.

I'll just take a very quick look, I promised myself, heading for the tunnel. *If I can get round the back and see inside, if I can find*

out what William's doing in there . . . that's it. I'll just take a very
quick look, and then I'll definitely *go.*

The rain had flooded the tunnel, and I had to slosh my way
through a good couple of inches of dirty black water, but I was
already soaked to the skin anyway, so it didn't really make
much difference. On the other side, a narrow track ran all the
way along the back of the bridge, giving access to the workshops in the arches. In the gloomy darkness, I could just make
out that the track was bounded by a wire-mesh fence on the
left, beyond which was another stretch of wasteground, and it
was cluttered with all kinds of rubbish from the workshops –
old tyres, rusted engines, mouldy car seats, cardboard boxes. I
followed the track, moving carefully through all the debris,
trying not to make too much noise, and made my way to the
back of Warwick Motors. There was a metal door, heavily
padlocked and chained, and a small window, high up on the
wall. I went over to the door and studied it for a while, trying
to find some kind of gap to look through, but it had no keyhole
and was fitted flush to the wall. I stepped back and turned my
attention to the window. It was boarded up on the inside, but
there was a faint patch of light showing through a hole in the
bottom right-hand corner. And if the light could get out, I
assumed, I should be able to see in.

The question was . . . how to get up there?

The window was at least four or five feet above my head, and
the wall was a sheer face of brick – no ledges, no handholds, no
way of climbing up. I looked around, searching for something
to stand on, and saw a large oil drum a few feet along the wall.
It looked pretty old and rusty, but it was the only thing I could
see that was big enough to get me up to the window. I went over
to it and lifted the lid, hoping that it wasn't filled with anything
that would make it too heavy to move, but luckily all it contained
was a few screwed-up newspapers and some dirty old cloths. I
grabbed hold of the rim and carefully rolled the drum along the

wall until it was directly beneath the window. I made sure the lid was on tightly, pressing it down with the palm of my hand, then I took a deep breath and hoisted myself up onto the drum. It wobbled like crazy at first, and for a heart-stopping moment I thought it was going to topple over, but somehow – by crouching down and spreading out my weight – I managed to steady it. I waited a few seconds, praying that no one had heard anything, then – very carefully – I began to straighten up. With a foot on either side of the drum, and using my hands to creep up the wall, I slowly raised myself up until my head was just below the window. I paused for a moment then, looking up to locate the exact position of the gap in the boarding. As I'd thought, it was in the bottom right-hand corner – a fist-sized hole where the wood had rotted away.

And I *could* see through it.

I was still about six inches below the window, so all I could see so far was a small section of brick roof and one end of a fluorescent light-fitting . . . but as I inched my way up towards the window – holding my breath now, my eyes glued to the gap in the board – more and more of the workshop came into view: the far wall . . . shelves full of tools, machinery, car parts . . . posters of half-naked women, the far side of the workshop floor . . . a stripped-down motorbike, the shape of a car beneath a sheet of tarpaulin . . .

And then I saw them. In the middle of the workshop, four men sitting at a table. The man in the flat cap, the two younger men . . . and William.

They were talking, but I couldn't hear what they were saying.

Their faces glowed in the flickering light of a small paraffin lamp on the table.

There were other things on the table too: papers, maps, files, a bottle of whisky . . . electrical apparatus, wires and cables, switches, circuit boards . . . sawn-off sections of tubular piping, bags of nails . . .

And guns.

'Shit,' I whispered.

The guns were laid out on a sheet of sacking – two pistols, a rifle, and what looked like a machine-gun – and as I stared through the gap, not wanting to believe my eyes, I saw the man in the flat cap pick up one of the pistols and pass it to William. William took it from him and examined it, nodding his head. He said something to Flat Cap, and the other two laughed. Flat Cap drank from a glass, lit a cigarette, took the pistol back from William, then smiled and patted him on the shoulder. William took a cigarette from a packet on the table, lit it, and sipped whisky from a glass. He said something to Flat Cap again. Flat Cap looked at Ratty. Ratty nodded, said something to William, and gestured towards a pile of large plastic sacks stacked on a pallet against the wall. The sacks were printed with a picture of a ruddy-faced farmer standing beside a ploughed field, and underneath the picture, in writing that I could only just make out, it said AGRICULTURAL FERTILIZER.

Bombs, I thought.

Fertilizer bombs . . .

Guns, nails, pipes, switches . . .

'*Jesus!*' I whispered.

And then, just as I was raising myself up on tiptoes to see if I could get a better view, a huge flash of lightning lit up the sky, followed almost immediately by an enormous crash of thunder right above my head. The sudden explosion was so loud, and so close, that it made me jump, and before I really knew what was happening, the lid of the oil drum had come off, my right foot had slipped inside the drum, and I could feel the whole thing tottering over. I tried to steady it, flapping around with my right foot, trying to hold it down, but all my weight was on one side now, and there was nothing I could do to keep it from falling over. As the drum fell away from me, I reached up and grabbed desperately at the window ledge, but it was so narrow, and the wood so old and rotten, that I just couldn't get hold of it. With the oil drum crashing and clattering to the ground beneath me, I was vaguely aware, for a fraction of a moment, that I was falling . . . falling . . . and then – *THUD!* – a sudden jarring impact knocked the air from my lungs, and I felt myself bouncing off something, and then I was sprawled out on the ground, face down in a puddle, gasping for breath and feeling sick.

And the oil drum – which I quickly realized had broken my fall – was now spinning around all over the place like a giant top, crashing and banging into the fence, against the wall, making so much noise that even the rain couldn't drown it out.

As I struggled to my feet, still trying to get some air into my lungs, I knew that the men in the workshop had heard all the noise. I could hear the doors at the front opening, and raised voices – '*Quick! Round the back!*' – and then the sound of running feet . . .

I didn't stop to think – there was nothing to think *about* – I just pushed the oil drum out of the way and began to run.

I was a pretty good runner back then. I wasn't *lightning* fast or anything, but I'd always been fairly speedy, and – more importantly – I had stamina. I could keep going for a long time, at a reasonably good pace, without having to stop. So, that night, as I raced off along the track behind the arches, and the men from the workshop came running after me, I knew that as long as I didn't fall over, or get trapped in a dead-end, they probably weren't going to catch me. Of course, that didn't mean that I wasn't frightened – I was absolutely *terrified* – it just meant that I wasn't without hope. *Just keep going*, I urged myself. *Keep running, don't look back, don't fall over, just concentrate on where you're going* . . .

It was hard to know where I *was* going. There were no lights, it was raining hard, the sky was pitch black . . . all I could really see was the track right in front of me, and even that was hard to make out among all the puddles and potholes and piles of rubbish strewn all over the place.

But I kept my head down, kept my eyes open for obstacles, and kept going . . .

Don't look back . . .

Don't fall over . . .

Just keep running . . .

After about a hundred yards, I heard a sudden sharp *crack*, and for a petrifying moment I thought it was a gunshot, but as the echo of the sound rolled around the sky, I realized that it was only a short crash of thunder.

Keep going . . .

I slowed for a moment and risked a quick glance up ahead, trying to see where the track was taking me. The bridge itself seemed to go on for miles – a blurred black line, curving gently away to the right, disappearing into the bright city lights in the distance – but not too far up ahead, about fifty yards away, the track seemed to turn off to the left.

Don't look back . . .

I couldn't resist it any longer.

Slowing a bit more, I looked back over my shoulder.

They were about thirty yards behind me, a huddle of figures running in the darkness. I couldn't make out how many there were – at least two, maybe three, and it was too dark to see if one of them was William – but I could tell that they had no intention of giving up the chase. They weren't racing at top speed, they weren't waving their hands around or shouting out after me, they were just running . . . steadily, silently, patiently . . .

They were hunting me down.

I quickened my pace . . .

Just run . . .

I ran.

I had to slow down a little when I got to the point where the track turned off to the left, but after I'd swung round the ninety-degree corner, I picked up my pace again and carried on down the track. I was running *away* from the bridge now. The men chasing after me were diagonally across to my left, and there were houses on my right. The track ran alongside the back fences of the houses, so it was a lot less cluttered than before, *and* it was slightly downhill, so it was a lot easier to keep up a good pace.

Keep going . . .

I was really moving now.

From the corner of my eye, I could see that the men had just reached the turning, and I was pretty sure that I was beginning to leave them behind. All I had to do now was keep going and try to find a way to get off the track and get back to the streets. The streets meant other people, other people meant safety . . . and the streets meant taxis too. I had to find a taxi . . . I had to get to Islington . . .

And Curtis . . .

Oh, God . . .

The gig!

Don't even think about it . . .

I started to look at my watch . . .

DON'T!

I dropped my hand.

Just keep running, keep going, keep looking . . .

There were lights up ahead, in the distance. Streetlights, head-lights . . . a main road? I couldn't be sure . . . but what else could it be?

Keep going, keep looking . . .

I saw a lane then. On my right, a narrow grass lane between two houses, with tall hedges on either side . . .

I slowed and peered down the lane.

It led out onto a residential street. There was a car parked under a streetlight. There was a house, two houses . . .

Keep going?

I looked back up the track. The men were about fifty yards back, just approaching a slight bend in the track where a thick growth of ivy covered the wire-mesh fence. And as they ran round the bend, momentarily disappearing from view, I sped off along the grass lane.

The street at the other end was a secluded cul-de-sac, quiet and empty. There were lights showing behind closed curtains in some of the houses, but most of them were in darkness. It was late, people were in bed . . . sleeping, dreaming . . .

Keep going . . .

I ran down the street, heading towards what I hoped was a main road . . .

And when I got there, and I realized that it really *was* a main road, that's when I started to cry. It was just such a *relief* to see it – a real, proper road . . . with two lanes of traffic, cars and buses . . . shops, streetlights, traffic lights, people . . .

I'd made it.

Thank God . . .

I'd made it.

Now all I had to do was find a taxi.

I wiped the tears from my eyes and looked up and down the street, *willing* myself to see a black cab. I saw cars, a motorbike . . . more cars . . .

No taxis.

I glanced back up the cul-de-sac, willing myself *not* to see any running men . . .

There was no one there.

I turned back to the street again, looking to the left, to the right, to the left again . . .

There!

The black taxi was approaching me on the other side of the street, its yellow light glowing in the rain. I stepped off the pavement, raising my hand . . . and jumped back at the sound of screeching brakes. A car coming the other way had almost run into me, braking and swerving just in time. As it passed by, the driver hit his horn and angrily waved his fist at me . . . but I was already on the move again, running across the road, waving my hands at the rapidly approaching taxi, calling out to the driver – *'Taxi! Hey, over here! TAXI!'* I saw him look at me, and I saw the sudden surprise on his face, and I thought for a moment that he wasn't going to stop. I must have looked like a crazy person – soaking wet, sobbing, covered in mud and oil and God knows what else . . . wearing a big black donkey jacket and a biker's cap – so I understood *why* he might not want to pick me up, but there was no way I was going to let it happen. Not now. Not after all I'd been through. He *had* to pick me up. And I was perfectly prepared to do whatever it took to make him stop, even if it meant jumping out into the road in front of him, which was exactly what I was just about to do . . . when I saw him nod at me, and his indicator came on, and he pulled up right next to me in the middle of the street.

I yanked open the door and jumped in the back.

'Are you all right, love?' he asked me, genuinely concerned.

'Yeah, thanks . . . could you just get going, please?'

'What the hell happened –?'

'Please?' I said desperately.

He nodded, turned round, glanced once in his mirror, and drove off.

26

I didn't have much time to think about anything in the taxi. The main road I'd ended up on turned out to be St Ann's Road, which was only just round the corner from Seven Sisters Road, and from there it was only a couple of miles or so to Islington. So, by the time I'd assured the taxi driver that I wasn't hurt, and that I didn't need him to call the police, and that I didn't really want to talk about what had happened to me . . . and by the time I'd convinced him that the Screen on the Green *would* be open at this time of night . . . well, by then, we were almost there. And all I'd really had time to think about was the time.

It was 12.35.

I'd be there in five minutes . . .

And if things were running late, which they often did, there was still just a chance that everything would be all right. We'd have to play without William, of course . . .

My mind flashed back to the scene in the workshop – William at the table with the three men, talking and joking, drinking and smoking . . . William with a pistol in his hand . . .

No.

I couldn't think about it.

Not now.

I just *couldn't* . . .

The Screen on the Green was really crowded when I got there, and even though I ran all the way it still took me a good five minutes to get into the building and make my way to the dressing room. I could hear music blasting out from the auditorium, but it wasn't the sound of a live band, and I just hoped that meant that the gig hadn't started yet.

It's going to be OK, I assured myself as I opened the dressing-room door. *It's going to be OK, it's going to be OK . . .*

It wasn't OK.

Stan and Jake were sitting disconsolately in the corner, watching in silence as four young men bustled around the room talking excitedly to each other. They had Manchester accents, so I guessed they were the Buzzcocks, and they all looked hot and slightly out of breath . . . and I knew straight away that they'd just finished playing. I knew that look only too well.

I glanced over at Jake.

He just stared back at me.

'Am I too late?' I said.

Before he could answer, I felt someone grab my arm from behind, and even as I turned round and saw that it was Curtis, he started dragging me out into the corridor. I struggled, trying to pull my arm away, but he was holding me really tightly.

'Hey!' I yelped. 'You're hurting –'

'Where the *fuck* have you been?' he spat, pushing me up against the wall.

'Get *off* –'

'Do you *know* what you've fucking *done*?'

'Let go of me, Curtis,' I said, looking him straight in the eyes.

He didn't move for a moment, he just stared back at me – his eyes bulging, his teeth clenched tight – and it took all the self-control I had to stay calm, keep my eyes fixed on his, and not lose my temper.

'Let . . . go,' I repeated, slowly and quietly.

'Fucking *hell*, Lili,' he spluttered, throwing his hands up and stepping back from me. 'I just can't *believe* this . . .'

'What's going on?' I said.

He glared at me. 'What's going *on*? You're asking *me* what's going on?'

'I just meant, you know . . . can we still play tonight?'

'Oh, *yeah*,' he said, laughing unpleasantly. 'Yeah, it's no problem at all. I'll just go and tell the Clash that *we're* ready now, so if they wouldn't mind getting all their gear off the stage –'

'Can't we play after them?'

'No,' Curtis said. 'We can't.'

'Why not?'

He looked at me. 'Do *you* want to go and talk to Malcolm? Do you want to try explaining to him why we couldn't play when we were supposed to play? I mean, do you really think he gives a shit anyway?'

I sighed. 'Look, I'm sorry, Curtis –'

'You're *sorry*?'

'Yeah . . .'

'Hey, don't worry about it,' he said sarcastically. 'I mean, it's not as if this gig was important or anything. It was only going to change our lives for ever, wasn't it? So, you know . . . who fucking cares?'

'I *said* I was sorry –'

'Go on then,' he said coldly, lighting a cigarette. 'Tell me what happened. Tell me what you're so fucking *sorry* about.'

I hesitated then, suddenly unsure what to say. If I told Curtis the truth, if I told him all about William and the three men, and what had happened to me . . . well, it probably wouldn't make much difference to Curtis anyway, but at least I'd be telling the truth. On the other hand, if I *didn't* tell him the truth . . .

'Did you find him?' he said.

'Sorry?'

'Billy the fucking Kid . . . did you *find* him?'

'No . . . well, not exactly.'

'And what's *that* supposed to mean?'

'I found out where he lives . . . I mean, I went to his flat, but he wasn't there.'

'Really?' Curtis said, looking me up and down.

I stared at him. 'Why are you looking at me like that?'

'No reason . . . just wondering.'

'Wondering what?'

'How come you're such a fucking mess.'

'Well, if you'll just *listen* –'

'I mean, Christ, Lili . . . look at the *state* of you. You look like a fucking tramp.' He shook his head in disgust. 'Not that it matters *now*, of course –'

'Do you *want* to know what happened to me or not?' I said, beginning to lose patience with him now.

He sniffed. 'Where did you get those clothes from?'

'What?'

'You heard me.'

'Does it *matter*?'

'You weren't wearing them when you left here.'

'I know –'

'Are they his?'

'Whose?'

'Billy's . . .' He stared at me. 'They look like Billy's clothes.'

I frowned at him. 'Of course they're not William's clothes . . . why would I be wearing William's clothes?'

'You tell me.'

'They're *not* William's clothes,' I said, exasperated and confused. 'Chief lent me the jacket and the hat . . . you can ask him, if you want. And the T-shirt and jeans –'

'I've seen that T-shirt before.'

'Where?'

'On Billy.'

I shook my head. 'It's *Nancy's* T-shirt, not William's. Look, I was soaking wet when I got there –'

'Who the fuck's Nancy?'

'She's William's . . .' I sighed again. 'Well, it's a bit complicated, but she's kind of his stepmother . . .'

'*Kind* of his stepmother?'

'Yeah –'

'And she was there, was she, this Nancy? She was in the flat?'

'Yes.'

'Right,' he said, sneering at me. 'Of course she was.'

'You think I'm lying?'

'I *know* you're lying.'

'*What?*'

'It's pretty fucking obvious, Lili . . . I mean, you've been at Billy's flat for the last two and a half hours, and then you come back here wearing his clothes . . .? It's not *that* hard to work out what you've been up to.'

I stared at him, utterly speechless.

He said, 'I just hope you think it was worth it –'

'That's enough, Curtis.'

He smiled cruelly at me. 'Was he better than me?'

'No more.'

'Did you enjoy it?'

I slapped him hard across the face.

He didn't even move. He just looked at me for a moment, his eyes cold and empty, then he raised his hand and lunged at me. I instinctively stepped back, turning my head away and closing my eyes, bracing myself for the slap . . . but it never came. I waited a second, then cautiously opened my eyes. Curtis was standing over me, his arm raised, his open hand just inches from my face. With a scornful smile, he moved his face right up close to mine, stared into my eyes, and gave me a contemptuous pat on the cheek.

'No hard feelings, eh?' he sneered.

'Fuck you, Curtis.'

He grinned. 'Yeah, right . . .'

And then he turned his back on me and walked away.

My head was a mess of confusion as I headed back along the

corridor. I didn't know what I was feeling, I didn't know what had just happened, I didn't know what I was doing or where I was going . . .

I was just walking . . .

I was *so* tired.

So everything.

I was nothing.

After a while, I somehow found myself in the auditorium. The Clash were on stage, blasting away, looking and sounding really good, and everyone in the crowd was going crazy. I stood at the back for a minute or two, just looking around, listening to the music, watching the band, watching the crowd . . .

All the familiar faces were there. Jordan, McLaren, Vivienne Westwood . . . a bare-breasted Siouxsie Sioux. Steve Jones, Bernie Rhodes . . . the Bromley punks, Charlie Brown . . .

Flashbulbs were going off . . .

The whole place was rocking . . .

This was *it*.

This was the dream.

This was what it was all about.

It was nothing.

And as I left the auditorium and walked out into the storm-bruised night, all I could think about was William.

27

I slept until noon the next day. The sun was shining when I woke up – the pale August light filtering in through the curtains – and I could hear Mum and Laura pottering around in the kitchen downstairs, talking and laughing, making coffee . . . and, just for a moment, everything felt perfectly normal.

It was a nice sunny day.

Mum and Laura were in the kitchen.

And I was just lazing around in bed . . .

But then, of course, the illusion cracked and the events of last night came flooding back to me – Mum and Doc Sam . . . the kids at Cranleigh Farm, Nancy and Joe . . . William and the three men . . . the workshop, the guns . . . the men chasing after me . . .

And then Curtis . . .

God . . .

I rolled over, closed my eyes, and buried my head in the pillow.

I didn't really want to think about *any* of it, I just wanted it all to go away, but I knew that it wouldn't. It *couldn't*. It had happened, and things that have happened don't just go away. You can bury your head in a pillow and shed as many tears as you like, but it's not going to make any difference. It's never going to *change* anything. What's happened will always have happened, and eventually you just have to deal with it.

You have to stop crying . . .

Open your eyes.

Take your head out of the pillow . . .

And deal with it.

You have to ask yourself – those men with William, they were IRA men, weren't they? Pistols, machine guns, bomb-making equipment . . . what else could they be? And if they *are* in the IRA, what does that mean? Is William one of them? Is *he* in the IRA? Has he been lying to you about everything? About his mother, his father, about Nancy . . . the reason he came over to England . . . is that all just a cover-up for the *real* reason he's here? I mean, can you *really* believe that William is involved in an IRA plot to set off a bomb somewhere in London?

And, if so, you have to ask yourself – what are you going to *do* about it?

I don't know.

And what about Curtis? What are you going to do about him? Are you just going to assume that it's all over between you? Do you *want* it to be over? What if he were to apologize for the things he said, for the way he treated you . . .? Could you forgive him? Do you *want* to forgive him?

No . . .

I don't know.

And what about the band? What does all this William and Curtis stuff mean in terms of the band? Is that all over too? Are Naked finished now? And, if so, do you care?

I don't know.

What *do* you know?

Right now, all I know is that I can hear my mum downstairs, and that she sounds quite happy, and that might just mean that she's doing OK . . . and I could really do with something being OK at the moment . . .

I got out of bed, got dressed, and went downstairs.

*

264

It was always hard to tell with Mum. She could be reasonably normal one minute, totally crazy the next. Or she could be perfectly OK for a couple of weeks and then suddenly lose control again, and for the next few weeks, or even months, she could be virtually anything – drunk, depressed, hyper, horrible, asleep, insane, obsessed, unbearable . . .

But that day, when I went downstairs and found her sitting in the kitchen with Laura, I was as sure as I could be that – for now, at least – she really was doing OK. Her eyes were bright, she looked and sounded fresh and happy, and the smile she gave me when I went into the kitchen . . . well, it was *her* smile. Her *real* smile. And it was so good to see it that I almost began crying again.

'Are you all right, love?' she said, getting up to give me a hug. 'How was the concert last night?'

'Yeah . . . yeah, it was good, thanks.'

She held me at arm's length and looked into my eyes. 'Are you sure you're all right? You look a bit . . .'

'No, I'm fine . . . really. Just a bit tired, that's all.' I smiled at her. 'Are you OK?'

'Never better,' she said, smiling back. 'Especially now that you're here. Are you staying for a while?'

'Well, I don't know –'

'Do you fancy going shopping with Laura and me this afternoon?'

'Shopping?'

'We're only going to Hampstead, you know . . . just the local shops.' She took my hand and gave it a squeeze. 'Come on, Lili . . . we haven't been out together for *ages*. It'll be fun.'

It wasn't *my* idea of fun – traipsing around shops all afternoon, looking at clothes and shoes and God knows what else – but I thought it might help to take my mind off things, so I went along anyway. And it *was* kind of OK for a while. Mum was right, we hadn't been out together for a long time, and it felt good just being with her again – out in the sunshine, walking the streets, looking in shop windows . . .

It was nice.

It wasn't exactly *fun* . . .

But it was kind of OK.

And every now and then, just for a moment or two, it did actually help to take my mind off things. But they were only moments. And as the afternoon wore on, even the briefest of these occasional moments gradually faded away, until eventually I found myself thinking of nothing *but* the things I didn't want to think about.

William . . .

Lies . . .

The IRA.

Curtis . . .

William.

Curtis . . .

The thing that kept coming back to me about Curtis was, quite simply, why? Why had he accused me of sleeping with William? It just didn't make sense. Why would he *think* that? And the only answer I kept coming up with was that he *didn't* actually think that I'd slept with William at all – he'd just said it. He'd been so pissed off with both William and me for messing up the gig and ruining his dream that he'd just blurted out the first thing – and the *worst* thing – that came into his head. He knew perfectly well that it wasn't true, but once he'd said it . . . well, for him, that was it. There was no going back.

Or maybe he *hadn't* just blurted it out . . .?

Maybe it was a lot simpler than that.

Maybe he'd *wanted* us to break up all along. And rather than doing it the hard way, he'd just accused me of the worst thing he could think of, in the hope that I'd get so mad that I'd leave him, which would not only save him the bother of leaving me, but would also gain him all the sympathy.

Or maybe not . . .

I just didn't know.

And it was that that was killing me – the not knowing.

'Mum?' I said, as we headed towards yet another chic little shoe shop. 'I've just remembered something.'

'Sorry, love?'

'I have to go, Mum. There's a band meeting this evening . . . sorry, but I forgot all about it.'

'Oh,' she said, obviously disappointed.

'Sorry.'

She smiled. 'Well, if you really *have* to go . . .'

'Yeah, I'd better.'

'All right then.'

As I gave her a hug, I glanced over at Laura and mouthed, 'Is that OK with you?'

She nodded.

I let go of Mum.

Laura said to me, 'Will I see you tomorrow, Lili? I'm staying for another couple of days . . .'

I nodded back, letting her know that I understood, then I headed off to the underground station.

It was around five o'clock when I got to Seven Sisters. The sun wasn't shining any more, and as I left the tube station and walked down the road towards the squat, the skies were beginning to darken under a bank of heavy black cloud. A cold wind was blowing, scattering litter around the streets, and I could smell the spicy heat of takeaway food in the air.

I didn't know what I was doing.

I didn't know what I was hoping to find.

I didn't even know what I was feeling.

I'd reached the squat now, and as I headed up the path towards the front door, I remembered the night of the party, when Curtis had given me a piggy-back down the street . . . and he'd gone hurtling down the road, jiggling me up and down on his back, and I'd closed my eyes and screamed like a kid on a rollercoaster . . . and then we'd crashed into the hedge and tumbled to the ground and we'd both just sat there, laughing ourselves stupid . . .

I shook the memory from my head and carried on up to the front door. It was open, as usual – the only time it got locked was at night – so I just walked in and went straight up the stairs. There was music playing all over the place – Captain Beefheart from a room downstairs, some old Bowie stuff from somewhere else – and as I moved up the stairs, I realized how familiar this place had become to me. The same-old sounds, the same-old house, the same-old mixture of smells – marijuana, mould, unwashed clothes . . .

'Hey, Lili.'

I looked up at the sound of the voice and saw a frizzy-haired girl in a doorway on the landing.

'Oh, hi, Sinead,' I said, pausing for a moment.

I didn't know Sinead that well, but I'd spoken to her a few times, and she was kind of all right. She designed her own clothes and sold them at Kensington Market.

'Are you OK?' I asked her.

'Yeah . . .' she said, smiling.

But she didn't *seem* all right. She seemed nervous about something, hesitant, not sure what to say. Which was unusual for Sinead.

'Do you know if Curtis is in?' I asked her.

Her eyes flicked briefly upwards. 'Uhh . . . well, I'm not really . . .'

'It's all right,' I said, heading up the stairs. 'I'll see you later.'

'Uh . . . yeah . . .' I heard her mutter. 'Yeah, see you . . .'

Curtis's room was the first on the right at the top of the next flight of stairs. I couldn't hear anything as I approached it, but that wasn't unusual. Curtis didn't always make lots of noise, he'd quite often spend hours and hours sitting quietly in his room, reading or writing, or sometimes just thinking. Of course, he often slept during the day too, especially if he'd been up all night.

So I didn't give the silence much thought.

And I didn't even think about knocking before I went in. I *never* knocked on his door, I always just opened it up and walked straight in . . .

Why shouldn't I?

I virtually *lived* there. It was *our* room. I mean, you don't knock on your own door before you go in, do you?

So, no . . . I didn't knock, or call out his name, I didn't even allow myself a moment to stop and think, because I knew that if I did, I'd start wondering what to say, and how to say it . . . and all that would have done was confuse me even more. *Just open the door*, I told myself. *Open the door, go on in . . . and see what happens.*

And that's what I did.

The room was dim, the curtains closed, and it took a couple of moments for my eyes to adjust to the gloom. And when they did, and I looked down at the bed, it took another couple of moments for the reality of what I was seeing to sink in.

I knew that it *was* real.

And I knew that I *was* seeing it . . .

Because it was right there . . . *they* were right there. Right there in front of me.

Curtis and Charlie Brown, asleep on the bed together . . .

Naked.

It was obvious that they were both totally wrecked. There were empty bottles all over the place, ashtrays overflowing with dead joints . . . there were clothes strewn all around the room, sheets thrown off the bed . . . and when Curtis finally half opened his eyes and looked up at me, he was still so out of it that he didn't recognize me at first. He just kind of lay there, squinting through the darkness at me, his eyes all bloodshot and bleary . . .

'Whuh . . .?' he mumbled, rubbing his face. 'What's that . . .?'

I glanced at Charlie Brown. She was waking up too now, struggling hard to sit up straight and open her eyes, but as soon as she saw me standing there, she knew exactly who I was – and it didn't seem to bother her one bit.

'Oops,' she said, covering her mouth and smirking at me.

'Lili . . .?' I heard Curtis mutter.

I looked at him for just a moment, just long enough to see that he still didn't know what was happening, and then I turned round and walked out.

He didn't come after me. He didn't even call out to me as I ran down the stairs, the tears already streaming down my face.

Or maybe he did . . .?

Who knows?

All I could hear was the roar of the hurricane inside my head, the crushing emptiness, the anger, the sickness . . . the pounding of my own stupid heart. And as I stumbled down the stairs, blinded with tears, I could feel the walls of the house closing in on me, squeezing the air from my lungs . . . and I knew that I *had* to get out of there. My chest was being crushed . . . I couldn't breathe . . . I couldn't see . . .

Just keep going . . .

Keep running . . .

Don't look back . . .

As I clattered down the last few stairs and crashed along the hallway towards the front door, I caught a passing glimpse of myself in a dusty old mirror that was leaning against the wall, and just for a moment – a very brief moment – the image I saw was of a girl who was running away from herself. She wasn't running away from Curtis, or Charlie Brown . . . she was running away from *herself*. And I *knew* – with absolute certainty – that this girl in the mirror would never ever get away . . .

I knew that she'd be running from herself for the rest of her life.

And then, as I left the mirror behind and threw open the front door, I knew nothing again.

It was raining hard.

The sky was black, edged in yellow.

Just keep going . . .

I hurried along the path, wiping tears from my face . . .

I turned right, heading for the tube station . . .

And saw a familiar figure coming towards me. Slight, not that tall, his dark brown hair neither long nor short . . . dressed as ever in his tattered black jacket and washed-out shirt . . . and his eyes . . .

God, his eyes.

So clear and radiant, so full of life . . .

William smiled when he saw me. And then, almost immediately, as he realized that I was crying, his smile faded and he started hurrying towards me with a worried look on his face.

'Lili?' he said. 'All you all right? What's the matter?'

'I can't do this . . .' I heard myself mutter.

'What? You can't do what?'

'I just can't . . .'

'Lili?'

But I'd already turned round and started to run.

28

I was running through the rain again, running through another summer storm, and the hurricane inside my head was roaring ever louder, and my stupid dead heart was pounding ever faster, and I was blind with tears and soaking wet and sick and empty and sick and angry and I knew once again that the girl in the mirror would never get away from herself . . .

She'd never get away from herself . . .

She'd never stop running for the rest of her life . . .

I knew nothing.

It was raining hard.

The sky was black . . .

Just keep going . . .

Keep running . . .

Don't ever look back . . .

Just run.

I ran.

I didn't know *why* I was running any more. I didn't know what I was running from, or to . . . I had no idea where I was going. I was just running. I couldn't stop. I knew that if I stopped running, even for a moment, I'd never be able to move again . . . I'd just sink down to my knees and sit there in the pouring rain, and that would be it. I'd never get up again. I'd stay there for ever. And if I stayed there for ever . . .

Just keep going . . .

I kept going.

*

I'm not sure how long it took for the madness in my head to subside, but gradually – very gradually – the roar of the hurricane began to fade and my senses began coming back to me. I could feel the rain in my face, I could feel the cold. I could feel the tiredness in my legs, the pain in my side, the ache in my lungs . . . I knew that I couldn't run any more. I had to rest. And I knew, as I slowed to a walk and then stopped and looked around, that I'd run all the way up Stamford Hill, over the crossroads at the top, and now I was heading down the other side towards Stoke Newington.

It was a long way to have run.

But at least I'd stopped.

I hadn't kept running for ever.

And that was something.

And there was something else too . . .

As I stood there on the pavement, sucking in great gulps of air, it suddenly came back to me *why* I'd run all this way in the first place . . . or, at least, why I'd *started* running in the first place.

William.

I'd run away from William.

And it felt *so* weird, realizing that I'd actually forgotten something that had happened no more than fifteen minutes ago. I'd seen William outside the squat, I'd turned round and run away from him, and then . . . the next thing I'd known . . .

I hadn't *known* anything.

And now . . .?

Now I was looking back up the road in the forlorn hope that he'd followed me, and although I was still too confused to know whether I really *wanted* to see him or not, when I *did* finally see him, jogging over the crossroads at the top of the hill, I knew – quite suddenly – that not only did I *want* to see him, but I wanted to see him more than anything else in the world.

Whatever he was, whatever he'd done . . .

However confused I was . . .

The sight of him lifted my heart.

He slowed down when he saw that I'd stopped and was waiting for him, walking the last fifty yards or so down the hill towards me. I was still trying to get my breath back, and I could see that William was puffing and panting a bit too. I could also see that he was keeping his eyes fixed on me, just in case I decided to start running again.

He needn't have worried.

I wasn't going anywhere.

The rain had begun to ease off now, and I was starting to shiver. It wasn't particularly cold, but I wasn't wearing a coat, and I was soaking wet, and the sweat I'd built up from all that running was now cooling me down too much . . .

I jiggled my shoulders . . .

Wrapped my arms around myself.

Stamped my feet.

I felt stupid and ugly and wet . . .

Embarrassed.

'Lili?'

I looked up as William came up to me.

I didn't *know* how I felt . . .

'Here,' he said, taking off his jacket and gently putting it round my shoulders. 'God, you're *freezing*. Come here . . .'

He put his arms round me and held me close, sharing his warmth with me. I was really shaking now, trembling all over, my teeth chattering, and as I held him tight and buried my head in his shoulder, I was sobbing like a baby.

I told William about Curtis and Charlie Brown as we walked down Stamford Hill towards Stoke Newington, heading for a Greek café that William knew about. He didn't say anything as I talked, he just listened, and when I'd finished telling him what had happened – which didn't actually take very long – he still didn't say very much, he just put his hand on my shoulder and told me, quite genuinely, that he was sorry for me.

'Yeah, well . . .' I said. 'I should have seen it coming, I suppose. I mean, it wasn't as if I didn't *know* that he fancied her . . . and then, you know, what with everything that happened last night . . .' I looked at William, realizing – of course – that he didn't *know* what happened last night because he hadn't been there . . . he'd been with three IRA men in a car-repair workshop under a railway bridge, a workshop full of guns and explosives . . .

'Nancy told me that you came round looking for me,' he said.

I didn't say anything, I just carried on looking at him.

'Look, I'm sorry, OK?' he said. 'I mean, I'm sorry for lying about Joe's birthday party and everything, but it was just . . .' He sighed. 'Well, I had to see some people . . .'

'Yeah? What kind of people?'

He looked at me. 'I didn't *mean* to miss the gig, Lili. I thought I'd be able to get there on time. But things changed at the last minute . . .'

Again, I didn't say anything, I just kept walking . . . waiting to see if he'd tell me the truth, or anything near the truth.

'What happened anyway?' he asked me. 'At the gig, I mean . . . did you play without me?'

'No.'

'Why not?'

'Because I didn't get back in time.'

He frowned at me. 'But I thought you left my place at just gone eleven? That's what Nancy told me –'

'Yeah, I did.'

'So how come you didn't get back to Islington in time for the gig?'

I stopped walking and looked at him. We'd reached the bottom of Stamford Hill now, and were standing on the pavement opposite the entrance to Abney Park Cemetery. The rain had stopped, and a glint of sunshine was just beginning to show through a gap in the clouds.

'You didn't answer my question,' I said to William.

'When?' he said, feigning ignorance. 'What question?'

'Just now . . . when you said that you had to see some people on Sunday night, and I asked you what kind of people.' I looked into his eyes. 'Listen, William, are you going to tell me the truth or not? Because, if you're not . . .' I shrugged. 'I mean, it's up to you what you want to tell me, and if you *don't* want to tell me the truth . . . well, that's fine. Just tell me that it's none of my business, and I'll walk away and leave you to it. But if all you're going to do is keep *lying* to me all the time –'

'I haven't lied to you,' he said. 'I've *never* lied to you.'

'Yes, you have –'

'When?'

'You lied about Joe's birthday party.'

He shook his head. 'I didn't lie to *you* about that, I lied to Curtis –'

'Oh, come *on* –'

'All right,' he said. 'When else have I lied to you?'

I stared at him. 'You tell me.'

'I *am* telling you . . .'

'Go on then.'

'What?'

'*Tell* me . . . tell me where you were on Sunday night. Tell me who you had to meet. Tell me what you were doing.'

He looked thoughtfully at me for a while then, not saying anything, and I wondered what I'd do if he *did* tell me to mind my own business. Would I just walk away and leave him to it, as I'd promised? *Could* I just walk away?

'Not here,' William said.

'Sorry?'

'I can't tell you anything here, it's too public.'

'All right, what about this café you were telling me about?'

'Even worse,' he said, glancing around. I saw him gaze across the road at the entrance to the cemetery, and then he turned back to me. 'Have you ever been in there?'

I shook my head.

He smiled. 'It's a beautiful place . . . nice and quiet, calm, peaceful . . .'

'It's a cemetery,' I said. 'It's full of dead people.'

'Exactly.'

I'd heard about Abney Park Cemetery before, and I'd seen the entrance in passing a few times, but I had no idea just how big it was, and as I followed William through the pillared gates, and we headed off along a hushed, grassy track, it took me a while to take it all in. It was such an amazing place. A vast labyrinth of trees and pathways, with great masses of tangled vegetation growing wild over ancient gravestones and tombs . . . it was like being in some kind of enchanted forest. As well as all the gravestones, there were countless stone monuments and statues dotted all around – angels, saints, lions, crosses – some of which were no more than crumbled ruins, covered in lichen and moss, while others leaned precariously amid the shrubs and trees. Although it wasn't raining any more, the whole place was still saturated with moisture – raindrops dripping from trees, the sweet smell of damp earth filling the air. But perhaps the most surprising – and wonderful – thing about the cemetery was the silence. We were in the middle of London, right next to a busy main road, and yet, after walking for only a few minutes, all I could hear was the sound of birds singing and the gentle drip-drip of raindrops falling from trees.

It really was quite beautiful.

'Shall we sit down?' William said, indicating a wooden bench at the side of the path.

I nodded and sat down.

William sat beside me.

'It's nice, isn't it?' he said, gazing around.

'Yeah, it is.' I looked at him. 'How come you know all these places? I mean, the café . . . this place. Do you know people around here or something?'

He shrugged. 'No . . . I just like walking around, you know . . . not *just* here, although I do come here quite a bit, I suppose. But I just like walking around London . . .'

I nodded. 'It's a big world.'

He smiled. 'Yeah . . .'

I looked at him. 'Lots of places, lots of people . . .'

He looked back at me. 'Do you remember at the party, when I told you about my mum and dad and everything?'

'Yeah.'

'And you promised not to repeat anything I told you to anyone else?'

'Yeah . . .'

'I need you to promise me the same again.'

I didn't say anything, I just carried on looking at him.

He said, 'It's the only way I can tell you the truth, Lili.'

'All right,' I said.

'Promise?'

Without taking my eyes off his, I held out my hand. He held my gaze for a few moments, and once again I saw that trace of sadness in his eyes, and then – with a quiet nod of his head – he took my hand, gave it a shake, and began telling me about the three men.

'I first heard about them from some of the kids on the estate,' he explained. 'This was quite a while ago, maybe a year back. I'd got to know the estate kids pretty well by then . . . you know, we'd done a few bits and pieces together, helped each other out, that kind of thing . . . and I'd kind of spread the word around that if anyone ever came looking for Nancy or me, I wanted to know about it. Especially if they were Irish.' William shrugged. 'It wasn't a big deal for the kids on the estate, because they're really wary of strangers anyway . . . they won't talk to *any*one from outside the estate.'

'Yeah, I know,' I said. 'They gave me a pretty hard time.'

William grinned. 'So I heard . . . that was Mikey, by the way. The black kid you spoke to.'

'The one who wanted my watch?'

'He was only messing around. He's harmless really.'

'Right . . .'

William had fished a damp and crumpled cigarette from his pocket and was trying to straighten it out. I watched him as he fiddled around with it – breaking off the dampest bits, trying to make it smokeable – and eventually he ended up with a two-inch stub of mostly dry, and mostly unbent, cigarette. He put it in his mouth, pulled a lighter from his pocket, and cautiously lit it, doing his best not to burn his lips in the process.

'So, anyway,' he went on, blowing out smoke. 'About a year ago, a couple of the older kids told me about these three Irish guys they'd seen in a pub in Green Lanes. They hadn't been asking about Nancy or me, the kids said, but they were new to the area, and nobody seemed to know who they were, and the kids just thought I'd want to know about them. Which I did, of course. So I asked the kids what these men looked like, and what time they usually went to the pub, and then I started checking them out. I didn't actually go into the pub at first, I just hung around outside, waiting for them to show up so I could get a good look at them, you know, to see if I recognized them. But I didn't. I'd never seen any of them before. When I went inside for a closer look, they were sitting at a table in the corner, just talking quietly and drinking, and although I couldn't hear what they saying, I could tell from their accents that they weren't from Belfast. They were from Derry.'

William took the cigarette from his mouth and peered at it. It had gone out. It was too wet to smoke after all. He dropped it on the ground.

'I didn't *know* they were IRA then,' he continued, 'but I was pretty sure that they were . . .'

William's voice trailed off as a big black collie dog came trotting along the path, followed by a scruffy young man and a pretty young woman with spiky blonde hair. They were both eating ice lollies. The collie came up to us, wagging his tail, and William said hello to him and stroked his head.

'What's his name?' he asked the young man.

'Floyd,' the young man said.

The dog trotted off, and the young couple strolled past us, carrying on down the path. William waited until they were out of sight, then he started talking again.

He told me how he'd slowly got to know the three men from Derry. How he'd started off by cadging a cigarette off them in the pub one night, just to let them know that he was from Belfast . . . and then, over time, he'd just gradually let things progress. He nodded at them when he went into the pub . . . they nodded back; he spoke to them occasionally . . . they muttered back; they bought him a drink one night . . . he bought them one back; they invited him to join them at the table . . . he joined them at the table; they began to talk about this and that . . .

'I told them that my father was killed by the UVF when I was five years old,' William said. 'And that after that my mother brought me to London to live with her parents.' He smiled at me. 'I could tell then by the questions they asked me that they were definitely IRA, and it was also pretty obvious that they weren't here looking for Nancy or me . . . but I knew they were up to something. So I just kind of strung them along, you know . . . I let them think that I was this displaced Belfast boy who hated Loyalists and Prods in general, and that I'd do anything to get back at the bastards who killed my father . . . and eventually, after three or four months, they began to realize that they could use me.'

'What do you mean?' I asked. 'Use you for what?'

'For whatever they were planning. I mean, they still didn't actually *trust* me, and it took them another couple of months before they finally told me that they *were* IRA, and even then they wouldn't tell me anything about what they were doing, they just asked me if I'd be interested in helping them out now and then.' William looked at me. 'Do you know what a "clean-skin" is?'

'No.'

'It's someone without a criminal record, someone who's not *known* as a terrorist, someone who terrorists can use without raising suspicion.'

'Right,' I said. 'And that's what you are to them?'

'Yeah.'

'Why?'

'Well, like I said, they can use me to do things without raising suspicion –'

'Yeah, but why are you letting them use you at *all*?' I looked at him. 'Aren't you scared that they'll find out the truth about you and Nancy? I mean, if they're *not* after Nancy, if they don't know anything about her or your dad . . . why are you even *talking* to them?' I shook my head. 'I just don't get it. They're IRA . . . the IRA murdered your father, for God's sake. I mean, how can you sit down in a pub and have a drink with people like that?'

He didn't answer for a few moments, he just sat there, staring thoughtfully across the path . . .

I looked up at the sky. The sunlight had disappeared again, blocked out by a lowering canopy of rolling black clouds, and I realized that the air had suddenly become warm and very, very still.

'It's kind of strange really,' William said quietly, still staring distantly across the path. 'After my father was killed . . . I never really thought that much about who'd actually done it. I mean, I knew it was the IRA, of course . . . everyone knew that . . . but as to who actually pulled the trigger . . .' He slowly shook his head. 'I don't know . . . it just didn't seem to really matter. Whoever it was . . . well, they were just carrying out orders . . . just doing what they'd been told to do. Blaming them for my father's death seemed as pointless as blaming the gun they'd used, or blaming the bullet that killed him . . .' William looked at me. 'Does that make any sense?'

'Yeah . . .' I said. 'Yeah, I think so.'

He nodded thoughtfully. 'It was kind of confusing for a while, you know . . . you've got this terrible anger inside you, and you want to direct it at *some*body or *some*thing, but you know in your heart there's no point. I mean, I could spend the rest of my life blaming Franky Hughes, or the man who pulled the trigger, or the brigade commander who gave the order, or the whole fucking *philosophy* of the IRA . . . but where would any of that get me?' He shook his head again. 'It wouldn't change anything. It wouldn't make me feel any better. It wouldn't bring Dad back to life, would it?'

'No . . .'

'All you can ever do is try to get on with things, you know? Forget about finding someone to blame, forget about retribution and justice and all that kind of shit . . . just concentrate on looking after the people you love. Watch out for them, care for them, do your best for them . . .' He paused, running his fingers through his hair, and then he sighed heavily and went on. 'But then, one day, you come across these three IRA men from Derry. And all you're really concerned about at first is whether or not they pose any threat to Nancy and Joe . . . because that's all that matters. It doesn't *matter* that these men come from Derry, and that you know for a fact that the IRA's Belfast Brigade sometimes bring in outsiders to carry out their executions, and that after your dad was murdered there was a lot of talk around the Falls Road that the man who shot him was a killer from Derry called Donal Callaghan . . .' William paused again, looking sadly at me. 'When I found out that one of the three men from the pub calls himself Donal, I just couldn't help wondering, you know . . .'

'You think he might be the man who killed your dad?'

William shrugged. 'Not really . . . I mean, just because he calls himself Donal and he happens to come from Derry . . . well, so what? There must be thousands of men from Derry called Donal. And it's probably not his real name anyway. But even so . . . I don't know . . . I just can't seem to let it go. I *need* to find out, you know . . . just in case. I need to know for sure that it *isn't* him.'

'And that's why you're hanging around with them? To find out if this man killed your dad?'

'Yeah . . .'

I looked at him. 'And if he is . . .? I mean, if you find out that he *is* the man . . . what are you going to do?'

'I don't know, Lili . . . I honestly don't know.'

I sighed, not really knowing what to say. 'He just calls himself Donal?' I asked. 'No surname?'

William shook his head. 'First names only.'

'And how do you know for sure that they're *not* after you and Nancy and Joe? I mean, if this Donal *is* the one who shot your dad –'

'They wouldn't use him again, not for a hit on the same family. They'd give it to someone else. And besides, I mentioned Nancy's name once when I was talking to them, her real name, and there was no reaction at all. Absolutely nothing, not a flicker of recognition from any of them.'

I raised my eyebrows. 'That was a bit risky, wasn't it?'

He smiled. 'I didn't tell them who she was or anything, I just happened to mention the first name of a young woman from

Belfast who used to work behind the bar . . . just in passing, you know? Just to see if the name meant anything to them. But it didn't.'

'All right,' I said, struggling to come to terms with all this. 'But I still don't understand why you have to put yourself at risk by getting involved with these men. I mean, if you *know* they're in the IRA, and you think that one of them *might* be responsible for your father's murder, why don't you just tell the police?'

'I can't do that,' William said simply. 'No matter who they are, what they've done, or what they're planning to do, I can't turn them in. I just *can't* . . . I'd be no better than Franky Hughes if I did.'

'Yeah,' I said, 'but what if they *are* planning something? You can't just let them blow people up, for God's sake.'

'That won't happen,' he said firmly. 'I won't *let* it happen. If I find out that they're planning something that's likely to hurt or kill people, I'll stop them.'

'How?'

'I don't know . . . I'll think of something.' He looked away from me. 'But if they're here for any other reason, anything that doesn't directly threaten anyone . . . well, I'm not going to get in their way.'

I shook my head. 'I don't understand . . .'

He sighed again. 'I'm not sure that *I* do, really. It's just . . . I don't know. Part of me still believes in what my dad believed in, that it's a war, and that we have a right to fight back . . . I mean, we *have* to fight back. It's the only way.'

'Do you *really* believe that?'

'Yeah . . .' He nodded. 'Yeah . . . at least, I *think* I do. But the thing is . . . I don't *want* anyone to get hurt. I don't *want* anyone else to get killed. It's just not *right* . . . I mean, I know . . . I fucking *know* . . .' He paused for a moment, wiping his eyes. 'I know how it feels . . .' he muttered quietly. 'No one should *ever* have to feel like that.'

I put my hand on his shoulder.

He looked at me, his eyes moist with tears. 'I just have to do what I'm doing, Lili. I have to find out if this man shot my dad, and I have to do it my way. But I *promise* you that I won't let anyone get hurt, OK?'

I nodded silently.

He rubbed his eyes, cleared his throat, and went on. 'I'm getting closer and closer to them all the time now, they're starting to trust me . . . they're actually starting to let me in on what they're doing. That's why I missed the gig last night. They'd asked me to meet them in the pub, and I'd just assumed that nothing much was going to happen, as usual – a few drinks, a few questions, a few vague hints about what they wanted me to do – and then I'd tell them that I had to go, and I'd jump in a cab and get to Islington in plenty of time for the gig. But when I got to the pub, instead of just sitting in the bar and having a few drinks like we usually do, they took me to a little room upstairs, and once the door was closed . . . well, that's when things got *really* serious.'

'What do you mean?' I asked.

'They had a list of things they wanted me to do . . . it was mostly just errand-boy stuff – collecting packages, delivering stuff . . . nothing too heavy. They asked me if I could do it, and I said "no problem", and then they started slapping me around a bit.'

'Why?'

He shrugged. 'Just to make sure, you know . . . to test me, to let me know who I was dealing with, to give me a taste of what would happen if I fucked them over. It's what they do. They tape up your eyes and put an empty gun to the back of your head, and then they just scream at you for a while, telling you all kinds of scary shit, and then, eventually, they say goodbye and pull the trigger . . .'

'*Shit* . . .' I whispered. 'That's *terrible*.'

'Yeah, well,' he said, smiling. 'I knew the gun wasn't loaded, so it wasn't that bad. And the thing is, once they've done it . . .

well, then you're in with them. It's all handshakes and smiles afterwards, you know – no hard feelings, have a drink, have a smoke . . . all that kind of shit. Anyway, the next thing I know, they're telling me that they want to show me something, and I'm following them out of the pub, and five minutes later we're in this car-repair place under a railway bridge, and there's all *kinds* of shit in there – guns, explosives, maps, timers . . . everything.' William looked at me. 'That's where I was last night, Lili. That's why I couldn't get to the gig, you see? I just *couldn't* . . .'

I nodded. 'So did you find out what they're planning to do?'

'Not exactly,' he said, shaking his head. 'I mean, I know it's big, and I'm pretty sure it's going to happen sometime in the next two or three months . . . but that's all I've got so far. I think they *were* planning to tell me a bit more about it last night, but something happened . . .'

'Really?'

'Yeah, there was someone sneaking around outside the workshop . . .' He shrugged. 'It was probably nothing, just some local kid nosing around or something, you know? But Donal's a bit paranoid – he thinks MI5's after him – so he had us chasing this kid halfway across London –'

'Did you catch him?' I asked, struggling to keep a straight face.

'No, he got away . . .'

I started to laugh.

William frowned at me. 'What? What's so funny?'

'It was me,' I said. 'The kid you were chasing . . . it was me.'

William shook his head. 'I don't get it.'

I told him everything then, how I'd seen them all coming out of the pub and followed them to the workshop under the bridge . . . and when I'd finished explaining it all, William just sat there in silence for a while, slowly shaking his head in utter disbelief.

Eventually, he looked up at me and said, 'But you didn't look anything *like* you . . .'

'I was wearing Chief's donkey jacket and hat,' I said. 'And, besides, it *was* pretty dark . . . *and* it was raining.'

William shook his head again. 'So how did you get away from us? Where did you go?'

'I cut down a little lane between those houses, you know . . .? The ones to the right of the track? Then I went down the street and got a taxi in St Ann's Road.'

'Shit . . .'

'That's why *I* was late for the gig.'

'Right . . .' he said, nodding. 'And what did Curtis have to say about that?'

'Well, he wasn't very happy.'

'I can imagine . . .'

I looked up then as heavy raindrops began to fall, splatting down noisily through the trees. The sky was black with thunder-clouds.

'I think we're in for another storm,' I said, as the rain began to pour down.

William got to his feet, gazing up at the angry sky. 'Come on,' he said to me, holding out his hand. 'We'd better get away from these trees before the lightning starts.'

As I took his hand and stood up, the first crash of thunder boomed right above us, and the rain came down in torrents.

'This way,' William said, leading me off down the path. 'Come on, quick . . .'

Lightning streaked across the sky, and then – *CRACK!* – a huge crash of thunder ripped through the air, making us both duck our heads.

'Run!' William shouted, pulling me along now. 'Come *on* . . .'

It was actually quite frightening, the sheer *power* of the storm – the roar of the rain, the wind whipping through the trees, the rolling darkness looming over our heads – but as we ran down the pathway, hand in hand, clattering our way through overhang-ing branches, I couldn't help feeling exhilarated too.

'This way,' William called out again, leading me down another pathway. 'There it is . . . come on.'

The rain was coming down so heavily now, and the skies were so dark and gloomy, that I could barely see where we were going. I could just about make out that we were heading for some kind of building, but all I could really see of it was a blurred black shape looming up through the darkness in front of us . . . a solid stone wall, an arched doorway, a tapering spire . . .

'Mind your step,' William said, guiding me towards the doorway.

As I followed him through the door and down some stone steps, I realized that we were inside a derelict chapel. The windows were all boarded up, the ancient stone walls were falling apart, most of the roof was gone . . . it was basically just a ruined shell. Piles of rubbish were stuffed in corners, there were empty bottles and cigarette ends all over the place, the walls were scrawled with graffiti . . .

I looked up through the roofless roof, and all I could see was falling rain. I wiped my face and looked at William.

'It's all right,' he said, smiling. 'We'll be dry in a minute. Trust me . . .'

I followed him across the main part of the chapel and through another archway, and then he led me over to an opening in the wall on the right. Two stone steps led up to the opening, which was about half the size of a normal door, so we had to crouch down and duck our heads to get through it. William went first, and once he was through, he turned round and held out his hand to me.

'Mind your head,' he warned, helping me through the gap.

I crouched down, keeping my head low, and crawled warily through the opening.

'It's all right,' William said, once I was through. 'You can stand up now.'

I cautiously got to my feet and looked around. We were in a

small stone room. It had a stone floor, stone walls, and – thankfully – a fairly solid-looking stone ceiling. The ceiling was only about six feet high, so there wasn't a lot of headroom, and it took me a while to feel comfortable standing up straight with the roof so close to my head. It also took a while for my eyes to adjust to the gloom. The only outside light came from a small glassless window at the top of the far wall, which probably wouldn't have let much light in at the best of times. Now though – with the storm still raging outside, and the thunderclouds still blackening the sky – there was only just enough light seeping in to see anything at all.

'What is this place?' I asked William, still gazing around.

'I don't know . . . just an old chapel, I suppose –'

'No, I meant here . . . this room.'

He shrugged. 'God knows . . . some kind of storage place, maybe? A wine cellar . . .?'

'Have you been here before?' I asked him, peering through the gloom at some old sheets of sacking laid out on the floor in the corner.

'Once or twice . . .'

I looked quizzically at him.

'It's just a place . . .' he said, slightly embarrassed. 'There's nothing . . . you know, there's nothing *mysterious* about it or anything. I just . . . I don't know . . . I just come here sometimes, that's all . . . I just like it.' He looked at me then, smiling with all the innocence of a shy little boy. 'You probably think that's pretty weird.'

'Yeah, I do,' I said, smiling back at him. 'But weird's OK . . . I *like* weird.'

He laughed.

Lightning flashed outside, momentarily illuminating the room.

'Do you want to sit down?' William asked, indicating the sheets of sacking in the corner.

'Well . . .' I said hesitantly.

'It's all right . . . it's perfectly clean.' He grinned. 'Well, maybe not *perfectly* . . .'

'It's not that,' I told him. 'It's just . . .' And now it was my turn to be embarrassed. 'It's just that . . . well, I *really* need a wee.'

He smiled. 'Me too, actually.'

'I don't suppose there's a toilet in here, is there?'

He shook his head. 'If you go back out into the main bit of the chapel, then turn right and head up towards the far end . . . well, there's plenty of little nooks and crannies up there, you know, little hidey-hole places . . . you can use one of those.'

'Are you sure?'

'Yeah, why not?'

'Well . . . it's a chapel . . .'

'So?'

'I don't know . . . it just feels a bit disrespectful or something, you know? Having a wee in the house of God . . .?'

William smiled. 'I'm sure he won't mind.'

'I hope not,' I said, heading back out through the opening.

'You can always tell him the Devil made you do it,' William called after me.

'Yeah,' I called back, 'or I could tell him that William Bonney made me do it.'

'That's fine with me.'

As I picked my way through the debris on the floor, heading towards the far end of the chapel, I heard William chuckling. And then, as I paused to wipe a cobweb from my face, I thought I heard him mutter something to himself. It wasn't very clear, and I could have been mistaken, but I could have sworn he said that he was 'going to burn in hell anyway'.

When I got back to the little stone room, William was leaning against the wall beneath the window.

'All right?' he asked me.

'Yeah, thanks.'

He smiled at me, then headed for the opening in the wall. 'Won't be a minute,' he said.

I watched him leave, then I went over to the sacking in the corner and sat down. Through the window I could see that the rain was just beginning to ease off a little, and the thunder and lightning – while still crashing around – wasn't quite so close any more. The sky, though, was still as dark as ever.

I looked at my watch.

It was nearly seven thirty.

It would be nightfall soon. The warm air of the storm was already cooling, and before long the temperature would rapidly start to drop. Even now, with my clothes soaked through and my hair dripping wet, I could feel myself starting to shiver. I still had William's jacket draped round my shoulders, but as I pulled it tight, trying to keep warm, I realized that it was just as wet as everything else.

I started to think about lighting a fire then. It shouldn't be that difficult, I thought. William had a lighter, didn't he? And there must be plenty of stuff around here to burn . . .

I heard something then. Footsteps . . . in the chapel outside. The sound of someone running . . . I froze, listening hard as the sound got closer and closer . . . and then, all of a sudden, William came diving through the opening in the wall. He hit the ground, face first, then rolled over and quickly got to his knees.

'What the –?' I said.

'*Shhh*,' he whispered, putting his finger to his lips.

'*What?*'

'*Be quiet*,' he hissed, crawling over to me.

I heard another noise from the chapel then . . . more footsteps . . . someone walking . . . shuffling . . . coughing . . .

I looked at William. He was sitting right next to me now, his eyes fixed on the opening in the wall. 'Who is it?' I whispered.

'It's the man who locks up . . .'

'Locks up what?'

'The cemetery . . . he's just checking to make sure that no one's in here before he locks the gates for the night. Keep still.'

I leaned closer to William, peered through the opening, and caught a brief glimpse of a blurred figure passing by on the opposite side of the chapel. He was very short, no more than five feet tall, and he was dressed from head to toe in black waterproof clothing – Wellington boots, a full-length rain coat, a floppy-brimmed sou'wester hat.

I stifled a giggle.

'*Shhh!*' William said, but I could see that he was grinning too.

'It's the Grim Reaper,' I whispered.

'No . . .' William whispered in my ear. 'It's God . . . he's come to get you for having a wee in his house.'

I had to clamp my hand over my mouth to stop myself laughing. William was struggling as well, trying not to make a sound, his shoulders jiggling up and down . . .

After a few seconds, the God-Man passed back the other way, still on the other side of the chapel, and then, when he was out of sight, he coughed again – once, twice – and this time he made a disgusting hawking sound in the back of his throat and we heard him spit loudly on the ground.

'God . . .' I whispered.

And then, realizing what I'd said, I looked at William . . . and suddenly we both cracked up. Snorting and spluttering, grinning like idiots, and desperately trying to keep quiet, we ended up grabbing hold of each other and rolling around like a couple of naughty little kids at the back of the classroom . . .

After a while, I heard William whisper, 'I think he's gone.'

'Thank *God*,' I said.

And that set us off again.

Eventually, though, we managed to stop laughing . . . and then we were both just sitting there, side by side, trying to get our breath back . . . and, for a second or two, it felt kind of awkward. We were sitting *right* next to each other, our bodies touching, and neither of us really knew what to do about it. Should we stay like this? Or should we move away from each other?

It was one of *those* moments . . .

And then William said, 'You're shivering.'

I looked at him. 'So are you.'

'Am I?'

I nodded. 'I was thinking that maybe we should light a fire . . .'

'Yeah . . .'

'Or we could just . . .'

He looked at me. 'What?'

'Well . . . I think I read somewhere that if you're cold and wet, and you're with someone else, you can use each other's body heat to keep warm.'

'Body heat?'

'Yeah,' I said, smiling. 'All you have to do, apparently, is cuddle up really close to each other . . .'

William smiled. 'That sounds a lot easier than lighting a fire.'

'You think so?'

'Yeah,' he said shyly. 'I think so . . .'

We were both a bit fumbly at first, not quite sure how to get hold of each other, both of us a little embarrassed . . . but it was OK. We laughed quietly and smiled about it, and eventually we sorted ourselves out . . . and then we were just sitting there in each other's arms, holding each other tightly . . . and it felt just as wonderful as it had before, when we'd held each other at the party. It felt *so* right, so absolutely perfect . . . and, just like before, there was a sense that this was it, this was enough . . . that I didn't *need* anything else at all . . .

And I didn't.

But I *wanted* something else.

'William?' I said quietly.

He turned to me, and I kissed him.

His lips were sweet with rain.

'Is this all right?' I whispered.

He didn't say anything, he just smiled and kissed me back . . .
And then we lay down together in the fading twilight and we
went to another world.

29

Afterwards, as we lay there together in the growing darkness, William told me that it was his first time. I didn't say anything – there was no need to say anything – I just held him closer and rested my head on his shoulder.

I felt complete, content . . .

Just lying there, at one with each other . . .

Listening to the rain.

It was perfect.

It was also *really* cold . . .

I didn't *want* to spoil the moment by bringing us back to reality, and I lay there for as long as I could without saying anything, but eventually I just couldn't stand it any longer.

'Maybe we ought to light a fire after all?' I suggested.

'Oh, *I* see,' William said, smiling at me. 'So my body heat isn't enough for you now?'

'It was more than enough for me, thanks very much . . . but, in case you hadn't noticed, we don't have any clothes on, and it's getting really cold in here, and it's pouring with rain again –'

'OK, I get it –'

'And we need to dry our clothes as well. I mean, I don't know about you, but I *really* don't feel like putting on soaking wet clothes just now –'

'Lili?' William said, sitting up and looking at me.

I smiled at him. 'What?'

'The quicker you shut up, the quicker I can get a fire going, OK?'

I raised my eyebrows at him. 'Are you telling me to shut up?'

'I am, yes.'

I grinned. 'OK.'

Half an hour later, all wrapped up in sheets of sacking, we were sitting in the middle of the room in front of a makeshift fire. Our clothes were spread out around the fire, drying slowly in the crackling heat, and I was telling William what happened when I finally got back to the Screen on the Green on Sunday night.

'I wasn't *that* late,' I told him. 'It was only about quarter to one, but when I got there the Buzzcocks had just finished their set, so I suppose they must have gone on in place of us around midnight.'

'Couldn't you play after them?'

'That's what I thought, but apparently the Clash had already set up all their gear, so . . . you know . . . that was kind of it, really.'

'So what did Curtis say?'

'Well, he was already *really* pissed off with you for not being there, and then I didn't get there until about nine o'clock –'

'Why not?'

'My mum . . . well, it's a long story, but she wasn't well, so I had to stay with her for a while –'

'What's the matter with her?'

I looked at him. 'It really *is* a long story, William. I'll tell you all about it some other time, OK?'

'All right.'

'So, anyway . . .' I sighed. 'Curtis was mad at me for being late, and he was *doubly* mad at you for not being there . . . and then when I went looking for you, and I didn't get back until forty-five minutes *after* we were supposed to be playing . . .' I looked at

William. 'Well, you can't really *blame* Curtis for blowing his top, can you?'

'I suppose not . . .'

'I mean, it was supposed to be *the* gig, the one that made us . . . and that's all that Curtis has *ever* wanted. That's his *dream* . . .'

'Yeah, well,' William said quietly. 'You can't always get what you want, can you?'

'Well, no . . . but –'

'There's more to life than empty dreams.'

'Yeah, but music is Curtis's whole *life*. That's all he cares about –'

'No, it's not. If music was really all he cared about, he wouldn't give a shit about getting a record deal and "making it big" and all that kind of crap . . . he'd just want to play. But just playing *isn't* enough for him, is it? What he *really* wants is all the shit that goes with it – the fame, the celebrity, the adoration . . .' William looked at me. 'What kind of dream is that?'

'His,' I said simply.

William didn't say anything for a moment, he just carried on looking at me . . . and then, after a while, he nodded slowly and said. 'Yeah, maybe you're right . . . we all have different dreams, I suppose. And who's to say what's worth dreaming about and what's not?'

'You?' I said, smiling.

'Yeah, right,' he said, laughing. 'I mean, look at me – squatting on the floor of a derelict chapel, dressed in a dirty old piece of sack . . . I've *really* got my life sorted out, haven't I?'

'It could be a lot worse,' I said.

'Yeah?'

'You could be on your own.'

He smiled. 'That's true.'

'Or even worse . . . you could be sitting here with you-know-who.'

'Who?'

'You *know* who.'

He grinned. 'You don't mean . . .?'

'Yeah . . .'

'The God-Man?'

'Yeah, you could be sitting here with the God-Man –'

'In his waterproofs?'

'No . . . *without* his waterproofs.'

'No!'

'Just in his wellies –'

'*No!*'

'He'd be sitting right here,' I went on, 'all naked and blubbery, and then suddenly –' I moved my hand round William's back – 'suddenly you'd feel one of his Almighty hands on your shoulder . . .'

William yelped and rolled away from me as I grabbed his shoulder. I laughed and jumped on top of him, holding him down and moving my face towards his.

'. . . and then he'd try to kiss you with his Almighty lips . . .'

'*No!*'

'Yes!'

'No . . .'

'Yes . . .'

'. . . yes . . .'

'. . . you're not the God-Man any more, are you?'

'No.'

'You're just you.'

'I'm just me.'

'Good . . . because otherwise it might be kind of weird . . .'

'I'm just me . . .'

'. . . I mean, I know you *like* weird . . . but there's weird . . . and then there's *weird*, if you know what I mean –'

'William?'

'Yeah?'

'Shut up.'

'OK . . .'

The rain kept falling, and the thunderstorm kept drifting away and drifting back again, and William and I just sat round the fire and talked about things. I didn't tell him that Curtis had accused us of sleeping together, partly because it felt kind of strange now that we actually had, but mostly because there just didn't seem any point. All William needed to know was that I'd had a big row with Curtis on Sunday night and that the next time I'd seen him he was in bed with Charlie Brown.

'So what do you think's going to happen with the band now?' William asked. 'Do you think it's all finished?'

'I don't know . . .' I shrugged. 'Probably.'

'Will you miss it?'

'Yeah, I suppose . . . I mean, there's a lot about it that I *won't* miss, you know . . . all the stupid stuff that goes with it. I never liked any of that. But just *being* in the band . . . playing together, being on stage . . . yeah, I'll miss that.' I looked at William. 'We were *good*, weren't we? *It* was good.'

He nodded. 'Yeah . . . and I'm sorry, you know, if it *is* over, I'm sorry I messed it all up for you.'

'It's not your fault –'

'Yeah, it is. If I'd been there on time on Sunday, we wouldn't even be having this conversation.'

'Well, yeah . . . but –'

'It's *OK*,' he said, smiling at me. 'I'm not sorry for what I did – it was the right thing to do at the time, and I'd do it again if I had to – I'm just sorry that it messed things up for you, that's all.'

'What about Curtis? Do you feel sorry for him too?'

William shrugged. 'He's a big boy, he'll get over it.'

'Oh, right,' I said, pretending to be put out. 'So what does that make me?'

'What do you mean?'

'You don't feel sorry for Curtis because he's a big boy and he'll get over it, but you feel sorry for a poor little girly like me . . .?'

'I didn't mean –'

'Poor wittle me,' I simpered.

'No, I didn't *mean* it like that . . .' He looked at me, and suddenly realized that I was joking. 'Yeah, right,' he said, shaking his head, but smiling. 'Very funny, Lili . . . very *amusing*.'

I laughed.

He sat there smiling at me for a moment, and then I saw him glance over my shoulder. 'You know what else is really funny,' he said, looking back at me.

'What's that?'

He grinned. 'There's a rat on the floor, right behind you.'

I stared at him, smiling. 'You think I'm going to fall for *that*?'

'Well, it's up to you,' he said casually, glancing behind me again. 'But if there was a rat creeping up behind *my* bare arse, I think I'd probably want to do something about it.'

'No . . .' I said hesitantly, forcing myself not to turn round and look. 'No, I don't believe you . . .'

He shrugged. 'Like I said . . . it's up to you. But –'

I screamed then, almost jumping out of my skin as I felt something touch my bum, and as I leapt to one side, scrabbling across the floor towards William, I saw a furry dark shape scurrying away through the opening in the wall.

'*Shit!*' I gasped, grabbing hold of William. 'Did you see the *size* of that?'

'It's all right,' William said, putting his arm round me. 'The nasty watty's gone now . . . poor wittle you . . .'

I looked up and saw him smiling at me.

The rain fell . . .

The firelight flickered . . .

Time passed . . .

*

William told me about his grandparents, how they'd taught him almost everything he knew about music, and how he used to play with them in the pubs and shebeens around Antrim.

'What's a shebeen?' I asked him.

'It's a bit like a pub, really . . . except it's not licensed. I mean, everyone *knows* about them, they're just not . . .'

'Legal?'

'Yeah.'

'How old were you then?' I asked. 'I mean, when you were playing in these places with your grandparents . . .?'

'I think I must have been around five or six the first time I joined them –'

'Five or *six*?'

'Well, yeah . . . I was probably only bashing a drum or something, and I had to wait until I was a little bit older before they let me loose on anything else, but that's just how it was, you know? Music was just . . . I don't know. It was always there. It was a family thing, you know? Family and friends . . . you'd just get together, work out a few songs, and start playing.'

He told me about his grandmother's love of books too, and how she used to read to him all the time when he was a little kid . . .

'But she was always a great believer in not treating children like idiots, you know . . . so instead of reading the usual kids' stories to me, she'd just read me the kind of stuff that she liked to read.'

'Like what?' I asked.

'God, *all* sorts,' William said, smiling at the memory. 'Poetry, novels, history . . . a lot of it was Irish stuff, of course – Joyce, Pearse, Beckett, Yeats . . . Seamus Heaney – but she really liked some of the Russian novelists too – Turgenev, Dostoyevsky, Tolstoy – and she loved all the French stuff – Camus, Sartre, Rimbaud, Verlaine . . .' He laughed quietly. 'Sometimes she'd lighten up a bit and read me some Dickens or Wilkie Collins or something . . .

that was her idea of an easy read, you know? A bit of light relief. Granddad, though . . .' William laughed again. 'Well, he used to love Westerns, cowboys and Indians . . . and when Granny wasn't around he'd read me all this stuff about gunfighters and outlaws and cattle drives, and it was like our little secret, you know . . . no one else was allowed to know, especially Gran.'

I smiled at him. 'So you grew up reading Tolstoy and Westerns?'

'Yeah . . .'

The rain fell . . .

The night grew cold . . .

We huddled closer together . . .

'You still owe me a story,' William said.

'Do I?'

He nodded. 'You promised to tell me all about your family, remember? When we were at the party that night? I said that I'd tell you about my family on the condition that you told me about yours.'

'Oh, yeah.'

'But you never did.'

I looked at him. 'What do you want to know?'

He smiled. 'Whatever you want to tell me.'

'All right,' I said, snuggling up to him. 'Well, my mother's maiden name was Mari Ellen James, and she was born and brought up in a small farming village just outside Bangor in north Wales . . .'

The rain fell . . .

The firelight flickered . . .

I opened up my heart.

I'd never really talked to anyone about my mum and dad before, and when I'd finished telling William all about them – their history, their lives . . . what they meant, or *didn't* mean, to me – I was absolutely exhausted, both physically and emotionally. It was a really strange feeling, a mind-numbing mixture of relief, release, confusion, fear . . . a whirlpool of emotions that left me feeling ripped open and emptied out, but wonderfully liberated too.

'Are you OK?' William whispered, holding me close.

'Yeah . . .' I muttered, sniffing back tears. 'It's just kind of hard, you know . . . I mean, I know that in lots of ways I've had it pretty easy, so I shouldn't really –'

'It doesn't sound very *easy* to me,' William said. 'All right, so you've never had to worry about money, but everything else . . . I mean, *Christ*.' He shook his head in disbelief. 'Hasn't your father ever tried to get in touch with you or anything?'

'Not that I'm aware of . . .'

'What about birthdays, Christmas?'

I shook my head.

William looked at me. 'Don't you ever wonder about him?'

'I don't know . . .' I said. 'Not really . . . I mean, he's never been there for me, and I've never known anything else. I suppose it might be different if I'd known him before he left, you know, if I had some memories of him or something . . . but I don't.' I shrugged. 'So he doesn't mean anything to me, you know . . . he *isn't* anything to me. He's just the man who fucked up my mum.'

'Does she ever talk about him?'

'She used to tell me stuff about him when I was a little kid, but only really when she was drunk or something . . . and then she'd either start crying so much that I couldn't understand what she was saying, or she'd get really angry and work herself up into such a state that she'd end up screaming the house down . . . and then *I'd* start crying, and then she'd start yelling at me . . .' I smiled at William. 'You're probably starting to wish you'd never asked me about my family now, aren't you?'

He shook his head. 'How do you feel about her?'

'My mum?'

'Yeah . . . I mean, it must be really difficult . . .'

'She's my mum,' I said simply. 'She's . . . well, you know. She's what she is.' I shrugged. 'She's my mum.'

The firelight flickered . . .

My eyes felt heavy . . .

I rested my head on William's shoulder.

'Do you think the rain's ever going to stop?' I asked him.

'I hope not.'

I smiled.

'Tell me something else,' he said.

'What do you want to know?'

'Tell me what you were like as a child.'

I told him stories.

The rain fell . . .

The time passed . . .

And sometime in the early hours, we fell asleep in each other's arms.

30

I'm floating on the ceiling of the workshop, looking down at four men sitting at the table – Flat Cap, Ratty, the God-Man, and Curtis. They're talking to each other, but I can't hear what they're saying. Their faces glow in the flickering light of a small paraffin lamp on the table. There are other things on the table too: papers, maps, files, a bottle of whisky . . . electrical apparatus, wires and cables, switches, circuit boards . . . sawn-off sections of tubular piping, bags of nails . . .

And guns.

The guns are laid out on a sheet of sacking – two pistols, a rifle, and what looks like a machine gun – and as I look down from the ceiling, I see Flat Cap pick up one of the pistols and pass it to Curtis. Curtis takes it from him and examines it, nodding his head. He says something to Flat Cap, and Curtis and the God-Man both laugh. Flat Cap drinks from a glass, lights a cigarette, takes the pistol back from Curtis, then smiles and pats him on the shoulder. Curtis takes a cigarette from a packet on the table, lights it, and sips whisky from a glass. He points at the pile of large plastic sacks and asks Flat Cap something. Flat Cap looks at Ratty. And now Ratty isn't just a thin young man with long brown ratty hair, he's a thin young man with the head and face of a rat, a man-sized rat . . . and he's nodding his rat-head at Flat Cap . . . and then he turns and says something to Curtis, and they both look over at something in the corner of the room . . .

And then, all of a sudden, I'm not floating on the ceiling any more, I'm in the corner of the room . . . *I'm* what Ratty and Curtis are looking at. Me . . . and William . . . we're *both* in the corner of the room . . . in bed. We're lying in bed together, and the bed is made of sacking, and we're surrounded by guns . . . and we're naked . . . and everyone is looking at us . . . and there are empty bottles and ashtrays all over the place . . . and in the middle of the room a long-dead apple tree has been doused in petrol and set alight . . . and our clothes are spread out around the smouldering tree, drying slowly in the crackling heat . . . and *everyone* is looking at us . . .

I nudge William . . .

Wake up.

Whuh . . .? he mumbles, rubbing his face. *What's that . . .?*

Wake up.

He looks at me, his eyes all bloodshot and bleary . . .

And then someone, somewhere, says, *Oops.*

And suddenly I'm back on the ceiling again, looking down at everything, and now there's a bomb on the table . . . a big, black, cartoon-style bomb. Like a cannonball, with a fuse sticking out of it . . .

And the fuse is burning . . .

And someone, somewhere, says, *Oh, shit . . .*

And then . . .

KA-BOOM!

I woke up in William's arms, shaking uncontrollably and gasping for breath.

'It's all right, Lili,' he said softly. 'It's all right, it was just a bad dream . . . you're all right now. Everything's OK . . .'

My heart was pounding, I couldn't get any air into my lungs.

'It's OK,' William continued, holding me. 'Just take your time . . . breathe slowly . . . that's it. Nice and easy . . .'

I took a deep breath and slowly let it out.

'And again,' William said.

I breathed in and out again.

'All right?'

I nodded. 'Yeah . . . thanks.'

I looked around. The fire had gone out, and the room was bathed in a pale morning light. The skies were clear, the rain had stopped, and birds were singing in the trees outside.

I looked at my watch.

It was just gone seven o'clock.

William smiled at me. 'Do you always wake up like that?'

'No,' I said, yawning. 'It only seems to happen when I spend the night in a rat-infested cemetery.'

We cleaned ourselves up as well as we could – washing with rainwater, drying ourselves with sacking – and then we got dressed, said goodbye to the chapel, and headed off to get something to eat.

We were both absolutely *starving*, and when we got to the Greek café in Stoke Newington – which was not only open at that time in the morning, but surprisingly busy too – we both ordered the biggest breakfast on the menu. Fried eggs, sausages, bacon, fried tomatoes, fried bread, mushrooms, and plenty of toast . . . and big mugs of steaming black coffee.

It was the best meal I'd ever eaten.

We didn't talk to each other while we were eating, we basically just sat there shovelling it all down, and it wasn't until our plates were empty, and William was mopping up the last few greasy crumbs with a piece of cold toast, that I finally broached the subject that had been niggling away at me ever since last night.

'William?' I said quietly.

'Mmm?'

'About this thing, you know . . . with the men from Derry?'

He glanced quickly around, then turned back at me. 'Keep your voice down, OK?'

'Yeah, OK,' I said, moving closer to him and lowering my voice. 'Is this all right?'

'Yeah.'

'OK . . . well, the thing is . . .' I sighed. 'I just don't *like* it, that's all.'

'Neither do I.'

'So why don't you just leave it alone?'

He shook his head. 'I can't.'

'Why not?'

He looked at me. 'You *know* why not, Lili. I mean, we've already been through all this –'

'Yeah, I know, but –'

'Nothing's changed.'

'But these men . . . I mean, they're *bad*, aren't they? They're not nice people –'

'They're soldiers, Lili. They're not supposed to be *nice*.'

'I know –'

'Look,' he said, taking my hand. 'It'll be all right, trust me. I know what I'm doing. My guess is that they're probably planning some kind of statement attack, you know . . . just bombing a building or something, either when it's empty or with enough prior warning to give everyone time to get out . . . in which case, no one's going to get hurt.' He shrugged. 'And, besides, most of these things never come to anything anyway.'

'What do you mean?'

'These kinds of operations, especially the ones over here . . . the vast majority of them don't get any further than the planning stage. Things are *always* going wrong – logistical problems, problems with money, with personnel, munitions, information . . . people make mistakes, the police hear rumours, MI5 starts poking around . . .' William smiled. 'Whatever these three are planning, the chances of them actually carrying it out are virtually nil.'

'Really?'

'Yeah, really.'

'But there's still a *chance*, isn't there?'

'Yeah, of course, there's *always* a chance.'

I looked into his eyes. 'And there's nothing I can do to change your mind, is there?'

He didn't answer me, he just looked back at me with those bright hazel eyes . . . so clear and radiant, so full of life . . .

'Come here,' I said quietly, reaching for his face with a napkin. 'You've got ketchup all over your mouth.'

It was only a short bus ride from Stoke Newington to Dalston, and from there we took an overground train back to Hampstead. I told William that he didn't have to come all the way with me, that I'd be perfectly OK on my own, but he insisted. And when we got to Hampstead Heath station, and he offered to walk me back home, I suddenly remembered the night of the Valentine's Ball . . . when we'd all been hanging around London Bridge tube station, and I'd been really pissed off with Curtis, and I'd found myself thinking about going home on the tube with William, and I'd imagined him offering to walk me back home from the station . . .

And now, here we were . . .

Making it real.

I smiled at him.

'What?' he said.

'Nothing . . .'

He frowned at me. 'Is everything all right?'

'Everything's perfect.'

And it was. For about five minutes, everything *was* perfect. It was a beautiful day – fresh and bright, with a fine drift of mist in the air – and although I was really tired, it wasn't a *draining* kind of tiredness, but more the kind that makes you feel sort of floaty and light-headed, almost as if you're intoxicated. And as we walked together along the leafy Hampstead streets, I seemed to be seeing everything in a brand-new light. The houses, the trees, the roads, the views . . . nothing had changed, it was all exactly the same, but somehow it all seemed very different. It was clearer, brighter . . . with more definition, and more depth. I could see all the little details of everything – the bricks of the houses, the leaves of the trees, the lines and curves of the roads . . .

It was a good feeling.

A perfect feeling.

It only started to feel a little less perfect as we turned into my street and headed down towards my house, and I began to wonder what we'd do when we got there. Would William want to come in? Should I ask him if he wanted to come in? Did I *want* him to come in? What kind of state would Mum be in?

'It's all right,' William said, touching my arm. 'There's no need to worry about anything.'

I looked at him. 'Who's worrying about anything?'

He smiled. 'You are.'

'I'm not –'

'Yeah, you are. You're chewing your lip . . . you always chew your lip when you're worrying about something.'

'Do I?'

'Yep.'

I smiled at him. 'You think you're pretty smart, don't you?'

'Yep.'

We carried on walking.

He said, 'I'll just come with you to your front door, if that's OK. I mean, I'd like to come in and meet your mum, and I will . . . but just not today. Is that all right?'

I smiled. 'Perfect.'

'Right. So which of these fancy houses is yours?'

'That one,' I said, pointing down the road. 'The one with the tower.'

He paused, a look of surprise on his face. 'You live in *that*?'

'Yeah . . .'

'What the hell *is* it?' he said, grinning at me. 'Is it a castle?'

'No, of course not –'

'I mean, Jesus . . . that's *huge*.'

'It's not *that* big.'

He shook his head, still grinning. 'It looks like something out of a horror film.'

When I didn't reply, he thought for a moment that he'd offended me.

'Sorry, Lili,' he said. 'I'm only joking. I didn't mean –'

'Is that Chief's van?' I said, staring at a familiar-looking Transit that was parked outside my house.

William studied the white van. 'It looks a bit like it . . .'

'It looks a *lot* like it,' I said.

As we both started walking again, heading slowly towards the van, everything was suddenly a long way from perfect. It was definitely Chief's van, there was no question about it. I recognized the dent in the back door, and the broken tail-light, and the KEEP MUSIC LIVE sticker that Curtis had altered to say KEEP MUSIC EVIL . . . and as I saw the passenger door swing open, all I could do was hope and pray that it was Stan getting out of the van, or maybe Jake . . . but I knew in my heart that it wasn't.

I knew that it was Curtis, even before I saw him.

I just *knew*.

I stopped with William beside the van, and we both just stood there and watched as Curtis stepped out and turned towards us.

31

I was expecting Curtis to be angry, of course – seeing me with William, the two of us strolling back home together, first thing in the morning – and the fact that he didn't have any *right* to be angry with me any more . . . well, that was neither here nor there. And there was no doubt that he *was* angry. The way he looked at me, then William . . . the disdain in his eyes, the hurt, the bitterness, the sense of betrayal . . . it was all there.

But, surprisingly, he not only seemed to have it all under control, he also seemed to have more on his mind than *just* how he felt about William and me. Which was kind of confusing, to say the least.

'Hey, Curtis,' I heard William say.

Curtis gave him a cursory nod, then turned back to me. 'All right?' he said.

My first instinct was to say, 'It's not what you think, Curtis.' But, of course, it pretty much *was* what he thought. So, instead, I said to him, 'What are you doing here, Curtis? What's going on?'

He glanced at William again, then looked back at me, half-smiling. 'This is really awkward, isn't it?'

'Yeah, it is a bit.'

He came over to where we were standing, took out a packet of cigarettes, and offered one to William.

'Thanks,' William said.

Curtis lit one for himself. 'OK,' he said blowing out smoke. 'Here's the thing . . . it's about the Polydor deal, you know . . . the one that we all thought we'd blown by not playing on Sunday night?' He glanced at William again. William said nothing. 'Yeah, well,' Curtis went on, 'it turns out that the guy from Polydor who makes all the final decisions, a guy called Chris, he was supposed to be coming to the gig on Sunday, but one of his kids was ill or something, so he couldn't make it. I mean, he *knows* we didn't play . . . and, just so you know, Jake told him that you both had food poisoning . . .' Curtis looked at William again. 'OK?'

William just shrugged.

'Anyway,' Curtis continued. 'Jake had a meeting with Chris yesterday . . . and, basically, they still want to sign us.'

'Really?' I said.

'Yeah . . .' Curtis was smiling now. 'They've drawn up the contracts and everything . . . I mean, it's all there, just waiting for us . . .'

'What – so it's definite then?' I said.

'Yeah, yeah,' he said, unable to contain his excitement now. 'They want us to sign today –'

'*Today?*'

'Yeah, today. That's why we're here . . . I mean, I tried ringing you, but no one knew where you were . . .' His smile faded a little. 'So, you know . . . what do you think?'

'Well . . . it's a bit sudden –'

'Yeah, I know . . . Jake thinks they're probably rushing it through to make sure that no one else signs us up first. There's a new independent company called Stiff who've been showing a lot of interest, and A&M are still sniffing around –'

'How much are Polydor offering?' William said.

Curtis didn't say anything for a moment, he just stood there, staring coldly at William, as if to say – what the *fuck* has it got to do with you? But William didn't care what Curtis thought. He just stood there, staring back at him, calmly waiting for him to answer the question.

'It's a two-year deal,' Curtis said, pointedly talking to me, not William. 'They're offering a £40,000 non-returnable advance against royalties. We get half of it on signing and the other half in a year's time.'

'And how's that going to be split?' William said.

'The same as it's always been split,' Curtis said, reluctantly turning to William. 'We all get equal shares.'

'Including Jake?'

Curtis nodded. 'Is that a problem?'

'No.'

'What about Chief?' I asked. 'Does he still get *his* ten per cent?'

'Well, no . . . I mean, he'll still get paid when he works for us, but he won't get a share of the royalties or anything.'

'What about the music?' William started to say. 'I mean, who gets –?'

'Look, why don't you ask Jake, OK?' Curtis said impatiently. 'He's in the van, he knows all the details . . . you can talk to him on the way.'

'On the way to where?'

'To fucking Polydor . . . where do you think?'

I said, 'Are we going right now?'

He looked at me. 'The sooner we go, the sooner we'll get the £20,000.'

I looked at William, remembering all the stuff that we'd talked about – Curtis's dream, fame and adoration, music, the band . . . and whether or not I'd miss it, now that it was probably all over . . .

William smiled at me, shrugging one shoulder, and I knew that he knew what I was thinking about.

I smiled quietly at him, then turned back to Curtis. 'I need to get cleaned up a bit and tell Mum what's going on before we go, OK?'

He nodded, his eyes cold. 'Don't be long.'

I found out later that while I was in the house, Curtis took William to one side and had a few words with him. In short, he told him that if he ever missed another gig, or even just another rehearsal, he'd be kicked out of the band straight away.

'No matter what,' he'd added. 'Do you understand?'

'Yeah,' William said, looking him in the eyes. 'I understand.'

'Good . . . and whatever's going on between you and Lili –'

'That's between me and Lili,' William said. 'Do *you* understand?'

Curtis glared at him. 'Fuck you, Billy.'

William just smiled.

And when I came out of the house, Curtis was waiting for me at the front gate, and it turned out that he wanted a few quiet words with me too.

'I don't think that's a good idea just now,' I told him, glancing at the van to see where William was. I could see Jake and Chief in the front, but there was no sign of William, so I guessed he'd got in the back.

'I just want to make sure that we're both OK with this before we sign the deal,' Curtis said to me. 'I mean, are *we* going to be OK, you know . . . you and me, in the band –?'

'Can I ask you something?' I said.

'What?'

'When did you find out that the deal was definitely on?'

'Yesterday . . .'

'Monday?'

'Yeah.'

'*When* on Monday? What time?'

'Does it matter?'

'Was it before or after you fucked Charlie Brown?'

'Look,' he said, shaking his head. 'That was nothing, OK? I mean, honestly, it was just . . . I was completely *wrecked*, Lili, I didn't have a *clue* what I was doing . . . and anyway, I thought, you know . . . after Sunday night . . . you and Billy –'

'Nothing happened on Sunday night, OK? I *told* you that –'

'What about last night then?'

I just stared at him.

He said, 'Yeah, I thought so . . .'

I shook my head. 'It wasn't like that.'

'Like what?'

I sighed. 'I can't do this now, Curtis. I really can't.'

'You shouldn't have started it then, should you?'

'I *didn't* . . .' I started to say, and then I realized that he was right – I *had* started it – and I really wished that I hadn't. 'All right,' I said wearily. 'You're right, I'm sorry . . . let's just leave it, OK?'

'Listen, Lili,' Curtis said quietly. 'If you really don't think we can carry on in the band together, or if you're just not sure about it at the moment . . . well, we don't *have* to sign right now. I think it's better if we do, just in case Polydor start having second thoughts, but I don't want to *force* you into doing something you're not sure about.'

I looked at him then, caught up once again in the familiar confusion of not knowing what to believe – was he *really* being thoughtful and caring, or was he just stringing me along, telling me what I wanted to hear . . .?

I didn't know.

And I realized then that I never had.

'I'm ready whenever you are,' I said.

'Are you sure?'

'Absolutely.'

I don't actually remember very much about going to Polydor to sign the contract. I was still really tired, probably even more so by then, and everything was so sudden and so unexpected, and *so* confusing, that the rest of the day seemed to pass in a daze. I can't even remember exactly where we went to sign the deal. I've got a feeling that it might have been somewhere in Kensington, or maybe Hammersmith, but it's no more than a feeling. All I can really recall is going into an office building somewhere, then hanging around for a while in a really plush reception area – deep carpets, leather settees, gold records framed on the walls – and then eventually we were all escorted into an equally plush office where we were introduced to lots of men in suits. They were all smiling and shaking our hands, telling us how delighted they were, how excited, how thrilled . . . and then some of them left, and we all sat down, and the guy called Chris sat at his desk and talked for a while about options and publishing and recording plans and a load of other stuff that didn't make much sense to me, not that I was really listening anyway. Curtis and Jake seemed to know what he was talking about, and I noticed that William was listening intently to every word that Chris said, but I was just sitting there really . . . not listening, not concentrating, not doing anything.

My mind was somewhere else, a million miles away.

After a while, the talking stopped, and then it was just a case of actually signing the contract – sign here, and there . . . and once again, just here – and as we were all doing that, a couple of photographers came in and started flashing away, and William did his usual trick of making sure that his face was always at least partly hidden, and then the champagne corks started popping . . .

And that was pretty much it.

We'd done it.

Signed a record deal.

We'd made it.

Curtis and Jake were already celebrating – glugging down the champagne as if it was water – and even Stan was joining in, although I think he was a bit pissed off with Curtis because Curtis had told Chief to stay in the van, and Stan thought his brother should have come in with us . . .

But he seemed to be getting over it now, clinking glasses with Curtis, pouring himself another . . .

I had a glass in my hand too, but I didn't seem to be in the right mood for celebrating. I wasn't sure why. I wasn't really sure *what* kind of mood I was in. I just felt kind of quiet, I suppose. A bit deflated. A bit down.

'Hey,' William said quietly, sitting down next to me. 'Are you OK?'

I smiled at him. 'Yeah, you know . . .'

'Not drinking your champagne?'

I shook my head. 'I'm just a bit tired . . .'

'Yeah, me too.'

I smiled again.

He said, 'Why don't you just go home, get some sleep?'

'Yeah, I think I probably will.'

We both looked up then as another flashbulb went off across the room, the photographer capturing the moment when Chris handed over the £20,000 cheque to Jake.

'Welcome to Polydor, boys,' he said, before adding – with a smarmy look at me – 'and girls, of course.'

There was a slightly odd little moment then as Jake suddenly realized that a cheque for £20,000 is only actually worth £20,000 once you put it in the bank. And *he* certainly didn't have a bank account, and neither did Curtis . . .

'Stan?' he said. 'Have you got a bank account?'

Stan shook his head.

'Lili?'

'No, sorry.'

'How about you, Billy?'

William just laughed.

So then Jake had to ask Chris if we could possibly have some of the money in cash, just enough to tide us over until we'd set up a bank account . . . and Chris had to make some phone calls . . . and eventually, when we left Polydor's office, we had £1,000 in cash and a cheque for £19,000.

'All *right*,' said Curtis, standing on the pavement outside the office, triumphantly waving a handful of £20 notes around. 'Who's up for a drink then?'

While Curtis and Jake headed off to the nearest pub, and Stan went to fetch Chief from the van, William hailed a taxi and told the driver to take us to Hampstead.

'Don't you want to go for a drink with the others?' I asked him, settling down in the back of the cab.

He smiled. 'Not especially, no.'

'They'll be talking about us, you know.'

He looked at me. 'Do you think so?'

'Well, yeah . . .'

'Maybe I'd *better* join them then,' he said seriously. 'I mean, we can't have them *talking* about us, can we?'

I smiled at him. 'You're not funny, you know. You think you are, but you're not.'

He laughed. 'It must be the champagne . . . I'm not used to drinking stuff that costs more for a bottle than most people earn in a week.'

'Maybe you'd better get used to it. You know, if things work out with this record deal and we start making pots of money –'

'I wouldn't count on that,' he said.

'What do you mean?'

'Well, I'm only guessing really . . . I mean, it's not like I'm a lawyer or anything –'

'But?'

'I think Polydor are probably ripping us off.'

'What makes you think that?'

'Well, firstly, they should have advised us to consult a lawyer before we signed anything –'

'But Jake told us that he'd looked over the contract –'

'Jake knows shit,' William said simply. 'I wouldn't ask Jake to look over a wall for me, never mind a contract. I mean, I could tell it was pretty dodgy just by listening to what Chris what's-his-name said, or – more to the point – what he *didn't* say.'

'Like what?'

'Like who pays for everything – the recording studio, the engineers, the producer . . . transport, accommodation, wages, whatever . . . do you think Polydor are going to pay for all that?'

'I don't know . . .'

'They're not, believe me. We'll be swanning around in limousines, staying in posh hotels, thinking we've got it made . . . but even if we *do* make it, even if we *do* sell thousands of records, we won't actually make any money until we've paid back everything that Polydor have spent on us, including the £40,000 advance. And that could take years.'

'Why didn't you say anything about this before?' I asked him. 'I mean, if you knew they were ripping us off, why didn't you *say* anything?'

'Do you really think Curtis and Jake would have listened to me?'

'Well, no . . . I suppose not –'

'Curtis would probably have kicked me out of the band, right there and then. And that would have meant . . .' William looked at me. 'Well, the truth is, Lili . . . I really need the money. I mean, whatever happens with the band, whether we sell any records or not, I've got £200 in my pocket right now, which means we can pay the rent for a few more weeks, and then hopefully – once high-flying Jake gets a bank account sorted out – I'll get my share of the rest of the £20,000, and with a bit of luck that should just about be enough to get Nancy her new ID.'

'And what if we *do* make it?' I asked him. 'The band, I mean. If we start selling lots of records, getting our pictures in the newspapers . . . you won't be able to keep hiding your face for ever, will you?'

He shrugged. 'Well, we'll see what happens . . .' He smiled. 'We'll probably just sink without trace anyway.'

'I don't think so,' I said, shaking my head. 'We're too good for that.'

'You reckon?'

'Yeah.'

He nodded thoughtfully. 'Well, I suppose I could always start wearing loads of make-up, you know, like Kiss or something.'

'Yeah,' I said, smiling. 'Or you could call yourself Billy Stardust, and paint a big orange stripe across your face.'

He grinned. 'I like that, yeah . . . I could start wearing hot pants and thigh-length boots and pretend that I'm Ziggy Stardust's long-lost son.'

'Or daughter.'

'Even *better*.'

'You could go solo . . .'

'Or we could both leave the band and form a duo. You could pretend that you're my sister –'

'Or brother.'

'Husband?'

I shook my head. 'Wife, maybe.'

'OK, wife. And you'd have to wear all the glam-rock gear too, of course . . . all the make-up and glitter and everything.'

'What would we call ourselves?'

'Billy and Lili?'

'Why not Lili and Billy? Or Lili and Willy?'

'I *hate* being called Willy –'

'All right, Lili and Billy then. Or maybe just Lilibilly –'

'How about Mr and Mrs Stardust?'

I started laughing then.

'What?' William said mock-seriously. 'Don't you like it?'

'Yeah, I love it . . . Mr and Mrs Stardust . . . it's a really *snappy* name.'

'OK, so now all we have to do is write some really snappy songs –'

'No, hold on, I've just realized something . . .'

'What?'

'Ziggy Stardust didn't have a big orange stripe across his face, that was Aladdin Sane.'

'Are you sure?'

'Yeah, Ziggy had a big silver circle on his forehead.'

'No, I don't think so –'

'He *did*.'

'Really?'

'Yeah . . .'

By the time we got to Hampstead, I was feeling a lot better. I could barely keep my eyes open, and my head felt so mushy that I was beginning to slur my words, but I was nowhere near as down as I'd been when we'd signed the contract at Polydor. It seemed that joking with William about the possibility of being famous was somehow more enjoyable than experiencing the potential reality of it . . .

Which was kind of strange.

But I was too tired to think about it.

As the taxi pulled up outside my house, I said to William, 'Do you mind if I don't ask you in? I'm just so tired at the moment, I can barely keep my eyes open.'

'No problem,' he said, smiling. 'You go off and get some sleep.'

I looked at him, hesitating slightly. 'Will I see you . . .?'

'Yeah, of course. I'll ring you tomorrow, OK?'

I smiled. 'OK.'

He leaned across the seat and kissed me. 'See you soon, Mrs Stardust.'

'Yeah . . .'

When I opened the door and got out of the taxi, I felt so numb and wonderful that I thought I was going to float away.

32

I saw quite a lot of William over the next week or so. We didn't
see each other *every* day, which at first – having got used to being with Curtis almost all the time – I found quite strange. But
after a while, I realized that by *not* being together all the time, it
made the times when we were together all the more wonderful.

And they really *were* wonderful times.

The day after we'd signed the contract, for example, William
called me in the morning and we arranged to meet up later on in
Camden Town. I had no idea what we were going to do when I
got there, and I really didn't care . . . it was just so nice, and so
exciting, to be meeting up with him. I hadn't actually gone out
on anything like a proper date for ages, and I'd kind of forgotten
what it was like – choosing what to wear, fiddling around with
my hair, getting a bit nervous . . .

It made me feel how I was *supposed* to feel at my age.

Excited and stupid . . .

But stupid in a good way.

When I met William outside the underground station, he looked
a little bit anxious too. But even that was OK. It was *nice* that we
were both a bit nervous, it felt kind of natural, how it should
be . . . and, besides, it didn't last very long anyway. Once we'd
smiled at each other and shared a slightly awkward kiss – and
then laughed at the fact that it *was* slightly awkward – everything
was fine.

And we had a perfectly wonderful day.

We went to the zoo, had cold hotdogs and coffee at the sea lion enclosure.

We walked in Regent's Park, ate ice creams and fed the ducks.

We went back to Camden, looked round the shops . . . and William bought me a secondhand music box from a dusty little antique shop. He didn't let me see him buying it, he sneaked back into the shop while I nipped into a café to use the toilet, and when I came out of the café, he just shyly placed the box in my hand and said, 'I thought you might like this.'

It was only a tiny thing – a little wooden box, not much bigger than a matchbox – with a little wooden birdcage on top. Inside the birdcage were three tiny brightly coloured birds, and when you wound the handle at the side of the box, the birdcage revolved to the tune of 'Silent Night'. I'd always absolutely adored 'Silent Night', and it had always made me feel quite emotional, but when I stood there that day, holding that tiny little box in my hand, slowly turning the handle, the sound that came out of it was *so* incredibly beautiful, and *so* hauntingly sad, that I actually started crying.

'It's *lovely* . . .' I mumbled between tears. 'Thank you *so* much . . .'

It was probably a bit embarrassing for William, standing with me on the pavement while I sobbed like a baby to the sound of a music box, and it was probably even more embarrassing for him when I flung my arms round his neck and buried my snotty face in his shoulder . . .

But he didn't seem to mind.

And after that . . .?

Well, that was about it really. We didn't go home together, we didn't spend the night together, we just thanked each other for a wonderful day, hugged and kissed, said our goodbyes, and went our separate ways. And when I got home that evening – feeling happily worn out and content – I couldn't *wait* to see William again.

And that's pretty much how things continued.

William would phone me every other day, we'd arrange to meet up, and then we'd just spend the rest of the day together. Sometimes we'd just hang around with each other, not doing very much at all, other times we'd get on a bus or a train and go somewhere . . . it didn't really matter where. Anywhere would do. One day we went to Epping Forest, another time we took a trip to the Natural History Museum . . . we even took a train out to Southend-on-Sea and spent a day at the seaside, eating candy floss and playing on the slot machines. I went round to William's flat a couple of times, once for a meal with Nancy and Joe, and another time when it really was Nancy's birthday, and we all went to the cinema to see Clint Eastwood in *The Outlaw Josey Wales*, which I didn't think I was going to like, but I actually really enjoyed it.

I always felt very comfortable at William's flat. There was no awkwardness, no embarrassment . . . none of the usual family tensions. In fact, it was more like being with a group of good friends than being with a family. It just felt perfectly *normal*.

Which, for me, made a really nice change.

My home life *was* awkward and embarrassing, and although I was used to it, and I could deal with it, the prospect of sharing it with anyone else had always scared me to death. And while William wasn't just 'anyone else', and he knew all about my mum's problems anyway, I still found myself making excuses every time he talked about coming over to my place. I didn't *like* myself for doing it, making up pathetic stories all the time – we've got the builders in, the house is a mess . . . maybe *next* week – in fact, I *hated* myself for doing it, because I knew that William knew that I was lying. But I just couldn't help it. Mum had become even more unpredictable than usual recently, and there was simply no way of knowing what state she'd be in on any given day. So while it was perfectly possible that I could have asked William to come round and she would have been on her best behaviour

– the ideal host, the ideal mother – and she would have made him something lovely to eat, and they would have had a nice chat, and everything would have been fine . . . it was also equally possible that William could have come round and she would have been drunk out of her head, or stoned, or – God forbid – she would have tried to seduce him or something . . . and I just couldn't bear the thought of that happening. Not *just* for my sake, and not just for William's either . . . but for Mum's.

So I kept putting him off.

We didn't sleep together again. I'm sure we *could* have if we'd really wanted to, and perhaps if the opportunity had arisen, and everything had been just right, we would have. But it just didn't seem to bother us all that much . . . if it happened, it happened. And if it didn't . . .?

It didn't.

And as for the band . . . well, on Thursday 2 September, we went into a recording studio just off Tottenham Court Road and began work on our first single. We were booked into the studio for four days, from noon to midnight each day, and although that wasn't long – at least, not in comparison to the vast amounts of time some bands spent in the studio – it was still a long time for four people to be together all the time, working in close proximity . . . especially if there were tensions between some of those four people. Which, of course, there were. So although I was really excited about going into the studio, I was also really anxious, because I couldn't see us getting through the next four days without something disastrous happening.

But, as it turned out, I was wrong.

There weren't any disasters.

There was a lot of tension, and plenty of awkward moments – mainly between Curtis and William, but also between Curtis and me – and, of course, there were disagreements and arguments, and every now and then the arguments escalated into shouting matches, but they never really got out of hand. And, what's more, they were always about the music – how things should sound, who should play what, who *shouldn't* play what – they never descended into anything personal.

And I think that was partly because William and I had previously decided that it'd be best if we didn't act like a couple when we were in the studio. So although we talked to each other a lot, and we didn't try to hide the fact that we were together, we didn't go round holding hands or hugging each other or anything.

But Curtis played his part in keeping things professional too. He stayed relatively sober, not drinking at all during the day, and – as far as I could tell – he didn't take anything apart from speed throughout the whole four days. This was his dream, after all – recording his songs, making records – and whatever faults Curtis had, there was never any doubting his commitment to his music, his energy, his passion, his unerring determination. All he really cared about when we were in the studio was getting it done, getting it right, getting it perfect.

And personal issues just didn't come into it.

So, in that sense, there was no need to be anxious after all.

Which meant that the only thing left for me to worry about was the simple fact that we were in a recording studio, we were surrounded by people who were used to working with professional musicians – sound engineers, technicians, producers – and although my bass playing had improved quite dramatically over the last twelve months or so, and I was fairly confident that I was at least reasonably competent, I knew that I was still a long way from being proficient. I was a proficient *pianist*, yes. But as a bass player I was still a beginner.

And maybe that shouldn't have worried me. We were a punk band, weren't we? Punk bands weren't supposed to *care* about musical ability . . .

Well, to be honest, I'm not sure if that sentiment was ever really true, because although a lot of punk bands might have started off without knowing how to play, most of them soon learned. You *had* to learn. Because if you can't play . . . well, you can't play. And, also, while you might just about get away with not being able to play on stage, you can never get away with it in a recording studio.

So, yes, I *was* a bit worried when we first started recording.

But, again, as it turned out, I needn't have been.

Our producer was a man called Edwyn James. He was quite young then, in his early twenties, and although he'd go on to become one of the most sought-after record producers in the business, at that time he was still virtually unknown. But he'd made a few records with other Polydor artists, which Polydor were really impressed with, and so they'd brought him in to work with us.

And he really was incredibly good.

He spent ages just talking to us, getting to know us, asking us what we wanted to do, what kind of sound we wanted, what kind of feel . . . and then he asked us to play through the songs we were going to record, and it was obvious that he really loved them, and he told us how great they were, and how great *we* were – both as a band and individually – and although I guessed he probably said that to every band he worked with, I had no doubt that – in this case – he really meant it. So from that point on, instead of worrying about whether or not I was a good enough bass player, I just got on with it.

Before we started any actual recording, Edwyn spent a long time working with us to get the right sound – the right guitar sound, the right drum sound, the right bass sound – and it really *did* take a long time. Trying this, trying that – different amps, different speakers, different mikes, different settings – I mean, we must have spent a good hour or two working on the drums alone – moving them around the studio, padding them out a bit, removing the padding . . .

It was actually quite tedious at times.

But, despite that, I still found it absolutely fascinating.

And when we finally got round to the recording process itself, I really enjoyed that too. The way Edwyn worked was really simple. Once he was happy with the overall sound, he'd just start the tape and tell us to play. We'd then play through whatever song we were working on (which on that first day was 'Naked'), in exactly the same way as if we were playing it live, and Edwyn would record it. Then he'd tell us how good it was, and make a few suggestions about how to make it even better, and we'd go through it again. And then he'd make a few more suggestions, and we'd do it again . . .

And again . . .

And again . . .

And again.

Until, eventually, after one of the takes – it could be the fifth or sixth . . . or the eleventh or twelfth – he'd suddenly jump up and shout, 'That's it! That's the one!'

And then we'd start working on what Edwyn called 'the fun stuff', which basically meant adding all the overdubs to the basic track – extra guitars, backing vocals, harmonies, maybe a bit of accordion here, a little guitar break there . . . I even got to put some keyboards down on a couple of tracks. We didn't go overboard or anything because we wanted to keep the basic sound quite raw, but Edwyn knew exactly what he was doing, and at the end of that first day, at just gone midnight, when he finally played us a roughly mixed version of 'Naked' . . . well, I remember quite vividly the looks on our faces as we sat there listening to it. We were like four little kids on Christmas morning who'd just opened their presents and not only got *exactly* what they'd always wanted, but much much more . . . we just couldn't stop smiling at each other, grinning stupidly . . . like four little children, drunk on sheer delight.

It was just *so* fantastic.

Over the next three days, we recorded 'Heaven Hill' and a new song that Curtis had written called 'Every Moon', which I thought was one of the best things he'd ever done. A slowish song, and quite long – almost five minutes – it consisted entirely of the same simple refrain, played over and over again, with a hauntingly hypnotic bass and drum rhythm that gradually grew into a great crashing maelstrom of noise at the end. The vocal line, which Curtis sang beautifully, was a really dark melody that meandered around the heart of the song like a lost soul, and the words themselves were – if anything – even darker.

> *A SLICE OF MOON, A SLICE OF HEART*
> *BROKEN*
> *A SICK MAN'S PRAYERS*
> *OF DOGS AND LIGHTS AND BLOODY THORNS*
> *OF LOVERS' HEARTS AND WHORES*
> *IN CHAINS AND BURNING CAGES*
> *I AM FUCKED UP AND DEAD*
> *AT EVERY MOON . . .*

Neither Polydor nor Edwyn thought that it was the right song for us to record at the time. I think they appreciated that, as a piece of music, it was really quite astonishing, but they weren't really looking for an astonishing piece of music, they were looking for a three-minute song that might possibly make the charts.

But Curtis was adamant that we record 'Every Moon', even going so far as to suggest that if we didn't, then maybe we wouldn't record *anything* for Polydor, which – given the fact that we'd only just signed with them and hadn't actually released anything yet – was a pretty risky, and possibly pretty stupid, thing to do. But, in the end, Polydor took the easy way out: they let us record 'Every Moon', knowing full well that when the time came to decide which tracks would appear on the single, they'd go for the other two.

So, anyway, by the end of Sunday night we'd recorded the three songs – 'Naked', 'Heaven Hill', and 'Every Moon' – and everyone was happy with the result. Edwyn still had to do the final mixing, and there were all kinds of other bits and pieces to sort out – sleeve design, promotion, printing, publicity – but Polydor had already set a provisional release date of Friday 24 September, so if everything went well, our first single would be in the shops in just under three weeks.

It was hard to believe that it was really happening.

It was also hard to believe – as I left the studio that night and got into the back of a waiting taxi – that it was already Monday morning, 6 September, and that in a little over seven hours' time I'd be on my way back to school.

33

It felt really strange going back to school again after everything that had happened that summer, and as I walked through the gates at quarter to nine the next morning, I wondered why I was bothering. I didn't have much interest in schoolwork any more, and although I was perfectly aware that – as William had said – the band could easily sink without trace, there wasn't anything else that I particularly *wanted* to do with my life just then, so what was the point of studying hard, taking my A levels, and going on to university?

Why not just leave school right now?

Just turn round, walk away, and go home.

I knew that Mum wouldn't mind. She'd probably pretend that she did, because she'd think that was how she ought to react, but I knew that her heart wouldn't be in it. Five minutes after I'd told her, she'd be asking me if I wanted to go shopping.

So if Mum didn't mind, and I didn't care . . . why *was* I bothering?

I didn't really know, to be honest. All I knew was that I didn't turn round and walk away, I didn't go home, I just carried on through the school gates and made my way to the sixth-form common room.

I thought I was going to find all the usual back-to-school gossip really boring – you know, the 'where did you go/what did you do in the holidays?' kind of stuff – and, in one sense, I was right.

I *did* find it really boring. Holiday romances, arguments with parents, boyfriends dumped, getting drunk . . . it all seemed so dull and predictable. But then, after a while, to my surprise, I began to realize that I was actually quite enjoying it all. Which, at first, I didn't understand. It hadn't suddenly become *not* dull and boring, so what was there to enjoy? But then it gradually dawned on me that the reason I was enjoying it was precisely because it *was* dull and boring. It was ordinary. It was normal. It had nothing to do with the IRA, nothing to do with record contracts, nothing to do with sex and drugs and rock 'n' roll . . .

And I think I'd kind of missed that.

But while I was quite happy to just hang around and listen to all the gossip – who's going out with who, who's finished with who, who's done what with who – I did everything I could to avoid being *part* of it. I just didn't want to talk about my summer, I didn't want to talk about the band, about Curtis, about William . . . but it was difficult not to. Although Curtis had left school almost a year ago, he was still something of a legend to a lot of people, and because most of the kids in my year knew about our relationship, I was always going to get asked about him. And I did.

How's Curtis?
Is he famous yet?
Are you still in his band?
Are you still going out with him?

I kept my answers as vague as possible.

No, we broke up . . .
No reason, really . . . it just didn't work out.
Yeah, I'm still in the band.

It wasn't that difficult to avoid talking about the band, because most of the kids at school were fairly straight and either didn't know anything about punk or didn't *want* to know anything about it. They were still into Bowie, or Roxy Music, or Led Zeppelin, or Status Quo . . . which was fine with me. There were

334

a couple of girls in my year who were kind of punky, and they'd been to a few of our gigs, so they had a lot of questions about Naked . . . but that was kind of OK. I still didn't tell them much, just that we were doing all right, it was going really well, everything was fine . . .

I didn't tell them anything about the record deal.

I'm not sure why . . . I mean, it wasn't meant to be a secret or anything. I just didn't feel like talking about it.

Funnily enough, I just happened to be with one of these punky girls when I left school that afternoon. Her name was Mo. I'd bumped into her on my way out of the main building, and she'd started talking to me, and we'd just kind of ended up walking across the playground together, heading for the gates. And it was Mo who first spotted William.

'Hey,' she said, 'that's the guy from your band, isn't it?'

'Where?'

'Over there, by the gates.'

I thought at first that she was talking about Curtis, and just for a moment I felt a brief flutter of panic, but when I looked over at the gates and saw that it was William, the panic quickly died. He was leaning nonchalantly against the wall, smoking a cigarette, and when he saw me looking at him, he smiled and raised his hand. I waved back at him.

'He's the one they call Billy the Kid, isn't he?' Mo said, as we carried on walking towards him.

'Yeah.'

She grinned at me. 'He's pretty cool.'

'Yeah, I suppose he is.'

'And cute.'

I looked at her. 'You think he's *cute*?'

'Who *doesn't*?'

I smiled, looking over at William again.

Mo said, 'Are you and Billy . . .?'

'What?'

'You know . . .'

I smiled at her. 'Why do you ask?'

'Well,' she said, glancing at William and lowering her voice. 'I mean, if you're *not*, you know . . . and if he's not, you know, with anyone else . . . well, I'm free at the moment, if you know what I mean.'

'Right . . .' I said. 'Well, I'll let him know.'

'Not right now, though,' she whispered as we approached him.

I nodded, my eyes on William now as we stopped in front of him. He put out his cigarette, smiled at me, then looked at Mo.

'This is Mo,' I told him.

'All right, Mo?' he said, nodding at her.

'Yeah, yeah . . .' she said, suddenly quite flustered. 'Yeah . . . it's really good, you know, to meet you and everything . . .'

'Mo's seen us play,' I told William.

He smiled at her.

She just stared at him, suddenly unable to speak.

I said, 'Well, I'll probably see you tomorrow then, Mo . . . OK?'

'Uh . . .?'

'I'll see you tomorrow.'

'Oh . . . yeah, right,' she muttered. 'Right, yeah . . .' She glanced shyly at William again, mumbled, 'See you then,' and quickly walked away.

I waited until she was out of earshot, then said to William, 'She thinks you're cool.'

'Yeah?'

'And cute.'

He grinned. 'Well, you know . . .'

'I had to tell her the truth, I'm afraid.'

'That I'm *not* cute or cool?'

'No, that you're gay.'

He smiled. 'Fair enough.'

*

'So,' I said to him as we started walking back home. 'What's going on?'

He shrugged. 'Not much.'

'That's not what I meant.'

He smiled at me. 'I just thought I'd come and see you, that's all.'

'Yeah?'

'Yeah.'

I shook my head. 'I know what you're doing, William.'

'I'm not *doing* anything. Like I said, I just thought –'

'You'd come and see me.'

'Yes.'

I looked at him. 'And I suppose you thought that once you were here, you might as well come home with me and say hello to my mum.'

'Well, now that you mention it –'

'And because I didn't *know* you were coming, I wouldn't have time to think up another excuse to put you off.'

'Yeah, all right,' he said. 'But if I *had* told you I was coming, you *would* have put me off again, wouldn't you?'

I shrugged. 'Probably . . .'

'I just want to see her, Lili,' he said, taking my hand. 'That's all. I mean, I *know* she's got problems, and I *know* it's really hard for you, but she's your mum, you know . . . she's your mother. And if I'm going to be part of your life, I just think . . . I don't know . . . I just think I ought to meet her, that's all. I mean, she's part of you . . .' He smiled at me. 'That doesn't really make any sense, does it?'

'Yeah, it does,' I said. 'At least, I *think* it does.'

'You don't have to *worry* about anything,' he assured me. 'If she's too ill, or if she just doesn't want to see me, or if it gets too difficult for you or anything . . . I'll just go.' He looked at me. 'All right?'

'Yeah, I suppose . . . but don't say I didn't warn you.'

*

When we got to the house and went inside, I knew straight away that something wasn't right. There was a strong smell of fruit everywhere, a steamy hot smell, and I could hear the clanging of pots and pans from the kitchen.

'What's that she's cooking?' William asked, sniffing the air. 'Fruit pies?'

I shook my head. 'Mum *never* cooks.'

When we went into the kitchen, Mum was standing at the cooker, almost engulfed in a cloud of steam, frantically stirring at a bubbling saucepan with a big wooden spoon. She was wearing an apron and rubber gloves, but – to my utter dismay – that was all. Beneath the apron, she was completely naked . . . except, that is, for the six-inch stiletto heels on her feet.

'Oh, God . . .' I sighed.

'It's all right,' William whispered to me. 'It doesn't matter.'

The whole kitchen was full of steam, the windows all misted up, and Mum was dripping with sweat. It was like a sauna in there. And everywhere I looked, all I could see was jam. Pans full of jam, pots full of jam, jars full of jam . . . there were jars all over the place. On the table, on the worktop, lined up on the shelf . . .

'Mum?' I said.

She stopped stirring and turned round. 'Lili!' she said, her eyes lighting up. 'I didn't hear you come in . . .' She looked at William. 'And who's this?'

'This is William. He plays in the band.'

'William! How lovely!'

'Hello, Mrs Garcia,' William said, smiling at her. 'Nice to meet you.'

'What are you doing, Mum?' I asked.

She looked at me. 'Sorry?'

'All this . . .' I said, looking around at the pots and pans. 'What's going on?'

'Nothing's going *on*, love. I'm just making some jam . . . for

338

your dad.' She looked at the clock on the wall. 'He'll be back from work soon.'

'But . . .'

She smiled. 'You *know* how much he likes his jam.'

'But, Mum . . .'

'Yes, dear?'

'You can't . . .'

'I can't what?'

I didn't know what to say.

Mum turned to William. 'How about you, William? Do you like jam?'

'What flavour?'

'Any flavour you like. I've made raspberry, plum, apple . . . strawberry. Do you like strawberry jam?'

'Yeah, I love it.'

'Oh, you *must* try this then,' she said, crossing over to the counter and picking up a jar of jam.' She looked back at William. 'Would you like a spoon?'

'Yes, please.'

She turned back to the counter, opened a drawer, took out a spoon, then brought the jam and the spoon over to William. 'There you are, tuck in.'

'Thanks . . .' He smiled at her. 'Would it be OK if I had a piece of bread with it?'

'Bread?' Mum said. 'Of *course* you can have bread.'

For the next hour or so, everything was kind of all right . . . or, at least, it was as all right as it could be. I mean, it's not easy to be *perfectly* all right when you're sitting with your boyfriend at the kitchen table, and you're surrounded by ludicrous amounts of jam, and your mother is wearing nothing but an apron, rubber gloves, and a pair of stilettos . . .

It's not easy at all.

But we did our best.

William ate far too much bread and jam, and kept telling Mum how good it was. She clearly enjoyed his flattery, and after a while she – thankfully – sat down at the table, which at least meant that she wasn't flashing her bare backside around any more. And then she just started chatting to William, quite normally really, about the band, about Belfast, about all kinds of things . . . and William just talked to her, equally normally, answering her questions, asking her questions, telling her little stories, making her laugh . . .

And it *was* kind of all right.

So much so that I almost forgot that it *wasn't* all right, and that for Mum it probably never would be.

And then, all of a sudden, as William was telling Mum something about the dockyards in Belfast where the *Titanic* was built, she just let out an awful groan, as if she was in pain, and she started looking fearfully around the kitchen, frowning at all the pots and pans and jars . . . and then she froze for a moment, staring straight ahead, and then suddenly she looked down at herself and let out another anguished groan.

'Oh, *God* . . .' she muttered. 'Oh, God . . . look at me . . . *look* at me . . .' She got to her feet, covering her eyes with her hands, and began backing away towards the door. 'I'm so sorry,' she sobbed. '*Please* forgive me . . . I'm so *so* sorry . . . I didn't know . . . I didn't *know* . . .'

She backed through the doorway, and then we heard her scurrying away, still sobbing, still muttering madly to herself . . .

I looked at William. 'Still glad you came?'

'Yeah,' he said, taking hold of me. 'Yeah, I am.'

'You don't have to go if you don't want to,' I told William as I showed him to the front door. 'I mean, Mum will probably be all right in a while, she just needs a bit of time to calm down –'

'It's not that,' William said. 'I just have to get back, that's all.'

I looked at him. 'The men from Derry?'

He nodded.

I said, 'Is that it?'

'What?'

'You're not going to tell me anything? You're just going to leave me guessing?'

'There's nothing much to tell, Lili . . . honestly. I think Donal's still worried about the other night at the workshop, you know . . . when you were there.' William smiled. 'He still thinks there's a chance that MI5 might be on to them, and he's told us all to keep away from the workshop and lie low for a while, just in case. So I haven't really been able to find out much more about him.'

I looked William in the eye. 'There must be some other way of finding out if he *is* Donal Callaghan or not.'

'Like what?'

'I don't know . . . can't you at least get a description of him from the people you know back in Belfast?'

William smiled again. 'I've *got* a description of him . . . in fact, I've got about a dozen. The trouble is, they're all slightly different, and they're all so vague that they're hardly worth bothering with. He's medium height, medium build, somewhere between thirty and fifty years old . . . he's either cleanshaven or he's got a beard, or sometimes a moustache . . . his hair's dark . . . maybe brown, maybe black, maybe grey . . .' William shrugged. 'He's a killer, Lili . . . it's in his best interests to make himself look as ordinary and forgettable as possible. That's why I have to keep doing what I'm doing, you know . . . getting to know him, trying to draw him out . . . I just need to spend a bit more time with him, that's all.'

'Right . . . so you're seeing him tonight?'

He nodded. 'It's just a quick meeting in a pub in Hornsey, and I doubt very much if I'll find out anything useful, but you never know . . .'

'Right,' I said.

He took hold of my hand. 'Next time I come round, I'll make sure I can stay for longer, OK?'

I nodded, doing my best to smile, but it wasn't OK. It wasn't OK at *all*. I really didn't like what he was doing, it scared me – and I still wasn't a hundred per cent sure that he was telling me the truth anyway. At least, not the whole truth. But every time I thought about it, every time I asked myself – *what can I do? what should I do?* – I kept coming up with the same answer.

I didn't know what to do.

'Lili?' William said.

I looked at him.

'I have to go,' he said. 'OK?'

'Yeah,' I said, kissing him goodbye. 'Be careful, all right?'

He grinned. 'I'm always careful.'

34

Punk music, at this time, was still a few months away from hitting the big time, and it didn't really become a national phenomenon until after the Sex Pistols' notorious live TV appearance on the *Today* programme in December (when they made the headlines by swearing at the host, Bill Grundy), but some would say that the event that really brought punk into the wider spotlight for the first time was the 100 Club Punk Festival.

The festival was another of Malcolm McLaren's ideas. Two nights of live punk music – Monday 20 and Tuesday 21 September – with all the big names taking part.

Apart from the Damned – who'd signed with Stiff earlier that month – we were the only band with a record deal, but all the record companies were there, checking out what was on offer. The press were all there too – the music press *and* some of the nationals – and the crowds were really huge, with hundreds of punks from all over the country queuing up to get in each night.

I mean, the whole thing was a *really* big deal.

On the night we played, the actual performance side of things was, for the most part, really good. Siouxsie and the Banshees (with Sid Vicious on drums) were absolutely abysmal, but it was their first ever gig, and they clearly didn't have any songs, or any idea how to play, so it wasn't really surprising that were atrocious. Everyone else, though – the Subway Sect, the Clash, the Pistols – they were all excellent. The Pistols especially. They were amazing, *so* much better than the last time I'd seen them. They really *sounded* like a band now.

But no matter how good the Sex Pistols were, they were nothing compared to us. We were simply *phenomenal*. I'm still not sure *why* we were so good that night – although I think it might have had something to do with the confidence we'd gained from the recording session – but it was, without question, the best gig we ever played. The sound was great, the audience was fantastic, and we just couldn't have been any better. Both individually, and as a band, we were stunning. Curtis was as good as he'd ever been – mesmeric, demonic, lurching and reeling around the stage like a man possessed. His guitar playing was out of this world, and his voice . . . God, the way he sang that night . . . it sends shivers down my spine just thinking about it.

And then there was William, doing *his* thing – jerking and jiggling, his head bobbing to the rhythm as he effortlessly strummed away, keeping everything going . . . occasionally changing from guitar to banjo, then banjo to accordion, then back to the guitar again. And his singing, too, was something special that night. He didn't sing a lot, just a few lines of harmony here and there, and he sang so softly that at times you had to strain to actually hear him. But it was worth it when you did, because for a few sweet moments you could hear the voice of the devil's own angel.

And then there was me . . .

That night, for me, was the night when it all came together. Up until then, there'd always been a nagging doubt in the back of my mind as to whether or not I really *belonged* in the band. It wasn't that I doubted my contribution, or that I didn't think I deserved to be in the band, and there was never any indication from any of the others that I didn't fit in or anything . . . it was just me, the way I felt. I just felt, for some inexplicable reason, that although I was in the band, I wasn't actually *in* the band. I was always just a little bit off to one side.

But that night, for some equally inexplicable reason, everything changed, and as soon as we stepped on stage and started to play . . . well, that was it. I wasn't just *me* any more – standing there, just a little bit off to one side, playing my bass – I was *part* of it all, I *belonged* . . . I was *in* the band.

I was right *there*, right in the middle of it all – playing my heart out, dancing around, smiling, singing, rocking and rolling . . . it really was the best time ever.

And last, but not least, there was Stan – pounding away behind us, driving us on . . . his arms flailing, his foot hammering up and down on the bass pedal, his bare chest dripping with sweat . . .

He was *awesome*.

We all were.

It was a truly unforgettable experience.

The only moment that wasn't quite perfect was the by now almost obligatory outbreak of violence, which that night occurred when we were playing 'Every Moon'. It was the first time we'd played it live, and if anything it sounded even more powerful than the recorded version. We were about halfway through the song, just at the point where it really starts to build up, and Curtis was hunched over his guitar, his eyes closed, completely lost in the hypnotic beat of the music . . . when, all at once, a thick-head punk at the front of the stage put his hands to his mouth and shouted out, '*Boring!*'

Curtis didn't stop playing or anything, he just slowly looked up, fixed his eyes on the heckler – who was now just standing there with a stupid drunken grin on his face – and moved across the stage towards him. Without missing a beat, he went right up to the front of the stage, stopped in front of the still-grinning punk, then leaned over and spat in his face. The punk, not surprisingly, took exception to this, and as Curtis turned his back on him and started moving back to the centre of the stage, the punk grabbed a pint glass from the person next to him and threw it at Curtis. Luckily for Curtis, it just missed his head, but unluckily for Stan it went sailing across the stage and smashed into one of the cymbals, showering him with splinters of broken glass, one of which nicked him just over his eye. Curtis immediately spun round and went after the punk again, but he needn't have bothered because William had already dealt with him. As soon as he'd seen the punk throwing the glass, William had run across to the front of the stage and kicked him in the head. It was a running kick, delivered quite brutally, and the punk went down as if he'd been shot. Everything went a bit crazy then – people were shouting and screaming, angry punks were trying to get on stage, Curtis and William were kicking them off . . . and then Jake and Chief waded in, pulling people away, and the punks turned on them . . . and then a bunch of big security guys showed up, and once they started throwing *their* weight around, everyone suddenly calmed down again.

It wasn't very nice . . . at least, not from my point of view anyway. That kind of thing was never very nice. But, the truth is, it wasn't any worse than anything else we'd experienced, and I'd got so used to it by then that once it was all over and done, I didn't really give it much thought.

Unfortunately, as I said, there were a lot of journalists there that night, and they were also there the following night when Sid Vicious threw a glass when the Damned were on stage. The glass hit a pillar at the side of the stage, shattered all over the place, and a girl in the audience was badly hurt when a splinter lodged in her eye. Sid was dragged out of the crowd and beaten up, the girl was taken to hospital, and Sid was arrested and driven away in the back of a police van.

And it was that – and the violence at our gig – that made all the headlines.

Which was a shame really.

But that's just the way it was.

We all knew that we'd put on an amazing show that night, and as we sat around in the dressing room afterwards, none of us felt the need to say anything. We were just like those four little kids on Christmas morning again – smiling at each other, grinning stupidly . . . drunk on happiness.

We probably would have been perfectly happy to just sit there in silence for the rest of the night, but after about five minutes or so, Jake came bursting into the dressing room, his eyes bugged out with amphetamine-fuelled excitement, and he immediately started jabbering away like a maniac.

'*Great* show, fucking *brilliant* . . . absolutely fucking *amazing* . . . are you all right, Stan? How's your face? Shit, that fucking idiot . . . hey, nice one, Billy, you really whacked the fucker, didn't you? Fucking shit-hole . . . I'll kill him the next time I see him . . . but, yeah, anyway . . . I mean, shit . . . you were *so* good tonight . . .'

Eventually, he had to stop jabbering for a moment to light a cigarette. But once he'd done that, and passed the packet around, he immediately started talking again.

'So, anyway,' he said, blowing out smoke and grinning, 'what do you want first? The good news or the *really* good news?' When no one answered him, he just carried on. 'Well, all right then, the good news is that I've just spoken to Chris, and the single's *definitely* coming out this Friday. They've decided to release it as a double A-side, "Naked" and "Heaven Hill", OK? And the *really* good news is . . .' He grinned again, barely able to control his excitement now. 'Are you ready for this? The day before the single comes out, that's this Thursday . . . you're going to be on *Top of the Pops*.'

'*What?*' we all said at once.

'Not bad, eh?'

'Are you *serious*?' Curtis said. '*Top of the Pops*?'

'Yeah . . .'

'Shit.'

It was an unbelievable way to end what had already been an unbelievable night. *Top of the Pops* was *huge* back then –

millions of people watched it every week. An appearance on *Top of the Pops* almost guaranteed you instant success. Of course, we all despised virtually everything about the programme – the stupid DJ presenters, the disco bands, the embarrassingly dumb dance routines – and no one with an ounce of cool would ever admit to actually watching it, even though we all probably did . . . but none of that really mattered. It was *Top of the Pops*, for God's sake. *Top of the Pops!* And *we* were going to be on it.

But, as good as that was, and as good as everything else was that night – the way we played, the togetherness, the passion, the music, the feelings – the most significant thing for me about that night was that it was the last time the four of us ever played together.

35

In those days, *Top of the Pops* was recorded on a Wednesday, the day before it was broadcast, which meant that after Monday night's gig we only had a day to get everything ready and work out what we were going to do. So the plan was to meet up at the warehouse on Tuesday afternoon, go through everything we needed to talk about, then get all the gear ready for the following day.

The meeting was scheduled for three o'clock.

And after ringing school in the morning to tell them I had a really bad cold and wouldn't be in for a couple of days, I arranged to meet up with William at twelve o'clock, at Abney Park Cemetery, so we could spend a couple of hours together before heading off to the warehouse.

The summer was well and truly over now, and the first signs of autumn were beginning to appear. The leaves on the trees were starting to yellow, and some of them had already begun to fall. The sun was out, pale and high in the sky, but there was very little warmth to the air, and what little there was seemed to flutter away at the faintest hint of a breeze. But that was fine with me. I *liked* the feel of autumn in the air. It felt fresh . . . dusky . . . it felt kind of hopeful, like something was coming. It felt good.

William was waiting for me at the cemetery gates when I got there, looking as good as ever. He was wearing an overcoat which

I'd never seen before. It looked reasonably expensive, a good-quality coat, and I wondered if he'd treated himself with some of his record contract money . . .

Probably not, I guessed.

It was more than likely stolen.

'Hey,' he said, as I walked up to him. 'You OK?'

I nodded. 'Nice coat.'

'You think so?'

'Yeah . . . you look like a rock star.'

He laughed.

I kissed him.

And we headed off into the cemetery.

'So,' William said. 'We're going to be on *Top of the Pops*.'

'Yeah.'

'Excited?'

'Well, yeah . . .'

He looked at me. 'But?'

'I don't know . . . I mean, it's great and everything, obviously . . . but there's just a couple of things about it that are bothering me.'

'Like what?'

We were sitting on the wooden bench at the side of the path where we'd sat together the last time we were here. Over to our right, half hidden behind some tall trees, I could just make out the tower of the derelict chapel. As I gazed over at it, remembering that night with William, a pigeon broke out from the eaves of the chapel, flew a ragged arc round the tower, then returned to where it had come from.

I looked at William. 'Do you watch *Top of the Pops*?'

'Well, yeah, I've seen it . . . I mean, I don't make a *point* of watching it or anything –'

'Did you know they have rules about who can be on it?'

'What kind of rules?'

'Well, you have to have a single in the Top 20, for a start. And the single has to be climbing the charts, not going down . . .' I looked at him. 'Do you see what I'm saying?'

He nodded. 'Our single isn't in the Top 20.'

'Exactly. It's not even *out* until Friday . . .' I frowned at him. 'What are you smiling about?'

He laughed quietly. 'I heard Curtis talking to Jake last night . . . Curtis couldn't understand it either. He just didn't get why they'd want a band like Naked on the show at all.'

'Well, yeah,' I said. 'That's what I thought too. I mean, we're not a "pop" band, are we? We just don't *belong* on *Top of the Pops*.'

William smiled again. 'Well, apparently, Jake knows this girl who used to go out with a guy who's got something to do with booking the bands for *Top of the Pops*, and she told Jake that there was supposed to be an American band coming over to do the show this week, but they had some kind of problem getting visas or something . . . I think it was something to do with drug convictions. Anyway, they had to pull out, and Jake found out about it, and then . . . well, he didn't go into any details, but it sounded to me like this girl told Jake that she knew something about the *Top of the Pops* guy, something personal that he'd do almost anything to keep quiet, and that, for the right price, she could get just about anyone on the show.'

'By *blackmailing* her ex-boyfriend?'

'Basically, yeah.'

'So Jake paid her?'

William nodded. 'I think so.'

'How much?'

'No idea.'

I shook my head. 'Well, at least that explains it . . .'

'Yep.'

I looked at William. 'It's a bit kind of *shabby* though, don't you think?'

'Shabby?'

'Dirty, shady . . . you know what I mean.'

He nodded. 'Well, yeah . . . I suppose so. But it's just business, you know, the same as any other business. Business is *always* dirty.'

'So it doesn't bother you?'

'Nope. Does it bother *you*?'

'I don't really know, to be honest . . .' I shrugged. 'And I don't suppose it matters anyway, does it? I mean, even if it *did* bother me, there's not much I can do about it, is there?'

He grinned at me. 'You could go on strike, refuse to appear –'

I smiled. 'And you'd support me, of course.'

'Of course. We could picket the show together, you know . . . we could stand outside the *Top of the Pops* studio with placards and everything, singing protest songs –'

'Here we go again,' I sighed.

'What?'

'You.'

'What about me?'

'Nothing,' I said, smiling. 'Just you.'

The other thing that had been bothering me about doing *Top of the Pops* was the effect that it might have on William. All kinds of people watched *Top of the Pops*, including – quite possibly – the kind of people that William didn't *want* to be seen by. And I remembered him telling me before that if things started getting any bigger for us, he might have to consider leaving the band . . . and things didn't get much bigger than *Top of the Pops*.

'I know we joked about it before,' I said to him. 'You know, all that stuff about disguising yourself by wearing make-up and everything . . . but it's not a joke now, is it? It's real.'

'Yeah, I know.'

'So what are you going to do?'

He smiled. 'I don't see why I *can't* wear make-up. I mean, Curtis does –'

'He wears a bit of eye-liner, that's all.'

'I've seen him in lipstick too.'

'Yeah, but –'

'Don't you think I'd look good in make-up?'

'Come on, William,' I said sternly. 'This is serious . . . if the IRA are still after Nancy –'

'They won't recognize me,' he said, his smile quickly fading.

'Why not?'

'Well, firstly, like I said before, I've changed a lot since I left Belfast. I was just a kid then . . . I look completely different now. And secondly, when we're on *Top of the Pops* the cameraman's not going to be concentrating on me, is he?'

'I suppose not . . . I mean, they *do* tend to focus on the singer –'

'It's *you* they'll be focusing on.'

'What?'

He laughed. 'Come *on*, Lili, you know what *Top of the Pops* is like . . . the cameraman spends most of the time looking up pretty girls' skirts –'

'Yeah, but –'

'And you're not only a *very* pretty girl, but you're also in the band . . . so, yeah, they might stick the camera on Curtis now and then, but most of the time it's going to be all over you.' He grinned. 'Me and Stan won't get so much as a look-in. Trust me, they're not going to waste any time filming us.'

'But what if –?'

'And *thirdly*,' he said, holding up a finger to let me know that he hadn't quite finished yet. 'Just in case they *do* happen to point the camera at me . . .' He reached into his coat pocket and pulled out a pair of sunglasses. 'What do you think?' he said, putting them on.

I couldn't help laughing.

'What?' he said indignantly.

'Nothing . . .' I giggled again. 'Yeah, you look really *cool* in those . . .'

He smiled. 'I've got a hat too.'

'A hat?'

'Yeah, a trilby . . . like the one Van Morrison wears.'

'Who?'

'Van Morrison . . . don't tell me you've never heard of Van the Man. He's a legend in Belfast –'

'Does *he* wear sunglasses too?'

'Yeah, as a matter of fact he does.'

'Well,' I said, smiling. 'That's OK then.'

He grinned. 'I'm glad you think so.'

'Let me try them on,' I said, reaching out for his glasses.

'No,' he said, playfully leaning away from me.

'Why not?'

'Get your own.'

I lunged across the bench, making a grab for the glasses, but William was too quick for me, scooting out of reach across the bench. I looked at him for a moment, both of us smiling, and then I lunged again, this time really flinging myself at him, but he saw that coming too, and in a flash he was on his feet and looking down at me as I sprawled like an idiot across the bench.

I looked up at him.

He smiled.

'You'd better start running,' I said.

'Yeah?'

'Yeah . . .'

'You think you can catch me?'

'I *know* I can catch you.'

He smiled again, shaking his head . . .

And I leapt off the bench . . .

And we ran through the wildness of the cemetery together, whooping and laughing like children.

36

Wednesday, 22 September 1976 . . . the date is seared into my memory. The *Top of the Pops* recording was scheduled to start at four o'clock, and we'd arranged to meet at the warehouse at two, giving us plenty of time to load up all the gear and drive across London to the BBC studios at Lime Grove.

'When we get there,' Jake had explained, 'you'll be allocated a time to set up the gear and run through the song, and then, when they're ready, they'll call you back for the actual recording.'

'But we're only miming, yeah?' Curtis said.

'Right.'

'None of it's live.'

Jake shook his head. 'All you've got to do is open your mouth at the right time and make sure you look good.'

When I got to the warehouse, at around one forty-five, Curtis and Jake were already there, and Chief and Stan turned up in the van about five minutes later. As we started to load up the gear, I found myself glancing up and down the road all the time, looking out for William. I had no *reason* to be worried – he wasn't even late yet – but there was just something . . . I didn't know what it was . . . but something didn't feel right. It was the kind of feeling you get when you're waiting for someone, and you keep trying to *imagine* them turning up – because somewhere, in some primitive part of your mind, you actually think you can make it happen simply by imagining it – and sometimes you just *know* that they're going to be here any minute, but other times, no matter how hard you try to imagine it, you just *know* that you're not going to see them . . .

That's how it was for me that day.

I just knew.

Deep down . . .

I knew.

But I wasn't going to admit it. Not to myself, not to anyone.

'He'd better be here soon,' Curtis said to me, lifting an amp into the back of the van.

'He'll be here, don't worry.'

'I *am* worried.'

'Well, don't be.'

Twenty minutes later, with the van all loaded up and still no sign of William, Curtis had had enough.

'Well?' he said to me.

'Well what?'

'Where is he?'

'I don't know.'

'Christ, he's your fucking boyfriend, Lili.'

'I don't *own* him.'

'Well, maybe you should.'

'Look, just give him another five minutes, OK? I'm sure he'll be here –'

'No.'

'Come *on*, Curtis –'

'I *told* him, if he ever missed another gig, no matter what, he'd be out.'

'Yeah, but –'

'We have to go,' he said, looking at his watch.

'All right, but let's just call round at his flat on the way –'

'No.'

'It's not far –'

'I said *no*.'

'But what if he's ill or something?'

356

'If he's not well enough to get here, he's no good to us, is he? And, besides, we don't actually *need* him anyway. We're miming. We can mime perfectly well without him.'

'But he might need *us*. I mean, maybe he had an accident on the way here, maybe he got hit by a car –'

'Yeah, and maybe he's just one big fuck-up. Have you ever thought of that?'

I looked at Curtis, trying to think of something to say, but my head and my heart were empty.

'Come on,' he said wearily. 'Get in the van. We're going.'

I didn't really think that William was ill, or that he'd had an accident, I just thought . . . well, that was the thing. I didn't really know what I thought. All I could think of was that he'd either been lying to me the day before, just pretending that he wasn't worried about being recognized, and that he'd never had any intention of appearing on *Top of the Pops*, or that he'd had second thoughts about it and changed his mind . . . he'd realized that it *was* a risk after all, and he'd decided not to take that risk.

I didn't want to believe that he'd lied to me.

If he'd lied to me about that, then everything else could have been a lie too – all the joking, the fun, all the seriousness . . . all false.

No . . . I couldn't believe that.

I *didn't* believe it.

And if he'd had second thoughts . . . well, he would have told me, wouldn't he? He would have *told* me . . .

Wouldn't he?

And, besides, the last time I'd seen him – when we'd left the meeting at the warehouse the day before – there was nothing remotely doubtful about him at all. I could still picture him – walking with me to the tube station, smiling at me, kissing me, saying goodbye . . . see you tomorrow . . .

'Don't forget your sunglasses,' I'd said.

And he'd laughed . . .

No, he hadn't been worried about a thing.

Had he?

No . . .

He'd been fine.

Which meant . . .?

What?

Why *wasn't* William here? Where the hell *was* he?

The only thing I could think of, the only thing that made any sense – and at the same time scared me to death – was that he was with the men from Derry.

There was a lot of waiting around to do when we got to the BBC studios. We had to wait to get in while they checked who we were, we had to wait around in the dressing room until they were ready for us to set up our gear and rehearse the recording, and then we had to wait for ages while all the other bands went through the same routine . . .

And it wasn't as if it was a particularly *pleasant* place to be either. In fact, as far as I was concerned, it was distinctly *un*pleasant. The studio itself was really small, for a start – much smaller than it appeared on TV – and it was so much tackier than it looked on TV too. There was no glamour to it whatsoever – no excitement, no magic – it was all just plywood and plastic, and miles of black cables, and big tinny cameras lumbering all over the place while dozens of slightly dazed teenagers were herded around by officious middle-aged men with beards and clipboards and head sets . . .

And Tony Blackburn in an awful cream suit . . .

And the dancers . . .

And the other bands . . .

God . . . the other bands.

The Wurzels were there – a novelty band, fat old men dressed up as West Country bumpkins who sang songs about cider and combine harvesters. And a band called Smokie – very white suits and very long hair. And Rod Stewart was there too, I seem to recall, and a singer called Kiki Dee, and the Drifters, and another old sixties band called Manfred Mann . . .

The whole thing was *totally* unreal.

It was like some kind of music-hall nightmare.

Curtis couldn't stand it, and as soon as we'd finished our rehearsal he went off with Jake and the other two in search of a bar.

'Are you coming?' he asked me, just before they left the dressing room.

'No, thanks.'

'Oh, come *on*, Lili . . . don't be like that.'

'Like what?' I said coolly.

'Look,' he said. 'I know you're pissed off about Billy –'

'His name's not *Billy*,' I snapped. 'OK? It's *William* . . . his name's William.'

'Yeah, all right . . .' Curtis said, taken aback by my sudden outburst. 'I was only –'

'Just *go*, Curtis, all right? Just fuck off and leave me alone.'

6.46 p.m. . . . the time is seared into my memory. I was alone in the dressing room. The Wurzels had just left to record their performance, and the long-haired man who'd been trying to chat me up for the last five minutes – I had no idea who he was – had finally given up and had gone off to 'get some chow'. So I was on my own, alone in the silence.

Except it wasn't very silent.

From the studio next door, I could hear the muffled awfulness of the Wurzels record – *I am a cider drinker* . . . – and the sound of people dancing and pretending to enjoy themselves . . . and from outside in the corridor, I could hear people talking about schedules and ratings and contracts . . . and from a small television mounted on the wall of the dressing room, I could hear the background babble of BBC regional news – human-interest stories, something about a car park, news of another train strike . . .

I could hear it all, drifting and droning all around me . . .

But I couldn't *hear* it.

As I sat there, staring at the floor, thinking about William, all I could hear was the saddened silence inside my head . . . the empty sound of hope. I didn't care *where* William was any more. I didn't care why he wasn't here, or who he was with, or what he was doing . . . all I cared about, the only thing that mattered, was that he was OK. Anything else, *every*thing else, was irrelevant.

Just be OK, I kept telling him.

All right?

I don't care about anything else.

Just be OK.

Please.

Just be . . .

I'm not sure what it was that made me look up at the television then – maybe it was something the presenter said, something that meant something to me . . . or maybe it was just the sudden change in the tone of her voice . . . I don't know. But when I looked up and saw the picture on the screen . . .

I just *knew*.

Immediately.

I just knew that William *wasn't* OK.

It was just a gut-feeling at first, a terrible shocking emptiness that I didn't really understand, because for a moment or two I didn't really know what I was looking at or what it meant. It was the kind of image I'd seen so many times before on the TV screen: a pile of smoking rubble, smouldering debris, the fire-blackened wreck of a still-burning car . . . police vehicles, ambulances, flashing lights, news reporters . . .

A scene of devastation.

A bomb blast.

Another terrorist attack somewhere . . .

But this wasn't just *somewhere*, I suddenly realized. This was under a railway bridge, at the end of a grubby little backstreet lined with dilapidated houses, and in the background I could see a patch of wasteground . . .

'No . . .' I muttered, hurrying over to turn up the volume on the TV. 'No . . . please, God . . . no . . .'

The picture on the screen had switched to a reporter now – a man with a moustache, standing halfway down the street, talking into a microphone. '. . . well, details are still very sketchy at the moment,' he was saying, 'but I can confirm that the explosion took place at approximately three fifteen in a workshop owned by Warwick Motors, a local car-repair business. The workshop was situated beneath a railway bridge, and as you can see behind me, the bridge above the workshop has been destroyed. As yet, though, we still have no information on the cause of the explosion or the extent of any casualties.'

'Are the police treating this as a terrorist attack?' the presenter asked.

'So far, there's been no official statement from the police, but sources I've spoken to are in no doubt that the cause of this devastation was a massive bomb blast, and that it does bear striking similarities to other bombings carried out recently by the IRA.'

'Was any warning given?'

'Not as far as we know. But it's possible that the bomb wasn't meant to go off here, and that what we're actually looking at is the result of a terrorist operation that has somehow gone wrong . . .'

Gone wrong . . .

Gone wrong . . .

Gone wrong . . .

What had gone wrong? How? Why? What had *happened* . . .? My head was spinning now . . . the whole room was spinning. I couldn't take anything in. The words and images were just tumbling around in my mind like confetti in the wind – the workshop, the pile of rubble . . . *owned by Warwick Motors* . . . the burning car, the smouldering debris . . . *a massive bomb blast* . . . *the IRA* . . .

And suddenly I could hear William's voice in my head: . . . *I don't want anyone to get hurt . . . I don't want anyone else to get killed . . . I won't let it happen . . . if I find out that they're planning something that's likely to hurt or kill people, I'll stop them* . . .

'No . . .' I muttered, shaking my head. 'No . . .'

The dressing-room door swung open then, and I heard someone say something to me, but all I could hear was the voice on the TV – '. . . and we'll be back with more news of the North London bombing in our late-night bulletin at eleven fifty . . .' – and then, as the weather map appeared, I reached up and switched over to ITV, desperate for more news, but there was nothing, just people talking about politics, and I stabbed frantically at the controls, switching to BBC2, but there was nothing there either, just an Open University programme . . .

'Lili!'

I tried BBC1 again . . .

'*Lili!*'

A sports programme was on now . . .

'Fuck!' I spat, punching the buttons. 'Fucking stupid . . . fucking *sports* –'

And then I felt someone get hold of me, and I spun round and started lashing out at them, stopping only when I realized that it was Curtis.

'Jesus *Christ*, Lili,' he said. 'What the hell are you *doing*?'

'William . . .' I mumbled.

'What about him?'

'I think . . .'

'What? You think what?'

What could I say? I couldn't tell him anything, could I? I couldn't tell *any*one anything. There was nothing I could do . . .

'Lili?'

Nothing . . .

I looked at Curtis.

'What is it?' he said quietly. 'What's the matter?'

I just looked at him, feeling utterly helpless.

Then Jake came rushing in, all panicky and flustered. 'Shit, *there* you are . . . come *on*! They're ready to record, they're *waiting* for you out there. What the *fuck* are you doing? Come *on* . . .'

Curtis didn't panic, he just looked me in the eye and said, 'Are you all right, Lili? Can you do this?'

I nodded, not really sure what I was doing any more. And the next thing I knew, I was following Curtis along the corridor, then through some doors into the studio, and I vaguely recall being blinded by the sudden bright lights as I crossed the stage and picked up my bass . . .

But the rest of it . . .

I can't remember.

I was in a trance, I was gone, somewhere else.

I wasn't there at all.

The next thing I can remember with any real clarity is sitting in the back of a taxi, staring out of the window, trying to convince myself that maybe William *was* OK after all – maybe he wasn't there when the bomb went off, maybe he had nothing to do with it all . . . maybe it was just the three IRA men in the workshop . . . and maybe, when I got to Cranleigh Farm, I'd find him safe and well . . . and he'd explain what had happened, and I'd pretend that I was annoyed with him for frightening me to death . . . and then he'd tell me how sorry he was, and he'd look at me with those hazel eyes . . . and he'd give me that wonderful smile . . . and everything would be all right again . . .

'I'll have to go round by Seven Sisters, love, all right?' the taxi driver called out over his shoulder.

'Sorry?'

'It's all closed up round Green Lanes because of the bomb, so I'll have to go round Seven Sisters. It shouldn't take much longer.'

'Right,' I said. 'OK . . .' I leaned forward and spoke though the hatch. 'Is there any more news about the bomb?'

'IRA, they reckon. Probably went off by mistake.' He shook his head. 'Bloody Irish –'

'Do they know if anyone was killed?'

'The police aren't saying yet, but I heard there was three, maybe four of them.'

'Three or four dead?'

He nodded. 'They reckon the bomb was in a car in the workshop and it went off with the bombers inside. Serves them fucking right, if you ask me.'

I leaned back and stared out of the window again, suddenly convinced now that William *wasn't* OK after all – he *had* been there when the bomb went off, he *was* with the three IRA men in the workshop . . . and when I got to Cranleigh Farm, I *wouldn't* find him safe and well . . .

I wouldn't see those hazel eyes.

I wouldn't see that wonderful smile.

And nothing would ever be all right again . . .

And then I remember telling myself not to be so stupid . . . just because a taxi driver tells you that he *heard* something, that he *heard* that 'there was three, maybe four of them' . . . that doesn't *mean* anything.

It doesn't mean *anything*.

He doesn't know anything.

And neither do you.

So don't even think about giving up yet.

364

Don't think about anything . . .

 . . . *I don't want anyone else to get killed . . . I won't let it happen* . . .

 . . . just believe.

37

It must have been around nine o'clock when I knocked on the door of William's flat. I'd started to cry in the lift on the way up, and by the time Nancy opened the door, I'd pretty much lost control and the tears were just pouring down my face.

'Lili!' Nancy gasped. 'What on earth's the matter?'

'Is he here?' I sobbed.

'William? No . . . I thought he was with you.'

I really broke down then, weeping and wailing so much that all Nancy could do was take me inside and hold me, letting me cry, letting me howl, letting me let it all out . . . until, eventually, the tears began to dry up, I stopped struggling for breath, and my voice very gradually came back to me.

'The bomb . . .' I muttered. 'The bomb . . .'

'All right,' Nancy said softly. 'Just take your time . . . breathe slowly . . . that's it. Nice and easy . . .'

I took a deep breath, slowly let it out, and looked at her. 'When did you last see William?'

'I don't know . . . sometime this morning, I think. He left around twelve –'

'Did he say where he was going?'

She shook her head. 'He went out a bit earlier to make a phone call, came back for a while, then went out again.' She was beginning to look worried now. 'Is he in some kind of trouble or something?'

'I don't know . . . I think he might . . .'

'What *is* it, Lili? What's the matter?'

'Did you see the news tonight?'

'What news?' She frowned at me, and then suddenly her face dropped. 'You don't mean the bombing?'

I nodded.

'No!' she cried. 'Not that . . . *please* don't tell me –'

'I don't *know* anything yet,' I said quickly. 'All I know is –'

'What? *What* do you know? Is William all right?'

'I don't *know* . . .'

It was her turn to take a deep breath now. She closed her eyes for a moment, steadying herself, then she breathed out slowly and looked at me. 'Tell me,' she said quietly. 'Tell me everything.'

I told her everything.

'God, what was he *thinking*?' she said when I'd finished. 'Why couldn't he just . . .?' She sighed, shaking her head. 'I should have *known* . . . I should have . . .'

'I'm sorry,' I said, crying quietly. 'I *tried* to change his mind . . . but he just wouldn't listen. And I didn't know . . . you know, I didn't know what to do . . . whether I should tell anyone or not. But I promised him that I wouldn't . . .' I looked at Nancy. 'I'm *so* sorry . . .'

'It's all right, love,' she said gently. 'It's not your fault.'

'I should have *told* you –'

'No,' she said sadly. 'A promise is a promise . . . there was nothing else you could have done.'

I sniffed, wiping tears from my face. 'Do you think . . .? I mean, do you think he's –?'

'What's going on?' a voice said suddenly, and I looked over and saw Little Joe in the doorway.

'Not now, Joe,' Nancy said, smiling at him. 'Just go back to your room for a bit, OK?'

'Is everything all right?'

'Everything's fine. We're just . . . we just need to sort something out.' She smiled again. 'Go on, off you go.' She waited until he'd gone and the door had closed behind him, then she turned back to me. 'Did William tell you what the other two men were called?'

I shook my head. 'I never asked him.'

'But you saw them all . . . you know what they look like?'

I nodded, looking at her. 'What are you thinking?'

She sighed. 'God knows . . . I'm just trying to get my head round this, I suppose. I'm just . . .' She looked at her watch, then got up and switched on the TV. 'I think we've just missed the ITV News, but there might be something on BBC.' She stood in front of the television for a while, watching as an MP answered questions about food prices, then the interview finished and the programme switched to a report about Concorde . . . and Nancy turned down the sound. 'Maybe it's already been on,' she said. 'I'll try the radio.' She went into the kitchen and came back with a portable radio. She turned it on, tuned into a local station, listened for a while, then set the volume to low and put the radio on a table by the settee and sat down next to me.

'What are we going to do?' I asked her.

'I don't know . . .'

'Shouldn't we get in touch with the police?'

She looked at me. 'If this *is* what it looks like, if it *is* an IRA operation . . . we can't go to the police.'

'Why not?'

'Because . . .' She sighed heavily. 'Well, firstly, whatever they've managed to find out so far, which probably isn't very much, there's no way that they're going to tell *us* anything. They won't confirm anything, they won't deny anything. And secondly, if we go to the police and tell them that we think William might have been at the workshop, all they'll do is pass us on to Special Branch or MI5 – because they'll be the ones investigating this

– and the chances are we'll be taken away and stuck in a cell somewhere, and then, when they're ready, they'll start asking us questions . . .' Nancy paused, looking at me. 'They'll want to know everything, Lili – about William, and me, and William's parents – and they won't stop until they've got everything they want, no matter *how* long it takes. And we still won't know anything about William.' She glanced up at the muted TV screen. The news had finished. A film was showing. Nancy sighed again. 'Special Branch or MI5 can do what they like to me, Lili, I really don't care . . . but I'm not going to let them get hold of you, and I'm not going to put Joe at risk either. Because if I'm not here to look after him . . .'

'Yeah,' I said. 'I understand.'

'Do you?'

I nodded. 'But we have to do *some*thing, don't we? What about trying the hospitals? I mean, he might have been hurt –'

'The police will already have checked all the hospitals. If he *was* badly hurt – and he wouldn't go to a hospital unless he was *really* badly hurt – the police would have found him by now. And besides . . .'

'What?'

She hesitated. 'Well . . . from what I saw on the news earlier on . . . I just think . . . I mean, if he *was* there when the bomb went off . . .'

'He couldn't have survived.'

She didn't answer me, but she didn't have to. We both knew that it was true.

'So what *do* we do?' I said. 'We can't just sit here all night –'

'I think that's all we *can* do, Lili,' she said, shaking her head. 'Just stay here, listen to the radio, watch the news . . .' She shrugged. 'I doubt very much if there'll actually *be* any news, not *real* news anyway, but you never know. And if William *is* out there somewhere . . . well, we need to be here for him when he gets back.'

I looked at her. 'Do you think he could be . . .? I mean, do you really think that he might be out there somewhere?'

She smiled sadly. 'Anything's possible with William, isn't it?'

I did my best to smile back at her, but I think we both knew that if William *was* still out there somewhere, if he *was* still alive, he would have let us know by now. And while I knew that Nancy was right, that anything *was* possible, I also knew that in the real world – and this *was* the real world – miracles don't happen.

No matter how much you *want* them to . . .

They just don't.

After Nancy had taken me down to a phone box across the street, and I'd called Mum to let her know that I was staying the night at William's, we went back to the flat and settled ourselves down on the settee.

We waited.

We listened to the radio.

We watched the news.

And Nancy was right, there wasn't any more *real* news. There were reports about the bomb, regular updates, but no actual news.

The police investigation was 'ongoing'.

Leads were being 'pursued'.

The cause of the explosion was still being 'examined'.

The extent of any casualties was still 'unknown'.

The time passed slowly, hours seeming to last for days, and as the clock ticked slowly away, I eventually began to drift in and out of sleep. I didn't *want* to go to sleep – it just felt *wrong* – and I did everything I could to stay awake, but I just couldn't seem to keep my eyes open, and at some point in the early hours of the morning – with my head resting heavily on Nancy's shoulder – I finally drifted off into a deep and dreamless sleep.

38

It was early when I woke up, the pale light of dawn just beginning to show through the window. I was cold. My neck was stiff. I was curled up on the settee under a thin woollen blanket.

'Lili . . .? Are you awake?'

Nancy was sitting on the floor beside me. Her voice was faint, her face was pale. She was crying.

I sat up. 'Nancy . . .?'

'Sorry . . . I didn't mean to wake you . . .'

'What is it?' I said quickly. 'Is it William? Have you heard something?'

She shook her head. 'I was in his room . . . I was just . . .' She wiped her eyes and looked at me. 'I found this . . .'

She passed me an envelope. I took it from her and looked at it. It was a plain white envelope . . . it was sealed. My name was written in black biro on the front.

I looked at Nancy.

She said, 'There were two of them . . . one for me and Joe, one for you. I found them on his desk. They were both inside a bigger envelope . . .' Sniffing back tears, she picked up a larger envelope from the floor and showed it to me. On the front, written in black biro, it said: *Only to be opened if I don't come back.*

My heart was dead now, dead and empty.

I could barely speak.

'Is that . . .?' I cleared my throat. 'Is that William's handwriting?'

Nancy nodded. We were both crying now. I looked down at the envelope in my hands. I didn't want to open it. I didn't want to know the truth.

I looked at Nancy. 'Have you . . .?'

She nodded again, holding up a sheet of paper. It was a letter . . . in William's handwriting. It was tear-stained.

'I'm sorry,' Nancy said, sobbing quietly. 'I'm so sorry . . .'

I looked down at the envelope in my hands again.

I didn't want to open it . . .

Nancy put her hand on my knee.

'I'm here,' she said.

I looked down at the envelope . . .

I didn't want to open it . . .

I didn't . . .

I couldn't . . .

I opened it.

There was a single sheet of paper inside, folded in three, with writing on both sides. I took it out, unfolded it, closed my eyes for a moment . . .

Then I opened my eyes, and began to read:

Dear Lili

With a bit of luck you'll never get round to reading this, but I need to ask you something now just in case I don't see you again. I'll have to be quick, I'm afraid, because I don't have much time. So I'll get straight to the point. It's 11.30 a.m. on Wednesday (22 September), and Donal's just told me to be at the workshop within the hour, so I'm guessing that whatever they've got planned it's going ahead today. I think they've probably been keeping it from me until the very last minute because they're still not 100% sure they can trust me. Hopefully, though, once I get there, I'll find out what the target is, and then I can decide what to do about it. As I told you before, if there's no chance of anyone getting hurt, I won't do anything, I'll just let them get on with it. But if there's any possibility of people getting killed, I'll stop them, I promise.

Either way, though, there's always a chance that something might go wrong, and that's really why I'm writing to you. Because if I don't come back, I need to ask you again to honour the promise you made at the party that night. All the stuff I told you about my mum and dad, especially my dad, and the IRA, and Nancy, it's really important – for Nancy's and Joe's sakes – that you don't repeat anything I told you to anyone else at all. And the same goes for everything you know about Donal and the others, and whatever happens today. I <u>know</u> that you wouldn't tell anyone anyway, and I feel really bad about asking you again, so please forgive me. But the IRA don't forget, and as long as Nancy's still alive, there's always going to be someone who wants her dead, and I'd never forgive myself if I didn't do everything possible to make sure that that never happens.

There's so much more that I want to tell you, Lili, but I really don't have enough time now. And, besides, I'm sure we'll be seeing each other very soon anyway, and then maybe we can go for another long walk in Abney Park, and I can tell you everything that I've been meaning to tell you, everything that's in my heart . . .

I'm sorry, I have to go.

Take care, Lili.

With all my love,

William xxx

39

It took me a long, long time to stop thinking that maybe – just maybe – William was still alive, and that one day he'd come back to me, and we'd take that long walk together in Abney Park, and he'd tell me everything that was in his heart . . . but, of course, it never happened.

The bomb blast was only in the news for a few days, and it would soon become just another small footnote in the long history of the IRA's military campaign, but while the media and the public may have lost interest in it, the security services certainly hadn't, and – very gradually – as their investigation continued, more and more evidence began to emerge. It was an incredibly slow and drawn-out process, with tiny bits of information being released one by one over many months and years, and even now, thirty-five years later, there are still lots of unanswered questions. But despite the laborious nature of the investigation – and the unwillingness of the security services to talk about it – the facts did eventually start to come out.

The explosion was caused by a 300lb homemade fertilizer bomb. The bomb, which bore all the hallmarks of the IRA, exploded in the boot of a car in the workshop.

In terms of casualties, the first official report claimed that two men had died in the blast, but according to another report, released some months later, there were 'at least three fatalities, possibly four'. Apparently, due to the sheer size of the bomb, and the proximity of those caught in the blast, it was proving very difficult to 'piece together and identify the human remains'. Nevertheless, the security services had little doubt that the bomb was the work of the IRA, and that the victims of the blast were all members of an IRA cell based in London who were planning a car-bomb attack on a prominent target somewhere in the capital.

It wasn't until the summer of 1979 that another report was released stating that two of the men who died that day had at last been positively identified. They were named as Liam Breen, 24 years old, a father of two from Derry, and Donal Callaghan, aged 47, also from Derry. Both were known members of the IRA's Derry Brigade, and it was further claimed that Donal Callaghan had been involved in a number of IRA-sanctioned killings throughout the mid-1970s.

It was never established why the bomb went off prematurely in the workshop that day, and because the only people who will ever really know what happened are the people who were actually there, the truth will probably never be known. Most accounts put it down to simple human error – someone made a mistake, the explosive was unstable, the wiring was faulty – and it's quite possible that's all it was. But there are other possibilities, of course, and over the years I've spent countless sleepless nights going over each and every one of them – imagining this, picturing that, trying to remember if William ever said or did anything that might give me a clue as to what had happened . . .

In my darkest moments, I sometimes wonder if he knew from the very beginning that Donal was Donal Callaghan, and that his only intention all along was to kill the man who shot his father as soon as he got the chance. It's a deeply troubling thought, but I've never really come close to accepting it because it would mean that William had lied to me, and he told me once that he'd never lied to me. I'd believed him then . . . and I still believe him now.

A possibility I *can* accept is that he only confirmed what he'd suspected about Donal at the very last moment. Maybe Donal said something that day in the workshop, something that only the killer of William's father could know, and William just acted out of instinct . . .

Or maybe he *never* found out the truth about Donal. Maybe what he *did* find out was that the planned attack was likely to kill or maim a lot of innocent people, and he knew that the only way to stop it was to deliberately set off the bomb . . .

Or perhaps none of these things happened.

I don't know . . .

To be honest, I try not to think about it too much any more, because I've come to realize that, in the end, it doesn't really matter. Whatever happened that day – however noble, stupid, brave, or just – William will always be dead.

I spent a lot of time with Nancy and Joe in the first few weeks after the bomb, and although we stopped seeing each other quite so much over the following months and years, I still spoke to Nancy on the phone fairly regularly, and we always made a point of meeting up at least once every other week or so. Sometimes I'd go round to her flat, and we'd just talk for hours and hours, other times we'd go out together somewhere for a cup of coffee or something to eat . . .

We became very close.

And she told me a lot about William . . .

Including the truth about his name.

'Did he ever tell you about his granddad?' I remember her asking me one day.

'Yeah,' I said, smiling at the memory. 'He told me that he used to love Westerns, and that when his granny wasn't there, he'd secretly read them to him.'

Nancy laughed. 'That's what he told me too . . . but what he *didn't* say was how much *he* loved Westerns too.'

'William did?'

'Yeah, he was always getting them out of the library, but he'd only read them when he was on his own, in his room . . . you know? Like it was still something that had to be kept secret.' She looked at me. 'To tell you the truth, I think he was a bit embarrassed about it.'

I nodded, smiling sadly . . . I could just picture him sitting on his own, in his room, with a paperback Western in his hands, lost in a world of gunfighters and outlaws . . .

'That's why he chose the name,' Nancy said.

'Sorry?'

'William Bonney . . . you know that wasn't his real name, don't you?'

'Yeah . . .'

She smiled. 'It was one of the names that Billy the Kid used.'

'Billy the Kid?' I said, staring at her. And I remembered that day in the warehouse then, the day that William had showed up at the audition . . . I remembered Curtis asking him his name, and when William had told him, Curtis had said, 'I can't believe it, you've got the same name as Billy the Kid.' And William had just looked at him and said, 'Really? I didn't know that.'

I looked at Nancy. 'So he called himself William Bonney because he loved Westerns?'

'Well, yeah, but there's actually a bit more to it than that. I only found this out recently, but Billy the Kid's father was called William Henry Antrim, and Billy sometimes called himself Henry Antrim –'

'And William's grandparents came from Antrim.'

Nancy nodded. 'But Billy the Kid's real name, the name he was born with, was actually Henry McCarty.' She looked at me. 'And that was William's real name too.'

'I don't understand . . .'

'William's real name, the name on his birth certificate, is Henry William McCarty.'

I frowned. 'And Billy the Kid was Henry McCarty?'

'Yeah . . . it's really weird, isn't it?'

I shook my head in bewilderment. 'So William was really . . . *Henry*?'

Nancy laughed. 'No . . . no one ever called him Henry. He was always known as William, ever since he was a baby.'

'Well . . .' I sighed, 'at least that's something. I mean, I really don't think I could ever get round to thinking of William as a Henry . . .'

'No,' Nancy said quietly. 'No . . . he could never be anything else but William.'

'William McCarty,' I muttered to myself. 'William McCarty . . .'

I liked the sound of it.

Nancy also told me that day what *her* real name was, but she made me promise never to reveal it to anyone, not even when she was dead. And, as she'd once told me herself, a promise is a promise.

And I've always kept my promises.

Which is why I'm only writing this now, a month after Nancy's funeral.

She'd been ill for a long time, in and out of remission since she was first diagnosed with cancer in the winter of 2006. It had looked for a while as if she was going to beat it, but when she went for her regular check-up in July this year, the tests revealed that the cancer had come back and was spreading rapidly . . . and after that everything went downhill very quickly.

She died in hospital on 21 September 2010.

It was the day before the thirty-fourth anniversary of William's death.

She was sixty-four years old.

And I miss her very much.

I know that Little Joe misses her too. He's not so little any more, of course, and he stopped calling himself Joe a long time ago. He goes by a different name now, a name that has no connections whatsoever with the past, and he lives a quiet life with his wife and children in a sleepy little place a long way from anywhere, a place where the past will never catch up with him.

The past caught up with my mother a long time ago. In the early 1980s her behaviour became so alarming, and sometimes even quite violent, that she was forever in and out of a series of 'special' hospitals and secure institutions. Every time she was discharged, the time it took before she was re-admitted became shorter and shorter . . . until eventually, in 1984, after physically attacking one of her neighbours (who she'd accused of having an affair with her husband), she was admitted to a long-term psychiatric hospital in Berkshire . . . and it was there, two months later, that she took her own life.

The last time I visited her, a week before she killed herself, she had no idea who I was.

Another life . . .

Another death . . .

Over all these years I've kept my promise to William, I've never told anyone the truth about him, I've never talked about his father or Nancy or anything else that might have put her and Joe at risk. It wasn't always easy, especially in the very early days after William's death, and perhaps one of the most difficult choices that I had to make was what to tell Curtis about William. I was so utterly devastated at the time, so eaten up with grief, that I didn't want to tell Curtis *any*thing. I didn't want to talk to him, I didn't want to see him . . . I didn't want to see *any*body. The truth is, I didn't want to *do* anything at all. Without William, I just couldn't see the point any more.

But Curtis kept phoning me all the time and calling round, desperate to find out what was going on, and the more I avoided him, the angrier he became . . . which, in hindsight, was kind of fair enough really. Our single was out by then, and after our appearance on *Top of the Pops*, it had gone straight into the charts at number twenty-three, so it was only natural for Curtis to want to know why I'd suddenly locked myself away and was refusing to talk to anyone.

And after a while I realized that if I carried on avoiding him, if I refused to give him at least *some* kind of explanation, it was only going to make things worse for me. So the next time he called round, I invited him in, took him up to my room, and told him that William had been run over and killed by a car.

It was a terrible thing to do – in every possible sense – and I despised myself for doing it, but I didn't know what else to do. I had to tell Curtis something, and I couldn't tell him the truth, so I told him a lie that was as close to the truth as I thought I could possibly get.

Curtis was genuinely shocked by the news, and it hit him a lot harder than I'd expected. I shouldn't have been surprised really, but I think I was so wrapped up in my own feelings about William that I'd forgotten just how much he'd meant to Curtis too. Of course, there was no denying that Curtis had also hated William at times, but I think, for Curtis, hating someone was almost the same as loving them.

So, yes, William's death was a massive blow to Curtis.

I think he had his doubts as to whether or not I was telling him the *whole* truth – especially when I explained that we couldn't go to William's funeral because his body had been flown back to Belfast the day after the accident, and that his funeral had already taken place . . . but, to Curtis's credit, he never pushed me on it. I always got the feeling that it didn't really make any difference to him how William had died, or where, or why – he was dead, and that's all there was to it.

I also told Curtis that day that I wouldn't be playing in the band any more, and that was when he *did* get a little pushy.

'Of course,' he said. 'I understand . . . it's only natural for you to feel like that at first –'

'No, Curtis,' I told him. 'I mean it. I don't want to do it any more, it's as simple as that.'

'All right . . . but why don't you just think about it for a while? I mean, there's no hurry –'

'I've already thought about it.'

'Well, OK, but –'

'I'm not going to change my mind.'

'Listen, Lili,' he said, looking at me. 'I know how you feel right now –'

'No, you don't.'

'. . . but the thing is . . . well, we've got commitments now. We've got interviews lined up, photo shoots, gigs, maybe more TV shows . . . I mean, if we don't make the most of this now –'

'I'm sorry, Curtis,' I said. 'But I really don't care. You'll just have to do it without me.'

'Yeah,' he said coldly. 'But it's not just without *you*, is it? I mean, there's only me and Stan left now –'

'Get out,' I said quietly.

He looked at me. 'I didn't mean –'

'Just go, please.'

'Look, all I meant was –'

'I'm not going to ask you again.'

He looked at me for a moment, and when I pointedly looked away, he got up and quietly walked out.

I didn't see him very much after that – at least, not in person anyway. He carried on with Naked for a while, bringing in a new bass player and a new rhythm guitarist, but it never really worked out. After the relative success of our first single – it eventually got to number twelve in the charts – Polydor had high hopes for the next one, an old song of ours called 'Crack Up', which the new Naked recorded in December that year, but it was nowhere near as good as our first record, and it didn't even make the top forty. Shortly afterwards, I heard that Curtis had broken up Naked and was recording a solo album. I also heard that, as well as everything else, he'd started using heroin now, and whenever I saw a picture of him, in *NME* or *Sounds* or *Melody Maker*, it was quite obvious that if he didn't sort himself out pretty soon, he wasn't going to live much longer.

For the next year or so, I didn't hear very much about Curtis. There were occasional reports that he was still working on his solo album – which was variously being described by those in the know as either 'a masterpiece', 'a modern symphony', or 'a pompous piece of shit' – and there were all sorts of rumours going round that the album was never going to be released due to contractual difficulties or legal wranglings or personal problems . . . but then, just as Curtis's dream seemed to be disappearing down a big black hole, everything suddenly started to work out for him again. First of all, Peugeot decided to use 'Heaven Hill' as the soundtrack to the TV advert for their new car, and it became so popular that Polydor re-released the original single, this time with 'Heaven Hill' as the A-side, and within a couple of weeks it was a huge hit. Number one in both the UK and America, played on the radio all the time . . . it was *massive*. And Curtis was suddenly hot property again. He was everywhere, promoting the record in newspapers and magazines, miming to it on *Top of the Pops* with an all-girl backing band . . . and he actually looked a lot healthier than he had for a while. Not *too* thin and gaunt, not *too* deranged . . . in fact, he almost looked as if he was enjoying himself.

'Heaven Hill' not only made Curtis a lot of money, it also made him a star, a genuine rock 'n' roll celebrity. And when his solo album – a double album called *Every Moon* – was finally released in 1979, his star status rose to even greater heights. It was an amazing record, absolutely stunning – dark, haunting, powerful, beautiful . . . the critics adored it, and the public bought it in vast numbers. It was number one in the album charts, both here and in the USA, for weeks, and it produced three hit singles – 'Stupid', 'Run For Ever', and 'The Dance Upon Nothing'.

Curtis was made. He'd achieved his dream, he'd got what he'd always wanted – fame, success, money, stardom. He was in the newspapers – not just the music press – and he was on TV. He made the news. He had beautiful girlfriends, he treated them badly . . . he got drunk, he had fights, he took drugs . . .

He was a rock 'n' roll star.

In 1981, he left London and moved to Los Angeles, hoping to break into films. He appeared in a few, none of which were any good – and even if they had been any good, it was generally agreed that Curtis wasn't – and in 1982 he announced that he was giving up acting to concentrate on music again. A new record was in the pipeline, a triple album this time . . . but then the rumours started again. Curtis was drunk all the time, he was back on heroin, hooked on cocaine . . . he'd beaten up one of his girlfriends, he was out of control, going crazy . . . he'd given away all his money and was living on the streets . . .

I don't know how much of this was true.

All I know for sure is that on New Year's Day, 1983, his body was discovered in a cheap motel room in downtown Los Angeles. He'd died from a massive heroin overdose.

The absence of a suicide note has fuelled endless speculation about Curtis's death over the years, and there have been countless conspiracy theories suggesting that it wasn't suicide, that it was an accidental overdose, or that he was murdered – by an ex-girlfriend, or the FBI, or the mafia . . .

I don't know if Curtis killed himself or not. But whatever it was – suicide or accident – it was always going to happen.

It was just a matter of when.

So I can't say that I was surprised when I heard about it . . . I was distraught, and stunned, shocked and confused, and I cried my heart out for a long, long time . . . but, no, I wasn't surprised.

He was Curtis Ray . . .

Fucked up and dead at every moon.

Life and death . . .

I don't know . . .

It's always really hard.

But you can't have one without the other, can you?

And, in a way, that's what this is all about. I can tell this story now *because* Nancy is dead, and Little Joe has a new life on the other side of the world, so I don't have to worry about risking their lives by revealing their secrets, because those secrets can't hurt them any more.

In the days and weeks after William's death, I was in such a state – both physically and emotionally – that it never even occurred to me that some of the things I was feeling might *not* have anything to do with my grief. The tiredness, the nausea . . . I didn't actually *assume* that it was all part of the grieving process, because at that time I simply wasn't capable of rational thought. It was just stuff that was happening to me, no different to all the other stuff . . . in fact, I barely even noticed it.

By early October though, after a solid week of being sick every morning, it finally dawned on me that perhaps there was something else going on. So I went to the doctor's for a test (this was before home pregnancy tests were available in shops), and within a few days it was confirmed – I was pregnant.

I was going to have a baby . . .

I didn't know what to think. Part of me was thrilled, elated, joyous . . . another part was scared, confused, unable to cope. I was still grieving for William, I was still in mourning, I was still consumed by his death . . . how could I now celebrate a life? And I was still only seventeen, I was still at school . . .

I didn't know what to do.

I just didn't *know* . . .

The only thing I was sure about was that William was the father.

I just *knew* it.

I could *feel* it.

There was absolutely no doubt in my mind.

And, besides, the timing was right . . . and whenever I'd slept with Curtis, we'd always taken precautions. But that night with William in the chapel . . . that was different. *That* was the night . . .

I knew it.

And even if there had been even the slightest doubt in my mind – which, to be perfectly honest, there probably was – when my baby was born, on 12 June 1977, and I held him in my arms for the first time and gazed into his eyes, I knew – without question – that he was William's son.

Our son.

His eyes were blue, of course – and they didn't become hazel until he was about eighteen months old – but they were undeniably William's eyes. Pure, bright, clear and radiant, so full of life . . .

Everything about him was just like William.

He *was* William.

He *is* William.

William Garcia.

There was no other name for him really.

He's thirty-four now, which I still find incredibly hard to believe, especially when it comes back to me that his father will always be sixteen years old. It's just so strange sometimes, knowing that my son is more than twice as old as his father . . . it makes me quite sad when I think about it.

But it can be very comforting too.

William is very much like his father, in all kinds of ways. He has the same eyes, the same hair, the same beautiful face . . . he thinks in a very similar way, he even sounds like his father, especially when he sings. And, just like his father, he's a naturally gifted musician. He's always loved music, ever since he was young, and as well as inheriting his father's musical ability, he also inherited William's *attitude* towards music. I've never forgotten the time when William was talking to me about Curtis's 'empty dream', and he told me that 'if music was really all he cared about, he wouldn't give a shit about getting a record deal and "making it big" and all that kind of crap . . . he'd just want to play.' And I know that he'd be proud of his son, because that's exactly how he's always felt about music. He just wants to write songs and play them. And that's pretty much all he's done all his life – write and play. He's done it on his own, in bands, for money, for nothing . . . he's never really cared if he makes a living from it or not. As long as he can play, he's happy.

He actually *does* make a living from his music now – in fact, he makes more than just a living from it – and although that means I don't get to see him as much as I'd like to, it also means that whenever I want to hear his voice, wherever I am, all I have to do is turn on my iPod and listen to his songs. And the most wonderful thing about that is that when I go to Abney Park Cemetery, which I do at least once a week, and I walk the pathways, soaking up the memories of William, and I sit on our bench, looking around at the trees and the statues and the great masses of tangled vegetation still growing wild over the ancient gravestones and tombs . . . I can, if I want to, listen to our son's music and imagine that William is listening with me.

40

I got an email from my son this morning. He's on tour in America at the moment, promoting his latest album, but he always keeps in touch with me, wherever he is – he'll phone or text or email me every day, just to let me know that he's OK. This morning, though, his email said simply, *It's about time you watched this, Mum.* There was an attachment with the email, a video . . . *totp/23976/Naked/Naked*.

It was a video of our performance on *Top of the Pops*.

I'd never seen it. For a long time, I wasn't even aware that the recording still existed – and even if I had known, I wouldn't have wanted to watch it – but I've known for a few years now that you can see a lot of the old *Top of the Pops* performances on YouTube, and that UK Gold has a lot of the shows too. So I guessed that if I'd really wanted to see our performance, I probably could have.

I just didn't want to.

But now . . .

Well, now that I've written this, now that I've gone back to those days and lived them again . . . it feels as if I've *exorcised* something. I know that I *can* go back there now, if I want to . . . I know that it doesn't hurt me too much any more. And when I read William's email this morning, and I realized that he'd sent me the *Top of the Pops* video . . . I knew that he was right.

It *was* about time I watched it.

So I did.

My heart was beating really hard as I downloaded the video and set it up to play. I was incredibly nervous, anxious . . . even a little bit scared. But I was excited too, in a scary kind of way. And when the video started to play . . . God, it was just *so* weird. It began right at the end of the Wurzels performance, the camera panning across the applauding audience to focus on Tony Blackburn, grinning his grin, dressed in his awful cream suit, flirting like an idiot with two teenage girls dressed in short skirts and tight tank tops . . . and then he turns back to the camera and says, 'Once again it's tip for the top time on *Top of the Pops*, and here's a brand-new group with a brand-new song . . . it's Naked . . .' He pauses, grinning again. '. . . with "Naked".'

As the camera pans back across the audience again we hear the opening four bars of 'Naked', and then we see Curtis – almost bent double over his guitar, hammering out the chords – and then the bass and drums come storming in, and *God* . . . I'd forgotten how good it sounds. Big and loud, stunningly powerful . . . and now Curtis is lurching up to the microphone, staggering and twisting all over the place, and he glares like a lunatic into the camera and opens his mouth and starts to sing:

> *IDLE BLACK EYES*
> *AND DRUG-YELLOWED SKIN*
> *THE DREAM FLOWERS DIE*
> *ON HER COLD NAKED SIN . . .*

He's miming, of course, but it doesn't really matter – it sounds fantastic, and he looks really good . . . and then the camera focuses on me . . .

And I look like hell.

I'm dressed all in black – tight black jeans, tight black vest – and my face is deathly white, and I look as if I'm in a trance. My hands are moving on the bass, but everything else is still. I'm just standing there, staring at nothing. My eyes are empty, my face is blank . . . I'm dead to the world. I don't even react when the camera pans down from my face to leer at my breasts for a few moments, I just keep staring straight ahead, staring into the void . . .

I'M NAKED!
YOU'RE NAKED!

It's a really odd feeling, seeing myself on the screen. I can see how I would have looked to others back then – I would have looked good, in an elegantly wasted kind of way . . . I would have looked cool, like I didn't care . . . I would have *looked* rock 'n' roll.

But I wasn't.

I was simply in shock.

WE'RE NAKED!
. . . NAKED!

The oddest thing about watching the video though – but also, for me, the most touching thing – is that although William isn't actually there on stage with us, you can see, quite clearly, where he would have been if he *had* been there. There's a clearly visible gap on stage, just to the right of Curtis, where William always stood, and whether or not Curtis is consciously avoiding that gap . . . I don't know.

But he doesn't go there.

Not once.

It's as if there's something there, something in the way.

And the more I watch the video – and I've seen it quite a few times now – the more I'm convinced that there *is* something there . . .

An energy, perhaps . . .

A force.

A spirit.

And, of course, I know that's ridiculous. I know it's *not* William . . .

But the last time I watched the video, no more than five minutes ago, I could have sworn that just for a moment I saw the ghost of a face looking back at me – a pale complexion, a beautiful smile, a pair of bright hazel eyes . . .

And just for a moment, I cried.

As **Robert** slowly wakes from a routine operation, he can hear, he can feel, but he can't **scream.** The operation isn't over. But **life,** as Robert knows it, is.

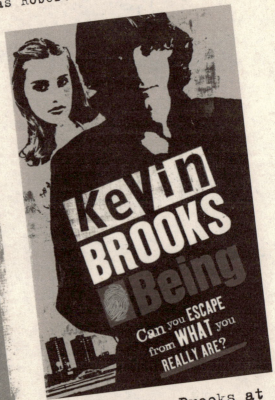

KEVIN BROOKS
Being
Can you ESCAPE from WHAT you REALLY ARE?

This is Kevin Brooks at his very best – powerful, intense and compelling.

'Violently enjoyable and worth catching' – THE TIMES

If you go down to the fair today...
you may not come out alive.

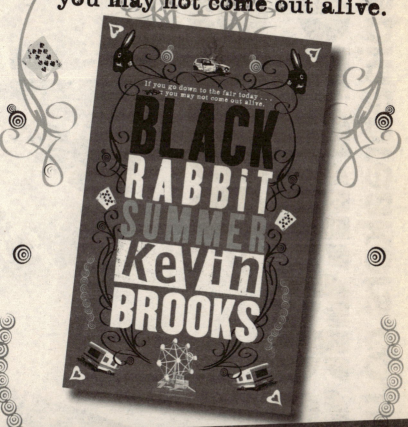

The dark, tense and gripping new novel
from award-winning Kevin Brooks.

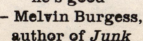

'Watch this guy,
he's good'
– Melvin Burgess,
author of *Junk*

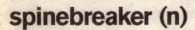